REBIRTH

TATTOOED ANGELS TRILOGY

Rebirth

Tattooed Angels Trilogy

Valerie Willis

4 Horsemen
Publications, Inc.

4 Horsemen Publications, Inc.
1497 Main St. Suite 169
Dunedin, FL 34698
4horsemenpublications.com
info@4horsemenpublications.com

Cover by Valerie Willis
Typesetting by Autumn Skye
Edited by Heather Teele

Library of Congress Control Number: 2022948986

Paperback ISBN-13: 978-1-64450-070-5
Hardcover ISBN-13: 978-1-64450-068-2
Audiobook ISBN-13: 978-1-64450-583-0
Ebook ISBN-13: 978-1-64450-068-2

DEDICATION

To my great-grandmother who taught me the importance of having Faith.

And to Shannon Whitlock for making sure this story got the attention and love it needed. Sorry it took so long to bring this trilogy to life!

Acknowledgments

A big thank you to those who backed this project on Kickstarter. It was amazing to see so many jump into the cause, and it only made me push harder. That includes the following awesome people:

Andrea Baker

Bill Arneson

Corey

David Sushil

Ryan O'Reilly

Sammy Smith

Richard Wentworth

Trudy Warman

Karen Webster

Secondly, another thank you to all my beta readers who gave me so much of their time. Without them, this story would have been lacking some much-needed love to get it off the ground completely.

Kay Kauffman for smacking me about and helping me clean up my mess! Love you and thank you!

TABLE OF CONTENTS

TRIGGER WARNING

This story contains themes of genocide, suicide, verbal and physical abuse, bullying, violence, murder, and similar, which may cause a reader distress. Read with caution, and please understand this is a fictionalized world, but some of the events are very realistic in nature. This is a trilogy about overcoming the tribulations of the past, present, and future as you uncover who you are and who you wish to be.

I

FADE TO BLACK

*H*otan's eyes struggled against the blinding light and searing heat. The intense white horizon of a desert landscape swallowed him. Sparkling sand, bright cloudless skies, and waves of heat obscured everything which lay beyond where he stood. Turning again and again, there was no end or means of knowing where this place was … or if it even existed at all. In the distance, he heard the sound of waves hitting the shore, but he could never make it over the hill when he came here. His ears began to pound with the beating of his heart until it deafened him.

His chest ached as panic filled him. *It's the dream again. Frantic, he searched all around. Where is he? He always comes for me. I never…*

"HOTAN!" a voice roared, closer than it should have been since he he'd been searching so hard for the inevitable attacker.

I never see him coming.

Hotan's nerves unraveled in his joints. Turning, his gaze fell upon a disrupted, blackened figure approaching him. It vibrated and wiggled as it closed the gap between them. It was as if this single component of his dream had poor reception, static of thoughts or emotions, and it kept him from seeing who stood there.

Just let me see his face this time. Is this a man or demon? Why do I feel like I know him? My instincts scream that this voice, this presence, is someone I should know by heart by now, yet…

"Hotan! I shall take my revenge." The animosity in the voice gripped Hotan's soul.

Not again. That aura of murderous intent is starting to weigh down on me. I know that I know him, but why do I also feel as if I have never met him? It's a haunting sensation of déjà vu.

"Revenge?" Hotan's mind flooded with questions as he tried to decipher the familiar voice. "Who are you? Why do I feel like I should know you? Have we met?"

"You know what blood runs in our hearts! This will be the last time you hide from me, the last time you'll hide from what you've done!" A long sword appeared out of the wavering blackness. Unlike the man who held it, this element of the dream was clear as it reflected the blinding sun, shining down upon Hotan like a spotlight on its kill. "I wish to thank you for my tortured life during all these centuries! I'll send you to a lonely darkness equal to the one you gave me!"

Hotan's heels scraped against something hard, and he fell backward. No matter how many times he changed his direction, he always fell back into the emptiness of this place. The sand, coarse enough to draw blood, burnt as his palms landed hard. It slowed, everything lingering between thudding heartbeats. The blade rose high, racing at him with astonishing speed as if it had broken loose from some time warp. Its edge ripped across his arms, and he released a blood-curdling scream. Blood sprayed into the air, the dark mist muddling the bright skies overhead. Falling back, it throbbed and stung.

All of this is so real; maybe I died this way in a past life, but…

The black shadow released a maddening laugh, the same one Hotan had heard a million times before in this nightmare. Wild eyes and a wide grin became clear on the shadow's vibrating face. The black static now carried a new color in its distortion; Hotan's stomach twisted as he saw the red tone of his blood blending into its very being.

Why? *he thought.*

Waves of slashes, not deep enough to kill, struck repeatedly. His screams were useless against the laughing man in this place where he found himself imprisoned. Suddenly, the blade plunged through his chest, pinning him against the sand, his heart aching against the metal which kept it from pumping. A coldness flowed through him as his blood soaked the earth, signaling his oncoming death. Darkness hid the blinding landscape, and a great weight of emotions pressed down on him for not recognizing the man he'd wronged in some way...

"Hotan!" Pushing her glasses back on her nose, the haughty teacher snorted in his direction.

He jerked his head up from his desk, breathing heavily after his nightmare. Sweat covered his face, palms cold and sweaty. Eyes pressed into him from all sides. *Did I fall asleep?*

"I would appreciate it if you stayed awake during my class." Scoffing, she turned back to the whiteboard to continue the math lesson on sine versus cosine.

"Feh." Rubbing the sweat off his forehead, he ignored the warning. *Of all places...*

"Psst, are you okay?" Wide-eyed, the light-haired girl in the desk next to him leaned closer. "You're looking pale today. Are you sick?"

"I'm fine." Annoyed that she had noticed his distraught expression, he cracked his neck before glaring out the window. *Great, now everyone thinks there's something else wrong with me.*

The girl sighed before returning to her notes.

I'm in no mood to talk to anyone. It wasn't uncommon for him to be antisocial, even with classmates. He spent most of his time in class looking out windows, waiting for the bell to ring. *I already know this. Why can't I just test out of it?* Despite the lack of focus, he passed his courses without any difficulties. *I just have no motivation to put extra effort into this.*

Hotan watched a gym class finish its last round of a basketball game. The view from the second-story window was the perfect escape from his math teacher's monotonous lecture. As the last of the kids disappeared, he shifted his focus to a pair of mourning doves sitting on the tennis court fence. A few more landed next to them, joining the line as the sun rose higher in the sky. The warmth of light hit his face as it pushed through the glass, a comforting sensation compared to the echoes of cold which still rattled through him.

It's strange how the birds are so clear and distinct from the rest of this gray landscape. Though he'd been born completely color-blind, there were occasionally strange moments where an object would appear in color. Despite having never seen colors before, he knew their names and how to describe them. One doctor had labeled him as a classic case of cerebral achromatopsia, a fancy term that meant he does see colors since he describes the world around him in shades of gray. The other theory came from a skeptic who claimed: "He sees color, but this is a clear cry for attention."

The doctor pointed out that the truly colorblind have no recognition of what gray is. It didn't matter; he couldn't tell you what color anyone around him wore, let alone the school's colors. He had other things to focus on than school pride. *Screw team spirit. Who was that man?* His thoughts reeled as the sounds of the classroom faded. Closing his eyes, the dark figure reappeared in his mind. *The same dream over and over again. This year has been the worst. What does it mean?*

"Class dismissed!" The teacher cleared her throat as students rushed the door. "Hotan Samuels, I need to speak with you."

Grabbing his book bag, Hotan approached her desk as the last student departed, leaving them alone. "Yes, Mrs. Bothirsen? Is there a problem?"

"Hotan…" She paused, waiting for the door to click shut before returning her gaze to him. "I know you are passing the exams with straight A's, but please, stay awake in my class. Just because you're smarter than the other students, doesn't mean you get special privileges, and it certainly doesn't mean you can nap in class. You'll never pass if you continue to just sit here staring out the window. You need to start participating."

"Sorry, I haven't been sleeping well," he confessed and turned away.

"Look, if you don't take my class seriously, I'm not going to give you an easy A." Mrs. Bothirsen cleared her throat as her tone grew stern and sharp. "The other teachers may give you special treatment, but I expect you to work for your grade."

"I got it. Understood." He started heading for the hall with no reaction on his face.

Her chair squeaked as she grew louder, offended by his even-keeled tone. "Look! I need you to take me seriously!"

Stopping a few steps short of the door, he glared back at her. "I apologized. I didn't purposely fall asleep, and I'm being honest with you. What more do you want?"

She opened her mouth to speak, but he interrupted her.

"Plus, who said I had special privileges? If that was the case, I wouldn't even bother showing up to class or school. I'd move on to more productive things in my life." Smirking, he glided out the door, leaving her unable to retort without risking someone overhearing her.

The hallways undulated before him, a churning of grays like boiling water in a silver pot. He kept his head low, silver bangs aiding in his efforts to ignore unwanted eye contact, especially after the debacle in math class. He just wanted to finish this last year of high school and move on with his life. Unlike the kids surrounding him, Hotan had no choice but to grow up. Memories of his mom made him bite his cheek as he continued the silent march down the stairs to the first floor. *I'm here because I promised her that I would graduate high school.* He sighed, passing through the mayhem like a phantom. The students around him seemed to fall silent as he lost himself to sour thoughts and memories. Panicked kids rushed past him, but he felt no urgency to make it to class on time—not anymore.

He paused in front of his locker. Tossing the math book on top of the stack, he huffed to himself. A smirk crept across his face. *There are only a few months left, and I'm done. I can move on once I do this for Mom.* He shut the door on the pile of textbooks, many of which he hadn't opened. Despite that, he was passing with straight A's. *It's like I was born with centuries of information programmed into every fiber of my being, but who am I to question it anymore? Not like I need someone to fix it.* Carrying the books to his classes had been a way to show his teachers respect and appear less intimidating to other students. At least bringing a book gave the impression that he studied or gave him a chance to follow along, though he wasn't interested in the slightest.

"Hey, there," a deep voice rang in Hotan's ears. Chills ran across the back of his neck as if Death himself had whispered the words. "I heard you were looking for me?"

"Hisota." Hotan turned and shoved the skinny, dark-eyed boy. "You haven't been to band practice. Are you even going to play at the club tonight? Or are you finally quitting the band? At least man up and tell me you quit."

With a coy smile, Hisota flicked his long, black ponytail off his shoulders. After a moment, he shrugged, increasing Hotan's ire. "What does it matter?"

"I need to know." Lately, Hotan had a tough time considering Hisota a friend. They'd met back in elementary school, and Hisota had followed hot on his heels ever since. "Cut the crap, Hisota. Are you leaving the band, yes or no?"

"If I say no, are you going to bully me into going tonight? Or would you prefer I say yes, so your cheerleader-wannabe girlfriend can take my place?" Twisting his face into a vinegary look, it was clear Hisota had a jealous streak when it came to Hotan's relationships with anyone else. "I hope you know pretty girls like her look like whores on grungy rocker boys like you. She's not—"

Hisota yelped as Hotan gripped him by the shirt and slammed him into the lockers. "Leave her out of this! Everyone knows you're jealous of her. Knock it off and grow up already."

"Don't flatter yourself." Hisota jerked out of Hotan's grip and stomped off into the wall of eyes.

"If you don't show, I'm counting it as you quitting!" Hotan shouted after him.

He doesn't get it. He's messing with my livelihood. Ignoring the chatter and giggles, Hotan pushed his way through the front doors of the old, brick school. *Unlike all of them, I have to make this work. I don't have parents to lean on, and I can't rely on Annie forever.* Aggravated, he tuned out the world and people around him as he made his way to the bus loop, marching silently down the sidewalk. He stopped a block down from the school where a strangely shaped shadow fell over him. Before him, he saw the old, broken church. *Yeah, I need time to think before I do something I might regret.*

2

LATERALUS

The church reminded him of St. Patrick's Cathedral in New York City, only half the size and with fewer embellishments. All he knew about the place was that it was built near the end of the American colonial period and abandoned for longer than anyone could remember. Not even his mother could recall how long it had been sitting on its weedy throne. Despite the church's small stature, it still towered over the quaint neighborhood, just as it had over the township since its completion. The modern homes neighboring it left the old monument stuck in a past no one wanted to remember. Regardless of its battered appearance, it was a solid piece of architecture and the perfect place to be alone.

Hotan couldn't remember what brought him here so long ago, but the peace it brought him when he walked through its rotting, wooden doors was refreshing. Slipping through the one working door, he stepped inside the dust-covered wreck. The church had once housed several angelic statues, but time and neglect had crumbled most of them. Two stone guardians near the front had broken limbs, damaged wings, and missing faces. Remnants of wooden pews scattered the floor. Behind the podium, in front of a shattered stained-glass window, lay a crippled wooden cross in a bed of rubble, having failed to uphold the savior it had once supported so proudly. The place would have been a sight to see in its prime. Only the finest materials had been utilized; fragments of marble, splinters of dark cedar, and hints of silver were evident in the little bit of décor that remained intact. What had once been a virtuous white, now lay in filth, grayed by dust, decaying and adding to the musky scent the air held.

Amid the wreckage, a few places to sit remained, and Hotan would often spend hours there, lost in thought. *This is my place. A year or two ago, the neighbors had questioned his coming and going from the church, but it didn't stop him. No "For Sale" signs had ever graced the lot in the time since he'd first noticed it, and oddly, no one he'd ever asked knew who owned the property. So much for getting permission to be here, but no one's heard from the owner, and the police don't seem to mind me being here since I am visiting a church.* He sat on a pew, staring at the broken, gray world around him as his muscles loosened. Leaving behind the conflicts of the day, he steadied his mind and his emotions, inhaling the pungent smell and finding harmony within it.

After several minutes, he sighed and walked back out the front doors. He pulled a cloth tarp off something large, exposing the motorcycle he had parked on the side of the building. A blue-flamed Suzuki Hayabusa—bought with what little money his mother's death had left him—glimmered in the afternoon sunlight. The school had thrown a tantrum when he attempted to register it as his senior year transportation. They revoked his parking permit at the very idea of such a thing, so he resorted to parking it here. Pulling on his helmet, he started the bike, gassing it softly so not to bring unwanted attention. The moment the back tire hit the asphalt, he opened up the throttle and roared toward the waiting city.

Shellie gripped his waist in a firm hug as they pulled off the busy downtown street. The front tire splashed through the puddles littering the back alleyway. He had picked her up on his way to the club, fearing Hisota's confrontation at school was his way of telling Hotan he wasn't going to be there again. The bike leaned heavily against the kickstand as he waited for Shellie to climb off. Removing the full-face helmet, he huffed and shook out his hair. Looking over the parking lot, he saw no signs of Hisota's bike. *It's down to either no show or a grand entrance at the last second.* Hotan bit his tongue as he dismounted his bike, stomping past Shellie through the back door of the club.

Anger crawled across his shoulders as he tensed and threw his helmet at the lockers. "Dammit, Hisota!" The thunderous noise caught everyone's attention, making them all flinch.

"It's okay. You know I'm perfectly fine with playing bass." Shellie gave him her best smile. "We all figured he wasn't coming after what happened at school."

"It still pisses me off that he doesn't take this as seriously as the rest of us." Hotan looked at her, a mournful look in his eyes. "I can't just replace him easily either. It gives me headaches just thinking about the drama he'd create. He must be going through some stuff, and he wants to do it alone. I can respect that, I get it, but I just wish one of us knew what the hell has him so worked over."

"Hotan, he'll get over it, just give him a few more weeks." Kyle, Hotan's best friend, flipped a drumstick in the air, twirling it in his fingers with uncanny ease. "We've got Shellie 'til he gets his act together. The last thing we need is for him to pull his power card in here. But I won't stop you from pounding his face in if it comes to blows."

"And whose face are we pounding in?" Chaz, the owner of the club, 7even, entered the room. He towered over the adolescents and grinned. After a puff from his cigar, he asked, "Still on for tonight, kids?"

There was a long pause as Hotan stared at Shellie and Kyle. They both nodded reassuringly. He relinquished the answer, "We're still on. Guess it's another night of me singing, if you don't mind." Sighing, Hotan picked up his electric guitar and flopped down on the bench to tune it. "We'll be out soon as we're all tuned. I'll let you know when to announce us."

"Fine with me." Cigar smoke billowed out of Chaz's lips as he walked back the way he'd come in. "See you on set in fifteen minutes," he chuckled.

It was a typical Wednesday night; regulars filled in the bar top and scattered between some of the tables. The band didn't always play on a slow night, but it was a chance to make extra cash—a concern for Hotan. *Being a cover band has its perks and opportunities. Unlike my fellow band members, I don't have the luxury of living at home with Mom and Dad anymore. Hisota is putting my livelihood at risk every time he throws one of his tantrums. Refusing to show up is his power card to make me bend in his favor. It worked the first few times, but I can't do this. I have to think about myself and my future. Unlike them,* Hotan eyed both Shellie and Kyle from where he stood on stage, *I don't have a safety net left.*

"Good evening, everyone." Hotan's voice was smooth and solid as he spoke to the crowd sitting silently in the darkness just beyond the stage. "We're going to start with my personal favorite cover, Tool's 'Lateralus.'"

As he picked the starting melody, he let his frustrations melt away. Playing music and reminiscing in the church seemed to be the only times he found some sort of peace within himself. In this moment, he felt like a real person instead of a constantly churning bundle of questions about every facet of his existence. Every element of his life was broken, or worse—lost forever. *Why would the world aim to destroy a person so much without some purpose or meaning behind it? My very nature opposes logic.* Perhaps he was overthinking, but a nagging feeling lingered at his core, telling him the reason was somewhere within himself, just waiting to be discovered. The dream, his knowledge, and his instincts drove him to keep going, to find the motivation behind his cursed existence. Despite everything, he'd made it this far.

Dropping Shellie off at home, he held her chin and kissed her slowly and tenderly. *At least I have this much left.* She was one of the very few people he trusted enough to share his feelings with, but there was still much that he kept to himself. He put his helmet back on and waited for her to close the front door before leaving the sleepy, suburban neighborhood. The cool night air comforted him as he made his way down streets and highways. Going home wasn't an option just yet. The day's events weighed heavily on his mind, and he wouldn't be able to sleep tonight. He found himself once more in front of the church as it sat in the shadow of the night.

He picked his way carefully through the trash and debris, awed by the beams of light sparkling down into this hallowed space. Odd shapes and shades of gray scattered across the dust-covered ruins like a colorless kaleidoscope. He sat down, drinking in the atmosphere. The wooden seat creaked and moaned as he shifted his weight. Closing his eyes, time paused to take a breath with him. Nothing seemed urgent or pressing anymore. Instead, he had all of eternity to resolve his problems.

"I've been waiting for you, Hotan," a rough male voice grumbled from the door.

Hotan's eyes widened as fear knocked the air from his chest. Flashes of his nightmare came to him, and he replayed dozens—no, thousands—of deaths. He wanted to run, but he couldn't bring himself to blink or even take a breath. Hotan stood frozen, every muscle taut and unable to move, not knowing if he'd see a man or demon just behind him.

"And here you are, right on time. You've walked right into the lion's den," chuckled the stranger. "If you want to stay hidden from me, you shouldn't be so predictable. What was that old Spanish proverb? Oh, yes, 'Habits begin as cobwebs and end up as chains.'"

The dream has come true! Jolting up from his seat, Hotan looked back at the entrance and met the wild glare of a large man. Hotan's voice failed him. Panic flooded him as his gaze took in every detail of the man. The broad-shouldered stranger had the bulk of a heavyweight fighter. Dreadlocks framed a maddening grin. He blocked the only exit. This sacred place of security had broken its oath to him, surrounding Hotan like a broken coffin. A cold sweat dripped down his temple as he watched the predator stalk its prey, taking slow agonizing steps ever closer. Laughter boiled out of the beast-sized man while Hotan's heart fluttered. *This can't be real. This can't be happening!*

"I've searched for you for centuries. Now, I can finally repay you for the hell you've put me through!" The man pulled out a large machete and swung it through the air, slicing the remnants of a marble statue with breathtaking rage. The exhibit of unnatural strength added to the soul-crushing fear that gripped Hotan.

"I can finally take you down and end the curse with which you imprisoned my soul!"

"Wh-who are y-y-you?" stuttered Hotan, barely getting the question out. He stumbled back, but his heel slammed into a piece of marble. He toppled backward, filling the air with clouds of dust. "How-how do you know m-m-my name?" *Am I really going to die here? Is this the end? I don't want to die! Not like this, not without something good happening in my life first!*

"Eh?" The man paused, dropping his machete slightly as his smile faded. "You don't remember me? Still?"

Panting, Hotan could only give the man a bewildered, terrified expression.

"Oh, that's just peachy!" A devilish grin crawled across his face as a cruel, deep laugh spilled forth. "You won't even put up a fight! Your own spell will be the thorn in your side! Karma's a bitch, ain't it, Hotan?"

"Please, I don't know what you're talking about!" Hotan shrieked, but the stranger laughed harder. "You must have the wrong person!" *Someone! Please help me!*

"No, you wouldn't know what I'm talking about." He stepped closer to Hotan, towering above him like Death, his blade held high. "You haven't awakened at all! Must be my lucky day. The fear pouring out of you is so sweet; I could drink from it all night."

Hotan pleaded with the zealot, "Please! I don't know what you're talking about."

"Hmm, where to cut you first?" The stranger ignored his outcry, smiling as he mused on. "Maybe I should start with your fingers and slowly work my way up the arms. What do you think, Hotan?"

Hotan's eyes widened, his body on fire. An intense heat filled him, spreading outward from his core. His terror shifted slowly into anger as he looked up into the eyes of his would-be killer.

Body, mind, and soul felt unexpectedly complete, despite the warmth emanating from deep inside. Flames wafted up from a deep unknown. As it grew, part of himself seemed forced to set itself to the side, ripping him from this moment of completeness. Someone else had taken the reigns. *Wait, I can't control or feel my body anymore? What's happening?* Flecks of color began to appear as he glared into Geliah's amber eyes. The sudden release of power had somehow changed Hotan.

"Back off, Geliah. I will defend myself if you do not cease this nonsense." *What is happening? Who else is here with me, inside me? Who is speaking for me? This isn't me. I don't understand!*

"You always were the party pooper, Hotan." Sighing, Geliah's wild grin vanished as he stepped back and allowed Hotan to stand. "This can't be healthy for you. The fear I felt a moment ago was not yours. Why endanger an innocent by hiding in a body that's not yours? Doesn't seem like your style. What would your big brother have to say about—"

"Silence!" Hotan's eyes shifted to bright green, and black lines snaked across his body like tattoos brought to life.

"Bah!" Geliah's skin reacted in a similar manner, like a chameleon changing its skin. "No offense, but I should have never been able to break that spell of yours."

"Do not question matters beyond your comprehension." Hotan's jaw muscles twitched as he spoke, "My soul slumbers within this new body, for it has no place in this world anymore. You should have stayed asleep, Geliah of Fear."

"You want me to tell you why your spell fell apart?" A wicked grin came across Geliah's face as he brushed back his dreadlocks.

Blue flames rose from Hotan's skin as he glared at Geliah. "I am reborn. I no longer exist. Only my essence remains," he insisted.

"That's all that's left?" Geliah scoffed in disappointment. "I was hoping for a good fight."

What are they talking about? This has to be another dream. I have to wake up! "I would gladly give up the last of my life to save this child from my past mistakes."

Geliah ignored the heat of Hotan's glare. "A shame you feel that way. Let me end this last piece of you then!" Geliah gave a primal scream as he swung the machete. "Now die!"

"Stop!" Hotan's voice echoed throughout the church as he caught the blade with a bare hand.

Glowering at Geliah, he tightened his grip on the blade. Paling, Geliah hadn't expected him to catch it unscathed. He took a step back, fearful of a counterattack. The blue flames painting Hotan's skin rose higher as rage filled his green eyes. The sword rusted and crumbled to the floor, leaving no mark on the hand with which he'd caught the blade's edge. A massive flash exploded from Hotan, blowing Geliah off his feet. The shock wave pulled Geliah across the marble floor and pinned him against the raised edge of the pulpit, following where Hotan's hand commanded him to go.

Another wave pulsed, and as it touched the ruins of the church, it seemed as if a miracle was happening. Missing marble materialized, its shine intact. Old woodcarvings appeared pristine. Angelic statues held their once missing shields in newfound limbs with pride on their found faces. As the wave rolled across, it returned the church to the peak of its glory. The pulse of power receded, leaving the final repairs doused in blue flames. *Did that come from me or the other Hotan? How is this possible? This can't be real. It can't be!*

Before him, the stained-glass window above the pulpit pulled itself back together. A large wooden cross rose to its rightful place, a resurrection unfolding like nothing he had ever known.

The statue nailed to the wooden cross stared down, passing judgment at the two of them. They glowered at one another as they convened in the unbroken cathedral. The sanctuary glowed in its newfound splendor as moonlight scattered the window's many colors around the room.

Geliah groaned and snarled as he stood. "Is that it? What a wasted display of power," he snickered. "I didn't come here to watch parlor tricks!"

"Geliah!" a new voice called from the front of the church where the doors had swung open.

A tall, thin man with silver hair dressed in a white business suit stood unphased. His silver eyes held Geliah and Hotan in place as he walked toward them. The church doors slammed shut, the thud echoing through the vaulted ceilings. *Another one? Where are these people coming from?*

The new stranger cleared his throat. "You know what you are doing is forbidden. Did I not warn you that there would be consequences for such actions? Did I not tell you never to force awakening on anyone else?"

"Oh, look, it's the Vulture of Judgment." Geliah's jaw visibly clenched. "We both know you can't pull power on me like before, Talib. Go pass your judgment someplace else."

"I wish to make you an offer." Talib straightened his tie a moment before glancing back at Hotan who nodded in recognition. "You are looking for a good fight and the ability to settle a score. I will give you the chance to do that … under my terms."

It's as if this other version of me knows what the offer will be. But who are these people? Why am I not in control of my body?

"You've got my attention," Geliah said, arching a brow. "What sort of a deal do you have in mind?"

"Give me one year to prep the young boy. If you kill him, you get what you desire, wiping all traces of Hotan off the Earth. If you fail to kill him or if you break our deal, there will be a devastating punishment in store for you."

Geliah considered the proposal. After a long moment of silence, he grunted, "You mean it?"

"I always mean it." Talib cocked his head. "Is this not what you want? A chance to kill Hotan without interruption?"

"Fine, it's a deal." Without further confrontation, Geliah marched past, slipping out of the newly repaired doors of the church.

"Thank you, *alef chet*…" Hotan thudded hard against the cold marble floor as darkness took him away.

ONE YEAR?! TO FIGHT THAT GUY?!

WAKE UP! WAKE UP! WAKE UP!

3

I DON'T CARE

At first, the muffled sounds in Hotan's ears came in the form of a tunneled shout down the longest hallway ever. With no sense of time, he strained to focus on the words. *Whoever it is sounds urgent and horrifyingly desperate.* Shivering, the coldness in his body did nothing to pull him from the darkness he sat in. Something warm and wet hit his cheek. Wiping it off his face, he opened his eyes, looking at the clear liquid in confusion. Fascinated by it, he rolled it between his fingers. More started to hit his face like tears falling from invisible eyes. The voice had stopped yelling and simply sobbed.

If these aren't my tears, then who do they belong to? Who's crying? Why are they so upset? What does this have to do with me? There's no reason to cry over someone like me.

"HOTAN!" His heart skipped a beat as the voice called his name, loud and clear. "Please! Wake up, Hotan!"

Shellie! He struggled to gain the strength, still tangled in his dreamlike state. Hotan tore himself from the pitch-black prison to truly open his eyes. As his vision regained focus, he stared into the brightest green eyes. For the first time, he saw her eyes and face in full color, the phenomenal, emerald green of Shellie's irises. They held small specks of gold which added to the rich earth tone of the green, but the tears falling from her flushed face made his heart ache.

"Shellie?"

"Hotan! You're awake! He's awake!" Shellie hugged him tight as her tears rained down on him. "What happened to you? I thought you were dead! You were so cold when I found you and I… Did someone do this to you?"

Attempting to sit up, the cathedral tilted and spun around Hotan as an agonizing pain filled his head. Looking back to Shellie's distraught face, he watched the colors melt away. *No, I want to see it for just a moment longer. The rosy peach tone of her skin, the natural pinkness of her lips… It's all fading away.* His miracle had come and gone so quickly, making his chest throb.

He opened his mouth to say something, but the words were lost in his sorrow. "I…"

"The ambulance should be here shortly, Shellie!" shouted Kyle as he walked into the cathedral with Hisota close behind. "Oh man, what a relief! He's awake!"

"Jesus, he looks pale." The surprised expression on Hisota's face let Hotan know how bad his current state looked. "What in the hell were you doing?"

With the help of his friends, Hotan managed to sit down on a pew. His head still spun as he struggled to remember how he got there. Another wave of shivering crawled across his skin as the sounds of distant sirens drew near. He tried to focus his thoughts, but all he remembered was leaving Shellie's house.

Looking up at his friends, he looked around, puzzled. "Where am I?"

"The church by the school. You don't remember where you are?" Shellie's words lingered in his thoughts as his stomach twisted into knots. They all looked at one another, concern visible on their faces. Shellie continued, "You come here all the time, Hotan."

The church? The broken place I come to all the time. Where I come to think? When did it ... but this can't be the same place? I must be dreaming... "The ... church?" Hotan's eyes scanned over the clean bright marble, the unbroken stained-glass windows, and lastly, the breathtaking crucifix statue on a wooden cross behind the podium. "But this can't be..." *Did someone renovate this place?*

"How long have I been missing?" A surge of panic flooded him as cold sweat raced down his back. "This isn't how I remember it! This can't be the same place! How long was I missing?"

"Well, I last saw you last night when you dropped me off." Shellie sat next to him as he looked at her, baffled. "You seemed fine when you left."

"When you weren't at school, we were all really confused." Kyle rubbed the back of his neck a moment. "So, when none of us had heard from you today, we got worried and decided to look for you after school ended."

"No offense, but in all the years I've known you, you've never called in sick," Hisota huffed as the church doors opened and the paramedics rushed in. "Anyway, let's have the experts take a look at you."

Hotan struggled to concentrate on the questions the paramedics asked him as they went about their work. The pressure of the cuff on his arm, the prick of the IV, and the forceful shove of the thermometer did nothing to disrupt his befuddled gaze. He was trying to take in every detail of the church in its current state. This was the peak of the cathedral's prime. The wood braces on the roof were each intricately placed and held unique carved scenes. The cedar pews were vibrant, even through his gray-colored world. The shiny embellishments made each seat like a throne, confirming what he had speculated about the décor.

A gurney rolled in, and with the help of the paramedics, he lay down on the rolling bed. Staring at the roof as they rolled him out, he witnessed not one cobweb on that ceiling. From his last memories, the rafters had barely been visible through the filth and spider webs. The sunlight blinded him as he made his way to the ambulance. Squinting his eyes, he continued to answer questions and reply to the information they gave him. He couldn't remember anything to assist the paramedics in figuring out what had happened to him. Hotan's body ached, his head pounded, and worse off, he felt sick to his stomach. *What happened to me?* No memories or hints presented themselves to him. Frustrated, he turned his focus to what was currently happening in the ambulance as it sped toward the hospital.

"Where have you been this last week?" Hisota leaned against Hotan's locker. "You couldn't call and update me on how you were doing? I had to get my info from Kyle, or worse, Shellie, the last several days."

"Like they told you, I was recovering." Hotan twisted his mouth as he nodded for Hisota to move out of the way. "I heard you actually made it to the club over the weekend. What brought on that change of heart?"

"I'm not that big of a dick." A smirk crawled across Hisota's face as Hotan slammed his locker closed. "I know that's your livelihood, and you're going to need the money to pay the hospital bills, right?"

"Don't remind me." Hotan glared at Hisota, trying to figure out what new angle he was trying to pull. "Does this mean you can play at the club as long as I'm not there?"

"Maybe." Hisota raised an eyebrow as he lost his smile. "At least your girl is a half-decent bassist, and Chaz had one of his guys play the guitar in your place. You're welcome."

"I'm not in the mood to talk about this." Breaking eye contact with Hisota, Hotan stared into the bustling hallway of students. *I still don't feel like myself. Last thing I need is to let my temper loose...*

Sighing, Hotan bumped shoulders with Hisota as he passed. He disappeared into the crowded hallway, leaving Hisota standing at the lockers alone.

"HEY!" Kyle bulldozed his way from the other direction. "HISOTA!"

"And here comes his majesty's dog," Hisota huffed under his breath as Kyle stopped, panting in front of him. "What on earth do you want?"

"I, I was wondering if Hotan made it back to school today?" Finally catching his breath, Kyle stood up straight. "My classes are way on the other end, and I was trying to catch him."

"Unfortunately, yes." Nodding down the hallway, he replied, "But he's already headed to his next class. You'll be able to catch him after school."

"Oh, thanks! Well, I better run back before I'm late to class again." Kyle started to run down the hall until he knocked books out of a girl's hands. "Oops! So sorry, here let me help you!"

Hotan stopped in front of the cathedral. Its outer walls were just as clean and bright as the inside. He'd kept his distance from the church, needing to build up his courage to dare see it again. Whatever happened that night, it left an unnerving sensation with no memory and a place he didn't recognize anymore. A jogging duo passed him, both commenting on the beautiful church. Hotan sighed; his sanctuary was now exposed to the world and no longer the invisible fortress where he could be alone. It stood out among the homes around it and shouted its existence today as the afternoon sun reflected off the white walls. Taking a deep breath, Hotan stood there with his hand against the new wooden doors. Calming his nerves, he walked inside.

Maybe coming here will help me remember what happened that night. I feel like a piece of me is missing, and my body still gets waves of shivers. The doctors insist its severe dehydration, but I can't shake the feeling that they're so wrong...

Walking down the aisle, he gawked at the miraculous renovations. It was as if the church had been reborn as he looked down at his own reflection in the marble floors. A surreal sensation grew with every glance he made as he paused in front of the podium. The crucifix was powerful as it hung in front of the rows of pews. It demanded attention to the front of the church, and the feelings it invoked were amazing. Hotan's eyes took in every detail as he observed the battered look of the cross. The granite statue painfully nailed to the wood stared down at him with a mournful expression. He admired the adaptation of the large granite wings that cast a shadow across the pews through the light of the stained-glass window. The statue would have seemed almost free with the wings spread so wide if it hadn't been tied down by an earthly possession. Shifting his attention, he heard a trickling sound. In the back right corner, a fountain of holy water flowed from what he assumed was a natural underground spring. Walking over to it, he investigated his own face in the shimmering reflection.

Do I look that sad? Maybe the statue and I have a lot in common. We just want to be free, but we're both being forced back to the ground.

"Hey!" Hotan jerked at the sudden sound of Kyle's voice. "I was hoping to catch you at school since Hisota said you were there today. How are ya feeling? You need help with anything?"

"I'm fine." Hotan took in a deep breath as he broke eye contact with his wavering reflection in the fountain. "So, what brings you to the church?"

"Figured you would come here, you know, fall back into routine. You've been extra quiet, lately. I mean you're the strong, silent type, but this is sort of scary silence stuff, ya know?" They both started walking back down the aisle toward the front doors. "Plus, I wasn't sure if I would find you passed out on the floor again."

"I should be fine." They paused a moment, and Hotan looked Kyle in the eyes, taking a firm grip of his friend's shoulder as a sign of reassurance. "They said I was super dehydrated. Most likely, a result of all the stress and not getting enough sleep lately. I'll take better care of myself since none of us really want a repeat of this debacle."

"Definitely, man. Well, guess you know I'm there for ya." Kyle sighed. "Did Shellie catch a ride with her friends today?"

"Yeah, I think they were going to go study." Hotan rubbed his jaw momentarily as they walked outside. "I feel bad, they were asking me to help them with calculus homework. I may be a genius, but I lack the patience to teach others. It's hard for me to pitch it in a dumbed-down version since it makes perfect sense to me when I look at the stuff."

"I think Shellie understands." Kyle started laughing as he watched Hotan straddle his motorcycle and strap on his helmet. "Plus, that one time you tried to help me was a disaster. You have a short temper when it comes to tutoring. Well, that and Hisota."

"Tell me about it," he muttered, starting the bike.

Hotan waved goodbye to Kyle before racing down the street. As he zoned into the drive home, passing through the endless rows of houses and subdivisions, he recalled the first time he met Shellie:

It was the first day of high school, and the freshman were all getting their fair share of harassment by the upper classmen. As usual, he'd kept a low profile and cold-shouldered all the encounters thrown at him. The day was nearing a close as he walked to his locker for one last book exchange. Turning the corner, he walked into a scene of two jocks pinning a girl against the lockers. Their grins and expressions clearly indicated that they weren't going anywhere until they got what they wanted from her. That girl was Shellie.

"C'mon, sweetheart. Why wouldn't a freshman like you want to go on a date with one of the senior football players?" The lead jock's grin faltered at this point, showing his frustration with her refusals. They had been at this for some time before Hotan came across them. He went unnoticed as they continued harassing Shellie. "Think of how popular you'll be when everyone finds out we're dating?"

"Get over yourself." Shellie tried to push through the two jocks, but a tight grip on her arm shoved her back against the lockers. "Ow! Let go. You're hurting me!"

"Darian doesn't just ask any girl out, you know?" Darian's friend scoffed at her. "And no girl has ever turned down the chance to date my friend here."

"Well, consider me the first." Shellie pulled her curly short hair away from her mouth as she jerked her arm away from him. "If you don't mind, I aim to be on time to all my classes today."

"I don't think so, doll." Darian pushed her yet again into the lockers, his smile was long gone as she continued to rebel. "You're not going anywhere until you tell me yes."

"Are you kidding me?" Her face paled as she began to realize that this was pushing beyond freshman bullying. "You can't go around forcing girls to be with you! That's messed up!"

"I'll do what I want, when I want." Darian placed his hand on her hip, and she slapped it away. "I dare you to do that again."

Sweat ran down the side of Shellie's cheek as she swallowed back her fears. Darian was massive, twice her size in height and probably weighed four times more than her petite frame. His short, dark hair and dark eyes only added to his menacing demeanor. Shellie glared at his companion, a slightly lighter-haired boy with light-colored eyes who started to shift nervously. It was getting too aggressive even for him. Once more, Darian placed his hand on her hip. Shellie grimaced as she tried to slap his hand away again, fearing he would hit her for the action. Her hand missed, but his hand was gone.

"What the hell?" Darian roared as Hotan tightened his grip on his wrist. "Who do you think you are?"

"It doesn't matter." Hotan's voice was calm and solid, as always. "Are you okay?"

Shellie stood in silence as she looked from Darian's face of rage to the stoic expression of Hotan. "I … yeah, now I am."

"Let go of me! Mikey, get him off me!" Hotan worked Darian's arm behind him, twisting it in a way that Darian couldn't break free from without some sort of pain, preventing any struggling. "I'm going to kill you for this!"

"Man, I didn't sign up for this shit." And with that, Mikey, his accomplice, rushed away, leaving the two boys and the frightened Shellie alone. "Fight your own battles, Darian."

"Now, apologize." Hotan tugged at Darian's arm, sending an excruciating agony to his shoulder. "Apologize and promise you'll never touch her again."

"What if I refuse?" Darian tried laughing through his discomfort as he gave Shellie a baleful glare. "You going to hold me here forever?"

"That was your plan." A smirk crawled across Hotan's face. "Tell her sorry and promise to leave her alone, Darian. You're not going anywhere until you tell her."

"Go screw yours—" Hotan slammed him into the lockers next to Shellie, causing her to squeal as she stood there in shock. "Dammit!"

"If you keep telling me no, I'll make sure you'll be kissing your football career goodbye before ever kissing another girl." Hotan's words stung Darian's ego as his shoulder throbbed and he glared at Shellie. "Now, let's try this one last time. Tell her you're sorry and promise to leave her alone."

After a moment, Darian sighed, looked Shellie in the eyes, and said, "I'm sorry. It will never happen again." Hotan shoved him harder against the lockers. "I promise! I'll never mess with her again! I'm sorry! Now let me go!"

Darian slid to the floor on his knees, rubbing his shoulder as he gave Hotan a sour look. Ignoring him, Hotan turned his attention to Shellie who still seemed stunned and confused. Rubbing the back of his neck, he finally looked her in the eyes, catching her attention.

"Do you need me to walk you to the administration office? Nurse's office? Class?" Mustering a sincere smile, Hotan waited for her decision. "It's up to you. I can just leave you here, but I won't do that until I know you're okay first."

"I, I think I'll…" She watched Darian stand up and walk away. He still held his shoulder, his face red with anger. Hotan had left a lasting message, and Darian wouldn't bother her anymore. "I don't want to go to class or go home…"

"Okay, that's a start." Hotan took a moment to read her expression and body language. "I'll tell you what, how about we go for a walk off campus? I'll be sure to get you back in time for the buses. I like to go to the old church around the corner to clear my thoughts. Maybe some place safe like that might help you relax?"

Looking him in the eyes, she weighed her options before she responded, "I would like that."

By the time they made it back to school, he had Shellie laughing and giggling. She was a happy person by nature, and he was relieved that he was able to snap her out of her shock. It felt so strange to feel the warmth of her arms around him as she hugged him goodbye. He hadn't expected it, and it took a minute before he wrapped his arms around her and hugged her back. Once more, she threw him off guard as her lips softly kissed his cheek. She left him behind as she boarded her bus, and it pulled away. He found himself standing there surprised at how much his own heart fluttered over those tiny gestures.

The next day at school, Hotan found that Darian avoided any hallway he was walking down, bitter to see Shellie hanging on his arm instead. It wasn't Hotan's intention to steal the girl away with a heroic act. At the same time, he couldn't ignore that level of bullying for anyone to endure. Shellie begged repeatedly to be his girlfriend, and no matter how many times he opened his mouth to say "no," he lost the will to do so with each smile and gaze they exchanged. Plenty of girls had passed him notes, asking if he had a girlfriend or that a friend of theirs had a crush on him. The hearts he broke every time he threw one of those letters in the trash grew every year. Perhaps it was time to let someone through the door. Besides, he admired her courage against Darian. Most girls would have given in, but she was brave and stubborn. It wasn't hard to fall in love with someone who made him happy by just being near him.

4

SAVE OURSELVES

The apartment's cold air welcomed him as he walked through the door and locked it behind him. He strode past the kitchen and flopped down on the couch. The blinds were closed on the only window in the living room, and the room grew darker as the sun continued to set. At last, he found himself sitting in the complete darkness, under the weight of the silence, trying once more to recall the events that had happened over a week ago. Hotan couldn't shake the feeling that something important was missing from his thoughts. Closing his eyes tight, he let out a groan of frustration. His head ached every time he came close to recalling whatever it was that he had forgotten. *Some part of me doesn't want me to remember, but why?* The only visual image he received was the crucifix and its mournful expression.

The sound of paper rustling met his ears. Opening his eyes, he scanned his door to see an envelope that someone had slipped into his apartment. Walking over, he paused, staring at the wax seal before taking a deep breath and steeling himself to open it. Inside, a single line of gorgeous handwriting read simply:

"Midnight at the Church"

A sense of alarm rushed over him. He unlocked his door as fast as his hands would allow. Running out into the hallway, Hotan looked right and left but found no one. Desperate, he ran down the stairs and through the main hall in hopes of seeing who left the letter.

"Are you okay?" Annie, his landlord, stood at her door with a laundry basket full of linens in her arms. "You look pale. Are you getting sick again? You're not going to pass out on me, are you? The doctor said…"

"N-no," Hotan stuttered as he made eye contact with her. "I just… well, did someone come walking out this way?"

"Not that I noticed. I just came down the hall and was unlocking my door after doing some laundry." She set the basket inside her apartment and came back out. "If anyone was out and about, I would have passed them for sure. What's wrong? You didn't get robbed, did you?"

"It's nothing." He sighed, rubbing the back of his neck, sorting through his thoughts. "I think lack of sleep is getting to me again. Sorry to spook you, Annie."

"Well, just call me if you need anything, Hotan." Annie gave him a warm smile as she went back into her apartment. "Good night!"

Making it back to his living room, he dropped the letter onto the coffee table. He glared at it, pondering who could've written it. No one he knew had the skills for such artistic writing. Furthermore, the wax seal ruled out everyone. *Not like I have friend in a letter writing guild or calligraphy club. Such an old-fash-ioned touch.* Staring at it gave him a strange, misplaced sense of nostalgia. *Who sent this to me? Why would anyone want to meet me, then set the place at the church? They must know me. The church isn't a vague choice, and I know which one they're referring to. And why meet at midnight? Is this what happened to me the last time? Or is Hisota or someone else trying to get under my skin?*

Picking the letter back up, he leaned on his knees and thumbed the writing. After several minutes, he closed his eyes, trying to remember. *How can writing look new and familiar all at once?* Chills crawled across his skin as he recalled the day on the church floor. *What happened to me?* Straining his concentration, he managed a glimpse of a memory. A shadowed figure had spoken something in a language he hadn't understood. Without a doubt, he wasn't alone that night in the church; there was a man standing over him. *Not a demon, not the man from my nightmares. No, someone I trust.* All he could recall were sad, gray eyes staring down at him. *Is that who sent this letter? What good is it if I can't recall what happened? Either way, how do I know if…*

A knock at the door jolted him from his thoughts. Biting his cheek, Hotan weighed whether to answer it. Another round of knocking barked through his apartment, demanding to be answered. Hesitantly, he opened the door.

"Well, it seems Prince Charming does know how to answer a door." Hisota's dark eyes gave Hotan a rebellious glare. "It seems clear to me you don't know how to answer a phone or email these days. At least I can confirm that, yes, you are alive, and yes, you are standing."

"Now's not a good time, Hisota." Gritting his teeth, Hotan pushed his annoyance back. "I'm not in the mood to entertain company, especially you."

"Well, excuse me for being the caring friend." Scoffing, Hisota narrowed his eyes at him. "I just wanted to apologize for giving you a tough time at school. There's no doubt you're still not feeling well."

Hotan was in no mood to respond; he glowered at Hisota from his doorway.

"Moving on…" With a sigh and smirk, Hisota finished what he had initially come to say, "Once more, I'm sorry, really. Call me if you need anything. I sometimes forget you don't have the luxury of letting parents deal with things like the rest of us. Get some rest and see you around, asshole."

"Thanks. I do appreciate you knowing that." It was a bland reaction on Hotan's part, but his mind wouldn't let go of the letter sitting on the coffee table behind him. *Great, Hisota is acting weird around me. He never comes to apologize for anything. I guess my hospital trip didn't just scare me and Shellie, but even his frozen heart, huh?*

Closing his door, Hotan leaned his back against it and stared into the pitch-black apartment. The walls and objects were nothing more than barely visible, dark gray blobs, and the air itself seemed to have frozen in time. The humming of the air conditioner kicking on filled his ears as he pictured the gray-eyed man's face once more. *The shape of his face was thin and gaunt as if he had lived a hard life, yet not a wrinkle grazed his skin. His hair glimmered, a silver-gray like my own or possibly white. At first glance, he looked like he could be blood-related to me, but I don't have any living relatives left. Actually, my dad might still be alive, but deadbeat fathers tend to keep their distance. Mom informed me that my grandparents passed away on both sides, and beyond that, no one really knows.*

I'll go. If I'm ever going to get some answers about what happened, this might be my one and only chance. I'll just have my cell phone ready and be on alert. Nevertheless, this all still feels like a dream. Nothing logical. And worse, I'm dealing with everything alone, again.

Exhausted from his dilemma, he decided to wash the tension off his muscles in the shower. Eyes closed, he indulged in the beating pressure of the water on his head, taking deep breaths of steam-filled air. Feeling the muscles loosen in his neck and shoulders, he cracked his eyes to watch the water and soap swirl down the drain. *There are days I just wish all my troubles would wash away as easily as that...* Frustrated, he slammed the shower knob, turning the water off in an instant. Toweling off, he approached the medicine cabinet and pulled out his cologne and deodorant. A dark symbol on his flesh flashed in the mirror, catching his attention, and he paused. Furrowing his brow, he slowly opened the cabinet once more, reluctant at first. He reached a point where he could see a black symbol in the mirror's reflection displayed on the wall mirror behind him. Something black swirled and stretched itself across his back.

"What the..." he stammered to himself, gaping at the tattooed image. "How the hell did that come about?"

Reaching behind him, he rubbed the discolored skin but could not differentiate it from the rest of his back. He studied the mysterious tattoo for some time. *If I had gotten this that night, I would have known. Tattoos sting for quite some time after you get them, and this is a back piece that takes up a lot of real estate.* There was no mistaking the tribal imagery: angelic wings etched into his back, abstract and organic in design. *What the hell is going on with me? Did I go through a rebellious stage and forget?* Baffled, he paced the living room floor for several minutes. *There is no logic behind it. When did this appear? Was it there all week, and I didn't notice? Or maybe it showed up this morning? It seems to be a tattoo, but no scabbing. No pain? What in the hell is going on? Am I losing my mind? Maybe I'm in a coma, and this is all some wicked ass dream...*

He stood there lost. Glancing over at the clock, he'd run out of time. Shoving on his jeans and a band shirt, he rushed out the door. Annoyed by his thoughts, he slapped on his earbuds as he straddled his motorcycle. As he took off down the quiet, late-night streets, his ears were greeted with The Blackout's song, "Save Ourselves." Music always had a way of reflecting his emotions and thoughts. *Please don't let this take away everything I have. I barely have anything left as it stands. I'm so tired of being alone…*

He parked in front of the church, and the half-moon draped everything in a light glow. Pulling his helmet off, the frigid night nipped at his face as his breath steamed in gentle puffs. He grimaced as stood there engulfed in the church's shadow. Inside, he would either get his answers or find himself laid out on the floor … again. A breeze cut across him as leaves slid and scraped across the sidewalk. He held his breath as he opened the heavy, wooden doors. Inside, someone had taken the time to light the candles that sat on tall, silver stands at both ends of the long pews. His eyes glided across every crevice visible in the wavering lights, but no one was present.

The nerves in his spine and shoulders tightened and tickled as he took slow steps toward the front. He aimed to sit in his usual spot, hoping some normalcy would calm the nerves that knotted with every passing second. *Am I alone or is someone watching me? Please don't let this be some sort of trap…* Making it to his seat, he was paranoid. Staring up at the statue on the cross, he noticed the expression was different from the sorrowful one he'd last seen. Tonight, that granite body seemed alive as it hung in its tortured place. The wings were outstretched wider than he'd remembered before, and in the moonlight, still shadowed the pews. He wondered whether it was shielding them or hiding them under those elegant wings. Hotan had never seen anyone associate wings with the crucifix. It seemed like a paradox in thought, but seeing it in practice was very much the opposite. The look was complete—moreover, correct. He continued admiring the artisanship, determining that it had a clear message of salvation and hope.

A movement caught his attention, and he squinted to focus on the statue's face. Something wet crawled down the cheeks of the statue. The color of red faded into existence; the crucifix was crying blood. *What is going on? Am I witnessing a miracle?* He opened his mouth, but no words would come. *Why does the color come to me for something like this? What is the importance of me being here to witness this?* It seemed as if the statue had a slight smile, and Hotan could feel his heart racing. Whether his reaction was fear, excitement, or panic was beyond his own understanding.

"It is not often we get to see proof of his existence," a mysterious and familiar voice spoke from behind him. "Sorry for running late, Hotan."

Looking toward the doors, Hotan saw the tall, silver-haired man from his memory. He wore a white business suit, dark tie, and eyeglasses which complimented his eyes and face. He approached silently and slowly, causing no alarm in his casual approach.

"Who are you?" Narrowing his eyes, Hotan couldn't shake the sensation that he should know this man. "What's going on he—"

He glanced back to the statue, but there were no more signs of red, wet tears down its face. The life had left the expressionless statue.

"Sorry if I startled you." The man paused, stopping a few rows from where Hotan sat. "I was hoping to take some time with you tonight to explain what is going on."

"Does this have to do with what happened to me a few nights ago?" Swallowing, Hotan continued with his questions, "You were here for that, right?"

"Do you not remember?" The man furrowed his brow and tightened his lips, concerned by the questions. "Or do you only remember some of it?"

"I only remember your face, nothing else." Trying to keep calm, Hotan stood in hopes of getting his nerves to stop tightening in his throat. "What the hell happened here? Who are you? What's going on?"

"My name is Talib." Hotan's heart skipped a beat as if he recognized the name from a past life. Talib pushed his glasses up as he spoke, "I am the element of Judgment, an immortal. What happened to you was a release of your powers when you were threatened. A built-in, defense mechanism that protects you when your life is in danger. As for what is going on, I am still trying to figure it out myself."

Immortal? Hotan wanted to question him, but something deep inside urged him to take the information as fact. He turned his focus to the only logical piece of information. "My life was in danger? How?"

"Geliah, the element of Fear, decided to take matters into his own hands. He has a vendetta against you, and now, he has found you. The man will not stop until you are dead. He believes that killing you will release the remnants of the spell, or curse as he refers to it. He suspects that he will become normal again as if the spell never happened. Unfortunately, he is sadly mistaken."

"A spell? Why would I have anything to do with a spell?" Hotan was skeptical as this crazy conversation continued. "I can only assume he's one of these immortals like you. I don't get how I could possibly have anything to do with his past. I'm eighteen years old; it's improbable for me to have anything to do with this."

"Do you remember anything about your former self?" Talib spoke cautiously and seemed to be paling. "Anything at all?"

"Former self?" Hotan was bewildered by the questions. *This sounds like a fantasy novel.* "What do you mean by that? I don't understand where this is going."

"You were the one that cast the spell. By the powers of the element of Rebirth, you set in motion a spell of continuous reincarnation on all of us in the hopes of allowing us to live a normal existence. Most of us agreed, understanding that we would never know who we were or remember one another." Talib turned his back to Hotan as he continued. "As your brother, I was left as a watcher. For some reason, you knew something might go wrong. Now, I have been desperately searching for you, as well as those who have awakened, in hopes of figuring out what has gone wrong. Does any of this sound familiar?"

"N-No," Hotan muttered, but his mind echoed the word *brother* as if it was a lost fact in his life. "To be honest, it sounds like a fairy tale."

"Perhaps it does since you do not recall anything at all." Hotan watched Talib pull a napkin from his coat pocket to clean his glasses. "Just know that we have much to do if you are to master your powers. I am sorry that I underestimated the severity of the situation, little brother."

"All of this is crazy. Why would you call me brothe—" It was as if the wind was sucked out of his lungs. *Every part of my being won't let me utter the phrase, so does this mean…* An overwhelming sensation of truth hit him as he caught Talib's glare. "You, you're my brother?"

"When was the last time you saw someone with natural silver hair, Hotan?" Talib closed his eyes as he took a deep breath. His voice was rich in trust and knowledge unlike anyone he'd ever heard. "This much is apparent: I need time to figure out a way around your inability to recall who you once were. Until then, take this time to continue to heal and digest the information I have given you. Perhaps when I see you next, a memory or two will have surfaced."

"That's it?" Panic came over Hotan as Talib started for the door. "You can't dump all this nonsense on me and just leave! Don't you know I've got no one! No one's left, Talib!" Hotan pounded his chest with a flat palm, his face panic-stricken as his heart raced away from home. "If you're really my brother, you must know that I'm all alone! Don't you even care?"

"Sometimes sacrifices have to be made…" Talib disappeared through the doors.

Hotan chased after him, but by the time he made it outside, there were no signs of anyone. The wind picked up speed, and in the distance, thunder rumbled. *Why does everyone leave me? When will this loneliness stop? What did I do so wrong that even my own brother and father keep me at a distance?*

5

WORLD SO COLD

Hotan woke to the buzzing of his cellphone as it danced on the coffee table. He rolled himself off the couch, standing to stretch his stiff muscles. Last night had been more of an annoyance and answered nothing. Worse, he had no means to contact Talib. His phone started another round of ringing and buzzing, demanding his attention. He sat back down and saw it flashing "Shellie." With a half-hearted smirk, he answered it.

"Good morning!" Shellie's voice was loud and bright like always. "Are we still going out for lunch today?"

"Crap, I completely forgot." He smashed his hand into his face, rubbing the sleep from it. "What time is it?"

"Noonish." He heard her sigh on the other end. "If you aren't feeling up to it, we can reschedule or do something else."

"No, just give me a few to wake up, and I'll get you. I stayed up too late last night." Yawning, he finished rubbing his left eye with the palm of his hand. "Long as you are okay with that?"

"Yeah!" Her voice perked back up. "I'll be here, ready to go! Bye, Hotan!"

"Bye, Shel." He stared down at his phone for several minutes. *I guess I'm not completely alone.*

It was frustrating that Talib hadn't left a number or even an email. *Anything would be better than nothing at all. How can he just leave me like this? You can't tell someone that you're their only surviving family member, then walk out the door! But that's exactly what you did. You told me some grand story and left.* Jerking off the couch, he stomped into the bathroom to splash cold water onto his face. Staring at himself, his youthful appearance didn't match the old and worn-out way he felt inside. *Former self? Is there some truth to it? Am I staring at a stranger in the mirror?* Closing his eyes, he pictured the tribal wings painted on his back. *Is that part of it? Do these wings hold the answer to me mastering these so-called powers of the element of Rebirth? What am I saying? Do I really believe this person's radical story?*

Grabbing his helmet off the table, he headed out the door. Distracted and absorbed in his thoughts, he barely had enough time to stop before smacking into Annie. Once more, her hands were full as she fumbled for her keys. She was overloaded with grocery bags this time; Hotan took them from her, so she could unlock her apartment.

"Thanks again." Annie opened the door wide and took the bags. "Wait here a second. I need to give you something."

"You need some work done?" Hotan leaned in, watching her as she placed her bags on the kitchen counter and grabbed an envelope. "What's that?"

"A note for you; it came to me with a check." Annie raised an eyebrow at him as she handed it over. "You didn't tell me you managed to get a sponsor."

"Sponsor?" Baffled, Hotan opened the letter. "I have no idea what you're talking about…" His voice trailed off as he read the letter:

Hotan,

Consider this a token of good faith. Your rent has been taken care of for the next year.

Your sponsor,

Jacob

"I, I don't know who this is?" Hotan was speechless. *I don't even know anyone named Jacob!*

"You don't?" Annie smirked bashfully to herself. "Well, whoever he was, he was hot."

"Are you kidding?" Folding the letter up, he tucked it into his back pocket. "What did he look like?" *Was it Talib? Does he have an alias?*

"Taller than you, very handsome," Blushing, Annie could no longer look Hotan in the eye. "Short, blonde hair, dark blue eyes that look purple, and this awesome tribal deer head with horns tattooed across his entire back. He seemed like a real nice and sincere guy."

"Was he shirtless or something? Are you sure the guy who delivered this was the same one who wrote it?" Confused, Hotan continued asking questions. "When did he come by? What time?"

"It had to be close to midnight last night. His name was definitely Jacob. Isn't that who signed that?" Red-cheeked, she sighed. "He left about six this morning for work, but I didn't catch where that was. All I know is he grumbled on about downtown traffic. He'll be back; perhaps we can do dinner together."

Hotan stood there in silence as he processed what Annie was implying. "Sometimes I wonder about your habits, Annie. Have you ever tried dating first?"

"Hush! If anyone else had said that I would kill them. Besides, I'm twenty-seven; I think I'm old enough to make my own decisions." Rolling her eyes, Annie waved him away. "Bye, Hotan. I need to get this stuff put away. My ice cream is melting."

"And so are you over someone you just met," Hotan scoffed, earning a heated glare from Annie. "Just be careful, that's all I'm asking." She shut the door, and he pivoted to exit.

As he made his way to Shellie's house, he weighed the information in his mind. *A sign of good faith? This has to do with Talib; I know it. Who the hell is this Jacob? Is he one of us? He did imply there were several immortals and looking for me specifically. A tribal tattoo across his back… Maybe there is a connection after all. Then again, every suave guy has a tattoo, if not across his back, then on his forearms. Why pose as a sponsor? Why even attempt to support me on a financial level? How much do they know about me and my situation? I can't help but think Talib is behind this, feeling guilty after what I said last night. I'm not into taking charity from anyone, and they knew to take it to Annie instead of me. Money isn't going to fix how alienated I feel or how estranged he's been with his only brother. Am I the only brother?* Hotan leaned into his last turn, sucking on a cheek as he pulled between logic and emotions. *Oh, Annie, you make horrible decisions at times. Sleeping with the messenger was a bit much. I don't think this can get any more complicated.* Slowing down and pulling into a driveway, he huffed. *I need a break from this bullshit and to enjoy some normalcy today.*

Shellie rushed out the front door, pulling her helmet on. Bracing on his shoulders, she slid behind him. In an instant, his tornado of panicked thoughts calmed to a dull roar. With her in place, Hotan headed to their destination. *A chance to escape the chaos.* At least taking her out to lunch allowed him to forget what he had no control over. Pulling into Benny's Place, a diner just a block away from the club where they played, his stomach growled. *When did I last eat? It feels like days…* The diner had been a popular eatery for ages since it was the only 24-hour, non-franchise restaurant for miles. From high school students to drunk crowds leaving the clubs after hours, there wasn't a local in town who didn't swing through the place once a week. The hostess smiled as she seated them at their booth.

The window looked out onto the main street; the skies were cloudless but still windy after last night's storms. They had missed the lunch crowd, and only a few patrons occupied the place. A woman shook her newspaper at the bar top as she took one last sip of coffee. Flicking her long braid off her shoulders, she walked out the door. At another booth, two men huddled around a laptop, discussing business over their late lunches. Hotan looked back at Shellie sitting across the booth from him, and she smiled. *Should I tell her about this nonsense? Would she even believe me? No, I shouldn't worry her; she's already paranoid about what happened to me. Maybe I can tip-toe around the crazier details?* Hotan found himself staring at the little bookstore across the street. Much like the church he admired, it was behind the times and stood out among the newer buildings. *I can relate. Lately, I stick out like a sore thumb. Even the teachers are starting to comment. No matter the situation, I just feel I'm paying for some past mistake in this life.*

Looking back at Shellie, she stared at him with her cute smile. She had no idea how much he wished to be normal like her. *How do I tell her that I'm not like her? Maybe it's true—I'm one of these immortals, no longer a human being. Was I ever human to begin with?*

"What's wrong with you? You usually speak a few more words than this." Shellie's smile faded. "Are you still sick?"

"I recently ran into my brother." Hotan gave her a skeptical expression, trying to decide what to say next. "Sorry, I'm feeling better though. Just dealing with … stuff."

"Brother? I thought you had no family left? You never told me you had a brother." Shellie leaned back in her seat, feeling she had missed something. "How many more secrets do you have?"

"Not many. As for having a brother, I had no idea I had one either. In fact, your face was the same reaction I had. It makes me feel … lost?" Shrugging, Hotan felt some relief wash over him as he shared his recent problems. "His name's Talib. Nice guy, but a little strange. He came out of nowhere, literally. I'm still in shock and confused about it. It's a lot to take in. I just don't know what to do with the information."

"A little strange? You two must be related. I assume he's older. I couldn't imagine your mom sneaking off to have another kid after you." Shellie grinned, trying to change the tone to a more positive one. "So, when do I get to meet this brother of yours? Is he still around, or is he a true Samuels and has mysteriously left?"

Hotan scoffed, "Yeah, he mysteriously left as fast as he came. Don't know where he went or if he even lives around here. Worse, I'm not sure if he's from my mom's side, dad's side, or possibly both. Definitely older than me. I guess whenever he decides to come back to town again, I'll see about introducing you to him. Apparently, he had to leave to take care of some things." Avoiding Shellie's gaze, he saw Kyle walk into the restaurant. A bouquet of flowers in his hands, he wrangled up their tall, dark-haired waitress. "Did I miss something? When did Kyle become a romantic?"

"Huh?" Shellie looked back and chuckled. "Oh, Kyle has had a crush on Jessica for quite some time. I've been pushing her to at least give the poor boy a chance. She needs a sweet guy for a change instead of all those jerks she's been dating."

"Oh really?" Hotan smiled as he watched the couple. Jessica blushed, and Kyle was undoubtedly saying something embarrassing. "He's a good guy and deserves a chance. Hotan turned back to Shellie, and teasingly asked, "I've been meaning to ask, do you know all the servers in town? It seems like no matter where I take you, you seem to know at least one employee."

"Anyway." Shellie waved off his comment, sticking with the original topic. "I just hope it works out between those two. They would make a cute couple, don't you think?" They both watched as Kyle and Jessica giggled as she placed the flowers in a vase. "Looks like it's off to a good start so far."

"Shellie." Staring down at his clasped hands, he started to think about things again. *This isn't fair to her. I'm so distant, and it's only getting worse. When we first started going out, it was amazing. But then my mom died, and I distanced myself. Shellie was the one who pulled me back from despair. Now, I'm doing it again, turning back into the recluse I was before she entered my life. It's not fair to her to be stuck in a relationship that I'm failing to maintain.*

"Yeah?" Her smile faded as she considered his solemn face. "What's wrong now?"

"If you want to end our relationship, it's fine with me. I know I don't take you out much, and lately, I've been a loner." Hotan looked up at her big, gentle eyes to read her reaction. "And on top of that, Hisota's been a real pain about us dating. I know it can be stressful, but I've got a lot going on and—"

"Hotan, if it bothered me, I would have said so or ended it already," Shellie cut him off, placing her soft hands on his with a warm smile. "I'll always want to be with you. You're not like the other guys at school. You let me have my freedom, and I merely do the same for you. If you want to be alone, that's fine. I can always make plans with my other friends; it's not the end of the world. Just remember, I'm here for you, and if you need to let things out, I'm willing to listen. We don't demand much from one another; we tend to understand each other's needs with no questions asked. I doubt I can get that sort of mature relationship with anyone in our high school. I mean, if it weren't for you, I wouldn't even feel safe walking the hallway; I may have dropped out."

Hotan covered her hand with his, enjoying the warmth of her touch. "I just don't want to tie you down. You deserve to be happy." *It's your nature to be happy, but my life is one of sorrow.*

"I know," Shellie snorted, chuckling to herself as she pulled away to address the approaching waitress. "Hey, Jessica!"

"Are you guys ready to order?" Jessica greeted them, giggling to herself.

"So, what did you say to him?" Shellie leaned over the table, grinning at her friend. "Yes or no? Or even a maybe at the very least?"

"I said yes. I've never had a guy bring me flowers like that. I don't know whether to be flattered or embarrassed." Jessica rolled her eyes at Shellie. "What do you guys want to drink today?"

"Coffee and today's special. I'm starving." Hotan handed her the menu, smirking. "Watch out, Jess. He might convince you to have those seven boys he wants. Kyle has plans you know, *big* plans for a *big* family."

"Oh no!" Jessica covered her mouth with the menu before laughing louder. "Shut up!" Turning her focus back to her job, she pressed, "What about you, Shellie? What do you want to eat today?"

"The usual." Shellie winked at her, following Hotan's lead in teasing her friend. "But really, Jessica, he's a good guy."

"I already said yes. Stop messing with me." Jessica shook her head and left for the restaurant's kitchen.

"Hey! Look who it is!" Kyle rushed over, finally noticing them. "I should have known I would see you guys here."

Shellie scooted over, and Kyle slid into the booth next to her. "Congrats, Kyle!"

Leaning onto the table, a goofy grin stretched across his face. "For what?"

"You finally harassed Jessica enough for her to say yes," snorted Shellie, nudging him with an elbow.

"Thanks!" Heaving a sigh, he changed topics. "So, what's happening, my homie?" Kyle nodded his head at Hotan, his expression serious. "You still not feeling good?"

"I feel fine, and I wish everyone would stop asking," Hotan grunted. "Other than that, I suppose the latest news bothering me is the fact that I found out I have an older brother. Still trying to figure out that ordeal and how it never surfaced before."

"No kidding." Kyle sat back into the seat, stunned. "So, is he, well, cool?"

"I don't know yet, barely got a chance to talk with the man. Let's just hope I get another chance." Jessica returned with their drinks. Taking his coffee from her, Hotan started adding sugar and cream to it as he spoke. "I'm still adjusting to the idea. There are questions it created that have no answers to them yet. It was so sudden; for once, I feel clueless."

"Hey, baby," Kyle lowered his voice, giving Jessica a seductive look, "how about you and I get married and have us some kids?"

"In your dreams, redhead." Jessica winked as she busted out laughing. "You're moving too fast for me! First flowers then skipping ahead to kids. Hell no!"

"Told you so." Grinning, Hotan took a cautious sip of his coffee. *Kyle always lightens the mood when I get too serious. Granted, they have no idea how much crazier my situation truly is. This stress is going to kill me.*

"Kyle, stop messing around!" Shellie chuckled, elbowing him in the ribs. "You're so ridiculous! You're going to scare her off before the first date."

"Okay, okay. Get back to work, woman." Kyle winked at Jessica, and she blushed in response.

"Their food is almost ready anyhow, and there are some customers heading in." Jessica headed for the entrance.

Hotan's attention followed Jessica as she neared the front doors. The bell rang as a new customer entered the diner, catching Hotan's attention. A tall, bulky man with dark dreadlocks walked in from the busy street. Hotan couldn't see his face, only the back of the man's dark trench coat. Something in the back of Hotan's mind screamed, *I should know this man.* Every nerve tightened, his body tensing against his will. The way the coat fit him indicated that the stranger was quite buff—a typical large brute. Hotan observed how he towered over Jessica as he followed her to a table near them. The man flipped his coat as he sat down, facing Hotan, his eyes shooting daggers at him. Amber irises glared at him. A smirk slithered across the brute's masculine face as they exchanged the unmistakable stares.

It's as if he knows I can see the color of his eyes. Why can I see his eyes so vividly? What is so important about this man that requires this much attention? Am I missing something? Do I know him? Like a flash of lightning, laughter and the nauseating memory of overwhelming fear sparked through Hotan's entire being. *It can't be...* Hotan's nerves unraveled. Unconsciously, he slammed his coffee down on the table, splashing some of it. Hotan failed his attempt to break away from the yellow-orange eyes. Another wave of tremendous fear silently shouted to him, warning him that if he looked away, he would miss an imminent attack from this behemoth. The man seemed amused by Hotan's paling face. This stranger didn't look familiar to him, but his very presence made Hotan feel tense and uneasy. Recognizable dread filled Hotan from the unfamiliar entity who continued to burn through him with his taunting glare. The man turned his playful look away to look at the menu, yet he was still watching Hotan's every move.

Who is this? I feel like my soul is screaming the answer, but I'm too scared to hear it. Why does this man terrify me so much? What am I so afraid of? My chest hurts from how hard my heart is pounding. Every thought seemed so loud as if the titan across the restaurant could hear each fear. Hotan swallowed hard as his heart hammered in his ears. The room darkened and muted around Hotan as if an explosion had happened. *I should run away. No, I need to run, but … why?* The muscles in his body ached under the pressure of how tense he'd become with each passing second. His breath quickened, his chest tightened, and his skin was clammy. Hotan was being crushed under the weight of his fear. He was thankful that the enemy was no longer staring him in the eyes. The invisible force of horror continued to invade him, drowning his very soul within it.

Finally, muttering to himself, Hotan realized what and who was causing him so much panic. "Geliah, the element of Fear."

"Hotan, are you okay, bro?" Kyle's smile had faded. "You going to pass out again?"

"No." Standing, Hotan dashed into the men's room, his stomach knotting and twisting.

Rushing into a stall, locking it behind him, Hotan lunged himself over the toilet bowl. Coughing and choking, cold sweat ran down the sides of his face. Everything felt like it had crashed down on him, bringing him to his knees. He watched what little nerve he had left swirl down the toilet. Closing his eyes, Hotan inhaled deeply, holding it there in an attempt to stabilize himself and push back the sickening sensation of his fear. Calming down, he tried to put things back together as he regained his composure. The pain in his throat brought no comfort as he desperately swallowed down the fleeting panic. The bathroom door creaked open. His hold on his nerves slipped, almost failing to control his vocal cords as he muffled the yelp he so anxiously wanted to let lose. Fear came rushing back, and he began to panic as his thoughts raced out of control. Frozen, he held his breath. A rabbit trapped in a corner, the stalking wolf with its hungry eyes ensnared him in his mind's eye. *This is it! Geliah has me! Here huddled to a toilet! I have no way of defending myself!*

6

FINE AGAIN

"Hotan?" Kyle's voice came as a relief, dissolving the horror, and Hotan could breathe again. "Are you that sick man? You shouldn't push yourself so hard."

Hotan came out of the stall and walked over to the sink, depleted of his energy. "I guess so. I don't know what's wrong with me lately."

"Man, I don't ever remember you getting sick; it hit you hard out there." Kyle watched as Hotan rinsed his mouth out and splashed cold water on his face.

Slouched over the vanity, Hotan stared into the white sink. "It's been a really strange week. Very strange. I don't know what to think about anything anymore."

"No kidding." Kyle sighed, clearing his throat. "So, what really happened that night at the old church? No matter how I mull it over, it's impossible for that place to be renovated over-night, am I right? It's like David Copperfield came in there and did some of his crazy mojo stuff. I was just there a week ago with you. Work like that takes months, and there weren't any signs of repairs when I was there, so..."

"It's hard to say. I still can't remember anything. I don't know if I'll ever remember, and last night didn't answer my questions like I had hoped." Looking up at his reflection, Hotan yearned for his former self to give him answers. *If this is all true, please let me wake up and remember.* "Meeting my brother was strange. He had a lot to say, but I don't know what to believe. It all sounded so crazy."

"Last night?" Crossing his arms, Kyle gave him a grave expression through the bathroom mirror. "Where last night? What all did he tell you?"

"The church. He asked me to meet him at midnight last night. I wish I knew a way to explain, but I can't. All I can figure is it has something to do with this mark on my back." Hotan straightened himself. "I can't help but feel this is the only proof I have that something is happening to me. Everything just seems irrational, no matter how many ways I run it through my head."

"What proof is that?" Puzzled, Kyle gawked at him as if he'd lost his mind. "You're sounding weird, dude. Not that you've ever been normal, but this is out of character, even for you."

"I guess I might as well show you. Just don't tell Shel." Hotan pulled up the back of his shirt to expose the angelic tribal tattoo on his back. "This tattoo thing; we both know I've never been interested in tattoos, let alone had one."

Kyle's eyes widened in surprise, picking it apart in dead silence.

"Well?" Hotan's heart sped up, finding Kyle's distraught expression unsettling.

Shaking his head, he met Hotan's gaze in the mirror before replying, "That thing covers your entire back, holy shit."

"See, I don't know how, but it appeared after I passed out." Pulling his shirt back down, Hotan faced Kyle. "I just didn't see it, or it didn't surface until the other night. I feel like I'm losing my mind, Kyle."

Kyle cracked a nervous smile. "Heh, and I thought mine was big. I've been trying to talk to you alone, but every time I've chickened out on bringing it up. See, after the night you passed out, I started having weird dreams, and like you, this freaking huge tattoo just appeared on my back."

"What?" Hotan watched as Kyle pulled his own shirt up to expose a marking of a tribal phoenix across his back. "How? Kyle, you weren't there, or were you? Why didn't you say something sooner?" *What on earth is going on?*

"No, I wasn't there, but it showed up that same night. You got any clue what it means? It's clearly not a tattoo, man. I think we both would have felt that for a month."

"Yeah, but, but, how in the hell?" Hotan fumbled his words as his mind filled with more questions. *What are the odds? My best friend, too? I must be in another realm.* "I just don't understand. None of this makes any sense…" *I just want this nightmare to end.*

"What does it mean?" Kyle gave Hotan a suspicious glare. "You have something to do with all of this, don't you? It's the only thing I can think of."

"Apparently, it has everything to do with me … or who I used to be. This seems too coincidental." Hotan headed toward the door, wanting to find more answers. "Let's see if we can locate my brother. If anyone has answers, it's him."

"Your brother?" Kyle followed close behind him as they left the bathroom. "You have to know more than that. How does this all fall back on your brother?"

Hotan watched Geliah from the corner of his eye like a mouse sneaking past a sleepy cat. Geliah's stare was unbroken as he watched Hotan leave the bathroom. He grinned as he took a sip of his coffee, which made Hotan's heart flutter. *There's no mistaking that Geliah is amused to see how sick I just was.* Hotan and Kyle went back to their seats, both silent as they sat there awkwardly. No longer overwhelmed by fear, Hotan glared at Geliah with a sense of rage. *It's obvious he used his abilities of the element of Fear against me. Now, I understand their powers. He's the element of Fear, and he can control that in other people. He's so strong, and he's twice my size in height and muscle. Talib made it clear that Geliah won't let me too far out of his sight, but why hasn't he tried attacking me? Doesn't he want me dead? If that's how the power of Fear works, then what exactly does Rebirth do?*

"Are you two okay?" Shellie took a bite of her salad, chewing it slowly as she shifted her eyes from Hotan to Kyle. They both looked drained. She placed her fork on the plate and made her voice louder, "What's wrong? Are you two dying or something?"

"We're fine," they responded as one, only adding to her suspicions as she arched a brow at them.

"What's wrong now?" Shellie twisted her mouth, expressing her irritation. "Are you two planning on leaving?"

"Yeah, I need to leave." Hotan broke his stare with Geliah and gave Shellie an empty smile. "I should have cancelled. I've got an upset stomach still." *She's not buying my excuse, but I know she'll let me go without any push back. I'll owe her an explanation or make up for it some big way.*

"Hey! Jessica!" Kyle waved her over to the table. "Do you mind taking Shellie home? I'm going to ride with Hotan, make sure he makes it home okay."

"Yeah, I guess. Why?" Jessica looked at Kyle puzzled but noticed the awkward atmosphere. "My shift ends in about thirty minutes anyhow. Maybe we can hit the mall or something, huh, Shellie?"

"Figures." Shellie sighed as she picked at her salad. "You need to take better care of yourself, Hotan. I suppose when you feel better, we can sit and talk some more."

"I'm sorry." Hotan stood, observing Shellie's flustered face. "I'll make up for this later, okay?" *Hope I didn't hurt your feelings, Shel. You're a strong person, but it's not nice for me to rely on that one component of who you are.*

Shellie's brow rose high, signaling that she wasn't convinced of his plight. "Go ahead and go."

"Thanks, babe!" Kyle hugged Jessica. "I'll make sure Hotan gets home in one piece, Shellie."

"See you, Shel." Hotan kissed her gently on the lips and left money on the table. "We'll talk later, promise."

Kyle followed Hotan's Suzuki across town in his green convertible mustang. They came to a stop in front of the old church and stood in silence, staring up at the building. Both of them wanted answers, but they were unsure if they were truly ready to hear them. Two mourning doves flew out from under a pew, startling them as they made their way to the front of the cathedral. They sat, looking up at the crucifix with its granite wings towering over them; it seemed as if it was protecting them from some unseen danger. Hotan sighed, thinking about how complicated things had gotten within the last twenty-four hours. Staring at the statue, both remained silent and deep in thought. Hotan's eyes locked onto the wooden pegs nailed into its wrists and driven through its feet. A slate at its base held an elegant engraving:

> "Unto you that fear my name shall the Sun of
> Righteousness arise with healing in his wings.
> ~Malachi 4:2a"

Hotan smiled to himself, engrossed by the saying. *I wish that sitting here every day under those stone wings could heal me and take all the dreadful things away? It's a nice thought. Righteousness is so rare in the world these days. Whatever happened to morals and those of divine justice and law? If it still existed, I don't think I would be dealing with so much turmoil in my life now. Everyone makes human choices and, naturally, the mistakes. No one can accept the responsibility of their poor choices anymore, not when pointing the blame elsewhere is easier. Well, sometimes it's not your choice at all, and you're put in a corner with only poor choices to pick from. Even then, not choosing was always an option, wasn't it?*

When did I lose control of my own life? It doesn't even feel like I have a say in any of the events that are happening to me. Where does that leave me in the equation; am I just a pawn in destiny's game? I've been thrown headlong in the most bizarre situation I've ever heard of. I feel like Alice in Wonderland, fallen into some other dimension. All I can do is be careful about what actions I make. I need answers, explanations. Hell, anything at this point would be beneficial. There's no way for me to judge things when I feel so naive about what's going on.

If I am one of these so-called immortals, then what new rules will I need to follow? How big will my mistakes and wrong decisions be? Will it hurt those around me or something on a larger and more universal scale? How much damage can my actions cause once I master the power of Rebirth? When I make one wrong choice, one selfish unrighteous choice, how wrong can everything go? Who pays the ultimate price? Me, people around me, or the world? Will that horrible choice take me down or just leave me all alone in my dread?

"So!" Kyle blurted, jolting Hotan from his thoughts. "Are you going to explain things or leave me hanging? Are we waiting on someone?"

"Just trying to think of a way to contact my brother." Hotan continued staring up at the monument in front of them. "I don't really have any answers for you, but I'm hoping he will have some for the both of us. Then again, I hoped to find him here for some reason. Otherwise, I have no way of contacting him."

"Dude, that sucks." Kyle leaned on his knees as he stared down at the marble floors. "Really deep stuff, huh? You really think you have a chance of finding your brother here? What makes you think that?"

"I don't know. Somewhere deep inside me, I can't help but feel if I wait here, he'll show up. All I got from him was that I'm supposedly an immortal and should be remembering my former self." Hotan shot Kyle a grim look. "He went on about elements; like I'm Rebirth, and there are powers involved. I didn't really take it all in, to be honest. It just didn't seem logical, but the man at the diner, Geliah, made me aware that this may not be as farfetched as I initially thought." _My stomach and nerves are still churning at the thought of Geliah. Fear is a terrifying power for someone to control._

"Immortal? Are you serious? Do you believe—" Kyle stopped abruptly.

They both paused as the sound of footsteps clacked on the floor behind them.

"I figured you would return once the information had time to soak in. You are back sooner than I expected. Does this mean you are ready to hear more?" Talib stood in the aisle, once again sporting the white business suit and dark tie. "I see you have brought Kyle along with you."

"Yeah. Kyle, this is Talib, my older brother, apparently." Hotan rolled a shoulder to break the tension. He was relieved that his gut had been right about Talib being close by. "He's the one I got all this crazy information from."

"No shit." Kyle scowled, rolling his hands into fists as his tone shifted to anger. "You're an ass for leaving Hotan hanging like that, man."

"No, it's more like easing me into the story and forcing me to mull it over in my head. But we forgot to discuss one minor detail: the tattoo." Hotan glared at Talib, annoyed he didn't mention this in their first meeting. "You knew I would come back when I was ready to accept what little you gave me as some sort of truth, right?"

"Precisely." Talib cleared his throat. "And yes, the marking across your back is part of it. My question to you is: Are you ready to hear more?"

"Please. Will it be a problem with Kyle here?" Hotan glanced back at Kyle.

"There is nothing wrong with him being here. He is one of us, whether he is fully aware of it or not." Hotan's heart skipped a beat at Talib's reply. "As you suspected, we all bare markings much like tattoos across our backs. It signifies that we are immortals and symbolizes what we are. For instance, Kyle bares the image of a phoenix because he is the element of Fire."

"So how many immortals are there?" Furrowing his brow, Hotan waited for the answer. *What are the odds of Kyle being one of us? That means me, Kyle, Talib, and Geliah are immortals all in the same little city.*

"There are twenty that I am aware of after walking this Earth for centuries. I know each face and element along with its marking. Though we have lived a long time, the state in which they are awakening has weakened them drastically. It is unknown what triggered this in the last four hundred years or so." Crossing his arms, Talib lectured, "As far as our origin story, I will have to save that for later. For now, we must focus on regaining your memories, or at least the ability to control your element, Hotan. Of all the elements, yours is the most dangerous. Rebirth affects life and death itself, as your marking implies. That is why you bare a wing of life on the right side and the wing of death on—"

"You're wrong." Hotan's abruptness caught Talib off guard. "The wings are the same on both sides." *This doesn't sound good at all.* "Is there a chance they can change?"

"Never. Not even a slight change has ever happened before. Show me." Talib furrowed his brow as he came closer to Hotan, who pulled his shirt up.

Talib stared at Hotan's back for several moments. *Wish I could see his face, gauge the expression.* Hotan's heart fluttered as the silence went on, only hearing the shuffling of a stance and feeling the hint of breath hitting his bare skin. *He's taking in every detail.* The growing concern on Kyle's face made Hotan anxious. *Why is he worked up? Is it possible he made a mistake. Does this mean something is wrong? With me? With the power I'm supposedly holding.*

Talib spoke slowly, "You are right. It is not the same."

"What does that mean?" Kyle cut in, the uneasiness growing. "You knew mine; did you forget his? Were you mistaken, Talib?"

"I would never forget something about my own brother." Talib turned away from them, gaining a private moment to think. "It still has both wings, but they are overlapping on both sides. This is why you cannot recall anything about your former self. Life and death intertwined and created something … new. *Someone* new," Talib's voice trailed off, and they stood in silence.

Hotan shifted nervously; the tension in Talib's back was clear even through his business coat. *Something isn't right. This guy doesn't seem like the type to not know a crucial detail like this. Whatever is wrong with me is my fault somehow. Or it's the old Hotan's fault, whoever and wherever he is now. Am I a different person, and he gave me his powers? Or am I truly his reincarnation who has forgotten who I am?*

"This is definitely the source of the problem." Talib's voice jerked Hotan from his thoughts as he turned to face him and Kyle. "What it means, I have no idea. I will need time to research this. I have never seen anyone have a change in their element's mark before. I am confident that you are slowly becoming immortal and sense the dormancy of Rebirth beginning to stir deep within you. Normally, immortality is instant upon the first use of your powers, but with you, it is a small trickle. Just be careful. Your powers are fading into existence, and it may pick up speed at any moment. You are the embodiment of life and death, and if you are not aware that your abilities are present, you can bring serious harm. This cathedral was restored in a matter of seconds when your powers awakened for only a few minutes before reverting back to a state of dormancy."

"Does that mean we're not human? A different race or something else?" Kyle crossed his arms. "We're not human, right?"

"We are human, or, at least, started that way." Talib cracked a slight smile, his cold expression broken for the first time. "We each have become our elements, and like them, immortal and never-ending. In order to keep natural order, all aspects of the element are within our reach."

"So that's how it happened…" Rubbing the side of his face, Hotan spoke his thoughts. "That's why I got so sick." *That's why the church seems reborn, and that's why Geliah was provoking fear so easily. He is Fear itself in human form.*

"What made you sick at the restaurant?" Kyle asked Hotan, and Talib's smile faded. "I've never seen you sick. Never ever have you been sick before."

"The guy in the trench coat." Hotan took a deep breath, feeling uneasy as he recalled Geliah's devilish smirk. "Geliah was there in the restaurant."

Hotan took note of Talib's uncomfortable shift.

"Geliah?" Kyle questioned.

"All I know is that I'm safe, for now. He seems content with torturing me from a distance and making me miserable." Huffing, Hotan sat down, his thoughts spinning into a hurricane of concerns and theories. "He's the element of Fear, and he's very strong, inhumanly strong."

"This damn thing on my back is going to get my ass killed. At least we're in it together, right? Watch each other's backs?" Kyle gave him a half-hearted smirk, failing at his attempt to break the tension.

"Yeah." Taking a deep breath, Hotan liked the thought of not being entirely alone in the situation. *Is it selfish to be at ease knowing someone else is being dragged into the deep end with me?* "What are your thoughts on Geliah, Talib?"

"He will become a problem, but for the time being, avoid him." Talib turned from them once more and started for the door. "I will find you again if anything new happens. If something urgent comes up, contact Jacob. He can take care of your needs and should be by to visit soon enough with a better means to communicate with us."

"I assume Jacob is one of us, too." Talib froze at Hotan's statement. "I was starting to get suspicious. It seems there are a lot of us in town."

"Yes, he is one of us. And yes, they seem to be drawn by the unstable power you hold. I cannot explain why or how." Talib started for the door again. "See you when I find out more."

"I hope so." As the doors closed, Hotan's only hope for answers left him. *And just like that, I'm back to square one.* Looking back at Kyle, Hotan managed a reassuring smile. "At least I'm not alone in this, right? I suppose we should call it a day."

"Cool with me. See you around, man." Kyle gave him a quick hug. "Watch yourself. Stay safe, and call me when you find out more. I'm here for you. You have a friend you can talk to about it; I want to know what's happening to us, too."

7

THE RED

"Hotan! Hey, Hotan!"

"Eh?" He stopped unlocking his apartment door and looked down the hall. Annie was walking up with another letter in her hand. "Hey, Annie! Another note? This is getting ridiculous."

"I couldn't get a hold of you, but your sponsor stopped by again. He left like an hour ago." Annie blushed, grinning to herself. "Sorry you missed him again."

"It's okay, thanks." Taking the letter, Hotan paused, recalling how Geliah and Talib looked. *They don't really come across as an average person.* "Hey, did you notice anything unusual about him?"

"No, like I said the other night, he seems like every other guy. Only thing is his purple eyes, but he has a very sweet personality. I wonder if he wears contacts." She reddened, looking away from him. "And I can't really say much more, except the tattoo of a deer on his back is pretty hot. I've never seen such good tribal work."

"His tattoo?" Hotan furrowed his brow at her. *He is definitely an immortal with a tribal buck tattoo.* "Wait, that means you've seen him shirtless," guffawed Hotan.

Annie shook her head, waving her hand to reassure. "I can handle myself, so stop worrying about me. Anyway, I know this is your first sponsor, but my love life has nothing to do with it. Strangers meet and get together all the time."

Hotan rolled his eyes at her and replied, "Just don't get your heart broken over this guy." *Annie, it's not always about you when I fade into my thoughts.*

"I won't." She started to walk away. "Don't feel bad that you haven't met him. I hope you don't mind that I might start dating him. He's so dreamy!"

Annie disappeared down the stairs, and his thoughts started back up. *Dating my so-called sponsor does seem rather fast, Annie. Who is this Jacob guy? What element does the stag represent?* Hotan finished unlocking his door and sat on the couch. Opening the letter, he continued thinking about the stranger. *Who in the hell is he? I can't believe he's dating Annie. What kind of element is he? Is it possible he used his powers on Annie? Why is he delivering the letters in the first place instead of just coming by and introducing himself? Why would Talib send someone else in the first place? Could it be he doesn't know how to use today's technology? It can't be just because of his looks that she's fallen for him. On second thought, she's brought guys home from the bar and stuck with them for longer than they deserved. Then again, there might be a chance that I'm related to more than one immortal. Could Jacob be related? I'm sure he has his reasons for handling things this way. For now, I should go along with Jacob being my sponsor. Just go along with their plan until it proves dangerous.*

He unfolded the letter and began reading.

Hotan,

I know you are still shaken from your encounter with Geliah and learning that Kyle is an immortal as well. I apologize that I cannot deliver these letters in person. Jacob will pose as a sponsor for the time being until we can sort everything out. It will make things less suspicious since I wish to be able to provide you with some help. Please do not see the financial support as a means of forcing you into anything. It will be a while before I am able to meet with you again. You can confide in Jacob, so feel free to ask him for any help you may need.

My Apologies,

Talib

Leaning back, Hotan considered the possibilities of what to ask Jacob. Looking across his tiny living room at the entertainment center, the idea of listening to the radio was a chance to unwind. The idea of music was more appealing than coming up with which of his billions of questions should come first. Laying the letter on the coffee table, Hotan stepped over it and turned on the radio. He sat back down, looking over at the only window besides its twin in his bedroom. *When was the last time I actually slept in my room instead of crashing on the couch?*

Listening to the ending of Chevelle's "The Red," the announcer came on with her signature enthusiasm. *"Hi, this is your six o'clock DJ, Becky. It's a lovely Saturday evening, and I have some awesome news for all the local bands out there. The Big*

Band will be held in a few months, a showdown of local rock bands and one of the largest music events in town. We're officially open for submissions! The top winner will receive a record deal from P&D Record Company, one of many sponsors looking to support our little city's talent. Come down to the studio and grab an application! Speaking of which, next up..."

Her voice faded as his thoughts began to take him away again. *I completely forgot about the Big Band competition, the biggest battle of the bands event of the year. I look forward to it every year, but it almost disgusts me that it came up during all of this chaos. Maybe I should cancel the idea of competing. Trying to get the band ready while figuring out this crazy shit about immortals and elements is overwhelming. Hell, am I turning immortal? Do I just give up now?* Groaning, he covered his face as his frustration grew. *Then again, it would keep my mind off this crap. Yeah, that sounds like a great idea. Keep my mind on something else for a while when this gets tiring. Not like I know what's really happening with me or these powers. I should sign us up for it, guaranteeing an escape when I don't have answers. At least I can reserve that much normalcy in my dwindling life.*

Stretching, Hotan took off his shirt and tossed it to the side. His kept his bedroom dark; there was no point having light in a room when he couldn't see color anyway. Flopping down on his frameless, futon mattress, he looked up at a Tool poster. It blocked off the window, helping his belief in complete bleakness for the colorblind. *My mind always feels calmer in complete darkness.* Most of the space in the small room was overtaken by scattered books and piles of clothes. With no carpet on the floor, the hard concrete met his bare feet. Hotan closed his eyes, allowing himself to relax; he needed rest. Sleep took over quickly, and he started to dream as the last of his senses became numb.

Hotan sat at a table under an excruciatingly bright spotlight. His eyes stung as he looked around, blinking a few times as everything in view had color. The yellowish wood on the huge bookshelves encircled him. The books filling the shelves came in all colors: greens, reds, blues, black, and even the occasional white. Several dark, eerie aisles spread out with him at their center like spokes on a wheel. Movement caught his attention, and he turned to his right, the light above him hindering his ability to focus on anything beyond the table. Damn, is someone here? Mouth running dry, he licked his lips and tried to swallow back his anxiety. I don't think the shadow has ever attacked me in any other dream. Could this be Geliah trying to scare me again? His heart thudded hard as he recalled how the other dreams always ended. Is this another version I haven't experienced yet?

"I need to tell you where to go to find answers. I am sorry I left you on this Earth without the knowledge of my past, but I suppose those memories aren't meant to be shared." Hotan narrowed his eyes to see a darkened figure, but his face was blurred by the bright light. "No, I suppose it's because I'm too ashamed to let anyone see such memories. This is my responsibility, not yours, and I cannot let you suffer for mistakes I have made."

Hotan watched as a copy of himself walked out with bright, blue eyes. A thick, red leather-bound book slid across the table. Chills ran down his spine as he watched his doppelganger shift nervously, seeming anxious about their meeting even here in this dream. So, this is my former self. Why is he so nervous? Something isn't right; I've got knots in my stomach, but I can't shake the feeling.

"You're Hotan." He paused in astonishment, still baffled by the stranger who looked identical to him. "My former self, the person I'm reincarnated after."

"Yes, I am the last of what remains of myself. You will not see me again unless some sort of miracle happens. You are the rebirth of the element itself. I willingly ended my own life to create a new life. In doing so, I was able to strengthen the powers of Rebirth." Sighing, he slid the book closer to him with a heavy, burdened expression in his tired, blue eyes. "Find this book. It is called The Book of Ancients. It contains our history, where we came from, and what we became. There, you will find the answers to aid you as you come into your immortality. I no longer exist outside of this dream, outside of this body, other than a ghost of my former self. The last of my soul will be swallowed by yours in order to complete your transformation in becoming immortal."

Looking at the older version, he seemed sad and unsure. "Why are you staying behind? Did it ever cross your mind that the reincarnation failed because you still somewhat exist?" It's a hunch, but he's too on edge.

"In this book, there is written history of the individuals of our tribe and their elements. You may not know who they are," the former Hotan ignored him, continuing to explain, "but this will give you knowledge that I was unable to carry over. As their leader and the main element, it is crucial to know who is responsible for which elements."

Hotan slapped his hand over the book and glared into the startled blue eyes. "Answer me! Why can't I use the powers?" He searched the face that looked so much like his own, yet worn down and gaunt. "Is it because you're still here? Why do I not feel any connection to you? To the power?" Hotan gave a stern glare. I need advice; moreover, I need guidance from the one person who holds all the answers. If he made the spell using his abilities originally, then he must know what's currently happening. "I don't understand why you chose to stay unless something didn't go as planned. Something tells me the power hasn't shown itself to me. Is that your doing? Because you're still here spiritually, are you holding it back on purpose? Talib doesn't even know what's going on. Isn't he your brother? Why not explain—"

"Our powers are triggered by what we desire the most. I know my own desires, but yours are different. I am not you." The old Hotan's blue eyes drifted to some long ago time of pain. Hotan knew the look all too well after losing his mother so suddenly. "Your power surpasses my own in many ways," he confessed at last. "It works completely different, and nothing I say can help you, or even Talib, in your own discovery of your abilities. I can only hope that you choose to do good with your powers. Unlike…" he snapped his lips closed, a guilty expression flashing across his face before adding, "many of us who became greedy to satisfy our own desires."

"Yet, what I desire triggers this power?" Hotan drummed his fingers on the table, looking away in thought before insisting, "I don't desire anything, and I don't think my current needs and wants are sufficient triggers. If they had been, I definitely would have noticed something by now, before now even. My life has barely started in comparison to an immortal. I have no experience in what true desire is in comparison. Not to mention, Geliah threatening my life doesn't exactly help matters."

"Sometimes desire is complex; your true desires may scare even yourself." The ancient Hotan paced to and fro like a swinging pendulum. "It is a reflection of our deepest and darkest wants and not always something innocent. You have a stronger sense of life and death than I ever had, and I wish I could bestow you with all the memories I have acquired. There is so much I wish to share with you, but my time here is done." He seemed eager to leave as he nodded goodbye to Hotan. "This is goodbye, child. I wish you good fortune and much bravery. I, on the other hand, am too heartbroken to be of any use for you. My very being was weathered *down and shattered centuries ago. Before long, my soul will fade further into your own, and my self-awareness will no longer exist. From here on, I will not be able to protect you as I have done in the past. It falls on you to figure out how to manage the new form of Rebirth."*

"Wait!" Jerking up from the table, he watched the old Hotan disappear back into the darkness between the bookshelves.

A poster of Tool took the place of the black aisle as he sat there on his mattress. Sharp, paralyzing pain shot through his head. Eyes shut tight again, he clenched his teeth, trying not to scream in agony. After several excruciating minutes, it became shallow and barely noticeable. *Is this him fading? Is the absorption of another soul a painful event for both sides? I've had these before, growing up with headaches that made me curl up. How many times did Mom take me in for unbearable headaches? All this time, I assumed it was related to my colorblindness. Were the migraines caused by the old Hotan? If it's this painful for me to absorb him, then what has he been experiencing? My soul is slowly devouring his, one piece at a time.*

Shivers rattled his shoulder as the last thought hit his nerves. Stiff and wobbly, he made his way into the living room. The neighborhood lay in silence under its dark blanket; the clock on the wall read 11:44 p.m. He moaned and wiped sweat from his face, his thoughts spiraling into dizzying circles leading to nowhere. A laundry basket sat in the corner, reminding him he had chores to do. He quickly picked up piles of clothes, desperate for a distraction. Stuffing them all in the basket, he headed out and down the stairs. Passing Annie's room, he found the laundry room. He crammed his clothes into the washer, poured an obscure amount of detergent, slammed it shut, and turned it on. He leaned back against the washer, disgruntled to be left alone with his thoughts again.

Ugh! Do I even tell anyone? He avoided my questions, and when I brought up Talib, he practically ran away. That look of guilt. What the hell did he do to be afraid to face his own family or even say anything? What about Jacob? Should I tell him or wait and tell Talib directly?

A lighter flicked three times, breaking his concentration and thoughts. A tall man came just around the doorway, lighting a cigarette, leaning his right shoulder against the doorway. His shirt unbuttoned, the man stared at Hotan, his purple eyes a stark contrast to the bland gray of the room around them. *Purple eyes? Could this man be Jacob? I hate being colorblind and seeing colors at random. I hate that I know the name of the color is purple. What a schmuck coming in here all suave and lighting a cigarette.*

"There's a no smoking policy here," Hotan drawled, pointing to a sign on the wall behind the man.

"You're Hotan, right?" The man's voice was low and soft as he ran his left hand through his short spikey hair, releasing a puff of smoke from his lips. "Hotan, right?"

"Yeah, why you ask?" Hotan narrowed his eyes at him. *This has to be Jacob.* "And you are?"

"Oh, just heard about you. That's all." Pushing himself off the doorway, he opened the dryer, pulling out some sheets. "Nice to meet you, Hotan. Sorry, was doing late night laundry. Won't bother you anymore, night."

"Night…" Hotan watched as he disappeared followed by a trail of smoke.

He ignored answering the question as to who he is. Heard about me? I can't shake the feeling that he is Jacob. Maybe he's pulling information about me from Annie. Sighing, he wondered why he happened to be a topic in any conversation. Sitting on top of the washer, he continued his random chain of thoughts. He went back and forth from simple school life to the chaos. Finally, he remembered what the DJ had said right before he fell asleep. *Last year, I wanted to compete in the Big Band, but I didn't meet the minimum age requirement. This year, I'm eighteen. I have a chance at making the top three, at least, especially with the added advantage of improving my guitar skills over the last year.*

One problem, I'm short a bass player since Shellie is only seventeen. He sighed again, rethinking all the rules. It required each group to have a minimum of three people. Unfortunately, Hisota was only a lead vocalist and didn't do anything else except be a nuisance. *Instead, I have to become lead singer since I sucked at being able to do both for more than two songs back to back.* He would have to throw an audition at the club and find a bassist that way. Once they found someone, they would decide the songs that they would perform. The washer buzzed, and he chucked the wet clothes into the dryer. Back upstairs, he shuffled into his room and flopped on the mattress. Lying on his belly, he fell asleep peacefully.

Someone knocking on his door brought him out of his sleep. Swaying past his couch, he opened the door and leaned on its frame. Annie smiled sweetly and handed another letter to him. After closing the door, he walked into the kitchen and grabbed a glass from the cabinet. He lumbered over to the fridge, pulled out a carton of orange juice, and gulped it down before picking the letter back up. Inside, he found a short message in a stockier handwriting.

Just wanted to say hi last night. You looked irritated so I left. I'll catch you later when you're ready to talk.

Jacob

Crumpling the letter, Hotan huffed as he threw it in the trash. The glass clanked into the sink as he grabbed his empty laundry basket, annoyed by the note. *What a douchebag.* Returning to the laundry room, he thought about Jacob. *He's not like Talib at all. Suave, flirty, and worse, careless. What happens if trouble starts and that's who I've got to back me up in a pinch?* Geliah's grin crawled its way across his mind, and he shuddered uncontrollably. *I knew who Geliah was just by the flood of emotions that washed over me. I had a similar reaction with Talib when I met him. Oddly, I never had a reaction with Kyle like that. Is it because he hasn't awakened? Or perhaps the old Hotan had a stronger relationship with them and not the others?*

Coming to a dead end, he changed topics. *Desire is the key to unlocking the elements. There's too much happening in my life for me to waste time focusing on things I want or desire. I guess I'll have more luck finding* The Book of Ancients.

It can't be too hard to find a book, but then again, how often does someone find something from a dream? Flustered, he pulled out his cell phone and started flipping through the contacts. Pushing the talk button, he waited for someone to answer.

"Hello?" a groggy voice mumbled over the line. "Mmm, who is it?"

"Kyle, what are you doing today, man?" Hotan leaned against his wall. "I need your help."

"Nothing. Jessica is working this morning and planning on helping her dad move after that." Yawning and groaning invaded the phone for a minute. "Why? What's up?"

"Well, I have some clues and a possible source for answers. I was wondering if you wanted to come and help me find it."

Looking across the room, he watched a dove land on the windowsill and stare at him.

"Hell, yeah!" There were sounds of items falling followed by breaking glass. "Oops."

"Good. Be there in twenty minutes." Hotan smiled as he watched the dove fly away. *I have a good feeling about this.*

8

FOR YOU

Hanging up the phone, Hotan snatched up his helmet and headed out to the street. Rottweilers in the nearby junkyard barked and lurched as his motorcycle took off onto the busy highway. Accelerating, the front tire rose before hitting the ground again as he shifted gears. The wind pushed against him as he leaned into the turns along his route. He left his thoughts behind and enjoyed the ride. Smoothly swerving through traffic, Hotan soon stopped in front of a beige house. Wasting no time, Kyle strapped on the spare helmet, climbed onto the back of the bike, and away they went. After driving through skyscrapers for a while, they made it to an old, white building. The main library sat among the silvery towers in the heart of downtown, and considering its age, it was their best chance of locating *The Book of Ancients*. They walked up the huge row of steps and entered the dark, dusty building.

The librarian cleared her throat, demanding their attention as she nodded to the "Keep Quiet" sign on her desk. She was well into her sixties, sitting at a little desk, staring at them with twisted lips and a sour face. Their very presence seemed to be ruining the old woman's day as they stopped at her desk.

"Man! I don't know why I insist on riding on the back of that rice burner! My nuts get all crammed!" Kyle's words bounced off the walls of the building as he grabbed at his crotch. "Why didn't we take my car?"

"Stop it." Hotan's face turned red as he stared back at the annoyed librarian. *Please stop embarrassing me, Kyle! It's bad enough this woman makes me feel like I'm on trial.* "Excuse me. I was wondering if you might have an incredibly old book called *The Book of Ancients*? It's possibly older than the town itself. Do you have any books like that here?"

"*The Book of Ancients*?" Pushing her bulky glasses up on her nose, she contorted her lips to the right side of her face. "Never heard of it. We have books that old, but that's not one of them."

"Umm," Hotan's forehead creased as he gave her a baffled expression. *I think that's the most preposterous answer I've gotten this month.* "I'd feel more confident about your answer if you'd at least attempt to search the card catalog or something. You can't possibly know every book in this library. I'll be more than happy to do it myself if you're too busy. Just let me know where to start looking."

"You don't want to make him angry, lady." Kyle leaned over her desk with an overly serious, low-brow expression on his face. "Start answering."

"Fine." The old woman narrowed her eyes. Opening her desk drawer, she handed an old rusty key to Hotan. "If it's as old as you say, then walk to the back of that middle aisle there. Follow the path until you hit a dead end. There is a gate to the right containing a spiral stairway which leads to the attic. That's where the original library's collection is kept from when the town was a small colony. Nothing significant, anyhow. When you're done, lock the gate and return the key. Be careful; no one's been up there in years."

"Thanks."

Hotan walked down the dark aisle past a college girl, her hair in a tight bun filled with pencils. *She's completely engrossed with that book she's flipping through. I don't think she even noticed we had to squeeze past her.* Her glasses slid down nose as she closed the book and added it to her stack. She fumbled with her armful of books and started to lose them as the top one hit the floor. Kyle took a second to help, winking at her as she sighed in relief. *I've heard of a bookworm, but she takes the cake. Too bad Kyle stopped to help. I was curious to see how far she could make it before dropping another one.* Hotan smirked as he waited for Kyle to catch up to him.

At the dead end, a rusty gate awaited. Unlocking it, Hotan jerked it open. It groaned in protest, exposing the stairs it protected. To say it hadn't been opened for years was an understatement. He took one soft step on the rust-covered stairs, and they creaked in reply. Testing his weight again, no more protesting followed. Holding his breath, Hotan cautiously made his way up to the top where a heavy, oak trapdoor awaited their arrival. The attic was dark as he eased it open against the will of its stiff hinges. Light barely filtered through the thick dust caked on the window. Kyle entered behind him. Not able to see anything beyond his feet, Hotan stood still, perplexed as Kyle brushed past him. *Where does he think he's going? I can't see anything besides the faint glow of an old attic window.*

"Whoa! And I thought my room was a mess!" Kyle's steps went deeper into the musky room. "It stinks in here. How old is this crap?"

"What?" Hotan took a deep breath of dust-filled air. Coughing, trying to focus his eyes, he saw nothing. "How can you see? I can't even make out my own hands." *Are my eyes getting that bad? I didn't think colorblindness inhibited my night vision.*

"Huh? You can't see?" Kyle's steps moved to the right. There was a *click*, and a bulb flickered on. "Is that better?"

"Yeah." Looking around, stacks of cobweb-covered books lined the narrow attic. "How were able to see any of this?"

Kyle shrugged, "I've always had excellent night vision."

Maybe it's the element of Fire and the ability to provide his own light source? Maybe heat sensory like snakes? Hotan's shoulders shuddered, and he focused back to the task at hand. "This is going to be hell to go through. No one's been up here in an awfully long time."

"Hmm." Kyle began to walk down the aisle looking at all the stacks. "Well, the good news is that the stacks all start with the same letter. It might take us a few minutes to find the B's. Here's H."

"Good, at least its organized chaos. Maybe my luck's starting to change after all." Hotan started with the stack to his right and began working his way to the window. "Here's S… J… found them! Here's the B's! Come help me look through these. It looks like there are two stacks of them."

"Sweet!" Kyle knelt next to one stack. "Now what's the name of this book we're looking for?"

"It's called *The Book of Ancients*." Hotan took one book at a time, reading the titles. After a while, he scoffed, "It's not in this stack, nothing even close to that title. I was hoping I would get lucky, but all I see is a billion copies of *Beowulf* and the Bible. No wonder they sent these to the attic. I don't think it's practical to have more than ten copies on the shelf at the library."

"No way, there has to be another stack of B's around here. Here's the T section, but it's about the same with copies of *Tale of Two Cities* and *Treasure Island*." Kyle started scouring through nearby stacks. "Man, this sucks. It's like we found the old English class books."

"There aren't any signs of a mixed pile, and it seems they are all in title order. I already looked through the rest on this side." Huffing, Hotan mulled over his thoughts as he glared at the dusty towers of books. *Why did I think it would be easy to find?* "Figures, wishful thinking on my part. Sorry."

"Man." Crossing his arms, Kyle scrunched his nose as he thought long and hard. "Maybe Jessica has an idea of where we can look next; she reads stuff all the time. You should see the bookshelves of classic literature at her house, dude. In fact, she should still be at the restaurant if we hurry."

"I'm hungry anyway. Let's go." *I need to come up with a game plan. I can't keep rushing into things like this. If I wasn't acting crazy before, I'm definitely looking the part now.* Hotan rubbed the back of his neck, trying to relieve the tension.

They headed back down the rusted, spiral stairway and locked the gate behind them. Through the towering shelves of books, they passed the college girl once more. She waved as she lipped another "thank you" to Kyle, and he nodded in acknowledgement. Hotan handed the key back to the librarian. Grinning in victory, she dropped the key back into the drawer. Hotan still thanked her for her time. At least he knew her word was indeed solid. They headed for the diner.

I'm supposed to find a book that I'm not sure even exists. It was just a dream. Maybe the stress is starting to get to me, and I'm losing my mind. I wish I could say I was crazy. I hate feeling obligated to solve this insane mystery, but I can't shake this instinctual sensation that there's truth to all of this. Every time I attempt to convince myself it's a hoax, it boils over and overrides logical thought. At least I have my best friend to help me through this. We just have no way of getting through it any faster.

They parked on the side alley of Benny's Place. Sitting at their usual booth, Hotan stared out the window into the street. Jessica greeted them warmly to take their orders.

"Coffee," Hotan said bluntly; he needed something to keep himself moving at this rate.

"A hamburger with a side of fries." Kyle never ordered anything other than a hamburger and fries, no matter where they went.

Handing the order over to the cook, Jessica grabbed up a coffee cup and carafe and returned to them.

"Hey, where's mine?" exclaimed Kyle as he watched Jessica pour Hotan a cup of coffee.

"You can wait your turn. What? Would you rather have coffee?" Jessica laughed as she sat down next to him. "So, what are you two up to today?"

"Looking for this really old book." Rubbing the back of his head, Kyle gave her his best puppy dog eyes. "But we don't know where to find it. We've had no luck."

"Did you try the big library?" She looked over at Hotan, who took a sip of his coffee. "They have a rare books section; most libraries do."

"Yeah," Hotan replied, meeting her gaze, "but they didn't have it, so now we don't know where to look next. If you have any place in mind, let us know."

"Really?" Jessica propped her elbow onto the table and rested her head in her hand. "Hmm, no, not really."

"Oh, well." Kyle leaned back, watching her leave. "Another dead end."

"Sorry I can't help you guys." A bell rang from the kitchen, and she came back swiftly with Kyle's drink and meal. "Enjoy, babe!"

"It was worth a try." Kyle grinned at his plate as it slid in front of him. "Thanks! I'm starving!"

"Thank you, Jessica." Taking another sip, Hotan froze as he stared out the window. *I don't have to go looking for it, it just has to find me.*

Hotan looked across the street at a sign with its paint bleeding down in bright red; it simply read "SALE." The forgotten bookstore was short and much older than the neighboring buildings. A clutter of cobweb-covered books filled the store's front window, and it seemed dark inside. He'd noticed the little store before but never thought about visiting it. Everyone had assumed it was closed because no one ever saw customers going in or out of the place. After all the times he sat there staring at it, lost in thought, no signs of life were ever evident. *Strange that a sign would be out on the sidewalk on the day I start to look for* The Book of Ancients. Beckoning him to walk in, he couldn't break his stare from those red letters shouting loudly over the grays of the landscape around it.

"I'll be right back." Hotan set his coffee down abruptly. "Something's been brought to my attention." *Did you set this up for me, Hotan? How much of this failed reincarnation did you plan ahead of time? Why is this not in the hands of your brother, Talib? What kind of mistakes did you make that are still washing up into the present day? Did you really think deleting yourself from existence would make everything go away? I'm no immortal, but even I know drastic measures only create bigger problems. What the hell did you do?* A gust of wind blew his gray bangs into his eyes, blocking his view. Brushing them back, Hotan gathered enough nerve to head across the street. Pausing, he glanced at the red letters with curiosity. *Who is this person? How did they know I was looking for the book? That is what this is all about, right? I only barely started my own efforts, and here is a sign shouting for me to look here. It has to be here.*

Taking in a deep breath, he entered the mysterious bookshop. A bell rang to announce his entry into the stale-smelling room. The small store was a sea of dusty books, the atmosphere dark and heavy. There was only one overcrowded aisle in the store, bordered by overloaded bookshelves and stacks to the ceiling. A desk by the entrance was the only sign of human activity, though there were no signs that anyone was there. Leaning against the desk, Hotan watched the store's door, waiting for someone to show up. *Perhaps they stepped out to go get some lunch? I mean, who would dare rob this place? Everyone thinks the joint is closed, and last I checked, no one steals books.*

"There you are!" a voice shouted from behind him, causing him to jerk away from what he had assumed was a vacant desk. "You're late!"

"What the!" Hotan stared wide-eyed at a dark-haired girl who grinned wildly at him. She crawled up from the ground and stood behind the desk. Cobwebs and dust covered her black shirt and hair as if she had been one of the books. "Where did you come from? Who, or what, are you?"

"I've been waiting for you!" she repeated, glaring at him through her glasses and holding a dusty book in her arms. Nothing he'd asked seemed to matter to her as her unnatural moment of glee continued. "You're running late, mister-mister."

"Waiting? Right, and you are?" Hotan swallowed the last of his nerves, mustering some courage to persevere. *Maybe I was wrong to come here. This poor lady has lost her mind; she's clearly in need of medication. It all makes sense why no one dares to look at this place, let alone come inside.* "What's your name? And why have you been waiting on me? Who do you think I am?"

"Tiiiiiiiiiiinnnnnnnaaaaaaaaaa." Squeezing the book in her arms, she twisted side-to-side in bliss. "My name's Tina. You're so silly. How could you forget my name? Hahahaha."

"Tina." He blinked. "Well, I saw the sign out front." *Do I really want to ask her about this? I mean, will I even get a legitimate answer from an insane person? She thinks we've met before.*

"It was for you. I knew you'd come if I made you a pretty sign. You like it?" Hotan jerked as she slammed the book onto the desk. Clouds of dust rolled across the desk before settling as she spoke. "Here's my baby. Isn't it beautamis? You have to be nice to her. I like you. You're different. He said you would be different! The same, but not the same. Yes, yes, yes. He never lies about these things!"

"Huh?" Hotan slowly approached the counter, refusing to take his eyes off her Cheshire Cat grin. "Man. You're a little obsessed with this book, and a little, crazy, too. So, someone told you I was coming for this?" *She claims she was told I was coming. She acts like she was expecting me. Part of me wants to ask her a billion questions, but it's obvious I won't get a straight answer, if any at all, from her.*

"Maybe, maybe not." Her face went serious as she slid the book over to him. "You hurt her, you die. Take as long as you need with this, but she must come back. Must, must, must!"

"Okay." Reading the title of the book, he paled. The worn-out embossing was still legible—*The Book of Ancients*. "How did you know I was looking for this book? This is *The Book of Ancients*. Who told you I needed this book? Who told you!" *Is there someone else watching me? This can't be coincidental. This all happened within twelve hours. Maybe I can track down who is pulling the strings!*

"Because I'm one of you," Tina whispered, leaning closer as if telling a grand secret. "I'm the crazy one! Just be sure to bring her back. She's my book. He said I could be its new owner as long as I let the new him, the different him, read it. When you bring her back, bring me chocolate. You have to bring me chocolate!

I want chocolate for being a good girl! Bring her back with my chocolate!"

"The new one? Chocolate?" Hotan lifted an eyebrow. *I'm not going to get any answers from her, but clearly someone knew that a new immortal would be looking for this. Did the old Hotan really plan this? Is it possible he gave her the book before he… Forget it. I'll need to look at the book to see if I can find some answers.* Curious, he continued the conversation. "Why chocolate, if you don't mind me asking?"

"Yes!" She slammed her hands on the desk, sending more clouds of dust into the dry air. "And! If you don't return it, I will come for it. And I want my chocolate! Or I will follow you until you give it to me!"

"Don't worry, I'll bring your book back and bring you some chocolate." Hotan took the book, wiping the dust off the red cover. *There's no doubt. This is the exact same book from my dream. What secrets are you not sharing, Hotan?* "See you later, Tina. Thank you for helping me find this."

"Have a very gloomy day!" She waved at him as he left. "Aww, he and the different one are gone now."

Hotan crossed the street, stopping at his bike to grab his bookbag from the compartment under the seat. He slid the book in and slung it over his left shoulder. Returning inside the restaurant, he sighed in relief. Kyle's mouth was full, but he shot Hotan a questioning face. Hotan grinned in response as a sign that he got what he wanted. Glancing over at the bookstore, he watched Tina kick her sign around the sidewalk before ripping it apart. She was a complete mental case; she paused to bark at an old woman who made the mistake of stopping to stare. As she returned to her store, he noticed the sign pieces fluttering away in the wind, the letters no longer red to his eyes.

"Why are you so happy all of a sudden?" Jessica came back to the table, pouring him more coffee in a fresh cup. "Did we miss something?"

"I found it. It was in that little bookstore." Hotan took a sip, enjoying the steamy cup of coffee. "I can't believe it was so close after all."

"No way!" Kyle exclaimed, swallowing the last of his food. "You mean that insane chick had it? That place gives me the creeps. The whole town talks about how there's a madwoman who runs the store."

"Yeah, well, I've never heard anything about the place, but she had it." Hotan cracked his neck, relieving the built-up tension. "She's crazy, no doubt about that."

"Well, glad you found it." Jessica smiled, grabbing Kyle's empty plate. "So, what's the book about?"

"I don't know yet, but someone suggested it for a research project I have," Hotan lied with ease. "Time to start reading, and see if it's worth all the trouble." Hotan took one last sip before laying enough cash on the table for both meals and a tip. "I want to see what kind of information this book has and if it can help me."

"Bye, babe!" Jessica blew Kyle a kiss as they headed for the door. "Have a good day!"

"Bye Je—" Kyle slammed into the door that had closed behind Hotan. "Ouch!"

"Oh, hell, no!" Jessica busted out laughing as he fumbled with the door, managing not to further harm himself. "So freaking clumsy."

Getting back onto the bike, they headed for the main highway. Pulling away from the red light (though colorblind, he was able to see lit signals and from his test, the top or left light meant stop), Hotan noticed a slight red image reflecting in one of his mirrors. Looking back, he could see Hisota's black Yamaha with red flames trying to catch up to them. *Not sure why he would be giving me colors. I don't need his crap right now. I have the book and don't want to waste time tending to Hisota's tantrum. I'm going to try to lose him in this traffic. I hate doing this; it's just asking for an accident to happen, but…*

"Hang on tight, Kyle. I'm going to lose Hisota." Kyle tightened his hold.

Leaning into the bike, Hotan accelerated through the traffic. He swerved past the vehicles as cautiously as possible, gaining distance between them and Hisota. The cars felt as if they were sitting still as the wind roared around them. Making it through a yellow light, they managed to leave Hisota behind the stopped vehicles. They had blocked him in, making his attempt to follow them futile. Hotan redirected their route and headed for Kyle's house. *I'm positive he'll head straight to my apartment after seeing me with Kyle. It was pure luck that I saw the red and orange flames on his bike. Otherwise, my colorblindness would have hindered my ability to pick him out. I suppose my mind agrees with my feelings of keeping any additional stress at arm's length for the time being.*

"Thought we were headed to your place?" Kyle said as he unlocked his door. The house was empty while his parents were out doing their normal routine. "What happened? Change of plans?"

"Change of plans. Hisota knows where I live but not where you live. In fact, he's always refused to come to your place for some reason." Hotan followed Kyle to the back of the hallway. "I'm not in the mood to deal with him today. This is more important to me then catering to one of his rants."

I need to know what this book contains. What sort of information does this thing have? Why is so important that I use it? Hotan closed the door behind him, and a *Playboy* model smiled at him from her poster. He looked at it for a moment, shrugged, and turned back to the task of seeing what mysteries *The Book of Ancients* held. The bedroom consisted of a chaotic closet, a messy twin-size bed, and a desk with a lamp. Sitting at the desk, he pulled out the book. Kyle flopped across his bed and watched Hotan thumb through the aged pages. They were yellow, stiff, and fragile. Being delicate with the aged, worn paper, Hotan came to the first chapter. The entire book was hand-written and appeared to be a personal journal of some kind. Kyle leaned over Hotan's shoulder as he started to read.

THE BOOK OF ANCIENTS

The Beginning

In the beginning, we were nothing more than a tribe of spirited people fighting to survive. History has rubbed out our existence, but there were truly thirteen tribes of Israel. Many died, more were enslaved, but we last few survivors did not fall under these fates. Labeled as the Levites, Sons of Levi, we were known for our abilities in training diplomats and priests. The land we called home had been given to us in good faith, despite beliefs that we were not landowners. Even this was taken from us years later when fear and greed destroyed the act of kindness. A time in history marked by my people's enslavement to the tabernacle, their freedoms forgotten.

At the time of this enslavement, there were two brothers in charge of the village. It had been decided, following the chief's death, that the younger brother would be the head of the tribe, while the older brother would serve as his advisor. It was an unorthodox move, and the rate of its success scared the other tribes since it had never been done before. Whispers of conspiracy among the larger tribes claiming that they would soon fall under control of the Levites began to spread like locusts. Fear devoured hearts, and with it, our hope. It was not long before communications went silent. Our brothers and sisters in the nearby territories stopped sending messages. The end was inevitable.

The elders within our tribe argued whether action should be taken to check on the status of our silenced priests and diplomats in neighboring lands. In the end, no action would be allowed. The brothers pleaded for someone to attempt contact, but none would disobey the elders. This was when the system, the trust in our leadership, failed. Some of the elders had been paid off. They were promised land and riches in exchange for sabotaging plans of defense and urging that all was well despite the silence. These elders were among the first targets in the slaughter inching ever closer to our home. Despite my nightmares and the sensations that wrenched deep in my gut each night, shadows grew darker, and we failed to push the issue further.

It was during a spring festival; the time was 928 BCE. The other tribes rushed in, sinking their fangs deep into the village. People, children even, were thrashed. Any refusal to comply with demands led to losing one's life. The general, an exiled Levite from our ranks, made a personal effort to locate the brothers. His only desire was vengeance for the excommunication given to him by their father. With what little time they had, Hotan and Talib gathered who they could and fled their homeland. Screams of their loved ones beckoning rescue echoed behind them. Haunting images remained with them. An elder groveled at the feet of the general. Bleeding, dying, he screamed, "Where is my land? I kept my promise! Where is my gold? I did what was asked of me! I earned my place!"

The Devil had snaked his way into the hearts of the people, and the brothers were dismayed that they did not recognize it.

The journey to freedom had its own costs and horrors. Crossing the dry lands led to death from thirst and exhaustion.

At one point, a pack of starving lions stalked and picked off any who fell too far behind. The sea was not a comforting sight as the salty air stung at our blistered skin. The water only brought more fear and death. Our lives were cursed, the land around us a plague, killing us in its slow and painful method. We stalled here for some time, trying to decide how to salvage what was left of our existence. Our choices became death, either by drowning or by being eaten alive by the four-legged vultures that circled within view. Roughly one hundred started the journey, but less than half continued the struggle to live. Still catching our breath, we were forced to cross the sea when the army appeared on the horizon. The shadow had not fallen far from its aimed target: the brothers. The exiled Levite, fueled by the devil himself, had chased us over treacherous land.

Reluctantly, we took to the sea.

The sun was blistering on the water more so than it had been on land. A breeze added to the torment as salt stung at our wounds and cracked skin. We watched our remaining members drift off to an eternal sleep, one-by-one freeing themselves from the torture in which we were trapped. Thoughts of Purgatory rattled our minds. One man leapt into the water, willingly drowning himself to escape his rotting flesh. Storm clouds rolled over us so quickly that it felt like a dream. Lightening boiled the water where it struck around us, and the waves grew to the size of mountains.

This was Purgatory.

We were neither dead nor alive.

This was the last test given to us. This horrendous act of nature would separate who was worthy from those not meant to survive the night. Many of us lost what we had left when we washed ashore. The pain that weighed on our hearts those first days on the island will forever stain our souls. Only twenty of us remained.

Twenty.

After so much blood, sweat, and tears, this was not merely survival; this was a new beginning, and the past cut savagely into our minds. Faces of our loved ones haunted our dreams. Gruesome last moments and memories of suffering was the last stride of who we were as a tribe.

Why were we punished so?

What was the purpose in leaving so few alive? Why was God angry with us? Or was this a sign of his mercy? So many questions flooded my mind. My heart was broken from losing my wife, carrying our first child, in the storm. I will never know the blessing of holding my own child in my hands.

The island was a prison made in the image of paradise.

We referred to it as Eden since it was so much like the stories read or told to us as children. Food and shelter were easily acquired, but the guilt of being the only survivors was seen on every face. Shoulders heavy, we focused on mending and strengthening what we had left. It was slow at first; we didn't notice that we were changing, becoming immortal. Our dedication to survival had distracted us from the passing of time, and soon we discovered new abilities.

Was this a reward for making it so far?

As I write this retelling, I can assure you, it was a curse in the end. A continuation of Purgatory that would not allow us to be claimed by death.

I would have gladly fallen into Hell rather than accept what was given to me.

Speaking without words was the first phenomenon. It was confusing how long we had been doing it without acknowledging the process. The natural sensation of using it was frightening, but we soon realized the importance of being able to easily contact each other despite distance. Cassandra was the first to discover her other special ability. She had been frustrated with her crops; attempts to domesticate the plants on the island had proven difficult. In anger, she struck the ground, causing seedlings to become full-grown, fruiting plants. We all gathered to watch her first attempt to recreate this miraculous moment. Insisting she had done it, she described the power she had felt flowing through her. She failed to perform this act a second time. Gathering her focus, she replayed the emotions and thoughts in her heart and struck the ground. Markings painted her skin, and she had a miraculous glow—the glow of saints about her. After that, we became more cautious, more aware, of what we did and how nature itself reacted to us.

We had become embodiments of nature and humanity.

There were ten elements of Nature and ten elements of Humanity. Nature consisted of the Mind, Body, and Spirit as its strongest point, but Rebirth was the all-encompassing factor. This also included six elements: Fire, Earth, Wind, Light, Water, and Metal. The elements of humanity were those which could persuade one's heart. These were labelled as Fear, Anger, Lust, Judgment, Insanity, and Clarity. Lastly, the remaining three elements related to the body: Sight, Hearing, and Touch. These elements could be manipulated to one extreme or the other. Touch could numb you or make the slightest breeze against your skin feel excruciatingly painful. Earth could change soil, make plants grow, or even promote decay. Rebirth could rewind or speed up a life span, or even go as far as reincarnation.

I cannot say how many centuries had passed when we made the decision to leave our Eden. We wanted to use our abilities to aid our fellow man and show God that we held no grudges in hopes that we would one day be welcomed into Heaven.

Immortal, we were truly in Purgatory, and we vowed to repent. We wished to shed the curse of never-ending life and follow the teachings we knew from heart. With the ability to perform miracles, we sought to do the world good.

Unfortunately, we only found chaos.

The world had turned violent in our absence, and our efforts fueled new wars. Our return brought centuries of disasters and death to mortal lives. Please forgive our ignorance. We were no better than children as we scoured the land, not realizing how devastating the smallest use of our abilities could be. Tired of our miseries, Hotan aimed to shield his people from any more pain. It was not fair that the others were being punished for his own faults. They debated for quite some time before everyone agreed to what was offered. With the use of the powers of Rebirth, he could wash their souls clean and bring them close to mortality in an endless cycle of reincarnation. They would not know themselves or each other. It was a means of blending back into the rhythm of the world, leaving behind the memories of their cursed life. One would have to stay behind, be left out of this spell to watch over them. The fear of awakening, possibly not remembering themselves, and causing more disasters pulled at all of them. Talib, the eldest brother and element of Judgment, volunteered to stay behind.

May God bless him and mend the pain that it caused him to watch both his wife, Saphellia, and brother, Hotan, disappear from existence.

May my sins be forgiven for what I have done.

9

TODAY

"That's deep." Kyle furrowed his brow before falling back onto his bed once more.

"There's the problem, though. We're under a spell that's falling apart for some reason. I'm Rebirth, and technically, the one who originally cast it." Hotan closed the book, staring at the worn, red leather cover. "Regardless of why this is failing, I'm slowly becoming immortal. At the rate things are going, it's going to become harder to blend in with normal society. If you never age or die, someone is bound to notice. I wonder how long ago this awakening started. Who was the first to wake up and regain immortality? Maybe we can figure out what went wrong if we figure out who snapped out of the spell first." Hotan's mind raced, and at last he muttered, "Perhaps Talib knows. I imagine he would sense another coming into existence."

"Yeah, it does seem strange. Did you lose your powers at some point? A bad reincarnation along the timeline?" Kyle looked at Hotan, who stared out the window at doves pecking at the grass. "It has something to do with you right? You're the reincarnated version of the man who cast this spell in the first place."

"All I know is that I'm not the Hotan in this book." With a heavy sigh, he looked back to Kyle. "The Hotan who initiated the spell is dead, and I'm what's left. He used his powers to remake the element of Rebirth, but I don't know why." The dream flashed in his mind—the look of fear on the old Hotan was unmistakable. "He was tight-lipped about why he needed to do this, other than making the element stronger. If he was so powerful, why the need to be stronger?"

"What are you saying?" Kyle sat up, alarmed as he digested the information. "How do you know what Hotan intended? You sound like you met him somehow. There can't be two of you…" Kyle paled, swallowing before adding, "Or is there?"

"No, there aren't two physical versions of me. It's the same reason why I knew to look for the book. It wasn't Talib who told me about it." Hotan held up the book as he confessed, "It was the old Hotan himself." He put the book into his book bag, and cut off Kyle before he could ask or say anything, "In a dream, he came to me. It wasn't an ordinary dream. I felt something there… I can't seem to find the words to describe it. It was like a locked section of myself came to life for that small moment and then faded to nothing."

"Hold on, you're not making any sense, man." Kyle watched as Hotan flopped the book bag on, ready to make an exit. "You're talking all crazy again, dude. This is insane."

"I've got to go." He opened Kyle's door. "See you tomorrow at school."

"You better explain to me what the hell you're talking about." Kyle watched as he left, closing the door behind him. "This is taking a toll on him, Talib. Why aren't you helping him?"

The English teacher finished his lecture and passed out dittos. As usual, they needed to be finished before class ended. It was one of those casual, laid-back days when the teacher just wanted to relax while grading projects that students had recently submitted. Hotan couldn't complain; it was nice to enjoy some quiet class time for a change. He zoomed through the paper, answering correctly without studying or flipping through the book like the rest of the class. Shoving it to the side, he took a deep breath. The feeling of mental exhaustion flooded over him. He had no desire to engage himself in anything that required thought. Shellie scooted her desk closer and stared at his unusual empty glance.

"What's wrong with you? You've been really weird lately, and it's got me worried." She sighed, grabbing his right hand to catch his full attention. "Are you okay? Are you still feeling sick?"

"I really wish I knew." He stared at her hand clasping his. His was much bigger; her fingers were thin and dainty compared to his fat stubby ones. He felt content and at ease while holding her hand. "I've got so much on my mind. I feel like it's eating me alive, inside out. There's no longer a definitive line between what's real or fantasy, and it's frustrating. I lose myself to my thoughts, driving myself crazy wading through what is fact or fiction. I'm exhausted."

"It seems that way." Letting go, she focused on her ditto to avoid the teacher's glance. She continued to whisper to him, "If there's anything I can do, let me know. I'm always here. You know you can talk to me. I just want to know what's going on, even if I can't help."

"I'll be fine." He laid his head down on his arms and closed his eyes. "Just wish you could help. I'm just so tired. I can't sleep lately. It's like my body is slowly losing its want for sleeping and eating. Physically, I feel fine, but mentally and emotionally, I miss the break from existence."

"This is not a group activity, you two." The teacher cleared his throat, watching Shellie scoot her desk back into place. "Thank you, Ms. Hoffman."

Feeling drained from his life crisis, Hotan let himself drift. His mind was constantly asking questions with no answers to be found. Sleep was impossible with so much left open and unresolved. Worse, everything seemed to cycle back to him. He was the problem and the answer, but no one could help him. Taking a deep breath again, his ears took in the sounds of papers rustling and someone occasionally coughing or swishing in their seats. Hunger and sleep, in a physical sense, wasn't affecting him like normal. Waves of anxiety hit him when twelve or more hours had passed, and he failed to feel hungry.

Is this part of becoming immortal? No more sleep or need to eat? Or am I just swamped with this whole chain of events? Please body, just let me sleep, so I can just stop thinking. I can't focus on anything when all I want to do is to lay my head down and make all these questions stop. If I can get some answers, maybe I could get some rest. Where is Talib? Why isn't he helping me? I haven't heard, seen, or even gotten a letter from him. What an ass. He came and threw this all in my face then left. I would write back, but I don't like that Jacob guy. Really ticks me off that Annie's in love with him. It's not right that these immortals play with people's emotions. Geliah can screw someone for life with the ability to manipulate a person's sense of fear. This whole ordeal is unfair. Heavy with his thoughts, they came to a stop as he began to fall asleep.

"Hotan," a voice called to him in the darkness of his mind. "Hotan, can you hear me?"

"Who is this?" Hotan answered, no longer able to hear the classroom. *Am I dreaming again? Did I finally fall asleep?* "What do you want?"

"Hotan." The voice was new to him but soft and desperate. "I need you to find me. I need help."

"Find you? Who are you?" *This wasn't the voice of the old Hotan or anyone he had heard before.* "Why me?"

"I can't leave from this place until you find me; I'm trapped here. I fear for my life. Geliah will not allow me to leave." The fear in the man's voice sent chills across Hotan. "My only hope is that you can pull me from under his control. I cannot push past the fear he instills on me; I'm too weak."

"Leave where?" Hotan thought loudly as if shouting out over a great distance. "How can I find you? Geliah is too strong for me to face!"

"Here. I am here in the city at the…" the voice faded, and Hotan's mind went silent.

Feeling a hand glide across his marking caused him to jerk awake.

"Don't touch me!" He yelled, and his shout bounced off the walls in the classroom. Shellie's startled face told him all he needed to know. "Shellie, sorry, I didn't mean to shout. I'm so sorry."

"It's okay. You scared me." Her eyes were sad and watery as she gathered her things. "The bell rang, didn't want you to be late."

"Uh. Shit." Throwing his things in his book bag, he collected her books from her. "Here, let me carry these."

"Hotan, I can carry them," she said curtly, glaring at him. "I'm fine."

"No, but…" He knew he had hurt her feelings by the anger in her face.

The violent reaction had broken her last bit of patience in figuring out what was wrong with him. *I have to tell her. Maybe talking about it will help me clear my head.* "I've got something to show you. Let's go someplace and talk," he whispered, beckoning her to stay close.

"Show me?" Shellie followed him out of the classroom through the crowded hall. "Show me what? Hotan, slow down! Where are we going?"

"Follow me." Taking a swift turn to the left and out an exit door, he led her through the courtyard. No one was present but the two of them. "I want to show you this. It might help you understand why I'm acting weird. Come on this way. Keep this secret."

"Show me what? Keep what a secret? You're scaring me…" She quickened her pace to keep up with him. "Where are we going?"

Keeping quiet, he led her into the school greenhouse and laid their things on an empty plant table. Far as he could see, they were alone.

"Why did you lead me here?" Closing the door behind her, she stared at him, baffled.

"I've got to tell you something. It's about what's been wrong with me these past few weeks." *I hope she doesn't tell me I'm crazy.* Sighing, he continued, "It's all so irrational, so talking about it just makes me feel crazy. I don't have any answers, and it's challenging for me to believe that it's even real."

"Hotan, what's going on?" Her eyes widened as she shifted her stance. "Is everything okay? Are you on drugs or something? Hallucinating? Delusional?"

"That's the problem. I wish I could say yes, even maybe, to some of those, but I can't." Hotan looked her in the eyes as his jaw tensed. "I'm not sure what kind of situation I'm in at the moment. It's not drugs. I promise you that."

"What is the situation then?" He could feel her growing uneasiness. "Are you involved in something really bad? A gang?"

"No." He rubbed his forehead, searching for something, anything. "We've been dating for what, like two years now, right?" She gave him a bewildered expression but continued doing her best to listen by simply nodding. "If I was doing something, you would know about it, right?"

"Yeah," she answered cautiously. "What does that have to do with what's wrong now? Is it me? Are we breaking up? Because you can just say that."

"No. Maybe if you see this, you will understand why I'm so confused. Things are so out of place and complicated." Taking off his baggy shirt, he turned to expose his back to her. "Take a look. As many times as we've spent at the lake, you know very well this was never here."

Silently, she gawked at the tattooed wings which spanned his entire back. "When did you get a tattoo? It covers your whole back! Where on earth did you get the money for something like that?"

"I didn't. I woke up, and it was suddenly there." He glanced over his shoulder to see her pale face. "I'm telling you. The things going on with me aren't normal. I feel like I'm in some other realm."

"It just appeared, but it's huge." She walked closer, hesitant to touch it. "Wow, looks like it's been there for years. It just surfaced? This is wild. It's beautiful, like tribal angel wings. When did it show up?"

"The day you guys found me in the church. It was just there, no scabs, oozing, or puffiness like you see with a tattoo. I'm stuck with it for sure." Hotan leaned on the plant table, afraid to even see her face. *She must think I'm blowing smoke up her ass. Who could believe something so ridiculous?*

"Is it okay to touch?" Shellie stared at Hotan, but he didn't dare glance back as he pondered the answer.

"Go ahead." Her soft, warm hands glided over his back, following the design gently, and he shuddered. "There's no difference between my skin and the mark. It's crazy. I can't find any information on chemicals or conditions that could cause it. I mean, silver nitrate exposure, but it's not permanent and—"

"That's weird," she chirped awkwardly as she examined him closely. "It, well, it's the same texture as your skin. No signs of scarring or anything, but—"

"What is it?" His stomach twisted and tightened, making him nervous. "What's weird?" *I should have had someone check it sooner!*

"The marking. It's icy cold on one wing and hot on the other." She ran her hand over his back again to ensure she wasn't mistaken. "Yeah, it's a completely different temperature than the rest of your skin, Hotan. That's crazy."

"Cold and hot?" An uneasy feeling washed over him. *Is that a sign that it holds power?*

"Seriously, Hotan, it's like ice on the left side and feverish on the right. It's wild. No wonder you've been so secretive; this is crazy. Have you seen a doctor? Maybe there is something going wrong with your body, or it's somehow chemical poisoning?"

"No, no doctors. It's not like I have the money, and with my luck, I would end up a lab rat." He put his shirt back on. "I just have to figure out what it all means." *Talib said I was slowly becoming immortal. Maybe this is part of that...*

"Do you have any idea why something like this would suddenly show up? Have you figured out what triggered it or why you passed out? I don't know where to begin to look for answers about something like this." Shellie was troubled by his reaction. "I would have gone to a doctor. Don't you think you should see someone?"

"It's nothing a doctor can help me with. It's a lot stranger, and I feel fine. If I figure this whole thing out, I'll let you know more. For now, I'll just clue you in." Hotan began gathering her books. "You deserve that much, but I don't want you getting involved with this whole mess. For my sake, I need you focused. I need to know that when I'm with you, this can be put to the side. It's nice not to have to think about it when you're around."

"I see." Shellie nodded, giving him a faint smile that quickly faded as her fingers glided over the mark again, hidden now under his shirt. "But at least I know sort of what's going on in that head of yours."

"Yeah." Hotan handed the books back to her and kissed her cheek, whispering, "Sorry for making you late to class."

"No worries. It's worth it." She hugged him tight, and he relaxed in her warmth. "You know I love you, right? Don't be afraid to talk to me next time. I don't care if I don't understand one word you say to me. Just hearing your problems makes me feel like I can do something for the person I care most about."

"Yeah, I know." A smile crept across his face as he caught the scent of her perfume. "You better get going."

They kissed, simple and sweet, before she left the greenhouse. A sense of relief washed over him. *It feels nice explaining this to Shellie. At least she won't think I'm ditching her now.* Hotan made his way through the empty hallways as classes were in full stride. Paying no attention to the janitor emptying out an overfilled trash can, he passed the classroom doors, peering in at the students' faces within each window. His steps grew slower with the weight of his thoughts. His chest ached with regret and longing, the conflicted feelings taut under the pressure of his past, his present, and the future he couldn't seem to grasp.

Only a few weeks ago, I was no different from them: Just a student with no real worries in this world. Nothing expected of me beyond simply being a kid, a high schooler preparing for the next part of my journey. Now, I'm stripped of that comfort, forced to find out who I really am … or who I was. I'm nothing like them. I'm a recycled version of someone else, nothing more. There's no hope until I figure out this puzzle. Either I pick up where I left off in my forgotten life or get back to making my own and salvage broken dreams. It all seems so unfair.

Going upstairs, he passed another student who paid him no heed as he quietly entered a door. Mrs. Bothirsen shoved her glasses up and gave him a displeased expression. He sat down, ignoring her burning stare. *I'm not here to cause trouble. Please don't pick a fight with me today.*

"Page 223," a soft whisper came through his thoughts.

"Huh?" He looked over at the girl in the desk next to him.

"We're on page 223. She assigned problems 1 through 50, but we're only doing even numbers today." She smiled sweetly at him as she leaned over her book, her pigtails covering her eyes from his view.

"Oh." Hotan pulled out his book and started to flip through it. "So, what's your name? I keep meaning to ask you."

"Metsy." She started to work on her problems. "That's okay. Nice to meet you, Hotan."

"Thank you, Metsy." He stole another glance at her. *She always supports me when I have a difficult day in this class. Makes me feel guilty for not learning her name sooner.* "You help me all the time, and I forget to thank you a lot. Sorry about that."

"No problem." Focusing on the assignment in front of her, he heard her chuckle.

The light color of her hair meant she was most likely blonde. She always dressed in a punk-rocker style: leggings, skirt, black boots, and a logo shirt over a long sleeve one. Several times, she had helped him out when the teacher had been condescending or refused to let him know what she wanted him to do. *She wants me to fail, but why the hell she wants to risk us being stuck together in a room for another year is beyond me. Without Metsy, I wouldn't be surviving the class.*

Metsy had always been nice to him, despite the risk it cost her with the edgy math teacher. When he and the teacher argued, it was obvious the other students became uncomfortable, shifting and whispering. No one understood why she had so many problems with a quiet, straight-A student. Intimidation was the only thing Hotan could conclude. Sighing, he worked on the assignment, zooming effortlessly through the problems. *I sometimes feel like I've done this before. Of course, past life. All that knowledge, those memories even, are still in my head somewhere, aren't they?*

He closed his papers in the math book, setting them to the side. Glaring out the window, he huffed.

Why does Metsy help me? I never talk to her. Until today, I never even thanked her for all the times she's come to my rescue in this class. Guess I should try to make an effort to talk to her, and others like her, some more. Glancing over, he watched Metsy groan and start to erase an entire equation. *She's struggling in this class, but I make a horrible tutor. Shellie told me to never attempt to teach anyone, not even her, ever again. Maybe I can see if Shellie can help her out or something. She's a natural at math once she catches the concept. Heh, I guess I'm learning a lesson of patience the hard way through Talib, but honestly, I hate waiting.*

10

THOUGH GLASS

Now curious, Hotan pulled out *The Book of Ancients* and ran his hand over its cover. The red leather was scuffed, scarred, and worn down; it had travelled far and long. Opening the cover, he stared at the faded, blotchy ink of his own name inside. Below it, there was a date.

"Hotan!" The teacher snatched the book from his hands. "Pay Attention!"

"Give it back," he said, his voice low and calm as he glared up at her and held out an expectant hand. "I wasn't doing anything wrong. My work is done if you want to see it, and I should be able to read a book in peace."

"What?" she laughed, sucking on a cheek. "This is what I can't stand about you. I'm the teacher, and I didn't give you permission to do anything but the work assigned." She grimaced, taking another look at the book before adding, "You might get it back at the end of the school year … if I feel you deserve it."

Standing up from his seat, Hotan snatched the book from her, roaring as the last of his patience snapped, "What the hell is your problem? I've done nothing to you. This is a joke! How many other kids do you treat like this? Or do I intimidate you so much that you try to pull power over me? Push me around in front of everyone to feel like you are in control of someone who might know more about math than you do!"

"Uh!" She stepped back, startled by his actions as the words stung. "Why don't you go to the office! I'm calling the principal! I don't have to take this from you, of all the kids! Get out of my classroom!"

"Fine!" There was no hesitation as Hotan grabbed his book bag and left, the door rattling as he slammed it behind him. "This is bullshit! I've done nothing to you!"

"You're not going to pass this class!" she threatened, hiding behind her classroom door as she screamed one last comment down the hallway after him. "You're failing! You hear me, Hotan! FAILING!"

"Well, too bad! Long as I don't see your face again, I'd rather fail! More than happy to repeat this class!" Giving her the cold shoulder, he made for the administrator's office.

I've never had issues with any teachers, not like this. Considering I've never had trouble like this in the past, they can't take her side. I wonder if Metsy or some of the other kids would speak up for me? Hard to say. She's probably threatening them with automatic failure if they say a word about what happens in the class between us. All those ridiculous arguments over nothing. Literally finishing my work and minding my own business. What a joke.

Dropping his stuff in a chair, he flopped down in the adjacent chair. The secretary eyed him every so often as she whispered on the phone. He felt like a murder suspect by the way she shifted nervously while he stared her down. Hanging up her phone, she turned her full attention to him. Shifting in her chair again, she cleared her throat.

"Let me guess," She asked, scrunching her face. "Hotan?"

"Yeah," he huffed, "that's me."

"Who's your counselor?" She started looking at a chart on her desk.

"Mr. Wyatt."

"Well, he's not here today." The phone rang, and she picked it up. "Good afternoon, Northside High School, this is Lydia, how may I help you?"

"That's too bad," mumbling to himself, Hotan allowed his rage to pour forward. "Maybe he'll be more useful now that he's not here. It seems that guy gets more vacation days than workdays."

Her voice cut through his bitter thoughts as he eavesdropped. *What will happen now?*

"Yes, are you sure? Okay, I'll send him in."

Who is that? Was it really about me?

"But she said … oh, well, no, but … I see. Yes, sir. He's here and no, no issues. Indeed … my apologies. Yes, right away." Hanging up the phone, she flicked her finger at him, motioning for him to stand. "That was the principal, Mr. Piedmont. He wants a word with you in his office."

"Piedmont? It's the room at the end, right?" *Good, maybe I can explain to him what's been going on. If anyone has the power to do something about this, it's this guy.*

"Yes, all the way down. You can't miss it." The phone rang again, and she answered it, shooing him down the hall with her hand.

Hotan walked down the narrow hallway, knocking on the principal's door. *This can't get any worse. I suppose if this goes sour, I have every right to drop out. Then again, I did promise Mom I would finish.* Rubbing his chest, he felt the aching weight of letting her down, even if she no longer could scold him over the idea.

"Come in," the old man's shaky voice thundered through the door.

"Hi." Walking in, Hotan stared at the wrinkle-faced man who gazed up at him with soft, blue eyes. *Colors again? Why here though? Always with the eyes.*

"Take a seat there, son." Mr. Piedmont gestured to a chair close by. His desk was cluttered, piled high with stacks of paper, and he fumbled with his computer's keyboard. "Just give me a moment. I'm a tad unorganized today."

"Thanks. I'm in no rush, Mr. Piedmont." Clearing his throat, Hotan sat in the chair and took the opening to explain. "I just hope someone in class will be nice enough, or at least brave enough, to speak up on my behalf. There's a means of making a formal complaint against Ms. Bothirsen, and I wish to follow through with one after today." Hotan took in a deep breath, his words smooth and confident as he watched the old man squint his blue eyes at his monitor. *Is this some sign I should be picking up on? What am I missing?* "Once you have a moment, of course, I wish to tell you what's been going on in class."

"Well." The old man's face stretched awkwardly as he grinned, shifting his eyes to side glance at Hotan. "Before we start such a nasty conversation, I would like your opinion on something." He gestured above and behind Hotan, his voice cooing, "What do you think about that painting over there on the wall? I just bought it this week, and I'm not so sure about it."

"Huh?" Slowly shifting in his chair, Hotan gave Mr. Piedmont a dumbfounded expression. *He completely ignored what I said. Why does he want me to look at his picture? Wait, this has got to be some kind of joke. How much more frustrating is today going to be?* At last, Hotan looked back at the painting.

Once again, colors came to life. He saw the painting in full color but nothing else in the room. *I've never seen art in full spectrum!* It was a large watercolor in a Japanese ink style with large brush strokes. Smooth lines showed the caliber of the artist's talent and control on the flow of paint and brush. Hotan examined the earthy greens and golds on the bamboo limbs where a colorful bird sat. The bird held many colors which blended beautifully with reds, browns, purples, and blues. *A peacock or something similar?* He turned back to Mr. Piedmont, who smiled proudly while also taking in his painting.

I don't understand what the message is here. Why the eyes and the painting? What's so important about an old man and his prized picture? Huffing, Hotan took a moment to shake the anxiety from his rattled nerves. *I don't think I can take much more of this today.*

"Well, what do you think?" Mr. Piedmont's eyes made a strong connection with Hotan's, the blue flashing in excitement. "Isn't it beautiful?"

"It's nice," Hotan mumbled, swallowing his unhinged feelings. *Where is this all going? Does he want something? Does he have something I need? Will I get an answer or only more questions like before?*

"Ah. Which color is your favorite?"

"Color?" Shellie's green eyes flashed in Hotan's head, a color much like the bamboo leaves in the painting. "The green. I really like the soft, earthy green tones."

"Really?" Opening a desk drawer, Mr. Piedmont put some wrapped candy on the desk, a pile scattering in front of Hotan. "Try the green ones; they're good. I've always had a sweet tooth and find that these make for a great ice breaker."

"The… green ones." Staring at the candy, Hotan could only see variations of gray. *Kyle talks about the red candies all the time. He is always getting in trouble, and all I ever hear from him is about the candy. Is this a trick?* "Right, the green ones, of course."

"Well, where were we?" Mr. Piedmont watched as he picked up a piece and started to eat. "What's this whole problem in math class? You have such a clean record, and your grades are off the charts, young man. I can't imagine you making a scene and acting rebellious in class so close to graduation."

"Oh, she doesn't like me. I try to mind my own business, but she literally picks on me constantly. I finish my work then sit quietly, but she starts an argument every time." Plucking a candy, he inspected it. *No name or flavor listed. Damn. Is he assessing me somehow? Does he know?* Mr. Piedmont's chair squeaked, and Hotan continued, "Nagging at me. She nags at me and threatens that I'm failing. When I left, she continued to yell at me in front of the class. It's always in front of other students. I've gotten straight A's on her exams; there's no reason for me to fail this class." Swallowing, he met the principal's face, trying to gauge any hint as he asked, "What flavor are these?"

"I don't remember. I just know I like the green ones." His smile stretched as he snorted and laughed. "So, what do you want me to do about the situation?"

Gnawing at the hard candy, Hotan tried to place the flavor. *Maybe watermelon. Why watermelon? That doesn't help.* "Well, I simply don't want to be in the same room as her. I'll do the work, or even extra work, but to not hear another word from her would make me happy."

"Hmm, I'll see if I can work something out. You've got an excellent record, my boy. Obviously, it must be her." Mr. Piedmont leaned back in his seat, looking at his computer, clicking here and there. "Squeaky clean, in fact. Just bad chemistry between you two. That's okay; it happens more than you think."

"You actually agree with me?" *Oh, thank God.* Hotan sat up straighter.

"Of course. Only thing I can really think of doing is give you some sort of extra curriculum during that time slot. I'll talk to her, and you can take her exams. I know you know the material; your past teachers have written detailed comments on your abilities. This way, you just need to test out of the class and call it done." Mr. Piedmont lifted an eyebrow at him. "How's that sound? Will that work for you? Never have to see her again."

"Fair enough to me. What are you going to make me do instead? Where should I go? I can always head home early. I'm okay with that." Hotan laughed and earned a chuckle from the principal.

"I don't know. I'll see to it tomorrow. Come straight here instead of her class." He smiled again. "No going home early. I'm held liable for you until school lets out. I can't have that, now can I? Maybe you can do some work for the school office or an off-job-training program if we find someone to take you on, something like that."

"I completely understand. Thanks a lot, Mr. Piedmont." Hotan offered his hand. "I've heard a lot of good things about you. It's a nice to see they were true."

Taking Hotan's hand, Mr. Piedmont gave it a firm shake. "Anything for one of my top students! How are your parents doing?" His hand squeezed tighter as he added, "I'm sure they're proud of such an outstanding scholar!"

Retreating from the handshake, Hotan's smile fell in an instant. "My mom was." Mr. Piedmont's own smile faltered. "Never knew my dad. Don't even know if he's alive, to be honest. Mom died two years ago, so I've been on my own for quite some time, sir." Hotan took another piece of candy. *I hate this. I hate talking about Mom and that deadbeat called my dad. You would think they put this stuff in the records, too. They need to and should label it "Do not ask" alongside those other notes they like to take down about me.*

"Oh, sorry to hear that. You're doing well, I hope?" Mr. Piedmont observed Hotan's solemn face. A few more clicks of his mouse, and he found what he was looking for before pressing for answers. "It says here your guardian is an Annie Kerbowski? No relation then? Foster home?"

"In a way. She was the girl who babysat me when I was little. For now, she lets me live in a small apartment at our complex, which she owns. My mom and her were fairly close, and she stepped up to the plate since I have no other family. In return, I'm the handy man. She really has no one else either." Sighing, Hotan rubbed the back of his neck, letting Mr. Piedmont know the inner workings of his hard life. "And I tend to keep myself busy with things, no point in getting upset over it. I don't like to dwell on the past. When it happens, that's it. Nothing can ever be undone. You move forward and hope to learn something from it."

"True and incredibly wise of you to say. You're not like your fellow students, and it's not your intelligence. You're particularly mature for someone your age, but tough times do that to you. You simply grow from them. I'm sorry you had to grow up so fast." Mr. Piedmont mustered a sincere smile.

"Interesting way of putting it. I like being more grown up." Hotan gave a half-hearted smile to lighten the mood. "It's a lot more work, and I enjoy being independent, but I don't make many friends at school because of it."

Mr. Piedmont glanced at his computer as if hoping it would give him something to reply with before sighing and relenting, "Well, I better let you go. School's about to end in five minutes, and I have announcements to do. You can always talk to me if you need to, anytime, Hotan. Take another candy if you like. I have more than enough."

"I appreciate your time, sir." Hotan stood up, and Mr. Piedmont stood to shake his hand. "Once more, thank you, Mr. Piedmont. Thank you for being on my side on this."

"A true sign that you've learned something and have received more wisdom than before." Walking around his desk, the short, old man opened his door. "See you tomorrow, Hotan. I'll put your time to good use. I promise you that much."

"I hope so, Mr. Piedmont," snorted Hotan, lugging his bookbag on a shoulder.

The receptionist paid him no heed, and he left the administration office without any further glares or mutterings. *The excitement is squashed as quickly as it started.* Hotan made his way to his locker as he heard Mr. Piedmont's voice thunder across the school's intercom system overhead. With haste, he abandoned the math book into his locker, happy at the idea of never touching it again. *Good riddance.* Flinging his bookbag back on his shoulder, still heavy from *The Book of Ancients*, he swiftly walked to the exit. *I just want to find somewhere to read this.* The classroom doors opened, and students flooded the hall in a ruckus of noise, gossip, and shouting. Down the front steps of the school, he headed to his left where the old oak stood tall. He leaned against it, waiting for Shellie to show. The horde of students piled onto busses and gathered in chattering circles in front of the school.

They were all red, said a voice in his head.

"What?" Hotan saw no one nearby. *Where did that voice come from?*

They candies were red. It was a test, the strange voice spoke again, echoing inside Hotan's head as if someone else's thoughts were invading his own. *You should be more cautious when seeing random color. If Geliah—*

Who are you? Hotan growled to himself. *Who's in my head? Answer me now!*

Now that Geliah has left, I can speak freely. I'm Callan, the element of Water. I need help, and I think you're the only one who can get me out of here and break his hold on me. There was a moment of silence before Callan continued. *If anyone can disrupt his powers, it is Rebirth. Hotan, you need to get your abilities under control. I can see what you see, and this connection shouldn't so strong. Even you—*

How are you able to talk to me like this? I don't understand. Why me? Why not Talib or someone else? I'm just a kid. Screaming internally was the only thing Hotan could think to do. *I can't help you, Callan. I don't even know who I am. I have no abilities!*

Your element flows through you. It's there, you just need to find the rhythm. Through this flow, we can communicate using our elements and their connections to the world. You'll understand later. His voice sped up, *For now, I request your assistance. Geliah will not let me leave by my own free will. Damn, my time's been cut short.*

"This is going to get difficult," Hotan said out loud. Head spinning, he took in a deep breath, trying to get his nerves under control. The connection between him and Callan had ceased, and he mulled over the conversation, but one element stood out. "They were all red!"

"What was?" Kyle interrupted Hotan's frenzy. "What was red?"

"The candy." Hotan stared at Kyle in disbelief. "They were red. How stupid can I be?"

"What candy?" Kyle's face scrunched up a moment, confused by Hotan's panic.

"The candy in Mr. Piedmont's office," Hotan explained.

"Oh! I love those watermelon things. Hey! Wait, why were you in the principal's office?" Excitement overcame Kyle.

"Finally! Someone was sent to Mr. Piedmont's office besides me!" A sheepish grin crossed his face as his eyes sparkled over the idea. "You're never in trouble, that's my job! I go just for the candy nowadays."

"Long story, but…" Hotan paused a moment before starting again, "I hope things will make sense tomorrow. I'll have to tell you about it later. There's too much hitting me all at once. Today has been a pain in the neck."

"I hope so because I'm so confused. Did you hear about the tryouts for the Big Band?" Kyle could tell Hotan needed a break from the chaos, so he changed topics. "Are we cancelling, or are we doing this thing as planned?"

"Yeah, I was going to take Shellie with and sign us up." Trying to forget everything, Hotan glowered at a group of laughing jocks. "But the problem is, we don't have a bass guitarist. We're short one person since Shellie isn't old enough."

"Man, that sucks. Got anyone in mind?" Leaning against the tree next to Hotan, Kyle kicked at the dirt. "I can't think of anyone."

"Nope, I haven't a clue either. Let's see if Chaz would let us do auditions for a day at the club. We can run an ad in the newspaper and put up flyers. Set a date for those who may want to try out for the spot." Hotan watched Shellie walk out, chatting happily to her friends. "Let's see if she's up for it, huh?"

"That would be cool." Kyle nodded to himself. "We could be the judges. Shellie might want to help judge since they'll be replacing her. Seems like the right thing to do. She'll have to collaborate and catch them up to speed about how she's been playing and adding her own flair here and there."

"That's what I was thinking." Hotan shifted his eyes to Kyle. "Hey, Kyle? Can I ask you something regarding our secret?"

Kyle's smiled faded and he furrowed his brow. "Yeah, what is it?" he asked, and his voice seemed to mature tenfold in an instant.

Does he always have such a sobering tone to his voice? "That tattoo of yours. Does it have any interesting qualities about it?" Hotan lifted an eyebrow at Kyle, who seemed relieved and nervous all at once now. "Change in texture, temperature, or anything out of the normal?"

"Temperature?" Pulling at his shirt, Kyle started to fidget.

"Well, for instance, my marking is ice cold in one section and hotter in the other part. There's something unnatural about how it feels."

"Heh." Staring at the ground, he shyly kicked up some leaves. "Something like that, I suppose. I ran into that problem today. It's definitely not the right, er, temperature. I wish I had paid closer attention to it."

"Problem?" Pulling himself away from the tree, Hotan waited for Kyle to continue.

"Well, if we walk down to the church, I'll show you. It's bad enough it happened in class. I just don't want to try my luck while people are around." He shot him a desperate look. "It was an accident, I swear."

"Okay." Staring into his eyes, Hotan could see how anxious the event had been for Kyle. *What happened to him today? I know I had a bad day, but I keep forgetting I'm not alone in this self-discovery of promised powers and immortality nonsense.*

"Hey!" Shellie ran up smiling. "Glad to see you made it through the rest of the day!"

"Hey, Shel." Hotan stepped out of the tree's shade.

"I'm so sorry." She hugged him tightly.

"Sorry?" Her hug got tighter. "I'm the one who should be saying sorry here lately. I haven't been talking to you, let alone telling you about anything going on with me."

"I was getting so angry over nothing. I wasn't helping your problems. For that much, I'm sorry." She released him and gave a starry-eyed expression. "Just please keep me in the loop. You never know if there's something I can help you with."

"Don't worry about it." A smile crept across Hotan's face. "So, you going to go to the radio studio with me, or do you have other plans?"

"Hmm, I don't know." She glanced back at her girlfriends, who giggled and blushed when Hotan looked in their direction. "I need to study…"

"Oh, come on." Kyle winked at her. "We can take my car. It'll be an adventure!"

"All right! But I'll call you afterwards. Seriously, we need to spend some time on this project, and besides, I need to go home and clean up before Mom gets home from her business trip. Chores first, then I should be free to run the town with you guys. Is that okay?"

"That's fine. Guess I'll let you catch a ride with Jen then." Hotan motioned to a girl waiting back on the sidewalk. "Looks like she needs you."

"See you, Hotan." She kissed his cheek and left.

"To the church?" Hotan turned to Kyle, face flushed.

"Yeah, definitely." A smirk on his face, Kyle shook his head before leading the way.

They walked across the grass as the yellow busses pulled away, one after the other. Walking down the sidewalk, they remained silent and lost in thought. A car drove by with some friends and, automatically, they waved in response. It was still strange to walk into the church with its interior shining and clean. Hotan stared at the towering crucifix once again. Walking to the front of the pews, he stood in front of the statue that seemed to smile down at him. It was like something magnificent had happened and a sense of pride was being shown. *So strange for an inanimate object to express so many feelings.*

He turned his attention to Kyle, who finally took off his backpack. Hotan's blood chilled as he laid eyes on the scorched shirt. Kyle's marking had burnt through his shirt, leaving charred holes which exposed the image of a fiery bird, a phoenix, with outstretched wings across his back.

II

PARABOLA

"You've got to be kidding." Hotan stood in disbelief, gawking at the charred shirt.

"No joke, man. I was in chemistry class when it happened. I was leaning back in my chair, sleeping like always, when I smelled plastic burning. For a minute or two, I thought that it was a Bunsen burner or something like that. Then I realized everyone was doing bookwork." Kyle sat down, slouching over his knees. "It didn't just burn through my shirt, dude. It melted the freaking plastic chair! It left an imprint of the marking until I smudged it. Mr. Mayer chewed me out, thinking I took a lighter to the chair … again. So, now I have in-school suspension for the next three days."

"Maybe it's because of your element: Fire." Hotan rubbed the back of his neck as he thought about it. "There must be a connection to what you were doing. Were you dreaming?"

"Yeah! I was driving this high-powered car. You should have seen it! Dark green with nitro and the works!" Kyle perked up as he described the car of his dreams. "I was like the fuel going through the pistons, you know, like in car chase movies."

"Firing of pistons, eh?" Hotan grinned as he exchanged glances with the angelic statue Geliah had sliced in half. "Power of fire. A moment of envious want, an emotional spike for you. I wonder…"

"What?" Kyle looked at the statue. "What are you mumbling? Did you figure something out?"

"Envy! That's how you trigger it. Just think about your precious high-powered engine and how badly you want it! You can use those powers Talib was talking about. In *The Book of Ancients*, the element of Earth was first discovered because she wanted something; she desperately desired to grow crops." Hotan was excited. *For the first time this chaos is making sense.* "You envy the power in an engine more than anything else. Kyle, if the dream is what set it off, why not focus on that! See if you can't get your power to work."

Kyle looked at him quizzically. "You think that's it? It's that simple?"

"Yeah, for you, it's simple. Give it a try." *I'm jealous he connected before I could.*

"What should I try doing?" Kyle jumped up. "I can't light a pew on fire."

"Try something simple." Hotan searched the church. The new candles on the floor around the crucifix were perfect conduits for the task at hand. "Try lighting those candles."

Kyle knelt by one, pausing for a moment. "How am I supposed to do this?"

"Recall the engine, and lock that image in your head. Remember how you felt and how badly you wanted an engine like that. Don't break from that emotional spike at all. Focus the energy toward the candles. It sort of works like an electrical system. That moment is the power source, and you're the lightening rod."

"Okay, engine in mind." Kyle held his palm out and sat there for a few minutes. "Hotan, it's not working. Nothing is coming out; my hands are cold. Any suggestions?"

"Hold a finger on the wick. Play through the dream in your head." *He was leaning on the chair, so it's possible that contact is necessary.*

"How's that going to work? Won't it put it out?" Kyle stared at the little, white wick on the candle. "Won't I get burned?"

"Just do it. Trust me on this, okay? After setting your own shirt and chair on fire today, I think you're fireproof." Sighing, Hotan watched Kyle put a finger on the wick, and after several long minutes, nothing happened. "You're not focusing enough. You need to think only about the pivotal moment when you smelt burning plastic. Come on, try a little harder." *Please, let this work. Some part of this failed reincarnation must understand how this works. If I do, then there's a chance I can unlock my own. But how can I practice the element of Rebirth? Don't I run a risk of taking or giving life or cycling it endlessly?* Hotan's chest tightened. *I shouldn't be excited about remembering how to use this power. Even if I'm not the old Hotan, it's reckless without a guide of some kind.*

Kyle relaxed, recalling the climax of his dream. "Then I was seeing sparks, an explosion, warmth, then came the flames…" He opened one eye, checking if anything had resulted in this ultimate focus. "Oh, snap!"

The little flame sputtered to life, flickering before calming itself and rising in an unmistakable soft orange teardrop. "Told you!" The flame danced on the candle where Kyle's finger remained. *Clearly, the heat of fire won't burn him; it accepts him as the same. Kyle's the element of Fire, flame incarnate.* "That's the kind of focus you're going to need for this," Hotan announced, crossing his arms.

"Dude! Let me do that again!" Kyle repeated the process until he had lit all twenty candles with ease. "Check it! I lit them all with my fingers! Forget playing with a lighter. I *am* the fire! This rocks!"

"Yeah." Hotan stared at the line of flames as they shifted and flickered in unison. "At least I was able to help you figure this out. Just wish I could help myself."

"How did you know?" Kyle stood up from his low crouch to face Hotan, a skeptical look on his face.

"Know about what?" Hotan broke his daze from the flames.

"How to trigger and use my power. What I needed to do to turn it on." Kyle glanced at him suspiciously before dropping his eyes to pump his fist. "What else are you hiding? What are you not telling me, Hotan?"

"It seemed logical," Hotan answered curtly. "After everything Talib's told me, what I've read in the book, and that weird dream a while ago, I should have it down by now." He took a slow, steady breath. "I just can't seem to figure out what my focus should be. I don't even feel the power in me, and I should sense something there." *It's like my reincarnation is botched, and I'm not completely connected to the power that I possess. Perhaps the old Hotan hasn't fully let go of it yet.* "I'm sure you started feeling something. Am I right? There's this void in your soul that's now filled. That's how I imagined it." *I've been thinking about it for so long.*

"Well, not at first. Today, I felt it when I woke up." Kyle nudged Hotan's arm. "Why haven't you been using your powers and doing crazy stuff? You fixed this church with your powers, right?" Kyle sat down on the steps in front of the pews. His full attention aimed at Hotan. "It's hard to believe you can't use your powers when you can teach someone else. I know I'm not the brightest crayon in the box, but come on."

"I haven't figured out what I truly envy," confessed Hotan. "It should be easy since so much has been taken from me, including my mother, and now, my life and dream career." Hotan searched the air to no avail. "In order for the powers to work, I need to focus on what I desire or resent the most, but I don't know what that is. That's where it comes from: the emotional spike of envy or even greed. For you, it's your envy for that powerful engine with the flames roaring through it. That envy can be anything, but only one thing will work, and it varies from person to person. I don't quite understand why power would come from desire like that. It seems dangerous, considering it's so closely attached to dark thoughts. Maybe sometime later, it will fall in place for me. Hopefully." Hotan looked back up at the statue which seemed to have lost its smile. *Yeah, I'm not happy about it either, big guy.* "I just wish I knew myself better. I don't know who I am anymore. Everyone wants me to be this other Hotan, but that's impossible. I don't want to be that person. Before all this started, I didn't exactly aim to be immortal. All I worried about was what I was supposed to do in life: graduate, get a job, settle down, and so on."

"Yeah, I guess it does make things harder when there's pressure to become someone you're not." Kyle observed the art carved in the lumber supports above them. Epic battle scenes were etched into them—a landscape of a war between angels and demons. "Life is a struggle against the good and bad we experience. A never-ending battle."

"Anyway, are you going to the radio station with Shellie and me? If so, we'll take your car." Hotan was tired of thinking about the complexity of discovering his immortality. *I want to fulfill my promise to Mom. Once I do that, just maybe I can see where I want to go more clearly. Besides, this confirms that my thoughts on the mechanics of how it works are correct. I just need to find my focus.* Hotan looked at Kyle, noticing that he seemed to be sliding into a more mature mind frame as of late. *When did Kyle get so philosophical?*

"Yeah, I'm going." Rubbing the back of his neck, Kyle took a moment to blow out the candles. "Better not leave these unattended."

"Good. We can grab something to eat on our way back." The cell phone in Hotan's pocket started vibrating.

"Is that Shellie?" Kyle watched as Hotan pushed ignore.

"No, it's actually Annie. I'll call you when I'm ready. You need to change shirts anyhow." Hotan smirked. "And take a shower; you smell like burnt plastic."

"Yeah." Kyle mustered a smile and chuckled. "Hey, Hotan, do you know who owns this place? Someone owns it right?"

"No clue. But I hope they like the free restoration." Once outside, Hotan sat on his motorcycle and snapped on his helmet. "If they even know it's been fixed. Then again, something tells me Talib might own this place." *That's the only explanation for all that's unfolded without question or disruption.*

"Well, I'm starting to see why you like to come here so much; it makes me feel safe."

Hotan shrugged and drove away without another word.

Kyle watched the bike take its usual route home, disappearing around the block. Looking at his black and blue sports watch, he rubbed the back of his neck. Shuddering didn't help cut the coldness he felt after using his power for the first time. "It is going to be hard to regain my power again. So much has changed…"

Hotan pulled up to the small apartment building. Kicking the stand down, he pulled off his helmet, and sweat dripped down his cheek. It was hot outside with no breeze, just clear blue skies.

The ride was soothing but miserable when driving on the main highway. Heat rose off the asphalt in torturous swells. It scorched his legs and arms as it flowed up and stung against his face. His helmet was agonizing with its thick padding. He dreaded stopping at red lights or stop signs.

Sighing, he looked forward to the air conditioning inside the apartment building. He paused under a main air vent, letting the cold air wash over him. Annie yawned as she sat on a ladder, waiting to gain his full attention. She wore patterned board shorts and a white tank top as if she had been sleeping the day away. Her hair hung messily off the back of her head in a bun held with two black chopsticks. Smiling, Annie stood to greet him with a hug.

"Hey! Glad you could come so quickly." Scratching her head, she looked up at the blown fluorescent tube on the ceiling. "That bulb went out, and I need you to replace it. I've had a few complaints about it already. You know how some of the tenants are around here." She deepened her voice and added, "I take pride in where I live and hate to see it turn into a dump!"

Hotan rolled his eyes, knowing exactly which resident she imitated. "Do we still have lights in the basement? It's been a while since I replaced one of these things."

"The basement's a mess, I had to shove some old boxes down there a while back." She patted him on the back as they walked down the hallway. "By the way, Jacob and I want you to join us for dinner tonight. He has a free night and wants to do something with you. I told him dinner at my place is always a good way to go."

"Dinner?" Annie made a face at the hesitation in his voice, and he added, "I do love your cooking, so I can't argue with that. Jacob has a free night again. I've got a lot of questions for him and lot of catching up to do." *Finally, a chance to meet Jacob! I want to see what kind of answers I get from him instead of Talib on this whole mess.*

"Well, we were talking. Both of us thought it'd be a nice idea to get together and discuss how you're doing. Jacob is bringing a friend over, and I thought, well, we thought, you'd like the chance to get to know your sponsor. He wants to be there for you since he knows what it's like to be the only one left in your family. You have a lot in common, to be honest." She unlocked a door with her cluster of keys and flipped a switch. The light struggled to turn on, buzzing and popping before barely shedding any light down the stairs leading into the dusky basement. "He feels so horrible about not having enough time to talk to you about things."

"I'll be there. What time?" Rubbing the back of his neck, Hotan investigated the grimy darkness. *I hate going down here…*

"Seven thirty-ish. Thanks again, Hotan." Patting his shoulder, she commented one last thing as she left, "It's a blessing having your help to keep this place in shape."

"No problem." Huffing, he started his descent.

The wood cracked and moaned under the weight of his footsteps. Chills raced up his spine with each mournful cry, teasing him that at any time, they could drop him into the endless abyss below. He pulled a string, and the hanging light bulb flickered on in the dark, musky room. He looked around the room, scanning the labels of the dust-covered boxes. Some had toilet paper, others had chemicals such as bleach, but the majority were illegible or not labeled at all. Starting to his right, he worked his way around. He moved boxes around the crowded room, trying to find the misplaced light bulbs. *A mess is an understatement.*

Hotan flinched as something scurried past his feet, and he quickly turned to watch the small, fast-moving object zoom between two boxes. *And now its infested.* Shrouded in the dim light of the cold room, he couldn't make out exactly what it was. *A mouse? No bigger. Rat? Or maybe someone's cat…* He shrugged to himself. Rats were common in basements of old buildings. *I'll let Annie know. For now, I'll get what I need and get the hell out of here.* He turned back and continued digging through the boxes. He found paper towels and the regular light bulbs, yet no sign of the long fluorescent that he needed. *Getting warmer…*

Opening an old, unlabeled box, he found some Christmas ornaments. *This seems a tad personal to store here since it has been the maintenance supply closet for decades now. Did Annie put these here? I've never seen her use any of it. Maybe it was left behind by a resident? I wonder.* He started to dig through it until something sharp stabbed into his flesh. *Ouch!* Yanking his hand free, he had cut it on broken glass. Walking closer to the light, it felt worse than it looked. It stung badly as he pulled a broken shard from the small gash, and a stream of dark-colored blood dripped off his hand. Grunting in annoyance, he sighed, firmly pressing his left thumb on it to stop the bleeding. *Can today get any more irritating?*

He turned back to the boxes to finish the job at hand. *I don't have much time to spare today, too much I need to get done.* Closing the Christmas box, he started to search somewhere else. Moving the labeled boxes behind him, he came to some that were even more questionable. *I know these boxes have been down here for a while, but I've never noticed them before. I hate to open personal items. Who do they even belong to?* Hotan glanced around, noticing all the empty space on the once full shelves. *Why are they all off the shel—!* His heart jolted when a box behind him fell off a shelf. The violent bang and clutter of it hitting the cement floor made every muscle in his body tighten. He turned back but saw nothing.

Cautiously, he walked over, mumbling to himself, "I'm going to bring traps down with me next time, rat. You've knocked one box too many off the shelves."

Out of curiosity, he opened the box and looked at the contents. Pulling out old books and photo albums, he shrugged to himself. *Well, this is weird. Why are there photo albums and things like this down here? I'll take it with me, dig through it, and see if there's anything worth keeping. Maybe I can figure out who owns them.* He started to search the shelves again, finding the tube lights near where the box had once rested. *Finally! I can get out of this basement!*

"I'm out, rat." Scoffing, he added, "And next time, the pest guy will be paying you a visit."

Heading back up the steps with the box and bulb, he flipped the light switch as he reached the top. Hotan glowered down the dark, eerie stairway as if hoping to see the rat. A chill snaked up his spine, and he shuddered. *Yup, still creepy.* Pushing the door closed, he could hear something. Right before it completely shut, he thought he heard a voice. It seemed as if someone, possibly a child, had giggled or whispered something as the door shut. *Is something or someone hiding in the basement, or am I freaking myself out?*

He shook his head in dismay. *I'm starting to really lose it now.* He felt paranoid. *I need this to stop before I go mad.* He sighed again and made his way back to the ladder in the hallway. Climbing the ladder, he slid the cover to the side. Unsnapping the burnt-out light, he quickly replaced it with the new one.

"Mmm! Aren't you sexy!" Hotan froze as a girlish voice broke his whirlpool of thoughts. "All hot and sweaty. Standing up there on that ladder like a statue of hotness."

"Hey, Kasie." The shorthaired girl who lived on the first floor was well known to all in the building for her flirtatious ambience. "What do you want? Need something fixed?"

"You! What else would I want, boy!" Kasie tilted her head with attitude, her body language always more exaggerated than the average person. "Are you single yet? Have you dumped that hoe of yours? Because you know I'm sexier than her. She can go to Hell."

"Unfortunately, I haven't dumped my girlfriend." Sliding the cover back in place, he slowly climbed back down the ladder. "Because I like her, and for some reason, she still likes me. So sorry, I'm still unavailable, Kasie."

"Oh. Is that so?" Seeing that she wouldn't get the attention she wanted from him, Kasie pranced off, hips swaying to draw attention to herself. "Whatever! I'm too good for you anyway!"

She looks like a ghetto runway model when she walks like that. He closed the ladder, carried it down the hall, and put it in its corner of the laundry room. He pulled his cell phone out and glanced at it. *Still no word from Shellie or Kyle.* Feeling clammy from the basement, he picked up the box of books and headed upstairs. Taking his time unlocking his door, he took advantage of being able to catch his breath for a moment. His thoughts raced between school, the band, and this puzzle involving immortality as he downed a glass of water.

Pulling out the first book, he wiped off layers of dust, revealing a worn photo album. *A decade or two old, for sure.* His interest was sparked by the battered, black cover. He noticed the signs of how often its owner had flipped through it prior to it being lost to the basement. *This somehow feels … nostalgic. I've seen this somewhere. Could it be some of Mom's old things?* The cover revealed nothing about what he might find inside. *I don't think I'm ready to open this and find out for sure what my gut is telling me.* His heart sped up as he fingers rode the book's edge, daring to open the cover to confirm what the goosebumps across his arms were screaming. *Should I?* His cell phone started vibrating, and Tool's "Parabola" broke the silence. Swallowing his heart back into place, he threw the book back in its box before answering the call.

"Kyle just picked me up; we're headed your way!" Shellie's cheerful tone brought a smile to his lips. "Did you finish up that work order for Annie?"

"Yeah, it was just a light bulb thing. I'll be out front waiting on you guys." After short goodbyes, he hung up.

Throwing his shirt to the ground with the rest of his dirty clothes, he pulled a nicer black shirt from his closet—one of the few actually hanging—and put it on. As he buttoned it up, he looked up at the Tool poster that was lit up like a night light from the sun it blocked. He cracked a slight grin as he thought about how much it was like him.

That's a clever way of seeing this whole thing. In my own way, I'm the obstacle in the way. I'm on the verge of seeing it all, but I can't step out of the way, so the information can move freely. Where's Talib anyhow? I really was hoping he would get back to me sooner than this. Not even one letter lately. They stopped as soon as they started, and I can't bring myself to write a letter to hand to Jacob without knowing exactly who he is. What could be so important to abandon me? Leave me to the wind like this when I am clearly the element that caused this mess. What else is happening that I am not aware of? I get the feeling it will still fall back on my shoulders, and the knots in my stomach tell me it's from mistakes made by the original Hotan.

He locked his apartment door behind him and headed down the stairs in silence, thinking deeply about things. Walking out into the bright warm sunlight, he sat down on the front steps of the old, brick apartment building and watched the neighbor-hood road. Hotan watched the doves as they sat, cooing softly, on a nearby fence. They moved on their perches every so often, ruffling their feathers. A car drove past, and all but one fled to the other side of the fence. He gave it more attention as he observed the soft, gray color of its feathers as it twitched its head as if staring back at him with the same sense of curiosity. The only difference it had from the rest of its comrades was a dark, black marking on the feathers on its neck, making it look like a collar. Another car drove past, and it flew off into the blinding brightness of the sun instead of the path that the other doves took. Sighing, he gazed at his bike, admiring the light gleam off the curves. He recalled a time when he worried more about it than himself, but now, there were more concerning things to think about.

What scares me the most is I still don't know if I'm going crazy? Maybe I'm stuck in my own reality, and I just need to wake up. How do I explain everything? Kyle was able to use his power. There's no explanation for it. It's intangible, yet there it is, screaming in my face. It's real. It wants me to know it's real. What kind of power sleeps inside me? Exactly how powerful is it compared to the others I've witnessed? They must know I have access to it. Why can't I use it? What kind of aftermath will it cause? Callan said that all the elements are connected. Nothing is ever going to be the same when I finally cross this threshold. Covering his face, he groaned in frustration at the thoughts. *This always happens to me. Why can't fate's changing tides leave me alone? I feel so naïve in this situation. Everything has purpose or meaning, but how am I supposed to interpret it all into one cohesive answer? I can't do this for much longer. Groping blindly through this is getting me nowhere.*

Kyle's car pulled up and slowed to a stop. Shellie was in the back, and she smiled happily as he shut the door, and the vehicle began to move. They all sat in silence, each of them thinking of the situation at hand, unsure how to start a conversation like normal. _This is painful. We all know._ Sighing, Hotan couldn't mistake that the tension in the car was due to the supernatural chaos which had invaded their lives. _Too many questions, not enough answers._

Kyle broke the silence, his voice deep as he started, "Should we tell Shellie? Tell her something about what's going on?"

Hotan shot a look at him, then looked to the back of the car at Shellie. "I kind of told her about it, clued her in at least." _Wonder what she said on the drive over that made him think she didn't know._

"Oh?" Kyle gave her a glance through the rearview mirror. "Okay, that makes things less awkward." His shoulders relaxed.

"Yeah, I know about it." Shellie looked down at her fiddling fingers. "It's definitely weird. That tattoo is massive, and the idea of it just appearing overnight is unnerving."

"Did you tell her about me?" A red light caught them, and Kyle slowed to a stop, before casting a sharp glance at Hotan, adding, "Or just about you?"

"No, I didn't mention you." Hotan returned his gaze to the window, watching the people walk up and down the sidewalk, chatting happily to one another. "I didn't want to say more than what was necessary." _It took a lot of courage to tell her what little I did. Now, Kyle wants to throw in the crazier side. I don't want to involve her._ Hotan sucked on his cheek and caught Shellie's furrowing brow in the reflection. _I can barely believe it myself, even if Kyle can somewhat use his element of Fire. Talib makes me think I should be feeling nostalgic at every turn, but this feels surreal, at_ *best. I can't handle her looking at me with those eyes that I love so much as if I'm crazy and a million miles away from reality.*

"What about you?" Shellie leaned in between them as the light turned green. Hotan received a fiery glare for a moment before she spoke. "What do you mean, Kyle?"

"I'm basically in the same situation." Kyle sighed as he switched into the left lane. "I have the same thing happening, so we can't just assume there's no truth to this."

Hotan arched a brow but remained silent. *Is he making sure that nothing I've shared should be taken lightly? Where the hell did this side of Kyle come from? When did he become so damn insightful?*

"You have tattoo-like marks on your back, too." She pleaded for more information, "Or is it something else?"

"Yeah," murmured Kyle, glancing at Shellie from the corner of his eye. "I have that, too. Markings."

"Strange, but does it have a different temperature from the rest of your skin like Hotan's?" She leaned back in her seat, but Hotan dodged looking her directly in the eyes and went back to gazing out his window. "His doesn't feel natural."

"That would be putting it mildly," Kyle answered angrily. "I melted a chair today, got in-school suspension over it."

Hotan cracked a smile, but it faded again. *The more I listen to him talk, the more he seems to shift. Is there something else happening to him?* Rubbing his chest, Hotan swallowed. *And why am I afraid to even ask? Maybe I'm getting paranoid.*

"What?" Shellie gaped. "Melted? A chair?"

"Yep," Kyle huffed. "And I won't need a lighter anymore to light my candles. Never again!"

"How come you have it though? You two are best friends, so…" Shellie paused, twisting her face. "You guys didn't join some satanic cult or something, did you? Is this thing contagious?"

"No," they replied hastily.

She finds it just as hard to believe as I do.

"Just woke up with it, just like me." At last, Hotan met her eyes with a calm, stern expression. *Please don't think I'm crazy, Shel.* "But there's still a whole lot we don't know. That's why I didn't say much else."

"Well." Shellie sighed, giving a soft, weak smile. The cracks of doubt were unmistakable in her voice as she said, "Just keep me informed, okay."

Kyle turned left into a parking lot. "We're here!"

12

GIVING IN

They walked up to the large, gray business building and pushed through the glass doors. They remained silent, avoiding eye contact with one another, distracted from their purpose for being there. *This is painfully awkward.* Questions rolled in their heads about the turmoil of the unexplainable events which haunted them. Head and hearts argued about how far one could push the boundaries between reality and the unknown. Hotan led them down the hallway to the row of elevators. He'd been there a couple of times but always felt the need to double check. A chart on the wall revealed what floor each business was located on, including the radio station. Hotan pushed the button for the fourth floor, and he leaned against the wall, watching the doors slide close. *This is exactly how closed off I feel about the world and what's happening to me.* It gave a slight moan as it started but met its destination in silence, smoothly slowing to a stop. Walking out into a small lobby, a secretary was stapling pamphlets, and they waited for her to gain a free moment.

"May I help you?" She nudged her glasses up on her nose.

"Yes, we're here about the Big Band tryouts?" Hotan watched as she straightened herself. "How do we sign up?"

"Oh. Umm, hold on, and let me see if Becca's busy." They noticed her name tag, "Mandie," as she walked through a door and disappeared for a few minutes. It opened once more, and she motioned them in. "She's waiting for you, third door on the left."

Hotan mumbled, "Thank you," as they headed toward the door. *This is the one thing in my life I have to look forward to, something that I want for myself. Not for Mom, not because I'm supposed to do it, not because someone asked me to do it or pressured me into this… I'm doing it for me. Even if I have to go into hiding afterwards, I want to do this much.*

"Hiya!" the short-haired girl greeted them warmly, her glasses propped on top of her head. "I'm Becca, and I'm in charge of the Big Band signups! I hear you're looking to sign up today."

"Hi. That's right." Hotan lifted an eyebrow as he observed her small, tidy office full of jars of candies and pop culture novelties. "We're the local band that plays over at 7even's, The Closet Hobos. I'm Hotan, the lead singer, and this is my drummer, Kyle, and bassist, Shellie. We want to enroll in the Big Band competition you've been announcing on your station."

"Ah, I see. Ready to see how you stack up against other bands, huh?" Becca flopped her glasses back onto her nose as she sorted through an open drawer. "So glad to see you here. I've seen you guys play over at Chaz's club, and you're one of the best cover bands around, but I won't be judging this competition. We have some special industry guys coming in to do that for us. People who may want to sign a band or two, hopefully. Regardless, I don't think there's anyone here who hasn't heard your covers of Tool or classical rock on occasion. Impressive stuff."

Hotan grinned at the praise. "What do we need to do?"

"Just fill out this application and drop it back off with a CD or USB with at least three songs. You can apply online, too, and drop MP3 tracks that way. They should be songs your group plans to perform." Becca handed Hotan a three-page packet. "In short, you may have three weeks according to the paperwork, but if we hit max capacity, it can be as short as two weeks."

Hotan scanned the papers, making sure to address any questions before walking away. "Why three songs? It says here that we only get to play twice."

"If you make it through the initial judging round and get past the actual concert part of the competition, you will need three songs. Two are for competing, and the last one is for the final showdown; normally, two to five bands are left at that point. Be sure to state where you found your resources, such as sheet music and lyrics." She leaned back in her chair and opened a jar of candy. "Any more questions?"

"Nope, I think that takes care of everything." Shaking hands with Becca, Hotan and the gang made their way back out of the building. *Finally, I can focus on something that I have control over. Crap, but we have to turn in samples.* Hotan flipped through the pages, rescanning the small print. It pained him to admit, "I don't think we can afford studio prices for this demo tape." *But I won't let that stop me.*

"I can record it for you guys." Shellie leaned into him as she offered up her solution. "It's the least I can do since I don't make the age requirement. In fact, if I remember right, we may be able to record it at 7even's before opening. The acoustics in there are great, and it should keep our signature sound intact. I recommend we double-down on the nostalgic card and our strong suits."

Kyle gleamed happily as they waved bye to the secretary. "Are you sure we can do that?"

"I figured we could do it at Chaz's club too. If we show up before opening, we can easily record three songs with no problems. He keeps telling me if we ever need anything to say the word." Hotan glanced at Shellie and smirked. "Promise you won't get jealous over the new bassist."

Shellie took the papers from Hotan and began to flip through them. "And since I have the best handwriting, I'll fill this all out, too."

"My handwriting isn't that bad." Hotan furrowed his brow as he looked at her coy smile. "It's very legible compared to Kyle's; at least mine looks like it's in the English language."

"Hey!" Huffing, Kyle punched Hotan's shoulder, and they started laughing. "At least I try!"

"Hotan, don't be so mean." Shellie hugged his arm, joining in their laughter, happy to see the tension in Hotan's muscles break.

"I still can't figure out how the teachers read anything he turns in." Hotan winked at her before adding, "Nothing mean about it, just being an honest friend, that's all."

"No worries, I'm used to it by now." A grin stretched across Kyle's face, and a sparkle came to his eyes. "But I did get a step ahead of him! First time that I, Kyle, am more superior than the all-knowing Hotan!"

"A step ahead, how?" Hotan looked over at him with great amusement, pushing the exit door open for Shellie. "I don't recall any time where you're one step ahead. Did I miss something?"

"At least I can use my power," Kyle bragged as he unlocked his car.

Hotan stopped dead in his tracks and struggled to swallow the knot that lumped itself in his throat. *No, Kyle! Don't say anything else! For a fleeting minute, I felt like none of this...*

"Power?" Shellie flinched as the tension returned to his arm, muscles hardening. "What power? What on earth are you talking about?"

"It's nothing." Hotan's abrupt response and heated glare made Kyle stiffen. *I can't think of anything to say!* Hotan's mind spiraled out of control. *How can I cover this up? If I stop panicking, I can crack a joke or laugh it off. What's wrong with me? Has it really gotten under my skin this badly?*

Kyle paused, deep in thought, before meeting Hotan's gaze in the mirror. The creased brow and lipped words, *I'm sorry,* were too late to untangle the mess he had sown. The motor purred as Hotan's distress physically manifested, becoming unmistakably visible while his thoughts and feelings collided.

At last, Kyle cleared his throat and said, "Guess I'll shut up now. You have a point, I'm never step ahead of you, Hotan, and I never think before I open my mouth." The car backed out of the parking lot.

"Ye-yeah." Hotan's thoughts crawled their way out of the whirlpool. *I need to get a grasp on myself. I can't shut down like this.* "I wish you had just kept your mouth shut this time."

"Hotan, you're such a jackass sometimes. I said I was sorry," Kyle mumbled as he pulled onto the road. "Always so smart, but careless about everything. I thought when you said you talked to her, you meant you told her everything. Next time, be a little more concise. Granted, we have a long way to go."

Hotan winced. "I know; I suppose this one is on me."

"I'm starving. Are you hungry?"

Hotan glared out the window, relieved that Kyle redirected the conversation. *Since when did Kyle start being so clever and witty?*

"Is someone going to explain to me what you are talking about?" Shellie leaned in between them. "You made no sense. What powers?"

"Nothing," Hotan and Kyle mumbled in unison, both avoiding eye contact with her.

Kyle's voice was filled with regret and almost inaudible. "Forget about it."

Shellie huffed, frustrated with all the secrets being held from her. "So, where are we going?"

"Jessica's restaurant." The car paused at a stop sign, and Kyle asked, "Are you two close friends? I don't think I ever asked."

"Haven't talked to her in a while and kind of miss her," Shellie said, pouting as she flopped back in her seat.

"When we get there, I have to run next door." Hotan watched buildings pass as they made their way through the city. *I need to clear my head. Maybe breaking off from Kyle and Shellie will help me gather my composure again.*

"No problem." Kyle had lost his normal cheerful mood. "Go clear your head, man."

Shellie looked over at Hotan, watching the reflection of his face on the glass of the car window. "Why? Is everything not okay?"

"I have to walk around the block to 7even's and talk to Chaz. After that, I want to stop at that bookstore across the street to ask the owner about something." Hotan turned to face her with a stern expression, still limiting what he told her. "Is that okay?"

"I was curious. I have no reason to worry. At least you have Kyle involved, and the fact you are no longer trying to deal with it alone makes me feel a tad better." Looking away, her body language revealed how angry she was about not being able to lean on his shoulder.

Sorry, Shel. I can't tell you about things that I still don't completely believe myself.

"We're here!" Kyle declared as he parallel parked a few feet from the entrance to Benny's Place. "Hooray! Hamburgers!"

"See you guys in a few minutes." Hotan was out of the car before Kyle even turned it off.

"But aren't you hungry?" Shellie struggled to get out of the back of the mustang. She smoothed out her beige skirt and straightened her petite, white shirt. "I haven't seen you eat any-thing today. In fact, you haven't been eating much at all!" she shouted after Hotan.

"Annie invited me to have dinner." Hotan cleared his throat to reassess himself. "Order me some fries," he corrected. *She's right. I'm forgetting to eat, and I don't feel hungry or tired like I normally would by now. Am I really becoming immortal? Or is my mind making me think I no longer need food?*

"Okay." She caught up to him and gave him a tight hug, kissing his cheek before walking inside the restaurant with Kyle.

Hotan headed in the other direction, making his way through the crowded sidewalk. As he walked past, a meter maid hummed a happy tune as she wrote a ticket for a car near a bum. *Sometimes I can't help but wonder about the irony in life. That bum has change in his cup, and the person who gave it to him is probably the one getting that ticket right now. Was that really worth the risk? Will you be compensated for taking a leap of faith, small or large, in the long run? How much risk do I need to take to see a positive result? I've never done anything risky if I didn't know the definite outcome. Have I been wasting my life this whole time? Am I thinking about life incorrectly? Am I not the aftermath of someone else's risk? How much longer will this recoil continue? He's not even here to see what he's done, let alone the destruction of my life.*

A groan escaped Hotan under the weight of questions which he had no answer. *I just get the unnerving feeling that this is more astronomical than what it started as. It's unfair that the person who put this domino effect into play no longer exists. I'm taking the heat for this, all alone, just because I look like him and inher-ited his element! What was supposed to happen? How can I fix someone else's mistake when I don't even understand how he used the power? What mistake was made in the first place to have to erase himself from existence? If I figure out what went so wrong with him, maybe I can put things in order. I may not be the original Hotan, but I definitely don't want to see this ordeal stretch out much longer. I want to be done with this whole otherworldly matter and go back to my simple day-to-day life.*

The crosswalk signal changed, and he crossed with a few other people. Walking into a nearby building, he was greeted by a gloomy, smoke-filled club. Loud laughter came from one of the large, corner booths and echoed throughout the empty space. Hotan walked over to see Chaz and a few of his employees in a thunderous chatter. A burst of laughter came from the group as he approached, almost startling him. It was a daily ritual for everyone to hang out before getting the day started.

"Hey, there." Hotan stopped at the edge of the table, slouched with his hands in his pockets. "You got a minute, Chaz?"

"Hey, Hotan! What are you doing here so early?" Chaz's loud voice echoed through the empty bar as he held his mug of beer high, cigar gritted in his teeth. "Come to join us?"

"No, actually, I need to ask a huge favor." Chaz sat his mug down and puffed on his cigar as he listened. "It's not too big of a favor, to be honest."

"No, no favors, not to the likes of you," a cocky guy spat, taking a puff of his cigarette, bellowing the smoke in the air toward Hotan. "You're just a spoiled brat. Chaz, you do too much for this kid. He thinks he has the run of this place all because he brings a few folks in the door with his guitar playing hobby."

"Why don't you shut up, Erik." A bartender sitting across from him flicked a peanut shell at him and giggled. "Stop teasing the kid! He works just as hard as us, and thanks to him, we stay busy on slow nights, getting a few extra hours and tips out of it."

Chaz leaned back in his seat, ignoring the others. "What's the favor?"

"I need to hold auditions for a bassist this weekend. Preferably Saturday morning before you open, if you don't mind. We want to enter the Big Band competition, but my current bassist is only seventeen." Hotan huffed his lungs clear of smoke. "If you can't, I understand. We'll just find somewhere else to do it. From past experience, I've had better luck on the weekends for auditions."

"Hmm." Chaz rubbed his chin with his left hand. "Let me think."

"Oh, let them do it, Chaz." The bartender took a bite out of her sandwich; her red hair mopped over her eyes, hiding her expression. "You know they deserve to compete," she muffled with a mouthful.

"No, it's a waste of time. They're not going to make it in the competition anyway." Erik put his cigarette out in the glass ashtray with a sneer. "Not like they can really play or sing. They don't have what it takes; I know from experience. No one wants to sign a contract with a high schooler."

"How about you light yourself another cigarette and shut your trap before I shove that ashtray up your ass." Hotan shot him warning glare, his cheek twitching from the growing tension. "We play just fine. I want to see how we measure up, not aiming to win." *He's been angry ever since his band failed in the first round and broke up before trying again. Don't compare me to you. I'm not lesser because I'm a kid.*

"What's wrong? Did I hit a nerve?" Erik leaned back with a sheepish grin. "Not aiming to win is like saying you're aiming to lose."

"Nerve? Never," Hotan countered with a casual smirk. "You should stop before you fall on your face again. Better yet, do yourself a huge favor by taking that grin off your face and showing some respect for a fellow musician. Stomping on others won't bring your band back together after three years."

"Why I oughta—" Erik started to say but froze when Chaz raised a hand.

"Okay, enough already." Chaz broke the tension, clearing his throat. "You can hold auditions if you're out of here before 2 p.m. and before I come to open at four. Make sure it's clean, deal?"

"No problem. Thanks a lot, Chaz." Waving, Hotan turned and headed out the door. "See you guys later."

Backtracking his route, Hotan made his way across the busy street to the front of the old bookstore. A gust of cold wind carrying the scent of rain blew past him. The sky was filling with dark gray clouds that sped past, slowly darkening the town. Taking in a deep breath to enjoy the smell, he turned to the bookstore and walked inside.

"Hello?" Once more, no one was within sight.

He walked over to the counter where he first met Tina, the bookstore owner. Cautiously, he leaned over it but found the other side empty. Nothing more than an old, cushioned stool. He took long, steady stare down the web-covered aisle, but it was hard to see much since it was overrun by books. Rubbing the back of his neck, he braved a closer look. Down its dark canyon, light from the front windows of the store failed to penetrate the dust-covered shelves. Books fell off the shelf near his face on his left, nearly hitting his cheek. Stumbling backward, Hotan smashed into the rock-solid shelf behind him.

"You!" Tina's voice rasped, sending chills across his body.

Slowly opening his eyes, her face glared at him from an opening in the shelf where the books had fallen. "How'd you get on that side?" blurted Hotan.

Tina grinned wide. "It's my store! I can go where I want!"

Hotan tried to focus on what he came to ask. "Are you familiar with, well, the powers?" *She must know. Between the book and the way she acts, I get the gut-wrenching feeling that she's aware of everything.*

"Powers? If you're asking if you're sane, yes. You are very sane." Tina erupted into laughter, causing Hotan to flinch, but she abruptly stopped, her wild grin gone. "Why are you asking that? You're so silly. You know what they are and what you are. Are you crazy or something? Oh! Did you lose yourself? I do that all the time; I think that's how I got behind this shelf."

"I don't know exactly how our elemental powers work. I lost that much of myself, if not most of who I'm supposed to be." Hotan inhaled deeply, hearing the confession out loud. *Whether I really believe all of this is still undecided.* "I figured you might know something since you said you are one of us." He started picking up the fallen books to avoid eye contact. "I can't feel anything. I don't even know if I'm supposed to feel anything?"

"Okay." She nodded, biting her bottom lip. "What do you know so far? I don't understand why you are asking me. Oh! Oh! Oh! A friend is coming; they can explain!"

"A friend? Who can explain?" Hotan's pulse raced. "I don't know if that's a—"

"You know him!" Tina spun in circles, still imprisoned behind the bookshelf. "He speaks in my head too!"

"Callan? The one who talked to me in my head. What could he help me with?" Hotan slid to the ground, covering his face with his hands. *Why did I think someone so mentally off-balance would give me coherent answers? She's asking random questions, and I'm only assuming she knows what I'm talking about.*

The bell on the front door jingled. Hotan's skin pimpled as he heard the door close again. Reluctantly, his nerves and muscles taut, he looked to see who had entered the long-forgotten bookstore. A tall, pale man in his twenties blocked the entrance. His straight, long, black hair was pulled back in a low ponytail, and he stared at Hotan with silver-blue eyes. His attire was gothic: a black shirt over fishnet sleeves and baggy jeans covered in chains.

Thank God it's not Geliah.

"Hotan." The man crossed his arms, his voice familiar. "I wanted to meet with you in person, but my time will be short."

"Callan?" Scrambling to his feet, Hotan knew without a doubt that this was indeed the voice that had echoed through his head earlier. "If you are here, then where is Geliah?"

"Indisposed for the moment." Stress riddled his gaunt face as he spoke. "Now that I am here, I can see what you were trying to express to me. I'm sorry to have burdened you; perhaps I can aid you in some way."

"I don't think anyone can help me at this point," Hotan spat bitterly. "Even Talib seemed clueless on what exactly is going on with me." Hotan stared down at his hands, feeling disconnected with his own body. "I cannot be the person who all of you need me to be. He's gone, and I'm left with powers I can't even use."

"You're feeling them, but the element of Rebirth is not in balance." A glow came from Callan's outstretched hand, and an orb of water formed. "Rebirth has always struggled to find balance between life and death." It took a moment before a flawless sphere of water floated there. "Our powers are normally smooth; they're naturally balanced with the aid of nature. Like this sphere of water, constantly in motion, but never conflicting with itself. Your power feels like this." The sphere contorted, spiked out randomly, and spun in a wobbled motion. "It's as if the element of Rebirth is in a tug of war or incomplete in some way. Something is interfering with your powers, but there's nothing that any of us are aware of that could disrupt the elements in such a way."

"Even so, shouldn't I be able to feel that chaotic instability in some way?" Hotan watched the water sphere ebb and flow, symbolizing the turmoil. *My whole life looks like that.* "Shouldn't I be in pain or accidentally casting magic spells or whatever?"

Callan's water ball evaporated in a blink of an eye, and he placed a knuckle on his chin, deep in thought. "I think you can only feel the parts that spike out, as if something deeper inside you is blocking the power. If those spikes are barely noticeable, like a passing breeze, it could prove dangerous for…"

"Voice, voice in my head! Gah!" Tina scrunched her eyes and fell from their sight, wailing. "No! Go away! Not you! I no like you anymore!"

Hotan backed away. "What's wrong? Are, are you okay, Tina?"

"He won't stop talking to me!" The shelf shook as she banged into it. "Damn you! Stop singing that song! Gah! No! Not this again!"

"Callan?" Hotan mumbled, backing into the other shelf again. Looking over, Callan vanished as if he had been a phantom. *So much for answers and help with my powers…* "Where? What's happening? Talk to me, Tina."

"Geliah!" Her face popped back up in the opening in the bookshelf, smiling. "Now, where were we? Oh yes, umm, power!"

Don't panic. Geliah's not physically here. Swallowing, Hotan tried to regain focus. "Is there anything else you can tell me?"

"I don't…" Tina said, stopping a moment as the tattering of rain started to fill the silence of the store. "Is it raining?"

"Umm." Glancing out her glass door, Hotan saw the monsoon unfolding, wind racing outside the restaurant and across the street as people barely kept hold of their umbrellas. "Yeah, it's definitely raining."

"Gah!" Her head twitched to the left as her right eye squinted. "My books! They'll all be wet! Must protect books from rain!"

Tina started shrieking and hissing as she shook the shelf. Books fell into the aisle and onto Hotan. He quickly shuffled out of the way and toward the door. *It's clear this was a bad idea. I won't get any answers from her.* Her screams and unrecognizable slurs pounded at his eardrums as he forced himself out into the commotion of the storm. The rain and wind hit him, and he squinted his eyes to see as he attempted to cross the street. Hurrying inside the restaurant, he shook the water from his shirt and hair. *I'm soaked.* Shellie was sitting at their usual booth, eating a hamburger and staring at him quizzically.

"So, how'd it go?" She paused from her meal as he sat down.

"Chaz said we could use the club Saturday morning." Hotan took a fry from a side plate. *Hopefully, she will feel better if I eat something. I hope I can meet with Callan again. He seems sensitive in detecting what's within me, and he might be able to help me balance and unlock the chains on the element of Rebirth.*

"That's good." Shellie took a sip of her Coke. "What about the bookstore? How'd that go?"

"I was wondering about that, too." Kyle slid back into the booth from wherever he had disappeared. "Did that bookstore loon have any more information?"

"Oh." Hotan creased his forehead and looked at the bookstore hazed out of sight by rain. "Not so well. She's not having a good day at all, and I got no answers."

Shellie took a bite of her food. Swallowing, she asked, "Why'd you bother to walk in there? No one ever does."

"Foosh." Kyle managed to swallow his food, then cleared his throat. "She's the one who had that rare book we were looking for. We were hoping she could give us some information on the author and where it came from."

"Really?" Shellie turned to the bookstore as the rain started to soften. "I suppose she would have some rare and unique books."

Hotan sighed and took a sip of Shellie's drink. "I'll let you know more later, Shellie, promise. I just have to clear my thoughts. Get everything in some sort of coherent order. It's hard to share when I have no concise answers to make heads or tails from."

"It's already confusing, from what I do know." She snuggled closer to him but grimaced at how wet he was. "Ah! You're soaked!"

"Heh." Hotan smiled. "I love you too! Just don't worry yourself to death about this. Let me take care of it. Plus, I've got Kyle to help me. I promise, I won't be solving this on my own."

"Fine." she huffed, but the worry on her face didn't subside.

13

SUNDAY BLOODY SUNDAY

Hotan knocked at Annie's apartment door and waited. The time was 7:28 p.m. Another round of knocking had him uncomfortably shuffling in place. Still, no one answered. Leaning his back against the door and crossing his arms, Hotan zoned out. Staring at a crack in the far wall, he let his thoughts wander aimlessly. *One of these weekends, I need to fix those and possibly repaint the yellowing white walls. Annie needs to make a no smoking policy around here, so I don't have to paint every year. Maybe she can just pick a darker color paint; anything but white would help. This building isn't getting any younger, ha! School's almost over, and I'll start doing heavier repairs this summer to get this place back up to speed like I promised her. I'll figure out what I want to do after, after…* Hotan couldn't finish the thought as a chill ran up his spine.

Today has been frustrating and confusing. He deflected, finding himself back to the things that hadn't been resolved. *It's been too long of a day for all that's happened back-to-back. A quiet dinner sounds amazing right now. Just a moment of peace. I can forget about sleeping tonight. Callan, Tina, this whole concept of power being locked up inside me. What is going on with me? What could be holding these abilities back with so much force? Hopefully, tomorrow will be better. Hell, seems like these last few weeks are starting to blend together. It's all rushing by, and I can't keep track of what day it is anymore. I can't manage much more, not when I'm having a tough time deciphering what's real anymore.*

"Hey, there!" Annie's voice broke his thoughts as she came around the corner carrying two grocery bags. "Sorry, had last minute shopping to do. Jake should be on his way."

"Jake?"

As Hotan grabbed the bags from her, she managed to get her keys in order to unlock the door. "Hope you weren't waiting long."

"No, but did you mean Jacob?" *Great, now she's got a casual nickname for this guy.*

"Yeah, Jake, Jacob, no big difference." Annie pushed the door open and flipped on the lights to reveal her Japanese-themed apartment. "Here we go."

"So, what's for dinner?" Following her to the kitchen, Hotan laid the bags on the counter. "Is it something simple or fancy?"

Annie threw her hoodie on the coat rack and slipped off her sandals next to it. "Umm, does spaghetti sound okay? With some garlic bread and meatballs," she added as if trying to convince him to comply with the menu.

"Sounds good to me." Shrugging, Hotan glanced around the apartment. "Can't remember the last time I had a home-cooked meal."

"Well, it'll be a good change for you then. It's definitely been a while since you've been over for dinner." Annie pulled a frying pan from its hanging place, set it on the stove, and turned on two burners. "Are you okay eating dinner with Jake and me? Because if you're going to feel uncomfortable, say so, and I'll just give you the leftovers. Don't feel forced to be here, Hotan. I think he has a friend tagging along anyhow. Guess it's hard for him to break from his job."

"No, it's fine." Watching her rhythm in the kitchen was entrancing and brought a wave of nostalgia of when he used to watch his mother.

Annie was the queen of multitasking: She boiled the water, rolled balls of hamburger meat, added various spices and herbs to everything, and still managed to chat to him. "I never want to pressure you into anything. On paper, I'm the guardian, but you're old enough and perfectly capable. Shoot, where did I misplace the salt? Ah, here it is!"

"Want me to set the table while you do that? Anything you need help with?" *She always seems to be doing a million things at once, but it never breaks her focus.*

"Yeah, the plates are in the cabinet behind me, and the silverware is in the drawer by the sink. I appreciate the extra set of hands; I'm running so late today." Annie smiled, turning the heat on the frying pan up and adding olive oil to it. "And if you don't mind, when you're through with that, I've turned the oven to 450 degrees, so when it beeps, pop that frozen garlic bread in. You can find a flat baking pan in the cabinet below the sink."

She's going to make an awesome mom later in life. Pulling out four plates and cups, he headed to the dining room table. "Thanks for making all these arrangements, so I can get to know … Jake. It's very awkward, and maybe it'll smooth things over with you here." *But there won't be a chance to talk about anything. Not unless … no. I don't know how to communicate telepathically like Callan.*

"Aw, no problem." Annie plopped the meatballs in the frying pan, poured the noodles into the bubbling water, and continued buzzing about the kitchen. "You're like a little brother to me, and even though we're not blood, we're family, Hotan. I mean that."

"So, are you and Jake serious about each other?" Glancing over at Annie, Hotan continued placing each plate and cup in its proper spot. She smiled to herself, cheeks growing red. "I take it I was right on that notion. I just think it's rather sudden."

"Hotan, it's the most sincere relationship I've had in a long time. Then again, we haven't been seeing each other long enough for me to say if it's just for fun or a solid deal. We have so much in common. Despite being a workaholic, he always wants to do stuff together when he has the time." Washing her hands in the sink, she continued, "And the … well, never mind. I kind of lost my train of thought. I told him he needs to spend some of that free time with you and figure out a way to get to know you. I've told him a lot about what you've been through. Hope that wasn't overstepping."

"No, you didn't overstep. Got to live a little, I suppose. And yes, I know nothing and would like to know him." Smirking, he walked up beside her and pulled out some silverware. "You're a big girl, Annie. Running an apartment complex and a caretaker of a teenage orphan. You can say you're a workaholic as well." *So Talib is aware of my past after all.*

"No, really, my train of thought just—" A knock at the door cut her short, and she immediately dried her hands on a nearby washcloth. "I've got it."

"Alright." Finished with laying the silverware, he walked over to the sink and opened the white cabinet doors below. As instructed, he pulled out a cookie sheet for the garlic bread. *Maybe having dinner here will give me a chance to get to know him instead of being overloaded with his whole crazy immortal thing. Who knows, I may end up liking him. A nice, sane conversation with the people who've shoved their way into my life.*

"Hey, Annie!" a familiar voice greeted her at the door. *That voice. Who's at Annie's door? Jacob?* "And this is my friend, Timothy." *Both are here…*

"Nice to meet you!" Annie's friendly voice responded, but Hotan was unable to make out Timothy's voice. "Please, have a seat in the living room while I finish cooking. Hotan's been here helping me already, shouldn't take much longer."

Annie walked back into the kitchen and stirred the noodles before turning her full attention to the frying pan and meatballs. Hotan glanced at her for a moment as she rolled the last of the meatballs and added them to the frying pan. Looking into the living room, he noticed one man was sitting and the other was standing. Both talked too low for him to hear. The standing man faced the kitchen, shooting an occasional glance in their direction. At last, Hotan identified him from the night in the laundry room. *The man with purple eyes, Jacob.*

Jacob laughed boastfully. Hotan could only see the newcomer's back. Concentrating, he failed once more to hear the man's voice. *Is Jacob's friend one of us, an immortal? Or truly just another acquaintance?*

Turning his attention back to the task at hand, Hotan continued his conversation with Annie. "So, I'm glad you two hit it off. Hope it works out in the end. You deserve to be happy."

"I hope it works out, too," she said, her words barely audible over the sizzling of the meatballs.

A distant look grew in her eyes, prompting him to speak up. "In case I forgot to say this, I've always thought of you as a big sister." Hotan remembered how often she joined them for dinner when she lost her dad to cancer and took over the complex. *Mom smiled and laughed more when she came into our lives.* "I've always considered you family, even before Mom's passing, during those days of having dinner or going to the park."

"I appreciate that." She flipped the burner with the noodles off and carried the pot to the sink. "Can you hand me the strainer hanging over there? I suppose I'm as much of a big sister as any. I did start off as your babysitter in the beginning."

Grabbing the strainer, he handed it to her and watched her drain the noodles. "Have you ever met his friend before? He seems soft-spoken." *At least they can't hear my questions from here over the faucet and meatballs.*

She plopped the noodles back into the pot and returned it to the stove. "No, I think it's more of a business associate than a real friend. Jake says it's hard to escape work; perhaps he improvised for tonight."

"Hmm." Opening the oven, Hotan placed the garlic bread in and the heat warmed his face and cheeks. "Guess we'll see tonight, depending on where the conversation goes."

"Always observing people. Why are you always so cautious? Do you ever relax?" Annie sighed as she opened a cabinet full of food and searched through it. "Now, where on earth did I put that big jar of sauce?"

"My life's been hard, and it's not getting easier. Caution and paranoia are part of the package. I used to have time to relax but not anymore." Hotan popped open the jar of spaghetti sauce which he had blocked from her view on the counter. "I don't think I'll ever get to rest or sit back and enjoy life. Every time it seems to slow down and settle, something comes along and kicks dirt in my face. I can't count how many times it's left a bad taste in my mouth."

"Really?" Grabbing the jar from him, Annie added it to the noodles and pulled the frying pan from the stove. "Maybe you've got things all wrong? I hope you're wrong. I know I've thought the same thing at one point, but things have gotten a lot easier since then. You just have to work a little harder to see the positive side of what's going on. Makes life a lot easier that way, you know. Take a deep breath and be positive."

"Hey, babe?" Jacob came into the kitchen, wrapped his arms around her, and kissed her softly on the cheek. "Is it done yet? I'm starving!"

"Hold on, all I have to do is mix it all together, and it'll be ready to serve." She smiled and kissed him on the lips before he released his wrap on her. "Patience is a virtue; now, go behave yourself."

"So, how are you doing, Jacob?" Hotan lifted an eyebrow as he leaned against the counter. Jacob wore a pair of iron pressed slacks and a white button up shirt. *Clearly, he came straight from work.* "Been a while since I've seen you around."

"Good, and sorry about that. I'm working on getting things changed, so I can get more time with you." Jacob's purple eyes glinted, demanding a solid exchange of glares. "How are you doing? Taking care of yourself? I hope you're staying out of trouble. Better yet, I hope trouble is staying out of your way lately."

"Fine, just fine." Narrowing his eyes at Jacob, he took in a deep breath. "So, what do you do for a living? I haven't had a chance to find more out about you. Our last visit was … short."

"Oh, me?" Jacob's coy smile crawled across his face as he ignored the condescending tone from Hotan, shrugging play-fully. "I'm just a simple businessman. I hate wearing a suit all the time at headquarters. Then again, I like being sent on special assignments, and the suit is necessary."

"Special assignments?" Hotan sucked on his cheek.

"Well, you would understand." Jake lowered his brow. "It's when protocol goes out the window that you can only rely on the old noggin." He chuckled, tapping on his forehead. "The fact that all the rules go out the window at that point is a refreshing break from the normal. I was quite a rule breaker when I was your age."

"You must have me confused with someone else," drawled Hotan. "I avoid breaking the rules, but it often screws me over despite that. Trouble just finds me."

"Interesting." Jacob opened his mouth to say more, but the timer beeped. "Oh! Bread's done."

"Yup." Annie carried the pot over to the black dining table. "Time to eat!"

"Yo! Timmy, food." Jacob glanced at Hotan before walking over to Annie. "Make me a plate, honey." Annie filled a plate, and he stretched his arms out. "Oh! It smells so good!"

Hotan grunted to himself as he grabbed a towel to retrieve the pan from the oven. Pulling a large knife from the drawer, he sliced it before carrying it over to the table. Jacob pulled out a chair for Annie, gently pushing her in like a true gentleman. Curiously, he took the seat across from her. Hotan sat next to him, hoping to avoid a stare down across the table. *I wish to keep my appetite.* Hotan's stomach rumbled for the first time in a long time, and he found himself captivated by the plate of spaghetti in front of him. *I'm starving. Finally, I'm feeling a little human. When was the last time I had this?* His belly ached as the smell of the garlic bread joined the symphony of smells and overwhelmed him. Breaking his attention from the meal, he looked up at Timmy taking the seat across from him. His hunger waned. *It can't be.* The muscles tightened in Hotan's jaws at he stared in disbelief.

"You okay, Hotan?" Annie's voice was soft and motherly. "You look pale all of the sudden. Are you coming down sick? You never get sick."

"No. I, I'm fine." Hotan glowered across the table, his stomach no longer aching. "I'm fine, just tired." *Was this the plan? To just waltz in and be a person in my life like this? I should have known the moment she mentioned he was bringing a friend that it was going to be him…*

"Hello, my name is Timothy Bithloa." Talib smiled gently at Hotan as he brushed his hair from the front of his face. "Nice to meet you, Hotan. I have heard a great deal about you from Jacob."

"Hi." Swallowing hard, Hotan glared into Talib's pale blue eyes, and Talib stared back with his overpowering aura. *This is bullshit.*

"Now, let's bow our heads for a moment of thanks." Face mottling, Annie added, "Sorry, it was something my dad always did, and now that he's gone, I like to keep it going." Annie broke the tension as her voice cut through everyone's thoughts, slicing peace among them. "Lord, I want to thank you for your love and comfort, and thank you for this moment of gathering in which we may eat together in your honor. I pray that the food you have provided for us will nourish our bodies, so that we shall remain in good health. Amen."

"Amen," they mumbled reverently, raising their heads and beginning to eat.

"Mmm." Jacob slurped a few noodles into his mouth and grinned widely. "Man, can you cook. You're amazing, Annie! If this keeps up, you'll have me fat and round like a turkey."

"I had to take care of myself, being raised by a single Dad and then…" She paused, drew in a breath, and started again. "My Dad became ill, and well, I had to take care of him before he passed away." Annie sighed as she twisted noodles around her spinning fork. "I don't mind it though. Brings back good memories. Food has a way of doing that."

"There is nothing wrong with such an ability, regardless of the circumstances which brought it on." Talib smiled at her as he sipped his iced tea. "It is very becoming of you."

"Makes you a well-rounded girl." Hotan managed a smile for her as he began to eat. *She used to make this for Mom and me, too.* "It brings back memories for me too." His hunger was overriding his urge to scream across the table at Talib. "Thanks for dinner, again." Hotan could only stare at Talib in disdain as he ate. *What would you know about abilities. You can't even help me with mine.*

"That's right. He's got a point, Annie." Jacob winked at her playfully as he took a gulp of his tea. "Wonderful to find a woman with a cooking talent, right, Tim?"

"Oh, you guys stop." Annie smiled again, finally eating some of her own spaghetti.

"Never going to stop flattering you." Hotan turned his attention to Talib once more. *Should I ask...*

"So, what do you do for a living, Mr. Bithloa?" Annie questioned politely, taking a bite of garlic bread.

"Well, I own a real estate company in the area," Talib continued, his smile cordial as if invincible to Hotan's heated glare.

Oh, really? I just wish you could hear me, asshole. In fact, I hope you can hear me, Timothy. What a name! Like there isn't anything weird about a guy in his late twenties with light gray hair who doesn't use contractions when he speaks. You sound like a misplaced medieval aristocrat. Sure, a name change will fix that, for sure. What is Talib? Sounds Arabic? Hebrew? Am I getting close?

"Wow. So, do you own any property in this area yourself? Or do you just sell it?" Annie paused her eating, becoming interested.

"Yes, I do. An incredibly old piece, in fact. It has been passed down in my family for generations, so I do not have the heart to sell it." Talib shot a quick glance at Hotan, his eyes wide. *When did you learn this? It is a little early for you to transfer your thoughts. Did someone teach you? I came here to discuss this with you, but we can wait until after dinner.*

"Oh wow, where?" Annie spun the fork again in her plate, wrapping it with saucy noodles as she continued the conversation. "What a wonderful thing to inherit!"

"Isn't it the old church by the high school?" Jacob asked, joining the conversation. "That massive cathedral?"

Well, I guess be careful what you wish for, Hotan hissed internally. *Let's just say Callan helped.* Hotan took another large bite of his food as he sat in complete silence. *Anyhow, why would it be too early? Isn't it good that I finally figured out how to do something, anything, on my own? I doubted this whole having powers thing, but this proves you're not pulling my chain.*

"Yes, the cathedral down on 24th Street; it is by a local high school." Talib ate his spaghetti with delight, his smile never failing. *Because it may cause you some problems, and it only gives Geliah an easier way of entering your thoughts. What did Callan want from you? I assume he wanted something.*

"So, being by the school, do you get many vandals?" Jacob took a big bite of food, chewing questioningly at Talib as the tension between him and Hotan grew.

So, you're the one who owns the old church. Go figure. Hotan paused, looking at him in surprise before lowering his brow. *Why did I think it wasn't connected? Regardless, Callan says he needs my help. To be honest, he needs me to help him escape. Apparently, wherever he is, he is unable to speak when someone else is around. I think he's trapped and in trouble with Geliah. I doubt Geliah's going to read my thoughts so easily.*

"Hey, isn't that where you go all the time, Hotan?" Annie looked at him, but he didn't respond, still exchanging a strange look with Talib. "Hotan? Are you sure you're okay?"

"Huh?" Breaking his concentration, Hotan turned to look at her, his face slightly red from embarrassment. "Yeah, I go there all the time. I enjoy the history." Hotan sat his fork down and gave Talib his full attention. "Sorry for trespassing; there were never any signs of it being an active church, so I didn't really think it was an issue."

"We mainly get visitors like yourself there, which wards off the vandals." A small hint of a smirk crossed Talib's lips. "I like to keep the place open to the public, since it is quite a sight to see. Recently, it was completely renovated in order to preserve the history." Talib took a sip of his drink, trying to hide the blossoming smirk aimed at Hotan. *Thank you for that, by the way. You most definitely saved me a small fortune.*

"I hate high school punks," Jacob mumbled, leaning back in his chair as he chewed a chunk of garlic bread. *Yeah, watch out for Geliah.* Hotan's head swiveled to Jacob as he heard his voice in his head. *He's a tricky bastard. Last we heard, Callan was on his side, but ole Geliah has been pulling some mean tricks over the last couple of years.*

"Oh, wow! It's been renovated?" Annie took a sip of her tea. "Why didn't you tell me, Hotan? I would love to see it now that it's been redone! Oh, how wonderful!"

"Uh…" Looking at Jacob, Hotan could feel the ghostly complexion taking over his face. *Wait, you can…* "I've been busy. Guess it slipped my mind. Um, anyway, I'm entering the Big Band competition." *You can hear me, too? Hear our conversation right now?*

"Hey, that's cool. I was hoping to hear that you and your band would take advantage of the competition. Let me know how I can help!" Jacob grinned at him. *What's wrong? Didn't know someone else was listening in Hotan? That's what Talib was trying to warn you about. We can't turn down the volume for you. We* _have no idea how long it will take before we can help you master this so you're not screaming from the top of a mountain. Until you figure it out, you're broadcasting your thoughts worldwide, buddy._

"That's right! You can enter this year since you're eighteen." Annie smiled, unaware of the alternate conversation circling the table. "How exciting!"

"Well, I wish you the best of luck." Talib took a bite of his food. _Jacob, stop taunting him. I think he now realizes the trouble. Your best approach is to master it to the best of your abilities. You can only communicate to other immortals, so who you can contact is limited. Perhaps Kyle can help you?_

"Thanks." Sighing, Hotan stared down at his half-eaten plate of food as his appetite faded. "But I need to find a bassist. Chaz is letting me use the club for auditions on Saturday morning." _So, now I have to master it, huh? I assumed that it only worked for them to contact me, not to broadcast to every immortal within earshot. Maybe I can practice it with Kyle, but wouldn't he have heard me? Does he even know how to do this?_

"That's nice of him. Chaz is a good man." Jacob took another bite of his spaghetti. _Teach him. At least he's trustworthy with your thoughts, right?_ Jacob arched a brow as Hotan's and Talib's faces grew sterner and more serious. _Well, you guys are boring. I figured you'd start up some sex stories or something worth listening to. Speaking of which, how's Saphellia doing, T-man? Is she adjusting well?_

"Cool. Wish I knew someone who could help you out." Annie stood up and walked her plate into the kitchen.

"It's fine. I think I can handle this." Hotan finished his plate. _Saphellia? Who's that? What else are you not telling me? How many are in the area who can hear me? Why are we all gathering in one place? Doesn't this seem strange? Even alarming? I want answers!_

"Man, Annie! This spaghetti's good!" Jacob's voice made everyone flinch. *Calm down.* He filled his plate again, grinning widely. *Uh oh, seems like big bro hasn't told the baby brother everything. How ironic. Don't you think that's uncalled for, T-man? We really can't afford to waste time. We can't wait for him to figure everything out and remember things. Who knows how long that could take or if it'll ever happen?*

"A bassist?" Talib swallowed hard and shot Jacob a cautionary glance. *She is fine, and I have not told him much because, simply put, I have shared only what he needs to know for now. I do not want to overload him with our whole history just yet, small pieces here and there. I am fully aware we are running out of time to prepare him and I … never mind.*

"Yeah." Hotan leaned back in his chair and narrowed his eyes at Talib. *Running out of time until what? What am I supposed to prepare for, Talib? I need to know more. I don't think I'll remember anything. Why leave it to chance? Just spit it out. The more I know, the better the chances are for me to figure this out.*

"Do you plan on making flyers and so forth?" Jacob stuffed his mouth full of food again. *You didn't tell him? Damn Talib, and here I thought you have the best judgment on these kinds of things. You've gotten rusty over time. We barely have a year to prep him!*

Silence! Talib choked on his drink and quelled it as fast as he could.

"Yep, got some of the school kids to spread the word." Hotan took in a deep breath. *A year for what? I would really like to know, especially since it involves me. What do I need to prepare for?*

"That's good." Talib left his last bite on the plate and leaned back in his chair, feeling the weight of Jacob's stare. *I have said too much. It is much too soon to bring up the matter. Too much at once would do more harm than good. For all our sakes, you will have to wait, Hotan.*

"Are you guys okay?" Annie cleared her throat, picking up Hotan's and Talib's plates. "You all keep acting weird and making these really strange expressions. Am I missing out on something? Do you two know each other?"

"What on earth do you mean, babe? I've been eating mostly." Jacob took another large mouthful of his spaghetti and chewed it in ecstasy. *Dammit, you two are going to get me in trouble with my girl here. If you do, you'll both owe me. Let's save this argument for when we are alone. Come on.*

"Uh, sorry if I have been rude somehow..." Talib laughed nervously at Annie. *This conversation is over. Go home. Now.* His voice resonated within Hotan's head, making every nerve tighten in his joints.

"Excuse me." Hotan stood up, looking reluctantly at Annie. *Fine.* "I've had a long day, and I'm not feeling so great. The meal was excellent, Annie." He turned to Jacob. "I've enjoyed eating with you. Sorry to leave. It seems every time we get a chance to visit each other, Jacob, it's cut short."

"Uh, okay." Annie followed Hotan to the door. "See you tomorrow, and good luck with those auditions."

"Th-thanks." Rubbing his forehead, he felt a tad confused. *Did I want to leave?*

"Bye!" Jacob waved, continuing to chew his food with his cheeks puffed out.

"Farewell." Talib's voice seemed parsimonious. *Rest well.*

Hotan walked out, feeling instant relief from the tension as soon as her apartment door clicked shut. Regret poured over him as he thought of Talib. *Jacob is looking better by the moment, besides his tendency to be nosy about everything. I didn't even figure out who this Saphellia person is or what is happening in a year. Why did I decide to leave so suddenly? In fact, I had no intentions to leave yet.* Hotan paused in front of his door, pondering. *Why did I leave with questions unanswered? I had him right there in my reach.*

Opening his door, Hotan slammed it behind him and stood in the shadow of the room. Staring at the box on the table, he sat on his couch and recalled the conversation that Annie hadn't heard. *Why did I leave?* Sighing, he leaned back into the soft, worn-out couch and stared at his ceiling. *I didn't even think…* Too many thoughts flooded his mind, and he couldn't keep them straight. Closing his eyes, he tried to slow down and focus. He needed to figure out when he had decided to leave in the first place. *Talib, that was why. Talib's the element of Judgment, and he can make others pass judgment to perform certain tasks, such as decide to leave. Talib made me leave. He said, "This conversation is over. Go home. Now." That was the moment he used Judgment on me and forced me to leave.*

A flashback entered his mind of Geliah's iniquitous smile and glare at the restaurant when he became sick with fear. *It wasn't the fact that I saw him, but Geliah who brought that strong feeling of fear over me. He controls Fear, and therefore he could make someone fearless or fearful enough to be overwhelmed by it. This means Kyle can cause flames and make them go away. He could make a nuclear explosion disappear without a trace or cause one with the blink of an eye. In that case, what are my powers and abilities? What can I do or take away from others? What did Rebirth do exactly? What the hell did the old Hotan do to disrupt himself along with everyone connected to him?*

A knock at the door interrupted his thoughts. He opened it slowly, unsure of who could be on the other side.

"Hey." Jacob had a solemn look on his face as he stood there holding a container of leftover spaghetti. "Sorry about that. T-man can be harsh sometimes."

"What do you want?" Hotan huffed, walking away from his door, allowing Jacob to come in. "I figured that was my cue that the conversation had ended."

"Just dropping the leftovers by. Annie was going to do it, but I volunteered. Felt someone owed you an apology." Jacob shrugged as he placed it on the counter. "Sorry about how sour things got at dinner."

"It's fine." Flopping on his couch, Hotan returned his gaze to the ceiling.

"Eh, Talib can be stubborn, and he's not the easiest guy to understand." Jacob sat down next to him, leaning on his knees. "I think this is the first time I've seen him act that way, toward you of all people. He's been through a lot, seen a lot. Despite that, I just don't know what is going on in his head. Usually, he has a plan, and … no, I'm sure of that much. There's a plan he's not sharing with any of us. Just what, I can't say."

"What do you know that he won't tell me?" Taking advantage of a possible second chance for answers, Hotan pressed, "What am I expected to do in a year?"

"Look, it's not my place to tell you. I'm not the one who made the deal. It's between you and him." Jacob ran his hand through his hair, feeling wedged between the brotherly argument. "But I'll do my best to do what I can for you. It's a really shitty deal. You need help, you're asking for it, and you deserve it. I can't overlook that fact."

"It's easy for you to say. I already know that I'm not going to regain the memories. Maybe that's why he's acting so stiff about it. I think he knows, too, and he's most likely lost on what to do.

I guess I can relate; Talib is also feeling the looming darkness of not knowing where to go next."

"What makes you say that? About the not remembering part." Jacob straightened his posture and gave Hotan a baffled expression. "You sound so sure."

"He said I was a rebirth of the element itself." Hotan took a deep breath as he stared at Jacob. *I met…* Hotan stopped the thoughts, the fear of broadcasting anything more.

"You mean?" Jacob paused. His face drained of color, and his eyes widened. "He killed himself. Hotan committed suicide! Are you sure?"

"What?" Hotan glared at Jacob, feeling the weight of realizing his situation was about to become worse. "Suicide? I, I never thought of it that way. He used his own power to destroy himself." *Why did I not let the idea sink in that my predecessor killed himself to end his immortality? Was it because the idea of immortals existing was still so surreal in my mind? Is this why Talib is struggling?*

"Shit, you have to realize we can't die like normal people. It's either we kill each other or die somehow by our own hand. If we are still under the reincarnation spell, we're mortals. I died from the flu once. We are immediately put back into existence as someone else in a new generation, and we don't remember any past lives." Jacob covered his face, trying to calm himself. "He would have had to create an updated version of himself to do it. Jesus, it goes against the teachings we live and depend on. What happened for him to send himself down that path? Oh God, and Talib, if he knows…"

"It was the only way for him to die." Hotan rubbed the back of his neck, watching Jacob's panicking body language. "We're all in a lot of trouble, aren't we? I mean, he did it to save everyone else … I think. He was simply being a leader who cared for his people, right? What was he trying to achieve with that though, Jacob? I assumed you guys would have the answers, but..."

"Don't tell Talib." Jacob shot him a fearful look. "No one, I mean none of us, would have let him do it if we knew he would die in the process, especially Talib. He was the only family Hotan had left, and Talib was brave enough to be our guardian, even knowing that his wife and brother wouldn't recognize him for all of eternity. At that time, he braved the decision for his brother. There's something wrong, very wrong. I have no idea why. Everything Talib has sacrificed is going up in flames. This is too much. He went too far. If Talib already knows, then so be it, but let's not break that news to him until we know for sure."

"What?" Wide-eyed, Hotan struggled with the idea of keeping anything from Talib. "Why not? Shouldn't we..." *Have I already let this slip?*

"It would absolutely break Talib's heart to know his little brother took his own life … that he hid the fact that he wouldn't be safe like the rest of us, as promised. Talib has given everything to his brother." Jacob wiped away a tear running down his cheek, turning away from Hotan's gaze. "I can't believe it. He's gone, and now you are tormented by all of this with no guidance as to what went wrong. Hotan, I'm so sorry this whole ordeal was left on your shoulders. I don't even know how to help you. You're just a kid. You don't deserve all this falling back on you."

"What should I do then?" Hotan felt vulnerable like he never had before; it was the only emotion he had left.

"I have no idea." Jacob sighed, standing up, trying to get rid of the uneasy sensation starting to overload him. "We'll just see what happens; it's all we can do. Handle it one piece at a time until we can figure out more. Maybe one of us could use our powers to help somehow."

"What element are you?" Jacob had shifted from a suspicious enemy to a fellow comrade in the confusion over the old Hotan.

Jacob managed to smirk before confessing, "Well … Lust, of course."

"Lust?" Raising an eyebrow at him, Hotan noted that Jacob was Annie's new boyfriend. "Love, huh?"

"Oh yeah." Jacob winked at Hotan.

"Every man's dream, eh?" A coy smile crossed Hotan's face, wondering if he had used it to get in good standing with Annie. "Make anyone fall in love with you at any given time."

"Well, not exactly," Jacob said as walked over to the door, "but it comes in handy sometimes. I don't take advantage of it, if that's what you're wondering. About Annie and me, she's a great girl, and I simply want to be there for her. Nothing beats the real thing kid, nothing. I should know; I had rotten times long before I became the element itself."

"Good to know." *No, he hasn't used his powers on Annie. That look in his face and tone in his voice tell me that he doesn't dare manipulate anyone's heart.*

"See you later. I'll get back to you if I figure something out." Jacob walked out, not giving Hotan a chance to ask any more questions.

14

BOTHER

Once more, Hotan laid on his couch, staring at the ceiling. Desperately, he tried to let everything settle. After a few minutes, he noticed his radio was still on and tried his best to zone out to the riffs and lyrics. Feeling overloaded, he didn't know where to begin. *He committed suicide.* Hotan stiffened. *If that's the truth, then why was I able to dream about him? Then again, was it simply because of the powers behind reincarnation and the element of Rebirth? Is it truly death when you're merely rebirthing, or reincarnating, yourself? It's confusing.*

Groaning, he held his head. *Things are getting worse. I have no one to turn to. There's no rational way to explain it to anyone. There are no answers for the millions of questions dragging me down. I could talk to Talib and Jacob, but they're nothing more than strangers to me. I blame Talib for putting me in this horrible dilemma.* His hands fell away. *It's taking over my life. The life I finally built for myself is being ripped away from me again.*

Hotan stared incessantly at the ceiling as if rummaging through the nighttime stars. Clues left more questions about this surreal dimension that he found himself now living within. Closing his eyes, slowing the flood he'd created, he listened to the radio as it transitioned into another song. Stone Sour's "Bother" came to his ears. They were one of many bands he enjoyed listening to from time to time. *Anything that I can relate to or reflect my status would be a warm welcome. Lately, it's the only link I have to the real world. If a song can still reflect the things I'm experiencing, then I must still be in touch with reality. It's so hard trying to keep everything under my skin and pretend I'm okay with what's happening to me. The old Hotan is the reason why everything turned out this way, yet I'm the one responsible for the events now playing out.*

Is there a difference in who I am and the first Hotan? Why is the finger being pointed at me for a crime I didn't commit? My own creator is framing me, someone who I'll never physically see, someone I've only once dreamed about. Even so, what evidence do I have of his existence? I'm in my very own biblical story, but where is my place, and what role do I play? Am I the hero or prophet in this tale or the fallen one needing help? Am I the one seeking the light? Or am I the dark one sent to destroy what everyone grew to love? He shuddered at the idea.

Rubbing his eyes with his palms, he rolled on his side. Looking at the stack of photo albums, he was frantic to stop the dark thoughts from resurfacing. Remembering he wanted to look through them, Hotan straightened himself on the couch and pulled the pile onto his lap. Wiping the thick dust from the covers, he hoped to find a clue about who they once belonged to. As he made his way to the last album, he paused, chest aching and frightened by the nostalgic sensation washing over him. *Mom's photo album.* He remembered seeing it as a child. His mother would bring it out on those lonesome nights to recall a life she had tucked away. He took a deep breath, hesitating to open it. *Forbidden, forgotten, and fractured this whole time—I was never allowed to see this.* Weighing the emotions building in his core, carefully judging each pang, he opened the monument of his mother's life.

A younger version of his mother with friends in arms was the first image that greeted him. She was laughing in the picture, and it was nice to see her smile for a change. Hotan slid a finger over her, a newfound sense of closure filling him. Echoes from the past brought a bittersweet sensation as he recalled how concerned and proud she was about everything he did. A scowl crushed the moment of joy, and chills crawled across his body. Looking to his wrist, it was 1:13 a.m. The dark memory seeped forward—one cold Wednesday night he would never forget.

Mom left for her night job and wouldn't come back home ever again. Heavy knocks at the door had broken the music in my earbuds at this exact time. Annie stood at the door with two police officers. She wiped tears from her face, and her body shook. My mom had just left. When the officers started to talk, the words shattered me. My heart stopped, my body shivered, and all I felt was pain. A pain that couldn't be described in any physical sense ravaged through me in that instant. There was no need to hear their words, I knew. My mother was dead. I had no one left— nothing left. Over and over, one word echoed in my thoughts:

Alone.

A drunk driver had crossed onto her side of the road. Considering the speeds involved, it was no doubt she had suffered life-threatening injuries. She died before they could get her out of the car crushed around her like a metallic coffin. I fell to my knees as my life was sucked away from me in a matter of seconds. It had been a hard life with just the two of us, and now it was just me. A kid out on the street with nowhere to go, no one who cared, and no existing family.

Alone.

During the following weeks, I packed my mother's things and sold what I could to gain money to give her a decent burial and headstone. Luckily, Annie helped tremendously with some of the funding. I insisted that she didn't need to help at all but couldn't turn it away either. I was just a kid, and she had to sign for everything. After that, I filed for my own guardianship in court, but the result was an agreement which made Annie my legal guardian. I managed to get a few small jobs near school, taking the city bus home or even walking on the nights when I worked past the last run. After a while, I managed to get a small, hand-me-down Yamaha motorcycle—a clunker, but I managed. Sleepless nights were often spent fixing the bike or repairing the miscellaneous items around the apartment complex, paying back Annie to distract myself. Living in an apartment at the complex was thanks to Annie who'd inherited it from her late father.

Alone.

Two years later, I saved up for a nearly new Suzuki motorcycle, had a great, full-time job performing at a club, and an amazing girlfriend—and finally, a curse of immortality. My bad luck continues to give me a tough time with no escape. Things pull themselves together only for something else to come crashing through, shattering the pieces of my life. Gluing them back in place is inconceivable now.

Flipping through the pages, Hotan saw what looked like his mother's high school friends: images of cheerleading squads, various cliché groups in a cafeteria setting, and even what looked like a drive-thru movie gathering. In one photo, she leaned on a black muscle car with the arms of a tall, well-built boy around her. It caught his interest, but the image was faded in the corner, and he couldn't make out the boy's facial features. The next few pages were graduation photos with grandparents he never knew or met. Both his grandparents passed away before he was old enough to remember who they were. His chest tightened and he sped up his flipping of pages.

Alone.

He paused when he reached a group of pictures with just her and the boy from the previous picture. *It's him.* Hotan shared the same features with the dark-eyed man: the jaw line, the build, and even the solemn posture and tone he held in each picture. Whether he was smiling or not, he looked so much like Hotan. Jet-black hair contrasted against the beach scene where he bore a tribal skull and crossbones tattoo across his back. *Why did you leave Mom and I behind?* Never explaining who he was, his mother had made it clear not to ask. *He scarred her heart and ruined her life. My life.* Continuing down the timeline of photos, he found wedding photos with the two of them, and his chest tightened. *She never told me they got married.* It was a simple wedding, a few friends in a small church with no signs of the heartaches to come. Soon Hotan came across pictures of her pregnant. At this point, there were no more pictures of the man.

Alone.

Did he really leave her because she was pregnant? Why marry her, then just leave her to care for your son, alone? Shouldn't it have been a happy moment in his life? This must be the reason why she never told me. She was afraid I would blame myself. I was all she had, and she would never blame me for this, but it seems as if she blamed herself. Why? Slamming the book closed, he huffed in frustration at the photo album. *Why did she keep this a secret? Where did he go?* A paper slightly sticking out of the back caught his attention. *Is he alive, out there somewhere?* Reopening the book, he found several pieces of paper tucked in the empty pages in the back. *Are these letters?* Hotan found the returned letters from when his mother had attempted to write to him. Among them was one bearing an unfamiliar writing. Promptly, he pulled it from the pile. *Did he reply?* Indeed, it was a letter from him:

> *Sorry, Loraine, I cannot stay any longer. I have failed you and myself. And as for the little one to be, I thought it was impossible. I am unfit to raise a family, let alone take care of you. Please forgive me for what I have to do.*
>
> *Love,*
>
> *I.*

That's it! That's all he left her with for a goodbye. Crushing the letter in his hand, Hotan threw it across the room. Tears flowing down his face wouldn't stop as the thoughts and memories flooded him. *I was the mistake and excuse for my father leaving. Why did she insist on still having me when she knew he would leave? Why would a child cause a man to walk away? Shouldn't her pregnancy have been considered a miracle and not a curse? Especially if it was considered impossible! I was a blessing, and he threw it away and my mother with me. He's right! He was unfit to take care of us! A coward willing to leave his child and lover to fend for themselves doesn't deserve them in the first place!*

The album slid from his lap and fell to the floor as he held his head in his hands to stop the tears. A chiming sound caught his attention as something metallic hit the floor. Hotan paused in his crippled state and stared down at the gold necklace baring a simple black pearl. As he picked it up, the chain tugged away from the pages of the book which had kept it for so long. He had never seen it before but remembered that his mother was always a fanatic for black pearls. *This must have been hers.* Unlatching the clasp, he put the necklace on. He had been forced to sell all her other jewelry. *At least this one remained. Maybe it will bring me some luck for a change.*

The alarm screaming from the bedroom brought him out of his heavy sleep. He spent most of the night boiling over everything but had dozed off at some point. Changing into fresh clothes, he scrambled to school. Hotan went from class to class, oblivious of the world around him. Nothing mattered anymore; he had concluded that his life was over. The lessons were irrelevant, there was no reason to uphold a conversation with anyone, and he ignored the blur of life buzzing all around him. Most of the time he stared out the windows, his mind jumping back and forth from the dinner with Talib to the latest information about his mother and so-called father. He couldn't decide which issue he should think about.

He walked into the principal's office with heavy shoulders, and anyone could see the vacant expression on his face. His body reflected the depression that had beset him overnight. Mr. Piedmont greeted him warmly, but it failed to breakthrough. Disconnected with everything, Hotan could not care less about upholding a good impression anymore. *My life is shit.*

"Here." Mr. Piedmont handed some files to him as he walked up to his desk.

"What are these?" Looking at the large folder, Hotan fought the urge to look under its cover. *I don't think paperwork is going to help me feel better about myself, old man.*

"I need you to take that file to the police chief. We're all tied up here today in the office, and it's a matter of urgency. I need you to deliver those downtown. You do know where the

Police Headquarters is, right, Hotan?" Giving a happy grin, Mr. Piedmont turned Hotan around and walked him back out the door.

"Yeah, it's across from the public library. Is there anything else you need me to do while I'm in town? Wait, should I even be leaving campus?" Hotan placed the file in his book bag between *The Book of Ancients* and his notebooks.

"Nope! But this is urgent," he insisted. "After you deliver that, don't bother to come back. I have too much to do here, and it's pointless for you to sit here for so long." Mr. Piedmont patted Hotan's back as he walked him out of the administrator's office. "I'll make sure to mark you present. Leave it to me." Clearing his throat, he motioned for the front doors. "Just be careful, sonny. As Socrates says, 'The unexamined life is not worth living.'"

"Uh, okay." Confused, Hotan walked away slowly, casting the occasional glance back until he pushed outside.

Leaving the school, Hotan made his way next door to the cathedral and parked his motorcycle. The heavy, oak doors shut behind him, and he stood inside and took a moment of peace. *I just need a minute to breathe.* Looking beyond the statue, he took in all the shades of gray from the massive, stained-glass window. Enjoying the moment, he observed the image it held: a classic Madonna with child. The piece was common in the Middle Ages, especially in places of worship. Some unique elements set it apart from most he'd seen in textbooks. In this picture, she was crying and looking up at the starry, bright scenery above. She held the child loosely in her arms, his legs placed as if to show him moving, struggling, almost as if afraid of being dropped.

A divine being left helpless in the arms of someone who didn't understand why she'd been chosen for such a delicate task. It's annoying seeing things illuminated in color at random. Always the eyes of the other immortals, never anything I would like to see.

I prefer to keep my moments of panic inside, but I feel so exposed when they show themselves. Whatever force controls that part, I would gladly give it up completely. At the same time, I feel like that child: the pure innocence of his own existence, struggling against the forces he has no knowledge of yet. I'm being held carelessly during my struggles, ignored by those holding me here, all the while given nothing more than pity.

Maybe I'm finally starting to trigger my powers when I see color, but they're putting me in danger. The dinner at Annie's came back to mind, and he snorted to himself. *Anyone could be listening right now, but I don't care. Could it be as simple as letting my emotions override logic, or is there something deeper, more hidden, keeping me from breaking loose the powers of Rebirth? Will I be able to even comprehend what's waiting to be discovered when I use them?* With that, he shoved out the door.

Starting up his motorcycle, he rode off toward the downtown area. Luckily, with everyone either in school or at work, it made for a soothing ride through the skyscrapers. Hotan pulled into a parking garage, grabbing the ticket from the machine. *He better pay me back if this takes more than an hour.* Jerking his helmet off, Hotan let out a huff from the heat. Hot days were one of the cons of being a motorcyclist. That, and the infamous sting of rain. Hooking the helmet to the back part of the seat, he walked toward the police headquarters next door. Pulling his hair back out of his eyes, he wiped his face free of sweat. *Not a cloud in the sky today, ugh.* The blast of cold air greeting him was a pleasant reprieve. Giving his book bag to the security guard, he walked through the metal detector. The lobby was huge and bustling with police officers, criminals, and witnesses mangled together in a cacophony of conversations and arguments.

The guard smiled as he handed him his bag. "Have a good day, sir."

"Thanks. Uh, where's the police chief's office?" The guard was the only available person for the question. "I'm supposed to deliver a file to him."

"Oh, well, why do you need to see Mr. Kendall for that?" He looked Hotan over. "You can leave it at the front desk over there."

"Mr. Piedmont, the principal at West Heights High School, sent me down here." Hotan kept to the mission and explained, "I was told to deliver this file to him directly and immediately. It was an urgent matter?"

"Oh! He said to keep an eye out for someone from the school!" A smile of relief crossed the man's face. "I was looking for a teacher or something, sorry about that. Just head to the elevator; you want the top floor. Once you're there, the receptionist will help you."

"Thanks." Hotan headed through the chaos as quickly as possible. *It's a mad house in here.*

"What floor?" a female officer asked as he slipped into the elevator just as the doors were closing. "What department are you looking for?"

"Top floor." Hotan leaned against the railing as the elevator creaked into motion.

"Wow, going to see the big wigs. You here to see Chief Kendall or the other guy?" She gave him an inquisitive look.

"Chief Kendall." Hotan shuffled as it stopped at her floor.

"Oh, this is me." They nodded to each other farewell, and Hotan continued his ascension to the top. The receptionist area was fairly large as the doors opened. There were three young ladies behind the huge counter, one busily writing as the other two chatted away on their headsets. Hotan quickly noticed that from this room, there were only two hallways on either side. The woman writing finished and looked up before making a sour face at him.

She seemed annoyed by the sight of a kid in her lobby as she drawled, "Can I help you?"

"Here to see Chief Kendall." Hotan ignored the harshness in her voice. "I was told to—"

"You have an appointment?" she huffed, cutting him off as she typed on her computer. "He's only seeing appointments today."

"No." Hotan's forehead creased. "I was told he should be expecting me." *Nothing is ever simple, is it?*

"You need an appointment," she repeated in a flippant tone. "And he's not available until next week, kiddo."

"No, I don't need an appointment." Hotan sighed, preparing himself as he pressed, "I was sent by Mr. Piedmont from the high school and told to deliver something to Chief Kendall directly. It's an urgent matter."

"Well, I'm sorry. We weren't informed to be expecting anyone." She leaned back in her chair and arched a brow. "I can make you an appointment. Morning or afternoon?"

A smug look surfaced as Hotan accepted the challenge. "Why would the security guard know about me and not you? Is it really that disorganized around here? I would have thought you, or the other two here, would know about it?"

"He must have mistaken you for someone else." She gave a sarcastic look and shrugged. "Do you want me to make an appointment or not?"

"No, I want you to call Chief Kendall and ask him for yourself. He's expecting me." Hotan leaned on the counter, and after a second of her not moving, he gave a shrug back. "Well, I'm waiting. I'm sure he can take one question."

"Keh, what nerve you have," she grumbled under her breath. "I'm sorry, young man, the chief is a terribly busy man, and I certainly am not going to disturb him over something so ridiculous, especially a smart-mouthed kid like you."

"Fine." Hotan sat down in a waiting chair, arms crossed.

"What are you doing?" Standing, she looked uneasy and startled.

"Waiting." Hotan's hands shifted to the back of his head, stretching his legs out in front of him. "I assume Mr. Kendall has to leave at some point. I'll just wait right here for him."

"That's absurd," she guffawed.

"Why not? He's going to eventually leave the office, isn't he? I hope he doesn't live here. Now that's absurd." Hotan waited for her next move.

"You can't be serious." Her face tensed as she began to unravel. "You're in the police station. I can call downstairs, and you'll be the one spending the night. Now if you don't mind—"

"Whoa! At ease, Rosey Doll!" a familiar voice came smashing into the room from the right hallway, catching Hotan by surprise.

That voice. It can't be. Could it? No way he would be…

"Oh, Mr. Kendall." The receptionist straightened herself while blushing uncontrollably. "So sorry for this whole matter. This young man refuses to make an appointment or leave. I was managing it fine, sir."

"Well, I was expecting him." The chief stayed out of view from where Hotan sat in the lobby.

I know that voice. I know who he is. I'm sure of it. This has to be some kind of joke.

"Send him in."

Jacob? Works a lot… I see why he says that now.

"Ye-Yes, sir," she stuttered, swallowing the mistake. She turned to Hotan and said, "Sorry for the misunderstanding. Please understand, it's my job to ensure he isn't disturbed. You may see him now."

"Understandable." Flinging his book bag over his shoulder, Hotan paused at the receptionist desk before entering the hallway.

"No hard feelings. You're just doing your job, and I respect that." *This makes life more interesting if it really is Jacob.*

She remained silent as Hotan walked down the hall. The chief had gone back into his office instead of waiting on him. *He's making me wait longer on purpose.* Hotan pushed on the large double doors and entered the colossal office. Its décor was full of artifacts and statues of all shapes and sizes. *They all look like fertility statues from my textbooks.* Swiftly, Hotan made his way across the room to where the desk sat with a wall of tinted glass behind it. Staring at the back of the king-sized chair, he anticipated if his guess was right. *It has to be him. The place, the setup. It all screams—*

"Sorry about the bulldog. She gets on a power trip and has a hard time settling down." The chair spun around playfully, and Jacob's bright eyes and goofy grin were unmistakable.

"No way. You're Mr. Kendall, Police Chief Kendall?" Hotan sat down in a chair, gawking at the chief in disbelief. "Why didn't you tell me? I can't believe you're the police chief!"

"I did tell you. I said I was a simple businessman, and as you can see that I am." Jacob laughed and raised his brows high. "What's so hard to believe? You didn't think I was the type? Come on! Got to give a guy more credit than that."

"Whatever." Pulling the file from his bookbag, Hotan dropped it on the desk. "From Principal Piedmont." *I wonder what this is about?*

"Yeah, I know." Jacob flipped through the pages in the file for a few seconds, occasionally whistling. "Not bad, not bad, you make some good grades, clean record. You're just a regular bookworm, eh? Makes my job easier in that case."

"Is that my file?" Hotan grabbed it from Jacob and frantically started flipping through the pages. "What the hell? Why do you want this? And how did you convince the principal to give it to you in the first place?"

"Well, the new issue is that you're aware of your abilities and have started using some. You've established your immortal age, or at least triggered the transition. We still don't know what locks in that final look." Leaning back into his chair, Jacob drummed his fingers on his desk. "We have to start cleaning up some of your paper trail. Otherwise, people are going to notice Hotan from high school still looks like a teen fifty years down the road." Jacob guzzled down his coffee. "I've done this for everyone who's awakened. In today's time, we must be more cautious, unlike in the past."

"Immortal age?" Leaning back in the chair, Hotan was intrigued at the opportunity to learn more about his situation. "What exactly are you trying to say? That I'll forever look eighteen?"

"We have a winner! Unfortunately, there's a chance you'll be eighteen forever, buddy." Jacob gave him a saddened expression. "Yeah, so, that explains why we're all different ages, such as Talib and me. We find it's best to dispose of as much documentation as possible to limit complications later in life. Usually when someone hits this point, they start remembering who they are. Unfortunately, as we already know, you're the exception."

"It's not going to be easy to keep it from Talib, is it? I'm sure he's already questioning the fact. He doesn't seem like a dumb guy or one to miss a detail like this." They exchanged a solid look with one another, and Hotan sighed.

"I don't know. I'm having a tough time keeping it under wraps. In fact, I can't figure out whether he knows already or not. He's a highly intelligent guy, considering he's the only one who was awake to witness the changes in society and the world." Jacob scratched his jaw. "And you're not the first awakened immortal he has dealt with during that time."

A flash of Talib's wary expression made Hotan flinch. "He has to suspect something."

"It might be why he's acting out of the normal." Jacob stared down at his cup of coffee as the conversation began to fall deeper into the subject. "You spend that much time on this Earth, I'm sure everything becomes routine. He seems to run short for answers on you and keeps his distance. I can't figure out if there's brotherly history coming into play, like a huge fight somehow unfolded. In the end, he's acting strange, and you're all we have as a Rebirth element."

"Does he ever talk about that time? I mean, considering his abilities and the fact he was to live out his life alone must have taken its toll on Talib?" Hotan watched as Jacob swirled his cup, both thinking about how lonely it must have been. *I know what it feels like to be alone, but not to that degree; I'm ashamed comparing myself to it.*

"He never speaks to me about it, not in great detail anyhow. All I know is that since we've started awakening, he seems to be more at ease. Granted, he is genuinely concerned with it; I'm sure it's a nerve-racking situation for him. Talib was supposed to ensure this couldn't happen, yet he's had no ability to bestow Judgment on those to stop the process. Plus, it doesn't help that Geliah's stirring things up. The bastard has an incredible ability to locate the unawakened. Fortunately, there's only a few left without the knowledge of their existence, and he's preoccupied since he found what he was looking for."

"Me, right?" Hotan shifted in the chair, feeling uneasy. "Geliah's been searching for Hotan. He seems pissed about being mortal for so long."

"Right," Jacob sighed, putting his coffee down and stretching out his arms. "But no worries, T-Man will figure things out. Or at least make sure you know all that you can about the whole situation. It's not easy news to break; we all know how it felt. Then again, once we all remembered who we were, there wasn't anything to explain. With you though, we have to explain what we do on an instinctual level. It's not easy to put into words."

"Yeah, well, at least this has been a great help." Pulling *The Book of Ancients* from his book bag, he slid it over to Jacob. "Not sure if you know about this book. It was sort of a farewell gift."

"What's this?" Jacob began to flip through it, his eyes wide in amazement. "Where the hell did you get this? This, this can't be right. It doesn't add up with everything else I know."

"Let's just say it was his parting gift. I got to meet the cause of this matter in a short dream, like I hinted to you last night." Hotan leaned back, taking a slow and heavy breath. "At first, I thought I was crazy for going around looking for something from a dream, but in the end, I found it."

"Really? So, he wasn't completely gone, but obviously, you're a completely different person. Oh my God, I..." Jacob paused, scanning through the pages of the book. "I had no idea this existed. Everything in here is exact. We're all here."

"I found it in the little bookstore across from Benny's Place. Tina had it." The shock on Jacob's face spoke volumes as he paused to read random excerpts in various chapters. *So, it's an accurate record of who they started as after all.*

"Really? The element of Insanity was keeping this secret from the rest of us. That woman can spin your questions into circles..." Frantic now, Jacob flipped faster through the book before stopping abruptly. The color drained from his face, and his jaw muscles twitched. "I can't believe it. It can't be possible. I don't understand why or how I. What happened all these years while we were sleeping?"

"What? What's wrong, Jake?" The room went cold, chills slithered across Hotan's skin as the fear in Jacob's eyes caught his own.

"Do you realize who wrote this book?!" Jake slid the book across the table with the pages open to where the author's signature laid elegantly across a back page. "Did you even look for the author?"

"You've got to be kidding. Dated in 1403?" Trembling, he stared at the signature that read "Hotan." *This shouldn't exist.* "You all were in a deep spell at that time, weren't you? That means he wasn't."

"Yeah, we were. I thought that included Hotan. The first one to awake was in the 1750's, and she kept herself silent and hidden for some time due to the turmoil during those times. It's hard to imagine this document exists. It leaves me questioning what is truly happening." Jake picked the book back up. "It's amazing though. He took such care in knowing who each of us were, both before and during the immortality. My only theory is that Hotan was indeed awake, but I must ask myself if Talib knew about this." Silence fell over him as he flipped to another chapter and scanned the pages. "I don't think he does, to be honest. The fact that Hotan wrote this himself in that time period… What the hell is going on? What would prompt him to log this information, then go as far as making sure you get it? He knew he was leaving this world at some point starting in the 1400s!"

"My only guess is something went wrong, horribly wrong. What, I don't know, and he sure in hell didn't say much. Although, this book clearly defines that it was an event in time and our immortality is real. It still leaves me questioning what happened and if Talib is aware of this." Leaning his elbows on the desk, Hotan continued his speculations. "He definitely knew he was going to disappear. 1403 was a mostly quiet time in history. It is after one of the biggest black plague hits, and other than a few crusades after that point, it seems like a good time for a runaway to buckle down in a hideout to write something. Even then, I still question if Talib knows something."

"You and me both, kid. I'm glad you showed this to me. As you can see, I have my own research in this whole matter. Not to say Talib's untrustworthy, but he loves leaving a lot unsaid. I definitely think there's more to this story than what meets the eye. For now, I'll let you continue to hold onto the book. When you're done with it, let me know." Jake rubbed the side of his face, trying to push the tension from his cheeks.

"You may have to acquire it from Tina since she was clear that it must be returned to her." Hotan slid it back into his book bag as he gave Jacob a sheepish smirk. "If that's okay?"

"Not a problem." Jacob stared into space before blinking himself back. "Well, let's call it a day. Let me walk you out and get you a pass for anytime you want to come by. I have a feeling you'll be visiting frequently."

They both jerked out of their seats, eager to leave the subject behind.

"Yeah, there isn't enough information to make any conclusions." Hotan followed Jake to the elevator. "Thanks for the help, by the way."

"It's my job, don't worry about it. Thank you for being so straightforward." Jake smiled, desperate to throw a feeling of comfort in the air as the elevator came to a stop. "I just wish I could help you … had some answers, or clues even."

"I appreciate the thought, at least." They stopped at the main counter. "I'll probably stop by when I come through this way, especially since I can find you a lot easier than Talib."

"Yeah, either here or Annie's place." Jacob handed him an ID badge. "Don't lose it or the security manager will blitz out. Security issues, bah!"

"Thanks." They made their way to the parking garage. "I still have a hard time with this whole situation."

"I don't blame you. If it weren't for the memories that came flooding back, I would be uneasy as hell about it. Honestly, I still have the small feeling of not wanting to accept the whole scenario." Jake jolted to a stop as they approached Hotan's motorcycle. "Shit."

Hotan's bike was lying on its side, tires slashed, and the whole thing looked like it had been dragged through a mud hole. "You've got to be kidding me. I just can't catch a break anymore."

"Good evening, boys!" An all-black motorcycle rushed to a stop between them and the bike. "Geliah sends his regards!"

Laughter poured from the helmeted woman on the bike as she peeled away. The screeching of the back tire was deafening within the parking garage. They cringed and turned their focus back to the dirt-covered motorcycle that lay on the concrete floor of the parking garage.

"Dammit," was all Jacob could mutter as they came closer to the devastated motorcycle. "I hate her with a passion."

"I can't believe this." Crouching down, Hotan assessed the damage on his only form of transportation. Worse off, it was the last item of value he owned. "That's strange; there's mud everywhere. It's like someone put potting soil in every nook and cranny. The fuel tank is full of the stuff!"

"Looks like Cassandra's work for sure." Jake shook his head. "Sorry, buddy, looks like Geliah's girl got you good on this one. He thinks you might try to leave town, I imagine."

"Who?" Hotan looked over at him. "Cassandra?"

"Yeah, take a closer look at the damage there. Since when do slashed tires leave dirt? In fact, I guarantee the engine's full of it too." Jake started digging into his pockets, keys and coins jingling. "Cassandra's with Geliah; she's his girlfriend, partner, bed buddy, whichever you prefer. Unfortunately, she's the element of Earth, and she can be somewhat of a nuisance, a real challenge to deal with since we're non-elementals."

"Great. You think she's been spying on me?" Hotan walked over to where his helmet laid on the asphalt and wiped dirt from it.

"Wouldn't surprise me." Jake lit up a cigarette, then grabbed his keys. "My truck is around the corner. I'll drive around, and we'll load your bike. I know someone who can fix it."

"Uh, I don't really have the money for these kinds of repairs. Or a new bike." Leaning against the parking garage wall, Hotan had hit a dead end. "And I don't think anyone has the skill to remove dirt from every inch of an entire motor."

"No worries. I'll pay for it. I can get work done there without a problem. Damn good mechanic too." Jake puffed on his cigarette, huffed out the smoke, and began walking around the corner. "I know they can fix this, trust me on that. They are always looking for a challenge, heh."

Staring down at the mess at his feet, Hotan managed to mumble, "Thanks again."

I5

SAVE ME

After a few minutes, a large silver quad cab pickup drove up and backed up toward the bike which lay in ruins. Jake climbed out of the vehicle, putting his half-smoked cigarette in his mouth. "One, two, three," they said in unison, and the two of them lifted the motorcycle into the bed of the truck and slammed the tailgate. Hotan climbed in, sliding into the smooth leather seats and letting the cool air conditioning hit his face. Jake turned up the radio as he finished the last of his cigarette. They drove in silence, pondering the details of everything they had discussed.

Now I have a new threat: Cassandra. I have no idea what she looks like or even the extent of what she's capable of. Would she go after someone close to me? Annie? Shellie? Kyle? Every corner I turn seems to make matters worse. I'm desperately trying to deal with life's everyday situations, but I'm overloaded with abnormal stuff like land mines in a sidewalk. It gets worse with every piece I learn. Every time I manage to fill a spot of the puzzle, something more dangerous rears its ugly head. Cerberus himself has crawled out from Hell to chase me down to drown in the Lake of Fire.

Shellie. I haven't talked to her in a while like we used to before all of this. The guilt is starting to get to me. She's left me alone to deal with it all like I asked. No harassing phone calls, just a simple yes or no question on it, nothing more. She disappeared quietly, giving me space and time to deal with whatever has interrupted our life together. It's one of the reasons why I like her so much: She doesn't need me to be there every day to know that we are a couple. We have a mutual and mature relationship unlike others I see at school. We accept that we both need our space and time apart. School and jobs take up much of our free time, but it makes our moments together a lot more special.

I should call her, check up on her.

"Check up on who? Your girl?" Jake flicked his cigarette out the window and rolled it up. "Shellie?"

"Uh, yeah," Hotan sighed, disappointed that he still hadn't mastered keeping his thoughts from being heard. "You heard that, huh?"

"Yeah, you're not as loud as when you first started over dinner but still there for anyone to chime in." Jake gave him a smirk. "So! How is your girlfriend?"

"Okay, I guess." Shrugging, Hotan looked out the window and watched the telephone poles zoom by. "Haven't really been talking to her lately."

"You guess? When was the last time you spoke to her, Hootie?" His smile faded when he glanced at Hotan. "Oh man, you need to call her or something more at the rate you're going. Life without love is just … sad."

"I think it's been a month. At least that long since I spoke to her normally anyhow." Hotan's guilt weighed him down even further. "I feel horrible about it."

"Holy cow! Are you sure you're even together anymore?" Jake gave him a distraught look. "Teenage girls don't take these things lightly, you know? Are you sure you're still boyfriend and girl-friend? That's far too long."

"Yeah, we're together." Hotan felt the pressure. "I feel bad about it. She knows that she can call me if she needs anything, but with all this stuff going on, it's been hard. I don't even know who I am anymore or if I'm still supposed to be someone else. The idea of dragging her through this bothers the hell out of me."

"Well, that's understandable." Jake drove through a more rural area of town with industrial buildings in the distance. "Don't you think that you need her right now? At least she's the solid point in your life. Sounds like you two really respect and care a lot about each other."

"Yeah, I guess you have a point." They passed the industri-al-type buildings on the desolate, weatherworn road; the build-ings were arranged in imperfect chaos, unlike the organized city blocks. "Where are we going?"

"Not too much further. The shop's at the end of this road, just around the turn." Once more, Jacob gave a smug expression.

"Gotcha." Hotan ignored it, letting his thoughts wander.

They pulled up to an aircraft-hangar-turned-mechanic shop. Directly behind it was a fenced-in junkyard, a resource for missing and hard-to-find parts. The sign for "Lilly Pad's Junkyard & Repairs" swung and creaked in the breeze. As the truck came to a stop, dust floated by, adding to the barren vibe. Hotan noticed no signs of anyone or if it was even open for busi-ness. Hotan remained in the truck while Jake got out and walked toward the open garage. After a minute or so, he walked back to the truck and opened the passenger side, rubbing the back of his neck.

"Looks like I'm going to need your help." Jake laughed ner-vously. "I can't see anyone anywhere."

Hotan blinked. "Help?"

"Yeah, we're going to have to search the junkyard for our beloved mechanic. Probably working on a side project again." Jacob sighed, leading Hotan around to the back of the shop. A gate teetered loosely on its hinges with the unlocked padlock hung lazily on the fence.

"Who am I looking for?" Hotan gawked at the stacks of stripped cars or those completely totaled from accidents. "And how am I going to see them in this place?" The injuries on the metal beasts were each unique and equally gut wrenching. "What do they look like?"

"It's the only other person out here, besides us." Jake passed Hotan, heading toward the right.

Hotan headed left, hoping he could manage his way out again from the maze of twisted cars. They came in all sorts of shapes, sizes, and conditions: some old, some new, and occasionally, one or two unrecognizable heaps. He traveled down the winding hallways of the morbid labyrinth that occasionally creaked or tinged as a gust of wind blew by. *It's creepy seeing all these vehicles. Did the passengers they once held survive? The damage is severe and horrific, and it was a safe place for someone to sit once.*

A rearview mirror crashed to the ground beside him from a car above. Hotan backed up, gaping at where it came from to find a black cat stalking him. After they exchanged glares, it flicked an ear and moved on. *Jake mentioned an incredibly good point. I do need Shellie. She's the only stable thing in my life. An anchor, my strong point, but I neglected ensuring it stayed that way. I hope she isn't upset with me.* Another scrap clunked down as the cat leapt between two towers. *I need her, but if Cassandra or Geliah would harm her...* Shaking his head, he walked in the opposite direction of the cat. *At this point, they've trashed my bike, but who knows what else they're willing to do. Cassandra is the element of Earth and the things she could do with that are unlimited. She could literally bury me ali—*

A muffler came smashing down in front of him. Hotan stumbled and fell backward, landing hard on the muddy ground. "Holy shit!"

"Eh?" a female voice came from far atop of the cars. "Who the hell are you?"

"I…" Hotan choked on his words as his heart pounded in his throat before he said, "Who are you?!"

"The property owner! That's all you need to know!" Steps could be heard coming across one of the cars above him. "Now tell me who you are and why the hell you're trespassing!"

"My name's Hotan, and I came here with Jake!" Hotan stood up and brushed himself off.

"Jake? Jake Kendall? As in the Jake Kendall that owes me money, Jake Kendall?" the voice chirped in disbelief like a bird in a tree.

"Yeah, Jake Kendall." Hotan ogled up at the towering giant of cars, shading his eyes from the sun to make out who he was speaking to. "I didn't know he owed you money."

"Yeah, well it's pointless with him. He thinks the world owes him everything and he owes nothing to the world!" She laughed, squatting down, still making it hard to see her from the sun glaring brilliantly behind her.

"Yeah, yeah, you can say that all you want!" Jake walked up behind Hotan and patted his back. "Were you trying to kill the boy?" Scoffing, Jacob kicked the rusted muffler.

"No, just stripping a car for parts. He happened to be in the way, that's all," she huffed, standing back up.

"I'm okay. It was no big—" Hotan's heart dropped when the person above them leaped off from what seemed to be a 25-foot drop. She landed without any complications with a *fa-thud* sound, squatting on the ground in front of them. "No way in hell."

"Feh!" The broad-shouldered girl stood up, wiped her heavy leather gloves off on each other, and brushed her overalls off with her muscular arms. "That's nothing. I've hopped down several stories before. It takes practice, but we're capable of a lot."

"Looking beautiful as ever, m'lady." Jake grinned as she adjusted the bandana which covered her coarse hair pinned back in its ponytail. "C'mon now, can't you pretend to be happy to see me?"

She twisted her grease-smudged face at him. "Depends on if you're here to pay me the two hundred bucks you owe me," she snorted, working her way through the skyscrapers of junk cars.

"Sure, I'll pay you today, doll face!" Jake raced up beside her and pulled out his wallet, handing over cash without further delay. "But I need another favor."

"What is it now?" She shoved the money into her pocket as she looked over at him nonchalantly. "Nitro? Lift kit? What project you got going and on which of your toys?"

"No, nothing like that, babe. This is for Hotan." She paused and glanced back at him with a ghostly complexion. "He's in a tight spot."

"You're… did you just say 'Hotan?'" She fixed her gaze on him, picking apart his every feature. "You may look like him … no, something is … wrong. You're not him at all."

"Yeah." Hotan returned her glare with a more questionable one. "And you are?"

"Lilly, but you're Hotan. You look like Hotan, but you sure don't act like him." Lilly walked up to examine him further. "And for you not to know who I am is even stranger. I can feel it's there, but it's different. You are completely different. Fresh even."

Hotan watched as she circled him once, leaning closer to him, exchanging forceful eye contact. "You're him, but…" Lilly finally stepped back and turned to Jake. With a concerned tone in her voice, she asked, "What the hell is happening, Jake? What kind of trouble is this?"

"Oh, I don't know what you're talking about, Lilly Pad." Jake shrugged and gave her his best smug look.

"Stop playing games; I know there's something up. Hell, this isn't Hotan." Lilly started stabbing him in the chest with a finger. "In fact, this is a kid with the same abilities, if not stronger! What in the hell are you and Talib going to do about this, Jacob?"

"Uh." Jake leered at her as she crossed her arms, sharp eyes slicing through him. "Oh, come on, Lilly. I really don't think this is the best time or place to talk."

"Now is better than never, spit it out, I don't care," she huffed as she tapped her biker boot impatiently on the ground, squeezing the answer from him with her gaze. "I refuse to do anything till you give me some sort of explanation of what's going on. I mean, obviously this has been developing for some time, but dammit, I need to know what we've gotten ourselves into."

"Tell her, Jake." Hotan broke his silence and fell under her glare. "Or should I try to explain it?"

"Why couldn't you just stay quiet?" Jake mumbled in frustration, rubbing the back of his neck. "If you think you can tell her, then go ahead, big boy. We still really don't know. Honest."

"Yeah, let me hear this from you." Lilly placed her hands on her hips. "I'm sure you're the one suffering the most out of this ordeal. You're an infant in this mess."

"Heh." Hotan took in a deep breath trying to give himself a moment to know where to begin. "Well, as you already figured out, I'm not the same Hotan. I'm a complete duplicate or remake. Still not quite sure why, and I haven't a clue what I can do. I don't have the luxury of remembering how to use these so-called powers."

"Is that all you know?" Lilly lifted an eyebrow, turning back to Jake, who nodded in agreement. *C'mon Jacob, what's really going on? Talib must know something, right?*

"Hey, it's rude to whisper like that." Jake started to walk further out of the junkyard in hopes of cutting her investigation short. "He's not completely void of abilities. He at least has that much going for him."

I can do it, but I'm not particularly good at controlling it. Hotan shrugged as she glanced back at him with an amused look on her face. "But there's a lot we don't know about what's going on. I'm still trying to deal with the idea that we exist, let alone that I'm one of you. On top of it all, I keep getting the impression that this whole mess is Hotan's fault, which ripples down to being all my fault."

"No kidding, but don't be so quick to blame yourself." Sighing, Lilly led them back through the decrepit gate. "I'm curious why he did this. He was so determined to make us disappear; it just doesn't feel right."

"Well, Lilly Pad, if you happen to find that answer, you be sure to call the rest of us," Jake scoffed as they stopped by his truck, and he lit up another cigarette and took a long drag. "What's got me twisted is the idea of Talib being awake for it all. Why did he let it happen? I know he knows, but the man hasn't said anything. Not one hint of how he feels or even a reaction to it all."

"Especially since you so easily picked up on the fact that I'm not who I appear to be." Hotan sighed as he leaned over the bed of the truck, scrutinizing his trashed Suzuki. "But I don't think Geliah gives a rat's ass whether I'm the old Hotan or not."

"Geliah? That ass needs to grow up." Lilly walked up beside him and peered over, curious why Hotan looked so remorseful. "You've got to be kidding."

"Yeah, I know, the bike's pretty rough," Jake commented with the cigarette hanging lazily in his mouth. "She's a dirty one, eh?"

"Cassandra's head is full of dirt, if you ask me, especially for being so wrapped up with Geliah. How about you two manly men carry it into the shop?" Lilly walked into the garage, disappearing from view.

"Damn, it's heavy," Jake growled through his cigarette as they laid the bike on the ground just behind the truck.

"Yeah, full tank of gas, well, mud." The two of them pushed the bike toward the shop with its flat tires dragging the whole way, leaving a distinct trail of dirt. "It's going to be a while before I get this thing back. Can you give me a lift home when we get ready to leave?"

"Sure, if you really think you need a ride." They stopped inside the garage lined with its shelves, drawers, and various tools. "I wanted you to see something firsthand." A heavy smell of oil and gasoline greeted their nostrils. "But she does fast work."

"Considering I have dirt encasing the inside of my engine, yeah, I'll need a ride, Jake." Hotan leaned against a table as Jake took one last drag from the cigarette and flicked it out the open garage door.

"You won't need to ride from anyone." Lilly came out of the office enclosure near them, gloves off and her face clean. "I do fast work." She tossed Jake a beer and opened her own against her arm like he had seen many guys at the bars do. "This should be an easy fix, but it's going to drain the hell out of me, fair warning."

"There's no way you can take this engine apart and fix it by the end of today." Hotan looked skeptically at Lilly as she guzzled down half of her beer.

"Who said anything about taking it apart?" She gave a smirk, winking in his direction. "Now close the garage door. Let's get this over and done with. This is what you wanted to show the kid, right?"

"You sure you want to do it that way, girlie?" Jake found a chair to sit on as he enjoyed the cold liquid pouring down his throat. "I know it's still hard on you."

"Practice makes perfect." She threw the empty bottle in a nearby trashcan, causing a loud clanking sound as it hit others. "It's getting better though."

"Are you—" Hotan looked at her as the garage fell into darkness. The chain-operated gate came screeching into its resting place, and the room illuminated from a few flickering florescent lights. "Are you going to do what I think you're about to do?"

"If you knew how to use your powers, it would have been an easy fix." Jake looked back at him smiling. "But she's going to push the dirt out by crushing the metal into a solid chunk, leaving the dirt to fall to the garage floor."

"Yeah, it may take me a while to do it, but it can be done." She cracked her knuckles and neck and took a steadying breath.

Hotan stood next to Jake, unsure of where he would be permitted during this delicate procedure. "Wait, but my bike's not completely metal. I know half the materials are plastic or rubber, so how is this going to work?"

"See that's the intriguing thing." Jake leaned back and took a sip of his beer. "We're a lot more complex than when we started all those centuries ago. Lilly of Metals has evolved in a most peculiar way, despite being in that Rip Van Winkle nap of ours. Her element has changed to match the times."

"Yup, not everyone adjusted or changed. It just depends on the element." She dug through a rather large toolbox full of various shelves. "It's really interesting, took me by surprise when I gained my memories again."

"So, what you're trying to say is that some of us have become stronger, despite the lack of use of our so-called elements?" Hotan tried to comprehend. "Adapted by default?"

"Exactly." She walked over to his grim-looking bike and started wrenching off the cover pieces, making the bike lose its smooth appearance piece-by-piece. "My abilities have gotten stronger, more advanced."

"And how did your powers become stronger?" Sadly, Hotan watched his motorcycle become a bare skeleton, showing nothing but the ragged insides which had endured a hellish blow. "Because I really don't see how metal could advance into something stronger."

"Well, let's break the idea of our powers down." She placed another cover piece gently on the table and walked back to the vehicle to continue the task at hand. "Keep in mind that overall, we are truly reflections of emotions or materials that make up a person and their life. I mean, there are emotions like lust or love that everyone yearns for and gives, and you have fear, which we all feel. Besides that, there is the basis of life itself, mind or spirit. Further from that, you have the environment that helps create that life: the earth we walk on, light that lets us see, and fire to give us warmth. It's what helps mold humanity."

"In short, Little Miss Can't-Be-Wrong is saying that metal has expanded into everyday life and is related to machinery more often than the element. Due to that fact alone, she has expanded her ability. Once, it was able to control the simple objects of metals and could make a knight's armor and weapons. Now, it includes more complex items such as guns, cars, and any other machinery she can possibly imagine." Jake proudly took a swallow of his beer as they continued to educate Hotan on this new finding. "We didn't realize it would be part of the package until recently. I'm convinced if she keeps at it, she may be able to do some high-tech computer stuff."

"Machines aren't one hundred percent metal. I'm able to manipulate plastics, rubber, and any other materials, depending on what I'm building." She clomped her tools back on a shelf and squatted in front of the bike, evaluating the damage.

"Huh, that's interesting, but it makes sense now that you put it that way. I didn't realize that society had such a big effect on us though." *Is he implying that Rebirth might be in the same situation?* "It's ironic considering your powers were impactful as they were."

"Yeah, it's a pain in the ass if you ask me." Jake sighed, leaning forward again, resting his elbows on his legs. "There's so much to adjust to and learn, but we're still human when it's all said and done. We just feel the flow of everyday life a million times more than the average person, and unlike them, we have the ability to manipulate the element of our choice."

Huffing, Hotan crossed his arms. "Of your choice."

"You heard right." Lilly smiled at him, but it faded as she released a heavy sigh. "But in your case, you had no choice."

"Yeah, and that just doesn't add up either." Jake looked up at him. "Anyway, let's get this show on the road, doll face."

"Like I said, it may take a while." She took in a deep breath as she stepped closer to the project before her.

Hotan watched Lilly as she stood there for several minutes as if nervous or reluctant about performing the ability. She had spoken so proudly of it just minutes before. Taking several deep breaths with her face solid with focus, she held her hands out toward the bike and gave her full attention to the motorcycle in its naked shape. Hotan's eyes widened as a bluish glow from the motorcycle broke his fixation on her. It seemed to grow from the very center of the bike, and within moments, the room was filled with the sound of metal and various objects bending and breaking. It was painful for Hotan to think of what was happening to the bike he had worked so hard to earn. The squeaking and groaning started to creep out, louder and more frequent.

I wish things could be normal again.

Turning his focus back to Lilly, Hotan saw black marks crawling across her face and arms as sweat ran down the side of her cheek. Soon, the bluish glow surrounded her as she continued her work. Parts and elements imploded into a mass which made up the heart of the bike. Dirt and mud began to rain down, finding no place to hide or contain itself. *This is truly an amazing event to witness*, Hotan thought as he looked down at Jake who was leaning back in his seat. Chugging his beer, Jake's grave expression told Hotan volumes.

He's worried about this. Obviously, this is still a grueling task on everybody. Getting accustomed to their new, weaker bodies has taken a huge toll on them. Maybe it's a good thing I'm starting from scratch.

The disintegration of his bike continued, crumpling like a piece of paper, slowly and torturously. It took several minutes before what used to be a working piece of machinery was merely a glowing blue ball of metal and various materials. A pile of dirt grew underneath the floating mass. It began to bubble and stretch itself awkwardly. Lilly maintained her composure even as more sweat collected on her face and arms.

She's pushing too hard… Should I…

She made a hollow metal case which imitated what the bike had looked like. It was an extremely slow process, but with so much detail, it was to be expected. Each component surfaced with every detail clear and defined as if it were brand new. Hotan held his breath as he watched his bike reappear from the deteriorated mass with grace within that blue glow. Upon completion, the tires filled themselves with air as they delicately touched the ground. The tread appeared like script across a page, like the tires had never touched asphalt. As it gently landed back on the garage floor, the glow started to fade.

Amazing, she rebuilt it in just minutes! "You're incredi—"

Lilly fell to the floor.

16

OPEN WOUNDS

otan and Jake scrambled to where she'd fallen. She was cold and clammy as Jake picked her up. Hotan followed close behind him as they busted into the office and laid her on the couch.

"Get something warm, a towel, rag, anything you can find!" Jake rubbed her face softly, saying her name to wake her up as tears filled his eyes. "Lilly, Lilly honey, snap out of it. You stubborn woman, you just had to push yourself too far once more. Please, Lilly, wake up! I swear you just want to meet Death himself sometimes..."

"What the hell just happened?" Hotan rushed into the bathroom, grabbed the hand towel, and impatiently waited for the sink water to get hot. "Is she okay?"

"It happens to all of us when we do more than we're used to. Now hurry!" Unable to wake her up, Jake pulled the blanket from the top of the couch and wrapped her in it. "We might be able to snap her back out if we can warm her up."

"Why did she even do it then?" Rushing back with the warm hand towel, Hotan caught sight of a tear sliding down Jake's cheek. *This is bad, really bad.* "I had no idea it was this extreme."

"She's stubborn." Jake snatched the towel from him and began slowly rubbing her face, returning color to her face as he did so. "She hates being like this, so she tends to rush it. She's been pushing her body to regain the stamina needed to handle the element. Stupid. Lilly, why did you have to do this to me today, honey?"

"Rush it? Hell, she's trying to kill herself." Hotan flopped into an old computer chair and tried to understand the situation. "This happens to everyone. This is insane." *How horrible.*

"At first, that is, until we get used to it again. Talib is the only one without this problem." Jake gave a sigh as Lilly started to moan and shift. "In fact, you've fallen into a similar state in the cathedral. Temporary memory loss, chills, cold, and even comas happen sometimes."

"Really?" Hotan watched Jake dab her with the hand towel to wake her from her unconscious state. "I guess that explains how I woke up and the church's new makeover."

"Shit," Lilly mumbled, grabbing her head. "That hurt. Ugh, I hate when I overdo it."

"Well, good morning, beautiful!" Jake exclaimed in relief. Even in Hotan's colorblind eyes, he could see color return to Jake's face. "Was wondering how long you were going to sleep on the job," he teased.

"Sorry if I scared you guys." She stiffly sat up, rubbing her forehead. "Ugh, can you grab my Tylenol from the medicine cabinet?"

"Sure." Hotan retrieved them. "Here you go."

"Gave us quite the startle when you didn't wake up at first!" Jake had taken Hotan's seat, and they watched her swallow the pills with no need for water.

"Yeah, I wasn't quite expecting it." Hotan crossed his arms, still feeling uneasy from the intense moment. "Why do you do it when it takes so much energy from you? That's pushing your luck, don't you think?"

"Heh, every time I push myself a few levels higher, it's easier the next time I do something big. As they say, kid, practice makes perfect." Lilly shoved the blanket off and stood up, wobbling. "I like pushing my luck, if that's what you want to call it."

"Yeah, she isn't the only one. Most of us made the mistake of trying something big once we remembered who we were. Woke up in the ER on IV for shock, malnourishment, or whatever other reason the doctors thought fit the cause of the sudden fainting session." Jake watched Lilly head to the kitchen where she leaned heavily on the fridge door. "It's just really hard gauging what we can or can't handle and how bad the outcome will be."

"I was thinking about that earlier." Hotan couldn't help but observe Jake's depressed and frustrated look. "I can almost say that I'm lucky to be starting from scratch."

"Anyone want a beer?" Lilly poked her head above the fridge door to see both of them raise a finger or two. "Alright, I can see that point, but in the end, you're facing as much, if not more, emotional trauma as the rest of us."

"Yeah, she's got a point." Jake took a beer from her as she returned to the couch.

"Here's yours, Hotan." Lilly smirked and winked as she handed him a Coke bottle. "I really think he's got more to worry about than us."

"You're telling me," Hotan huffed, enjoying the chilly liquid that flowed across his dry throat. "I have a lot on my plate, trying to figure out who and what I am. It's my fault this mess surfaced like it did. The only guy who can explain the whole situation doesn't exist anymore. On top of that, some other guy wants me dead over the whole thing."

"Damn, your life sucks." Lilly guzzled down her drink. "Must be hard being famous like that."

"Oh, Lilly Pad, go easy on the kid." Jake looked up at him. "Don't let her intimidate you. Her bark's worse than her bite. Trust me, I know from experience."

"Feh." Hotan grinned to himself, admiring her spirit. "I'm used to it by now. I'll finish putting the covers on the bike while you two catch up."

"About time you did something around here." Hotan could sense Lilly watching him as he walked out of the office.

Walking over to the open drawer, Hotan picked up the required tool. Next to the body panels, Lilly had laid the nuts and screws in plain sight. He picked up one panel and shoved the screws in his pocket. One piece at a time, he attached the outside jacket that gave the bike its aggressive look. As he wrenched away, he admired the chrome which made up the majority of the bike's metal components. As he went, he noted things weren't entirely in the spot they were before, and he could tell some new parts were in place. He hastened his wrenching on the panels, eager to ask Lilly what she had done to his motorcycle before daring to ride it all the way home. *Home is an hour drive, if not more, from where we are.* After several minutes, he finished, wiping the sweat from his forehead. Walking back into the office, they noticeably cut their conversation short.

"What exactly did you do to my bike?" Hotan glared at Lilly as she sat on the couch leaning on her knees, a fresh beer in hand. "You did more than I thought. It's not the same. Just looks like a Suzuki."

"Wow, you actually noticed." She smiled widely as her eyes lit up. "I modified the engine to maximize your output and changed the metal entirely to titanium. There's a lot more than that, but I think you know where I'm going on that note."

"Well, the question is: Am I going to kill myself trying to drive it home?" Hotan leaned against the door frame. *More speed isn't always the best.*

"Nope, but you'll notice it'll shift a lot smoother, and you'll feel it's got a lot more power behind it." She leaned back onto the couch, giving a quick glance over at Jake, who remained silent with his back to Hotan. "Be careful; she may feel lighter than the steel parts before. Take the turns easy."

"Just be careful, Hotan." Jake's voice was deeper, a fatherly tone giving his son worldly advice. "And call your girl. Take a break from all of this."

"Yeah, I know," Hotan huffed. "I'll be off then. Thanks for everything, Lilly."

"Anytime, kid." She raised her bottle to him. "Stop by anytime. I'll do what I can for you."

Hotan walked out to Jake's truck to grab his helmet from the passenger side. It was starting to get dark outside as he put it on and flipped up the tinted shield. He pulled the chain to open the garage door and hooked it in place to ensure it wouldn't come crashing back down. Sitting on his renewed motorcycle, Hotan felt nervous about driving it so far for the first time. Not knowing how it would work or feel, he started the engine, and it roared softer than what he was accustomed to. He kicked up the kickstand, and his legs welcomed the lighter weight of the bike; still, he felt anxious over the difference.

I'm going to wash out on this thing if I lean too hard on a turn.

Leaning a lot softer than before was going to be quite the challenge from the heavy beast he once rode. Hotan lightly pressed the gas and elegantly rolled out of the garage onto the isolated, industrial road. As the bike shifted, he felt the effortlessness of the changing of the gears and the clean feeling of the ride.

What an amazing job, Lilly!

Hotan made his way out of the dimly lit industrial section as the sun set and highway lamps began to flicker on.

I have to go see Shellie. I hope she's not pissed with me.

He made it to a familiar road which led to the expressway closer to home. Luckily, rush hour had ended hours ago. The cold night air hit his exposed arms and body through his thin shirt. He enjoyed how the ride was almost effortless with the redesign. The engine hummed softly as he made his way to the exit, taking caution as he made a right turn. As he pulled into Shellie's driveway, there were no cars, but the living room light was on. Approaching the door, Hotan hesitated at first before pressing the button. The doorbell rang behind the closed door.

Shellie has to be here.

He stood in silence, chest aching for several minutes. *Maybe I was too rash rushing here.* The clicking of the lock broke his thoughts as the door cracked open cautiously. A smile of relief crept across his face.

"Hey." Hotan could see she was indifferent about the sudden visit.

"Hey." Shellie smiled as she opened the door wider to let him in. "Mom and Dad are at a business party and won't be home 'til real late. What brings you here? Are you okay?"

"You." Feeling the weight of his guilt, he shook his head. "I was thinking about you today. Feeling guilty about not calling like I used to and not giving you a minute of my time in the last few weeks. Sorry, Shellie."

"You know I don't get mad about that kind of stuff. You're dealing with a lot and asked for some space. I can't blame you for being straightforward." She hugged him, taking in a deep breath of his scent. "But I'm glad to see you, much better than a phone call."

"I know, but it still doesn't give me the right to completely neglect you." Hotan lifted her chin up, staring deeply into her eyes. *I just wish I could see those eyes in color again.*

"You shouldn't worry so much, Hotan." She brushed some of his hair behind his ear. "I'm a big girl," she jested.

"Well then, forgive me. I completely forgot you were." Hotan leaned in and kissed her soft, warm lips. *I just want to think about the now.* Shellie's lips pushed firm against his own and sent his pulse running. *I'm so sorry for going so long without you.* Pulling her close and tight, Hotan let his troubles melt away, embracing her warmth.

She pulled away. "Are you okay, Hotan?" Her voice shook as she nuzzled his shoulder. "You're acting weird. You've never been this loving with me before."

"I don't know." A heavy sigh escaped him, and he confessed, "I don't know anymore. I just went too long without you and realized I wasn't being fair. I need you more than I'd thought. You're the only thing I have that makes me still feel human."

They didn't say much to each other as they snuggled on the couch, pretending to pay attention to the movie flashing across the television. A sense of joy filled him being so close to her and not thinking of anything. He had seen Lilly's amazing ability just hours before, but that didn't matter. Miracles, immortals, and their powers were no longer on his mind. He just wanted to swim in the warmth of Shellie's heart and be himself, not the boy trying to fill the place of the abandoned leader of the immortal Levites. He wanted to be plain Hotan—Hotan who goes to high school, has a band, and most importantly, has someone he loves and would do anything in the world to keep and protect.

Hotan... a familiar voice rang in his head.

Who is this? he responded, straightening himself on the couch, annoyed the moment with Shellie was interrupted.

Talib.

Hotan took in a deep breath as he sat silently. *What do you want? Didn't expect to be talking to you so soon again.* He held his breath, hoping his earlier thoughts were left unheard.

I want to apologize for the other night. Talib's voice was heavy with sorrow. *I … I am not sure if this is a good time to add to the stress you are already under with what Jacob and I had mentioned over dinner.*

Understandable. Hotan leaned back into the couch, staring at the ceiling. *But it seems I'm the one causing myself the most stress. We can start again if that helps.*

How so? Talib replied quickly. *What would you like me to do?*

I'm not up for talking about it right now. Hotan held back the millions of thoughts in his mind. *Maybe soon I'll be willing to share, but tonight's not going so well. I am tired and frustrated. We can meet later.*

Are you in some sort of trouble? A sense of urgency came across from Talib.

Nothing I can't manage. Normal life kind of trouble, nothing regarding my special abilities and what not. Hotan mentally kicked himself for the mess he was in with Cassandra's attack. *I'll be fine. Just need some rest.*

If you ever need me… There was a long pause from Talib before he finished, *you can find me at the cathedral.*

"You okay?" Shellie stared at him, observing the growing tension consuming the muscles in his face. "You look super tense. You feeling sick?"

"Uh." Hotan looked over at her slightly startled. "Yeah … I feel fine," he lied.

"Relax." Shellie smiled and kissed his forehead. "It's okay, Hotan. I'm not mad at you."

"Hey, Shellie?" Hotan grabbed her hand. *You'll never be the reason why I fall into despair.*

Furrowing her brow, Shellie met his eyes, concern washing over her face. "Yeah?"

Hotan laced his fingers with hers before confessing, "I love you."

"I love you, too." Her cheeks red, she grinned in her excitement. "But I still think you're acting weird."

For the rest of the night, Hotan sat there on the couch, holding her close as they watched movies. *I've tried so hard all this time to keep our relationship mutual and uncomplicated, but for what reason? For the first time, I feel like our relationship is complete and more stable. The question is: Does she truly feel the same?* He looked down at her head resting against his chest. *Of course, she does.* They sat in utter darkness with only the light of the television. She looked sleepy and secure as she focused on the movie. He pulled her closer and took a deep breath. The sound of two car doors shutting followed by the muffled sounds of chatter and laughter outside signaled the end of his short-lived peace. Keys rattled, and the door unlocked. Her parents came through the door in their formal attire from the evening's event.

"Well! Look here, Doris!" Shellie's father boasted, his cheeks red from alcohol and his mustache slanted across his face with his smirk. "We caught them in the act! Shame on them!"

"Oh, Henry!" Doris giggled, delighted that her little girl hadn't spent the whole night by herself. "Where have you been, Hotan? It seems ages since I saw you last."

"Oh, just working a lot, Mrs. Rubenstein." Hotan and Shellie straightened their posture. "Keeping busy with school, the band, grabbing side jobs where I can."

"You're just saying that." Henry gave him two hard smacks in the shoulder as they passed by. "But I like the sound of it!"

"Was everything okay, baby?" Doris kissed Shellie on the cheek and patted her on the head.

"Yeah, Mom. Hotan showed up not too long ago, but everything is fine." She stifled a yawn, stretching out her arms. "Would it be okay if I stayed the night at Hotan's?"

"Uh." Hotan looked down at Shellie, then back up to her parents, feeling his face turn red. "Wait, what?" *What is she thinking? They would never let her stay the night at my place. A teenage girl, staying the night at a delinquent's apartment, and she didn't even ask me!*

"Oh." Her mother gave a clueless expression, shooting a glance at her husband before meeting the baffled expression on Hotan's face. "Henry, what do you think?"

"Hmm." Henry stared down Hotan, and after a few minutes, cracked a big smile. "Well, Shellie's a big girl and smart at that. I don't see the harm in it. Just bring her back in one piece or else!"

My head's on the chopping block for sure. "Uh, yes, sir." Hotan shot a baffled look at Shellie at the sudden suggestion. *She must have known they would agree, but ... why all of a sudden?*

"Just bring her home tomorrow!" her mother added.

"Thanks!" Shellie jumped up and hugged her parents. "We have a lot to work on for the band. At least you don't have to hear me practice in the morning!"

"Oh yes! A quiet morning is needed after as much as I drank. I trust you'll take good care of her." Henry shook his hand, crushing it to send the unspoken message: *Don't lay a finger on her.* "She's the only daughter I have, Hotan," he warned.

"Yes, sir, I know." Hotan returned the firm squeeze, a silent exchange of respect and strength. "Besides, we have to go to 7even's early tomorrow for auditions. This saves me a trip. All business," assured Hotan. *I forgot all about the band auditions. Shit, I've really lost myself.*

"Oh! What are you auditioning for?" Her mother's face filled with interest.

"We're judging some people who are trying out for Shellie's place in the band." He sighed, scratching the back of his head, still perplexed.

"I'm one year under the minimum age limit, so we decided to give the band a chance, even if I have to sit out for this competition." Shellie shrugged as she glanced over at him, still smiling.

"That's very big of you." Her dad patted her on the back. "Well, your mom and I are exhausted. I'm sure you two are ready to head out by now."

"Good night, baby!" Her mom hugged and kissed her once more before stumbling down the hall to their bedroom.

"Okay, I'll be just a minute." Shellie raced off to her room. "Just need to grab a bag for the night."

Befuddled, Hotan stood up, stretching out his back. *She's out of her mind putting me on the spot like this.* Hotan found himself grinning, amused. After a few minutes, she came back with a black jacket and a backpack full of her things. They both took a minute to strap their helmets in place and headed for his place. She hugged his waist tighter than usual; then again, it had been a while since she'd ridden on the bike. *Maybe the bike feels different to her, too.* Shellie followed behind him, neither one of them speaking as they made their way upstairs. Unlocking his door, he allowed her to enter first and trailed in behind her. Tossing her bag onto the couch, she slid her jacket off. *This just hit a level of awkwardness I wasn't quite prepared for.* Hotan opened his fridge, leaning on the door as he scanned aimlessly through the items. *I'm not even hungry … or even thirsty. I need a moment longer to think. What possessed her to want to come home with me? Should I even have allowed this?*

"Thirsty? Hungry?" Hotan glanced over at her.

"No thanks, I had pizza before you showed up." Shellie stifled another yawn.

"Okay." Taking a quick swig out of the orange juice container, he walked into the living room, rubbing the back of his neck. "I don't know about you, but I'm tired as hell. You kind of put me on the spot there, Shellie. Um, you can sleep on the couch or the mattress, doesn't matter to me. Your choice." *I don't want to compromise us… I can't take this any further just yet.*

"Yeah, I'm pretty sleepy myself." Shellie stood up and hugged him. "If you don't mind, I want to snuggle with you tonight."

I hope she knows nothing is happening. Hotan's face heated. "Okay, a mattress on the floor isn't much, but it's big enough for us both." He led her into the bedroom where his mattress laid on the bare floor, scattered with clothes. "Though, it's a mess." With a sigh, he muttered, "And it's never clean."

"Wow, not into bedroom furniture at all, are you?" Shellie grinned at him. "No worries, I don't plan on doing anything with you tonight. I just wanted more quiet time with you, that's all."

Phew, that takes care of that awkward notion. "I promise the sheets and comforter are clean." He kicked off his shoes and threw his shirt to the ground. "Quiet time you shall have. I'm not going to be awake for much longer. Today was insane, yesterday even crazier, so for once, I actually want to sleep." *I hope this makes it clear that I have no intentions of making a move. Let's not complicate this relationship to the next level, not until we're both ready.*

"I'm not worried about that." She flopped onto the mattress, scooping up and hogging one of his pillows.

"I should've made you bring your own pillows." He flopped down beside her, pulling her close to him. "I can always use you as my pillow."

"Good night, Hotan." She kissed him on the cheek and snuggled herself on his chest and shoulder.

"Night, Shellie." Kissing the top of her head, he took in a breath of her scent and quickly dozed off.

The smell of food and sounds of cooking woke him. Shellie was no longer in bed with him, and he found himself hugging his pillow where she had been last night. *When was the last time I slept so deeply and peacefully?* Rubbing his eyes to remove the sleep from them, he stretched out his legs and arms. At last, he wandered to the living room. Shellie was busy over the stove, making whatever she could with the limited supplies in his fridge and cabinets. Seeing she didn't take notice of him, he circled back to bathroom. Turning on the shower, he waited for the water to heat up while shaving. Soon, his worn-down face looked fresh again. As the water pounded against his face, the rest of his worries washed down to the drain.

"Hey." Her voice made him jerk as if he'd been home alone and unaware of someone being there.

Did she just open the bathroom door to get my attention? His heart fluttered, and he swallowed. "Yeah?" He pulled the curtain back to make eye contact, once more baffled at how bold she was being. *Where did my shy Shellie go? Has she decided on her own that she wants to take this to the next level?*

"I, um." She blushed, averting her eyes as she tried to hide her sheepish grin. She tucked her head behind the door and said, "I made omelets, just, just wanted to let you know. Sorry. You didn't reply, so I thought if I opened the door … well, it, it's ready."

"Oh, yeah?" Hotan grinned to himself, enjoying the awkward moment she'd created and was now embarrassed by. "What kind of omelets? I didn't think I had enough food for that," he continued the conversation, teasing her.

"H-h-h-ham and cheese; it's all you had." Clearing her throat, she shut the door, no longer able to continue the conversation with him.

Pulling the curtain shut again, he continued his blissful shower. *I really don't know what's gotten into her since last night, but at least it seems to be all her choice. I'm enjoying seeing this newfound confidence from her. It's almost like we're an old married couple that's been together forever. In the past, she's only been like this toward her studies. Glad to know I haven't damaged what we have between us. Ugh. That's right, then there's Talib acting weird. He said I could find him at the cathedral. I wonder if he's been there the whole time. Maybe that's why I feel so safe there? I mean, I have this undoubting sensation to look up to the man for advice. It makes sense, considering he's supposedly my brother. If I were truly reborn again, what would that technically make me?*

He shut the water off and grabbed a nearby towel. Peeking out the bathroom door, he sighed in relief to see the bedroom door had been shut as well. Quickly dressing, he was eager to join her for breakfast. *I may not feel hungry or thirsty these days, but I am excited to have her cooking. This is officially the first time she's cooked something for me, and I can't get my heart to stop racing over it.*

"Took you long enough." Shellie was sitting on the couch, eating what little was left of her omelet as she flipped through one of the albums. "Wow, your mom was popular in high school. I don't think you ever showed me this."

"Yeah, I guess she was." Hotan sat next to her where his own plate and a glass of orange juice awaited him. "Thanks for cooking breakfast. I don't think I ate yesterday."

"No problem." She paused at a page in the album. "Is this … is this who I think it is?" She tapped a finger on a dark-haired, dark-eyed man.

"Is this what?" His mouth full, he leaned over and frowned. "Oh, him. Yeah." He continued eating.

Shellie gathered the nerve and asked, "Is that your dad? It's him, right?"

"Yeah, that's him." He took several gulps of his juice. "Uncanny resemblance, huh?"

"Wow." She returned her stare to the pictures. "No offense, but you look a lot like him. There's no denying that he's your dad"

"I know." Finishing off the last of the omelet, he shoved the dirty dishes in the sink with a loud racket. "The mirror almost taunts me since I found those pictures."

Catching the expression on his face, she shut the album and changed the topic. "Well, we better get to Chaz's." Walking into the kitchen, she began washing the dishes.

"Thanks." He kissed her. "It was delicious."

Her body went tight, and she dropped the dishes back in the sink. She kissed him back as he pressed her against the kitchen counter. Her wet hand cupped his face, their lips parting as their tongues tangled with one another for a fleeting moment. Pulling away, he held her in a tight hug as if his life depended on it.

"But I could not care less about my dad. I've got you in my life," he muttered as his pulse pounded in his ears.

All she could do was hug him back and give him the comfort he'd craved for so long. This whole time he'd been holding back, putting on the air of someone strong and invincible. For the first time, he allowed himself to be soft, no longer denying himself the security of being in someone's arms. Time froze and he could breathe with freedom, but deep down, he sensed that this might be the last time he would be able to come up for air. *I wonder if she knows how much this small moment means to me in my world of chaos.*

17

BY THE WAY

They admired the early morning air as they rode downtown. Kyle wasn't there yet, but running behind was normal for him. Hotan pulled out his keys to unlock the club's backdoor, letting Shellie in first. He took a cautious glance around the alley and shut the door tight, locking it. They quietly walked into the locker room and went about their tasks. Shellie smiled at him every time she passed or made eye contact with him. Grinning, he took a big breath. *Finally, some serenity and normalcy in my life.* Setting up the equipment with no one else, not even Chaz to make his remarks, felt awkward. Every noise and strummed string echoed all around the room, sounding foreign to Hotan as they made the necessary arrangements for a painless audition.

"Be sure to leave your spare bass up and a spot for them to plug into." Hotan looked over at her as she strummed a line or two. "It's hard to say if we'll get anyone who may not bring their own. People are weird like that."

"Okay. Should I set the sound up on the open line?" She pulled the bass strap off and gently placed it on a stand. "Or would that be pointless? I know everyone is different."

"That's your call. I don't see how it would hurt. They are replacing you, and well, if that's how you always have it when we play, then it makes sense for them to play your settings." He headed off stage to grab the sheet music.

He pulled a table closer to the stage and aligned three chairs. Dumping his book bag there, he unlocked the front doors as he listened to her strumming rhythms in the background. *I taught her that one.* He had taught her what he knew about the bass, and she absolutely took off with it. The one and only time he'd actually taught someone and managed to not lose his patience. *Glad I was part of something positive in her life, something she can remember me by.* Opening the door, he squinted at the sunlight, hot as it lay upon him, and he suppressed the bitter thought. There were still no signs of anyone, not even Kyle.

"Hey!"

Hotan whipped his head back to the left to see who had shouted. Blinking, he tried to adjust to the bright light blinding him.

"Hey, Hotan! I came to audition!"

"You?" Hotan's eyes focused revealing Metsy, the girl from his math class, skipping down the sidewalk with a bass case strapped to her back. "You play bass?"

"I've got a life outside math class, you know." Metsy straightened her punk, yoked skirt. "I saw the flyers, and well, I figured it was worth a try."

"Yeah, definitely." Hotan opened the door wider, letting her in. "I didn't realize you were eighteen. To be honest, I didn't think I would see too many kids from school because of that."

"Well, I guess that's the advantage of being labeled slow in elementary school," Metsy huffed as she swung the case off her back and hugged it. "I think I was held back twice."

"Really?" Hotan wasn't sure how to respond to the information she volunteered to him. "Well, we just finished setting up. If you want to sit and chill after walking all this way, you can."

"Oh, thanks, I appreciate it." Metsy flopped down in a chair, happy to rest her feet. "Hey Shellie! What's up?"

"Metsy!" Shellie chimed, waving from the stage. "It's been a while since I've seen you!"

"I know!" Metsy exclaimed. "We haven't had a class together in some time."

Hotan let them catch up while he dragged a heavy ashtray out to prop open the door. Kyle came around the alleyway, still rubbing sleep from his eyes and yawning. Mumbling to himself, Kyle was desperate to escape the morning light. *It's nice to have a normal day. Everything else just seems like a distant dream, despite all that happened yesterday.* Hotan didn't want to think about it. *There's plenty of time later to stress over the details and create new theories. Today, I simply want to be the Hotan with a boring life … at least while it lasts.*

"Well, we'll start when you're ready, Metsy. Hard to say who else will show today." Hotan smiled to himself as he walked back into shadowy innerworkings of the club. *Today I am me and solving the problems perfectly suited for who I want to be.*

"Sounds like a plan!" Metsy hopped up, full of energy as she unpacked her bass.

The day went by quickly despite how many showed up for auditions. There were some talented players, including Metsy. Hotan found himself not paying attention, staring at Shellie instead. He tried to gauge her reaction to the musicians on stage, enjoying every smile and giggle. *I want to immortalize this moment, this memory.* It stopped him from focusing on yesterday's overload, which kept knocking at the back of his mind. Kyle seemed divided between the auditions and watching Hotan. Half the time, Kyle would yawn or rub his eyes when Hotan caught him looking. *Is he dodging being caught staring at me? Why?*

Hotan sighed as he placed books in his locker. *At the rate my life is going, this could be the last time I see them. The only reason I'm even coming to school still is to see what Mr. Piedmont knows. School is one of the last places left where I feel partially human. Can I even consider myself human? I mean, we're technically people who adapted powers to help us in a time of need. Do any of us really know why we're here and have these abilities? Was this a mistake or flaw in nature? Maybe I should just…*

"Hey, are we still having a show tomorrow night?" Hisota's voice pulled Hotan from his thoughts.

"Yeah, why are you asking?" Hotan turned around surprised to see Hisota wasn't in his face. "You planning to show?"

"Well." Hisota smiled to himself and let out a gratifying sigh before admitting, "Yes, and I wanted to see if someone could come with me. I met her last week. Can you get her in?"

"Yeah … I can get … her in." Hotan raised an eyebrow at Hisota as his sentence fell apart awkwardly. "Who is she?"

"Her name is Charlotte." Hisota shrugged, smirking. "Let's just say, she caught me off guard."

"No kidding. Anyway, it shouldn't be an issue with Chaz." The bell rang overhead, signaling it was time to settle into class. "I look forward to meeting her. See you tonight."

"I'll bring her by and introduce her to you." Hisota jerked off the lockers and left in the opposite direction.

Hotan shook his head. *I'm happy Hisota has someone new to distract him. All these years, I've never thought of him as bisexual. I've been so far up my own ass, I've overlooked who Hisota really* is. Do I really know what he does and doesn't like? I mean as long as I can remember, he's always been flirty with me and jealous of any girl I showed interest in. He knew I didn't feel the same, but I didn't shun him for it.

In fact, back in elementary school, Hisota was the big, bad bully who got under everyone's skin and made the other kids flat out miserable. I was the silent kid in the background, a complete recluse. I'll never forget the day out on the playground when I watched Hisota take one kid down at a time...

I was sitting there eating a snack when I heard a scream from behind the pine trees and bushes next to the picnic table. It sounded like someone was in pain and hurt badly. With a sigh of annoyance, I walked over to see what had happened since the teacher was numb to the screaming kids playing all around. I came across Hisota and his latest victim, a boy who was new to the school. That boy was Kyle, and for the first time, a protective sensation washed over me.

Considering current information, looking back, it's amazing to know it was there at such an early age. I was so upset and angry, though I didn't understand why or what had pushed me into action when I had ignored it all this time before. It was by far not the first time I heard or saw Hisota lash out, but that day, the victim of choice ignited something new in me. Hisota shoved Kyle to the ground and began throwing pinecones at him. Tears streamed down his face, and a scrap of debris was across a cheek.

"Hey! Back off!" Hotan's voice shook as Hisota dropped the pinecone.

"Who are you?" Hisota was denser than he had given him credit for.

"Who cares?" Hotan helped Kyle up. "Why are you picking on him?"

"Because he's a meanie head!" Kyle sniffled, his bottom lip quivering as he cried further.

"Plenty of reasons: He's got red hair, and I want his gummy snacks." Hisota walked up, nose-to-nose with Hotan, poking him in the chest. "But since you're going to be in my way, I'll make you pay for it. This all would have been avoided if he'd just given me the—"

"No." Hotan ignored the little finger digging into his chest. "How about you give him your snack as an apology for what you did to him."

"What?" Hisota laughed, scoffing, "Yeah right."

"Yeah! Gimme yours!" Kyle antagonized from behind him. "Meanie!"

"How about I beat you up again?" Hisota shot a glare Kyle's way, and he withered back. "Just try me!"

"I don't think so." Hotan grabbed Hisota's shirt and slammed him against a tree. "If I ever see you picking on him, I'm going to beat you up."

"Ugh." Hisota was at a loss for words as a single tear made its way down a cheek.

"Come on, Kyle, let's go." Hotan turned and walked back to the picnic table with Kyle at his heels like a puppy dog.

"Don't mess with us!" Kyle tried putting on a tough guy act by puffing himself up.

They left Hisota against the pine tree as tears began to fall.

After that, Kyle had spent the following days trying to get me to talk. I'd forgotten about that. He was so insistent on being my friend. Could it be that he also sensed something? All day, Kyle made it his personal goal to sit next to me and talk on and on about anything in hopes I would respond. It was amusing to see how long Kyle would carry the process on. The most I gave him was a nod and a "thanks."

The teacher had marveled at the sudden change of behavior. The very next day, Hisota stopped picking on everyone and began following me religiously. It was bizarre how both Kyle and Hisota became my friends overnight. Kyle and I had a true friendship, but Hisota developed this odd obsession, creating a boyish crush toward me. I spent a lot of time trying to figure it out. Hisota worshipped the ground I walked on until high school, then it made a slow turn for the worse. Hisota became more like a jealous lover. He lashed out increasingly often, rage filling his eyes. Everyone concluded that Hisota was in love with me. In the end, I only replied in irritation or embarrassment to his tantrums.

I just hope he's not dragging this girl along to make me jealous. If that's the case, it's wrong. Hisota should know that I have no interest in him and move on. He's good looking, and there's no reason he can't snag a relationship with whomever he wants, male or female.

Shellie had seen her share of Hisota's schemes. He had coordinated the cruelest pranks, far outweighing the jocks and cheerleaders she'd faced before. Maliciously, Hisota used to attempt to drive a stake between me and Shellie. She'd fallen victim to dropped food, bubble gum in the hair, and even demeaning, childish rumors. Hisota once hung posters so vulgar, he damn-near got himself expelled over the chaos. How Shellie lasted through the antics was a miracle in itself.

Last year, the pranks faded away. I thought he had finally given up, but he turned his anger at me. Hisota would create confrontations with me, no one else, then simply disappear without warning. He thought abandoning me would hurt the most. He wasn't wrong, but I've been hurt by my mother's death by this point, and I was numb. Hisota soon tired of hiding away when no one seemed to care, or he found another opportunity to piss me off further. Perhaps I was the horrible and negligent friend, and maybe I can start to do that much for him before my life is no longer mine to live. I hope Hisota's new girlfriend is legitimate and a new outlet so he can move on. He'd do well with someone who enjoys doting over his every step. And in turn, I can say he'd return that unrequited love. It's clear that I could never give him that sort of affection. I can't necessarily label Hisota as a good or bad guy, but the day I witness a charitable act by him, Hell will have frozen over twice. It's not in his nature to be kind to others. I can't imagine him risking his own life for anyone, not even his own mother.

Snapping out of his thoughts, Hotan looked around his science class which was dragging as usual. Everyone was busy filling in answers on the five-page ditto on yesterday's lab. *Surely, the teacher is going to test us on these procedures later this month.* He sighed as he shoved the assignment to the side and eyed *The Book of Ancients* in his bag. Pulling it out, he continued his own research, jumping sections to look for the answers he wanted most of all.

THE BOOK OF ANCIENTS

Judgment

He is the most loving and forgiving man on Earth.

True to his title of elder brother, Talib should have been the leader of the Levites. He was kindhearted but had the impeccable ability to make sound judgments. Advising his younger brother with utmost wisdom and command came naturally to him. There was no disdain or jealousy about their father's decision to make him advisor and Hotan official chief. Instead, he became the backbone to his younger brother, Hotan. Together, they were strong leaders whose only mistake was trusting the council of elders. The council members were supposed to work in conjunction with them. The elders' selfish espionage led to the destruction of the thirteenth tribe of Israel, now labeled in the history books as the Levites.

Before their exile from the motherlands, Talib and his wife Saphellia had been attempting to produce a child. Despite the years of failure, they never lost hope or faith that someday they would be blessed with a child. That dream ended when the village burnt to the ground. It further died on the island of Eden when it became clear that our curse would not allow us the pleasure of continuing our lives or legacies through children or any normal means. I never understood where all that strength came from to hold such strong, happy faces. Perhaps, unlike myself, they were able to accept it as part of the sacrifice needed for the miracles we had been given.

Talib was the element of Judgment. It was fitting, and the control he had over his powers were far superior to everyone else. There were several visible indicators when abilities were actively used: markings across the skin, a flaming aura around the body, and in lower quantities, one's eyes would glow. When he invoked his ability, not even a shine in his eyes could be seen. Over the centuries, it was exciting and terrifying to watch how powerful his element became. In several cases, Talib shifted history with one judgment call. As with all the abilities, he controlled all aspects of this power. He could make it impossible for someone to make a choice, but more often, forced decisions for the greater good.

I was most amazed at how easily he was able to control a large quantity of people all at once. This was difficult for the other humanity-based immortals since it required an ungodly amount of stamina. I witnessed such a feat during the early attempts to colonize the New World. Unable to turn a blind eye, Talib saved hundreds of lives. That day as the first snow fell, they did not have enough resources or room to save the village with only one ship. He advised the captain and mayor to give up on the settlement and seek Croatan Island until they could return in a larger ship. Neither agreed with him. They were too proud to rely on the natives and would not entertain the idea of making such an alliance for their survival.

Death was coming, and he could not stop him, but he could make these people disappear or change their minds by force. It was the first time I witnessed him reveal his tattoos as his power spread out over the village. I watched in awe as everyone stopped what they were doing and marched for Croatan Island. The ship's captain and crew immediately turned back to the ship, having made a sudden decision to abandon the settlement in every aspect. With one last wave of his powers, he cast that they forever forget about Roanoke Colony. It was the last time I would ever see Talib, the element of Judgment.

This would soon be a place for Death to reside.

18

SIXTY-NINE TEA

Hotan froze as he finished the last line. He read it repeatedly. It made his insides twist every time. *Something isn't right. This book was written as his last will and testament. What was he doing in Roanoke Colony? What did he do that required this drastic of a solution? I need to know what you did, Hotan. I can't fix this. I don't even know what I'm supposed to fix. What went so wrong that no one but you knew about? Or does Talib really know? What is with all this impending Death? Was it Geliah? Or is there something else out there?*

Hotan focused on the terrifying statement: "*a place for Death to reside.*" It was becoming increasingly disturbing. Since Lilly's display of power, he'd pushed the issue of turning immortal, having powers, and the impending dangers off. *I need more information, but I'm not ready to confront Talib. Before attempting to bash heads with the most powerful immortal, I need to build an arsenal of information to push back with on a topic that I still don't grasp. Talib could twist me around before I even realize what's happening. I don't want to repeat that dinner incident again. Where can I look? Who do I turn to? Jake? Lilly? Is there someone else?*

"My goodness! You look older than me today." Mr. Piedmont wrinkled his face in concern. "Perhaps I can help?"

"No offense, Mr. Piedmont, but I don't think you can." Hotan slumped into the chair as the weight of his burden washed over him. "You wouldn't even believe me if I told you."

"Believe you?" Mr. Piedmont smiled at him and leaned over his desk. "Believe that you're the reincarnation of Hotan? Or that you feel an overwhelming obligation to fix a problem that neither you nor the rest of us, including Talib, have any information on? My boy, please remember you aren't alone in this matter. We want to find answers as much as you do."

"How, how do you…?" Hotan sat up, looking him in the eyes. *You, too? You're one of us, too?*

Yes, and I'm very worried about you. You keep going at this alone, but remember, we're just as lost as you are on the matter. Mr. Piedmont let out a heavy sigh as he leaned back. "I must say, I admire the brilliance of your mind. Hotan always had an amazing ability to take in the world around him and use that information to its fullest. Lately, you've been your own obstacle, which doesn't do anyone any good."

"I can't believe you're one of us, too." Rubbing his forehead, the room spun around him. "It's just, I've no idea who's who anymore."

"Please understand, I'm more of an observer. I've been watching over you, and I must say, you're not doing so well." It was the first time he'd ever heard a serious tone from the old man. "You need to be a little more aware of what's happening. If you keep going down this path, you'll fail to protect yourself, or worse, your loved ones. It's no grand secret that you're colorblind and have brilliant moments of seeing colors. I didn't confront you about it sooner because I was hoping Talib would take charge, speak up, guide us as he has done in the past." Mr.

Piedmont opened his mouth but snapped it shut, shaking his head before shifting in his seat and starting again. "Honestly, I think we've all been praying your memories would return. Until you unlock your powers, don't let it be known that you see any color. You made this mistake with me regarding the painting and the candy. If you're wondering why I'm telling you now, let me stress that it has never taken more than a month for an immortal to regain memories." *Except you, Hotan.*

"Never more than a month?" Hotan buried his face in his hands, agonizingly sickened by this truth. "It's been over three months since this all started, back when I passed out in the church. How many more times have I failed to take heed of the warning signs? How ignorant of me to put everyone at risk, letting my emotions trip me up. I'm so blind…"

"If imminent danger became a concern, I would have said something sooner, Hotan." Mr. Piedmont stood up, staring out the window where students ran the track aimlessly. "We have all come to the conclusion that our beloved leader is no more. Talib never told us. All things considered, he isn't with us anymore. For how long? We can't say, but I may be able to help you if you'll let me. We're running out of time, and I suspect that Geliah will not hold up to his own promises to leave you alone the moment he figures this out."

"Help me?" Dropping his hands, Hotan stared at Mr. Piedmont's back. "Do you know something that I can use? How can you help me?"

"I must apologize. I can't give you the information you seek or help you discover what powers lay dormant." Mr. Piedmont turned to face him with a gaunt expression. "However, I can use my power to help you control your current abilities and further your awareness of what you possess thus far. Being the element of the Mind, I can enhance comprehension beyond the normal limits. I guess that explains why I ended up being a principal of a school." He motioned to the office and mustered a half-hearted smile. "Watching all the kids explore the world around them and evolve in the way they think feels good to me. Ironically, it has helped me regain my strength, my confidence even, in my own abilities."

"Your power, the element of the Mind, is one of the three elements that make up a person as a whole, right?" Hotan realized this wasn't only his burden anymore. "How bad of a hit are you going to take to do this? How dangerous is it for you to use your power? Are there recoils for using them on another immortal? Have you even done this before?"

"In the past, the answer to these questions was unclear. I may pass out for some time after this, but I don't know what the overall reaction will be for us both." The old man closed his eyes, taking in a deep breath. "None of us knows what condition your powers are in, and even though I have helped others, Rebirth has always been much stronger than our own. In fact, it was powerful enough that the old Hotan could easily overtake all of us. There was never an instance where any of us would dare to even attempt to use our powers toward him. Likewise, I can't recall Hotan ever using his element against any of us, other than casting the reincarnation spell."

"He was that strong?" Rubbing the back of his neck, Hotan attempted to smooth the hairs back down as chills trickled up his spine. "Mr. Piedmont…" Searching the air for a moment, he met his gaze. "Don't do this if it will be a risk to your life. I've seen Lilly push her limits, and I know it's a painful ordeal. Rebirth is a power only the former Hotan understood, and I can't promise my own control or understanding of it. My power is about life and death, and—"

Mr. Piedmont threw up a hand. "We need you to figure this out for that reason. You have a strong enough mind and will, but you need help getting it on track. I'm doing this not only for you or myself; this is for the sake of everyone. The last thing we want is you using your power without knowing and aging someone forward, or worse. I know very well this is one of the many concerns you have weighed over and over in your mind. You're smart. Causing someone's premature death *is* a possibility with that unstable power you hold." Mr. Piedmont's voice shook as he continued, "Let me do this. It's the least I can do for you. You're suffering the most in all of this, and I want to do my part to help you. I honestly think Hotan didn't realize things would go so sour. He took all the burdens upon himself and gave us centuries of living out normal lives. Now, it's my turn to return the favor, and at least help you prevent a calamity if I can."

"Where do you want to do this?" Hotan made his decision on the matter. "I don't think here is a good place for it."

"No." The old man released a chuckle. "Of course, not here, goodness. I've talked to Jake. We'll go to his office when you're ready. Do you want some time to think about it? There's no rush."

"Let's do it tonight." Grabbing his book bag, Hotan gave a confirming look at Mr. Piedmont. "I'll meet you at Jake's office tonight. That'll give me time to settle my nerves. I can't afford to delay this any further. And more importantly, thank you."

"Thank me when the deed is done." Mr. Piedmont sat back into his chair, exhausted. "Thank me when I've done my job."

Hotan walked out, firm on the decision he had made. *I can't pretend this whole ordeal is my problem alone. I'm only a piece of a much larger puzzle and need to take advantage of any help. Amazing, Mr. Piedmont is one of us. How many more do I already know? Who has already attempted to show themselves to me in hopes that I would remember and recognize them? Never more than a month. Three months have passed, possibly longer. There's no denying that something's wrong, and they all are very aware of the bitter situation. Talib knows more, but he hasn't shared the details with anyone. Why is Talib making himself so distant over this? Is he mourning the loss of his brother? How much more complicated could this be? What am I not seeing that Talib is aware of?*

From habit, Hotan found himself walking into the cathedral to clear his head. He heard the distant sounds of school ending for the day as the door closed behind him. Talib was nowhere to be seen, and he was relieved to be here alone for at least a few minutes. All he wanted was to feel safe while he gathered his nerves. *Tonight will be intense. No one knows what kind of outcome Mr. Piedmont's power will have. What have I volunteered myself for? What is my end goal?*

Sitting in the front row, he tilted his head back. Staring endlessly at the towering ceilings above, many questions filled his head. He needed answers, not more riddles. The old Hotan was no more. There were no memories coming to his rescue. Worse, Geliah wanted his head with Cassandra by his side, and poor Callan needed help to break free. *The best I can do is blast my own thoughts out like a public service announcement.*

Talib, Piedmont, Jake, Kyle, and Lilly are immortals. That's nine, including myself. No ten. There is Tina too. That's half of the Tribe according to The Book of Ancients. *There are twenty in total, and I count ten so far. That isn't a bad start, but how many more have I encountered and not realized who they were? Fear, Earth, Metal, Water, Fire, Lust, Mind, Insanity, Judgment and Rebirth are all accounted for.*

Taking in a deep breath, Hotan missed the old, musky smell that previously filled the cathedral. This heavenly place had laid in ruin three months ago, and the mystery of how it looked in its prime had been solved. Leaning his elbows on his knees, he gazed up at the statue. Today, it gave him a stone-cold expression: no hope, no smile, no frown, no clue of emotion on that face for him. He indulged in seeing something different from time to time—a mirror of his own true feelings incarnate. *Then again, I'm trying to harden my nerves for tonight. Is that what I see reflected now? Encouragement to be stone-faced about the ordeal I'm about to endure.*

He smirked, silently hoping he would look just as regal tonight. The queasy feeling in his gut still hadn't eased.

"Hey, man! You alright?" Kyle came walking down the aisle. "I was a little worried when you weren't leaning against the tree."

"How long has it been?" Hotan's jaw tensed as his mind echoed one fact, *"never more than month," which means Kyle...* "How long have you remembered everything, Kyle? You remember who you are, right?"

"I…" Kyle fell silent for quite some time as he stood there, his head hung low. "I woke up remembering a lot of what I didn't know before. A day or so after the marking showed up on my back. I… I'm sorry, I didn't want you to know…"

"So, you've had all your memories back for almost three months?" Staring deep into his reflection on the marble floor, Hotan was unsure of how he should feel. *My friend has been missing this whole time. That's why his behavior seemed to be shifting as of late. He was shedding the mortal I once knew and becoming his true self.*

"Hotan, I'm sorry." Kyle's tone drastically shifted, sounding mature and experienced. It was beyond out of character for the Kyle he used to know. "I'm still your friend. I didn't want to take that from you or lose such a wonderful treasure of being your closest friend. You've done so much for me…"

"I'm not *that* Hotan." Hotan's throat tightened as he fought back the boiling upset clawing from his core. "I've done nothing."

"I'm not talking about *that* person." Kyle's feet stopped in front of him, but he couldn't face the stranger that stood before him. "I'm talking about all the times you went out of your way to help me. From saving me from being bullied to being a good friend when I had no one else to turn to. I may remember everything, but I'm one of the few who truly knows who *you* are. In my eyes, you're neither the old Hotan nor a remake of him. You're the friend I grew up with, someone who cares for those around him. I will never ask you to become anyone other than yourself."

"Kyle..." Gathering his nerve, Hotan looked up. He was shocked to see the tears streaming down Kyle's cheeks as he stood there solemn-faced. "You—"

"Please understand," Kyle cut him off as he continued his emotional plea, "I had no intentions of being misleading or deceptive. My aim was to return the friendship you've given me. It breaks my heart to see you going through this. Losing your only friend would have left you feeling alone; I know you well." Kyle rubbed the tears from his face, desperate to maintain what little composure he had. "I am so sorry you have to go through all of this. It's not fair to you. You're an infant in the terms of who we are. We mourn losing our leader, but the hardships laid upon you tug more so at my heart, my friend."

"I just wish you would have told me." Hotan was drowning in a sea of despair as he placed his hands on Kyle's shoulders. *I've lost yet another person, but perhaps...* "Thank you. Thank you for caring about our friendship above everything else. You've always been the one I feel closest to."

"Are you going to take Piedmont up on his offer?" The words fell awkwardly from Kyle's lips; the tone, accent, and presence of voice were a drastic shift. It was a stranger's voice, and it did not bring him the comfort he enjoyed in the past.

"Yeah, we're going to give it a try tonight." They sat down on the pew in silence before Hotan decided to reveal more. "We're meeting at Jake's office around midnight."

"I want to come. I want to be there to help." Kyle wasn't asking for permission. "What time should I pick you up?"

"I…" Hotan tripped on his thought, stunned at the in-charge attitude. "I'll most likely need a ride, depending how this goes." Glancing as his phone, he checked the new message. "Jake texted me to come at eleven tonight."

"I'll see you at your place then." Kyle gave him a few hearty pats on the back and left him in peace.

Sitting there in the cathedral, Hotan struggled to collect his thoughts and feelings. *That's no longer the friend I knew. No matter how much he comforts me, that's not my Kyle. He's as gone and dead as the real Hotan himself.* A gaping hole is all Hotan had left of the world he knew. *It will come down to embracing this new reality.* It had officially taken over his life. Hotan's depression sunk lower as emotions screamed inside him. The pain tugging at his heart competed with the night he lost his mother. *I am so tired of all the hurt…*

Hotan made up his mind. *I'm going to enjoy what's left of my normal life. For the remainder of this mortality, I will achieve getting my diploma and competing with my band. After that, I'll enjoy my last days of this old existence. I deserve to say farewell to the life I thought I would live before beginning as an immortal. Tonight, I will accept the help offered to me. Dammit, I feel like I'm falling into a black abyss that's swallowing my soul whole.*

I need to control the element of Rebirth. If I can do that, I can figure out what my predecessor did wrong. I have to become the replacement that Hotan's people need me to be. Talib has failed to step in, and the rest of them can only lend me a hand. I'm the key.

Someplace within me, I have the answers that none of us know. I have to turn on the light and see it.

Hotan kept Shellie in the dark again. *This is too much to share with her. Not until I can show her proof that this power I hold is something real, something tangible.* On a whim, he showed up at her house, took her out shopping, and to a fancy dinner. *A real date. I want to do this for her, for me. Just let me be normal for a few more hours, minutes, seconds.* Enjoying the moment, he allowed himself to lose track of time. He told her that he might disappear to take care of things and not to worry. *I want answers, too, but I have none to share with you.* Shellie simply smiled and encouraged him not to be gone for too long. His chest swelled with the aching of his emotions. Hotan couldn't stop thinking about it, about everything. *This might be the last time anyone sees a smile or hears a laugh from me. Not that I ever did much of either, but she always managed to get it out of me. How much am I going to change after this ordeal tonight? Will it be like Kyle? A completely different personality?*

Later, a silent ride with the strange new Kyle brought new concerns. Even Kyle's driving habits had changed. It felt wrong and foreign to Hotan as he rode beside his friend's doppelganger. Hotan couldn't even make eye contact with him, but Kyle's heavy body language spoke volumes. *He knows I hate this. That I'm mad and upset and … grieving.* Kyle felt guilty for not being that friend for Hotan anymore. The silence was suffocating. Desperate to drown out his thoughts, Hotan turned on the radio. The painful emotions boiling within him wanted him to act out, but he was stubborn. Focusing on the music, Hotan lost his thoughts to the lyrics as the rain on the highway grew thicker. Lightening shouted over the sounds of the traffic. Seether's "69 Tea" was starting, and his panicking thoughts started seeping through.

I won't die in there. I don't care if I'm lost. I just want her to be safe.

"Hotan, we're here." His body jerked away as Kyle shook his shoulder, waking him up. "You okay? You don't have to do this tonight. We can wait as long as you want."

"I'm fine." Rubbing his face, Hotan marveled that he had fallen asleep on the ride. "It's not like I've been sleeping much lately."

"Sorry, come on. Let's get this done and over with." Kyle patted him on the back as a silent form of inspiration. "This will at least keep you from broadcasting your thoughts like a radio station."

"Heh." Hotan finally looked Kyle in the eyes. "Is it really that bad? You really still hear everything?"

"Hate to say it, but yeah, man. You're very loud." Paying no heed to the rain falling around them, they grinned at each other. "Sometimes it's hit and miss now. You're improving, if I'm being honest." The front of the police headquarters was unlocked, and after flashing their badges, security waved them by. "It's clear this whole ordeal has weighed heavily on your mind and, other than that, Shellie. I never knew you put so much thinking behind everything you do."

"Oh, man." Hotan's cheeks grew hot as they walked onto the elevator.

"Don't worry. No one would dare say anything about it to you."

Hotan started to relax. *Maybe this new Kyle isn't as bad as I thought.*

"And if you decide to back out last minute, there's no shame. We're all nervous about this."

"The quicker we do this, the more I can focus on the next step." They stared at each other in silent reserve before he spoke the fear they all held. "If it even works."

Hotan took a slow, deep breath as they came to a stop on the top floor. As they walked off the elevator, he felt a tingle in his joints as his nerves began to unwind. It made each movement feel painful, even unstable. *Are my knees going to give out before I make it out of the elevator?* The dark, empty receptionist area added to the gloomy atmosphere. *An experiment was about to take place in the back room, and I'm the test subject.* Hotan walked through the valley of shadows that the hallway cast.

My tribulation is upon me, and I shall be judged before them all. Feeling miniscule in front Jacob's office doors, he thought, *This is it. There's no turning back.*

Kyle laid a heavy hand on his shoulder and pushed passed him, entering the office. *I've got you.*

"Hey there, Hotan." Jacob turned to face them. "If you want to back down for the night, don't be shy about it. This is no time to play it tough, kid."

"There's no telling what will happen when I use my powers to help focus your mind. I intend to enhance your perception, your comprehension of the power you can access." Mr. Piedmont had a solemn look on his face. "In the past, no one ever used their powers toward Hotan. I have used it to help others master their powers before, but that's as much as I've ever dared to try."

"I understand." It was getting harder to hold his composure as Hotan walked over to the chaise lounge where Mr. Piedmont stood. "Let's see if this does anything."

In silence, Hotan laid down as Jacob pulled up another chair for the old man to use. Hotan closed his eyes, too anxious to watch the taut faces surrounding him. Clammy, shaking hands gently touched his temples, making him flinch. Hotan desperately tried to steady his heartbeat. The thoughts in his head ran rampant as they spilled forward. *How bad is this going to hurt? What shape will Mr. Piedmont be in after attempting to dive into my mind? How much of my mind do I not know exists? Will this even work?*

Hotan felt himself drifting, as if free-falling into an empty void. It was a startling sensation that freed his thoughts from their despair. He felt disconnected with his body, besides the faint, warm sensation buzzing at his temples. Floating there, his mind swirled with questions. It echoed into the empty space, but his mind gave no reply. Looking around in the gray haze, nothing else resided there. As far as he could tell, nothing was happening. *This is going nowhere. I need this to work. I want it to work. I'll make it work.*

A wave shot through him. An electrifying pulse with great force resounded outward from his core. It was like a drop of water hitting a glassy surface. The waves amplified this drop a billion times, shifting it to become louder and more violent. It flowed through everything around it. His entire body heated up. Hotan was on fire, and it felt strangely right.

What's this?

Do not stop.

The gray melted away, revealing a mass of glowing, blue flames that swallowed him whole. Another wave of energy shot out.

There's something there. Something I need.

Do not let go, a voice within him urged.

Hotan's hand snatched up and grabbed a startled arm which had pulled away. Fear raced through the arm as a third pulse reverberated from Hotan's body. He drew upon something within his grip. Hotan used Mr. Piedmont's powers to his advantage, digging deeper into himself. If there was any shouting from the motion, he couldn't hear it. He focused within his own mind, not acknowledging what was going on outside of it. Something new was here. Without hesitation, he reached out to the white orb. There, inside his mind, was a burning ball of blue energy, its glow engulfing everything.

This has to be it. This has to be what I'm looking for.

Do not fail to open the door.

As his hand melded into it, another wave shot out. There was so much power there. A blinding flash took over. His body hummed as it poured over him. It was like being spoken to in every language humanly possible all at once. He desperately tried to catch the information, or at least pinpoint one line out of the flood.

What's all of this coming from so deep inside me? Why was this locked up? Was the real Hotan afraid of his own power? Is he still here?

Stop it. You are going too far. He heard an outside voice enter his thoughts, but he was too entranced to identify it.

Hotan heard someone else plead from inside the blinding light. *Keep going. Do not stop.*

I have to. I have to unlock this to fix everything. Hotan pushed further into the white energy searing his hand.

You're going to kill him if you… the outside voice buzzed in and out, ignored by him and this fractal of light.

I went too far and destroyed everything. I was selfish. The energy was burning him, attempting to push him out. *I deserve something worse than an end to—*

I won't make that mistake. Hotan broke past it, gripping the core.

Another pulse hummed louder than the ones before it. It shot out from the orb with more force, a scream riding on its wind. The original Hotan had shattered. It was true, he hadn't disappeared as he made everyone believe. He was hiding, imprisoned deep within his host, afraid of what he had done. *What in the hell did he do?*

With the former Hotan gone, he could inherit everything there was of the element of Rebirth. Information poured into him, and he could feel its knowledge within him. From everything he received, none were memories; those were not his to have. They belonged to the broken soul who had finally left him.

Stop it! Hotan, snap out of it! You have gone too far! Talib's infuriated voice ripped through him.

He could see lines of silver energy enter the glowing realm of his mind. Watching them as they glided over to him from all directions, he gently touched one. It clung to him, tugging lightly. Hotan smiled as he realized what he was seeing. *This is Talib's power creeping into my mind.* He could see it, feel it, and best of all, manipulate it. He waved his hand about, moving it around like puppet strings. The mechanics of how these powers worked were clear to him. *They are an extension of one's soul.* He felt the desperation in those appendages as Talib tried to pull him out of his own mind.

Wake up! I demand this of you! Talib shouted from the silvery tendrils.

This whole time another soul was blocking me from gaining access. There can only be one user, one soul to contain the element of Rebirth. The remnants of the old Hotan needed to be wiped out. Did Talib already know this?

Please! You need to come out! You are not physically strong enough for this! This is too much! Too soon! Talib's voice cracked and choked.

Is he crying?

Another pulse released, and Hotan gasped for air as he allowed himself to come out. He went from the comfort of the heat to the cold damp sensation of his body. Releasing Mr. Piedmont's arm, he rolled off the chaise. Hitting the floor, he succumbed to coughing and gasping for air. Frantically looking up, his vision blurred. The old man's blob staggered backward. Hotan's jaw was painfully grabbed and forced to look at another blurred face. He could only see the silver blur on top of a splotch of pale skin.

"What were you thinking?" Talib was furious, and his energy was fading quickly. "You went too far! Why? Why did you push so far?"

As everything started to go dark, Mr. Piedmont repeated, "He, he didn't let me use any of my power. I don't know how he did it!"

"Whose idea was this! This was naïve of you all!" Talib had dropped Hotan's jaw and was fuming after the others in the room. "To begin with, we have no idea how unstable he is!"

"It…" Hotan grabbed what he hoped was the back of Talib's pant leg. "It was my idea."

"You shouldn't even be conscious!" Jacob exclaimed. "Let's at least get the poor guy off the floor, Talib! We can discuss this when he wakes up."

That was the last thing he heard before going limp—no energy to even shiver the cold that consumed him.

THE BOOK OF ANCIENTS

Rebirth

Rebirth.

This is my curse.

"Ye are cursed with a curse: for ye have robbed me, even this whole nation."

Malachi 3:9

The last book of the Old Testament speaks volumes to what has happened to us and our people. My torture would not allow me to take back what I already lost, what had been robbed from me. It was clear I had cursed myself with my obsessions, yearnings to use the power given to me to fix all that was taken from us—no, from me. In the end, I fell into my own selfishness and set aside the teachings like a fool.

No matter how many times I tried, I could only use the forward momentum of Rebirth. I could bring age to all things, but no youth could be returned. There was no rewinding time to undo what was done. Even if I had accomplished this feat, it would not have filled the void in my heart. My curse had eaten my heart and soul by this point, and I have spent decades, centuries, repenting for the events I set into motion.

I blame myself. It was my doing that placed us all in purgatory. Perhaps I really did notice my powers first, but I was consumed by grief. The obsession I had over the loss of my wife had taken its hold. Our powers originated from my element, that much I can be sure of. It was not my intention to curse the others, to spread this disease that my corruption created. Perhaps trying to be mindful of everyone else was how I accidentally imposed the abilities on them. Constantly, I reminded myself to push back my sorrows and focus on those looking to me as a leader.

I failed.

Blinded by greed, I did not heed any of the warning signs. Instead, I spread my wickedness onto the innocent lives who were closest to me. Talib tried so many times to comfort me, but seeing him with his wife, Saphellia, ravaged my mind with jealous thoughts. The drowning depression of images of my wife, pregnant with our unborn son, followed. She almost made it here with me, but the sea swallowed her.

Where did I fail?

I wish I had been the one who drowned in that storm. If I had not survived, then the doom that I unleashed on Earth would have never come into existence.

I gave birth to Death.

Its rage in consuming the masses riddles the history books. I have sinned more times than I want to confess. I write this as an act of repentance. Death has followed my trail, seeking me out across lands, old and new. The element of Rebirth stirs within me as he gets ever closer. These people came to a new land, but I must find a means to persuade them to leave. I came here to separate myself from civilization in hopes of avoiding a mass killing yet again.

Talib is here, seeking to find me. Perhaps I should give up hiding from him. If any element was best suited for persuasion, it is Judgment. He does not know about Death. I pray I never have to explain my selfish actions. Maybe he knows of my Death and what is to come in this new world?

Before leaving our paradise, I made a grave mistake and hope to right the wrong. It was immoral for me to bring Death into this world and then cast him out of paradise. I am not God. It was not my place to decide who stays or goes. There is no shaking the feeling that this action is the reason none of us will ever be allowed to rediscover that island. This is why Malachi spoke: "I will not open you the windows of heaven." This is the warning and end result of what happened.

Centuries of thinking and planning and waiting have gone into this moment. In case it fails, I hope this book provides some light on the matter. This is not a request for forgiveness, nor hopes for understanding. My only wish is to confess my sins, to explain what I have done in hopes of stopping the plague I have fueled over thousands of years.

Talib, I am sorry I failed to take in your words of wisdom. If I had not been blinded by grief, perhaps none of this would have transpired. Even after bestowing the gift of Judgment on you, I still would not allow your power to persuade me. I was stubborn and ignorant. From you, I wish to be forgiven for what I have done and will do after I close this book for the final time.

Death has a name.

He calls himself Iapetos.

I cast him out from our island, and he raged war among the people. They called him a titan, a god of sorts, who aimed to defy his father according to the myths and histories from the Greeks. There are no words to describe the pain I feel to see his anger echoed in the history books so clearly.

I am his father.

It was me who willed him to life.

It matters not if it was unintentional. In a moment of greed, I attempted to bring my wife back and instead was greeted by a strange man claiming to be my son. Crawling out of the ocean, pale and shivering, he reached out to me with those dark, sorrowful eyes. My selfishness darkened my heart.

Enraged, I exiled him.

I was naïve to think that a power I could only control in a forward motion would not bring life to the unborn child. Why did I long for her over my own child? May she forgive me for casting our child to the side. Due to his condition, he had become the embodiment of Death.

There are twenty-one immortals in total.

After what happens when I face Iapetos for one final time, there may be only twenty. The things I have spent centuries deciding and experimenting with will be put to action here in the new world. One of us will dissolve into the unknown. Whether my power will be passed on to a new holder is a mystery still even to me. If that is the case, I pray he finds this journal and knows that I never intended for anyone to carry my curse as I have.

If I fail, may God protect the poor soul that will be met with vengeance intended for me. I am the one who brought Death to this world. I allowed him to consume so many lives. History may have labelled these atrocities as natural and man-made, but I know the truth. These waves of mass deaths were intended to ensnare me, but Iapetos failed.

Death cannot claim Rebirth,
and Rebirth cannot claim Death.

19

THE KILL

"Do you think he'll ever wake up?" Hotan could hear Kyle, but he couldn't respond. "That was the scariest thing to feel, let alone see. I've never seen anyone's powers pulse out in waves like that."

"I have no idea." Talib's voice was much softer than the last time Hotan heard it. "To be honest, I am not sure what he did or what exactly happened."

"This is my fault. I shouldn't have even tried." Mr. Piedmont's voice was heavy with guilt. "But he grabbed me when I pulled back. I still don't understand how he was used my powers on his own. It was amazing. I used none of my energy source. All that power. I had no idea he was that strong."

"I never knew much about my brother's abilities to begin with." Talib sighed, and Hotan felt a rag on his forehead, warm and comforting to the touch. "It was dangerous to attempt. Far as I knew, he was unstable. His power would rise and drop sporadically. I was trying to find a way to stabilize it before attempting to help him learn his abilities. He was a ticking time bomb."

"What kind of readings are you getting now?" Kyle mumbled as if hating to ask the question. "Is he… Is he okay?"

"Well…" Talib leaned back in a chair which gave out a mild groan. "He has been the most stable I have ever felt. I do not think my brother ever got his powers to lie as calmly as I feel Hotan has done. At the same time, it has made it hard for me to go in and feel around. He has managed to seal every leak which he had prior."

"You can't get in?" Mr. Piedmont asked. "You, of all immortals, can't find a crack?"

"Indeed, I cannot." Talib sighed again in frustration. "I have no idea when he will come to. It could be weeks, months, possibly longer. The waves of energy he released were massive. I have no idea how his body managed to handle the payload like it did. I am unable to even come close to one of those waves in power. You would think it would tear someone apart."

"My word…" Mr. Piedmont was rendered speechless.

"He's been down for over a week," Kyle's insisted. "Pushing two weeks in fact."

Two weeks! He was frantic at the information, but Hotan's body wouldn't twitch, and he was unable to open his eyes. Hotan's hearing and thoughts remained. *I've been unconscious for two weeks!*

"Oh my God!" Kyle exclaimed in excitement. "Look at that! He's awake!"

I can't move! They could hear him. *I can't do anything!*

"I would hope not," Talib scoffed. "You put your body through an immense exposure. The fact that you are awake is a miracle. We can only assume your power kept you from dying after the stunt you pulled."

"Don't be so harsh," Mr. Piedmont reprimanded Talib and released a sigh. It was as if he had been holding his breath for quite some time. "It is a relief to know you're okay! You gave us quite the scare, sonny."

You think not being able to move or open your eyes is okay? How do I fix this? I've wasted so much time. Is there any way to recover faster?

"Yeah, to take it easy." Kyle giggled. "Your mind obviously sustained the onslaught, but your body will need much longer to recover, buddy. Guess you'll be stuck here until you can get moving again."

Where is here anyway? I can't look around, help me out. It was depressing to know he couldn't speed up the process. *This is going to be a long road to recovery.*

"You are at my home." Talib did not give up his stern voice. "You will stay here for a while until we can get you back on your feet."

Oh, this sucks. If only I could sigh. It doesn't feel right not being able to sigh.

"I am the only one who has the time and space for it, as well as experience." Hotan could hear Talib leaving his chair. "Come on, everyone. He will never get to sleep knowing we are in the room. The sooner he goes back to sleep, the quicker his body can heal."

"Aw, man. Well, I guess we can talk later, Hotan." From the sound of his voice, Kyle was on the other side of him. "You don't have to push so hard, Talib!"

"Go!"

Hotan heard the door click closed.

At least I have time to piece together what exactly I managed to do for myself. It all happened so fast that night. The original Hotan had used what was left of his spirit to seal up a majority of the Rebirth element within his mind? No, body. That move caused the instability, among other issues. The old Hotan had grown afraid of his own powers, and now that they flow through my body without limits, I understand why. It's like sharing my body with something alive and godlike. His stomach turned as another thought surfaced.

Hotan was still in there. He was still alive in a way. When I unlocked the element, he shattered. I killed the last remnants of Talib's true brother, and in doing so, he died by my hand. How can I justify doing something so harsh? Was it even my place to take control of my own inheritance with brute force? The fact of the matter is that two people cannot share the same mind and body. It was causing a dangerous issue that could have ended a million times worse.

Hotan was far from knowing how to use his abilities, but there was one advantage he had gained: Any powers he had witnessed or been in contact with were now his own. *I can copy or manipulate anyone's abilities. That became clear when Talib attempted to pull me out while I was hijacking Mr. Piedmont's abilities. I may never master Rebirth, but at least I have a defense mechanism.* On top of that, he had sealed his mind. No more leaking his every thought to Geliah or whoever else had an open ear. Another advantage he obtained was that he could feel when someone attempted to use their abilities on him. Geliah's abilities would not be able to tweak Hotan's behavior. This freed him of the panic he felt about confronting both Geliah and Talib. He may be able to distort more information with mastering this new copycat ability.

Another attempt to move warranted nothing, not even a finger twitch. His body felt cold and dead to him. It was quite different from the fiery warmth the powers gave him when he released the white orb. It wasn't the mild shiver he had experienced after the church. Even his heart felt heavy with an icy, dead sensation. *This is the risk all the Levites face when overusing their ability. Lilly was so brave to even consider pushing herself too hard at the risk of enduring this lifeless sensation. Stamina was an excessively significant factor and perhaps came from their survival when they first inherited their abilities. In today's world, they haven't endured such a physical test, and it's a dangerous issue when using the elements.*

"I assume you are still awake." Talib hadn't left the room. While Hotan was startled, the jolt didn't echo to his body. "We need to talk."

Hotan's heart thudded hard, but he was relieved that Talib could no longer hear his inner thoughts. He turned his focus to his brother. *Well, I can't do much else. How must I endure these talks with you?*

"First off, what the hell were you thinking? You should have come to me," Talib said, his voice still soft and sincere; this wasn't the lecture he'd expected. "You could have killed someone else."

I had to do something. I was leaking information! My mind was wide open for anyone to just waltz right in. I need all the help I can get and in any form. It felt like the right thing to do. The urge to bite his lip went unanswered. Hotan thought to himself, *I just want to at least be able to give him a nasty glare! I need to push information out of Talib if I can.* He pushed to continue his reply to Talib. *I had no reason to come to you for permission. You've left me one time too many on the side, lacking information.*

"Consider your experiment a success then." The words were bitter as they left Talib's mouth. "You took advantage of the situation. I have no idea what exactly happened in there. You obviously waved me to the side and came out without my assistance. Congratulations. You won."

You could feel that, huh? Hotan longed to shoot a smirk at Talib. *I could see and feel it unlike before. I realized then that it is my sole choice to allow it, manipulate it, or even throw it back. You were desperate, very desperate.*

"You were sending out large waves of energy. You also had poor Mr. Piedmont's arm in your grasp." Talib sighed again. "And let us not forget that you have never previously expanded your powers. As far as I could tell, you were good as dead."

It's not like anyone died. Mr. Piedmont is still alive and breathing, as well as everyone else who was there. Hotan was annoyed. *Did you seriously come in here to lecture me against my will? I can't even move or look at anything!*

"Hotan." His voice sounded awkward, breaking slightly. "Hotan died. Someone died. Don't you ever forget that fact."

You knew? You knew he was still there? Why didn't you tell me? There was only the sound of a slamming door. *What have I done…*

A sickening sensation rolled itself into knots in his stomach. *Talib had known his brother was there the whole time. No wonder he struggled with how to deal with the situation. How could anyone choose a stranger over his own brother?*

I made the call that night to clear my mind and body of the old Hotan. Poor Talib has no chance of rescuing his brother now. He's dead. He won't be able to explain to anyone what happened. How can I ever justify killing off what was left of their beloved leader? I made a selfish move to gain access to this power. There has to be an answer among the information I absorbed from him to make this better. The new puzzle is how to open Pandora's box and obtain the knowledge and hope still held within my soul.

With much effort, Hotan cracked his eyes open. Hours passed before he managed to blink away the blurry eyesight. Focusing slowly, he realized he was on his side. *Did I do that? That has to be a good sign. How I managed it is a wonder since it takes all I have to slightly shift my fingers. Progress.* After the solar flare coming from the window started to recede, Hotan realized someone was in the room with him. She stood with her back to him, a long, loose braid of brown hair dangling from the center of her red dress. He could barely see her side profile, but she sipped from a dainty teacup while staring out the window. Moreover, he was fully aware he was no longer colorblind. Everything greeted his eyes in a symphony of colors. *Colors!*

"Good afternoon," she cooed elegantly without moving a muscle. "So sorry about Talib the other day."

There was no use in talking aloud; he still had a tough time moving his eyelids, let alone using his mouth and vocal cords. *I should be the one apologizing. I should have at least told him what I planned to attempt.*

"I don't blame you." Her movements were quiet and smooth as she seated herself in the chair next to him. "Talib lost his brother years ago. All that remained was a broken shell who gave up on life after losing his wife. You needed answers, and you went for it. I would have done the same. Honestly, I think we all would have taken the same path as you did, Hotan. Please don't let your guilt consume you while so many depend on your swift recovery."

He took it hard. She was beautiful with her tall features and big hazel eyes. *I had no idea that Hotan was still there. It was one last fragment of a long-lost puzzle.*

"Talib isn't as hard as he used to be." Her smile was comforting. "Centuries of being alone have damaged the wall he used to have. None of you knew that Talib was hiding the fact that a small piece of his brother remained. Hotan should have let the process complete itself. If he had, we probably would have never woken up."

I never thought of that. Pondering a moment on the concept, he finally realized she was right. *In fact, if he had dissolved completely and I had acquired the power out right, there would have never been instability of power. His power was the engine that kept the process of reincarnation going. The moment his abilities started fluctuating, it lost its ebb and started choking itself out. It still leaves out why he felt the need to do a partial reincarnation.*

"Ah, yes. You're right on that. Why he even needed a rebirth of his being is beyond us all." Sighing, she took another sip of her tea. "Just please don't be too upset with Talib's rant. You must understand he feels responsible for this mess, as well as other things."

But how could he stop any of it? Finally, Hotan was able to sigh! *I practically killed his brother.*

"Oh no." Setting her cup in its saucer, she leaned close to his face, smiling the whole time. "He was more afraid of losing you, my dear. You're so much like the original Hotan, before we were forced from our homes all those centuries ago. Talib had already come to terms with losing his brother, but losing you too would have been too much for him."

Of losing me? Hotan was shocked. He barely knew Talib; they were strangers, not even close to being friends. *Why me?*

"He's known you far longer than you ever could imagine, Hotan. I'll never forget the day when he told me that he had discovered you." She leaned back in her chair, her gentle smile mesmerizing him as she continued. "He was walking the neighborhood where you and your mother lived. You were just a small thing then, but there was no doubt who you were. He watched you intensely, but even that early on, he knew something was wrong. You were different, and his true brother was missing."

Why did he wait so long to show himself? If he cared so much, where was he when my mom died? I had no one, no one at all. He wanted to roll over and give her the cold shoulder, but he couldn't get himself to budge. *Why did he keep me in the dark on everything?*

"I wish I knew." Her smile faded. "Only Talib knows why he did things the way he did. Maybe he was afraid of pushing you away. He worked so hard to be there for his brother at every turn, and it got him nowhere. With you, he saw a second chance and tried doing the opposite, only to get nowhere again. Just be easy on him, for me."

Easier said than done, you know. He's edgier than I am these days. He managed another sigh, much to his relief. *You're Saphellia, his wife?*

"Yes. It's a pleasure to meet you, face to face." Gracefully, she stood up and floated out of his view. "Get some rest. You'll need to be back on your feet as soon as possible."

Thank you for the information and talk. He closed his eyes, feeling the exhaustion creep back into him. *I'll do my best not to give the old man a hard time.*

"Thank you. Call me if you need anything." The door shut, and he let himself drift off once more.

Sleep is the only recovery.

The sound of giggling brought Hotan swiftly out of his slumber. It sounded like a small child. He was able to open his eyes without much difficulty, but it was dark. Nothing could be seen beyond his bed. He managed to tilt his head one way, then stiffly the other way, attempting to see if someone was in the room with him. He saw nothing. At least he was on his back, allowing him the freedom to look around. Taking in a deep breath and closing his eyes, he felt like a kid again—afraid of the dark. Sounds of books hitting the floor from a shelf jerked him out of his peaceful regime. Another round of giggling followed as foot-steps echoed all around. Every hair on his body stood on end.

What is going on?

It was the basement all over again. It was no use; he couldn't get his voice to come out at all. A moment of silence added to the eerie atmosphere as Hotan felt imprisoned by his own body.

Who's there?

He stared hard in the direction of the noise. It was so dark; he couldn't see the door in that direction. The chair behind him squeaked, but he was too slow to catch what was sitting there. At least he could make out the chair where Saphellia had sat. He thought about the time Kyle saw in the dark. Concentrating, he hoped to recall that ability. *It's pointless. My body won't give me room to use any powers.* His skin rippled with a chill as some-thing on the foot of the bed walked toward his head. He spun around, panic engulfing his mind in his helpless state.

Oh, thank God… Relief gushed over him as he watched a black cat with yellow eyes approach. *I feel like an idiot.* Grinning, he exchanged glares with the feline as it sat down next to his face. It was a petite thing, possibly still a kitten, sitting silently next to him. Releasing a sigh, he closed his eyes. *I feel so stupid…*

"Why?" Every nerve melted as fear rushed back in reply to the tiny voice. "Why do you feel so stupid?"

What in hell is going on! Who's in here? The cat hadn't moved as he looked around and found no signs of anyone. *The cat is blocking my view. They have to be by the door.*

"Huh? By the door?" The cat turned and looked in that direc-tion. "No, I don't see anyone over there. Are you sure?"

The cat! It's talking! Am I dreaming?

"Huh?" It turned back, nose-to-nose as it giggled like a child. "Do you not like cats? I can be something different!"

What are you? He watched as the cat leaped from the bed. *Who are you?*

"I'm Abigail." Once more, giggles filled the room. "Would you rather I be a bird?"

What do you want from me? A mourning dove landed on his chest. *Why are you here?*

"Normally, I like to play games." The bird twitched its head a few times then flew off into the dark. "But I understand you're not in the best of shape."

Obviously, since I haven't been able to move a muscle, despite how much you've startled me. Frustration fueled his fury. *I never like it when I'm being toyed with, and that still stands now. What are you, Abigail?*

"Oh, no! Don't be mad with me." She walked to the bedside; with big blue eyes and golden hair that flowed to the floor in a curly mass, she revealed herself: an angelic child. "I came to make you feel better! Honest!"

Make me feel better? He was astonished at how pale-skinned and angelic she appeared. *I'm healing. There's nothing to do. I need sleep. Are you some kind of shapeshifter?*

"Oh, there's another way." She grinned sheepishly at him, batting her eyes. "I'm the element of Body. I can change forms, as well as control many aspects of the physical kind. Your poor body, what have you done to it? It's so tired."

I overused my powers. Her smile faded, and she lifted his hand to her cheek, nuzzling it. *I went too far, in fact. I think I've been in this bed a month. I have no way of tracking the time here. It seems when I sleep, it's for days…*

"I missed you around the apartment complex. My light bulb went out in the basement again, you know." She laid his hand down on his chest. "I enjoy scurrying about and watching you work on everything. You're so good at fixing things, Mr. Hotan.

I haven't had a chance to fly to the school and watch everyone there lately. It's not worth going unless you're going to be there."

Scurrying about? You're the rat in the basement? The mourning dove I see all the time? He thought to himself, *Abigail competes with Tina in the ballpark of insanity. So, I did hear giggling in the basement after all!*

"Sorry if I spooked you. It's so much fun travelling from place-to-place through the walls as a mouse or rat. You'd be so surprised of the things I find!" She clapped her hands gleefully. "I put them in the boxes there. Did you get the photo album? It had been thrown out, but the man in the pictures looked so much like you!"

The photo album had been tossed? You rescued it? The gold chain felt heavier around his neck. *Thank you, it meant a lot to me to have that.*

"Oh, it's nothing." Snickering, she snuggled herself onto the bed against him, once more nose-to-nose with him. "I need to fix you, but I want one thing in return."

What do you want? There is a catch after all. When will I ever be able to do something without a price to pay?

"Kiss me." He didn't hear her voice as he watched her eyes sadden and tear up, and she repeated the request louder, "Kiss me like a lover would."

Kiss you? That's a strange request and rather awkward. What would Shellie think? I don't understand why you want me to kiss you like that?

"You must understand, I was a small child when I became an immortal. Doomed forever to childhood." Her eyes spoke of the depths of her depression as her singsong voice dwindled. "I'm trapped at this age for eternity. I have lived like this for over four thousand years, and I have always looked up to Hotan. Admired how handsome he was … and how you are, too. I want to know what it's like to be kissed like a lover, not loved like the child I appear to be."

I'm so sorry, Abigail. Tears streamed down her cheeks as she looked away. *I'm sorry that you've been stuck as a child all this time. How horrible. I will do it, but you'll have to do me a favor. If you want this as sincerely as possible, I have to ask you to change your appearance. As horrible as that may sound, it's the best way for me.*

"You will?" She perked up, looking back at him. "Anything! Anything to make it feel as real as possible!"

I need you to look like Shellie. He kicked himself, but a month had passed. He had no clue if Shellie was okay out there with Geliah and Cassandra on the hunt for him. *I need you to look like the girl I love.*

"Okay." Abigail walked off into the dark once more. "It seems only right. That way, you are staying true to her. I'll honor your request, Mr. Hotan."

I hate to think what Shellie would do if she— His thoughts ceased as the Shellie doppelganger came to the side of the bed, including those wonderful emerald-green eyes. *My God, you... Not one detail missed.*

"You think about her a lot. It wasn't hard to hit all the details." Abagail leaned close, their lips hovering. The warmth from her nearness begged his own lips to meet hers, and he bit his bottom lip. "Sorry to ask this of you, I know it's selfish and—"

I'm the sorry one. Closing his eyes, Hotan's heart ached as he let his passion take over. *Please forgive me, Shellie.*

Their lips pressed firm as he sat up slowly, cradling her in his arms and deepening the kiss. *I miss Shellie terribly.* After his recent emotional blows, allowing himself to drink in the sight of the doppelganger didn't take much, though the guilt didn't let go of his heart. The heat of her lips and the lonesome compassion that ebbed from her was overwhelming and familiar. *They look alike, but her kiss is so much like my own…*

Abigail pulled away before he did, hid within the shadows of the room, and left him sitting there in bewilderment. *How can she…* Her centuries of loneliness still stung on his lips. "I had no idea someone could suffer so deeply," he muttered, touching his lips, shaken by the moment.

"Thank you," she sobbed. "Thank you for being true to your end of the deal. You gave me much more than you should have."

"It was only fair." Clenching his fists in front of him, he marveled at the ease in which he could move. "Thank you for healing me. I feel like I still owe you, considering this was quite the job to handle."

"Talib has no idea how powerful I am." Sniffling, a little girl came back into the moonlight with her straight black hair flowing to the floor and big brown eyes filling with large tears. *Before she was still pretending and changing into things that she thought were pleasant to look at. Now, now I see what she really looks like.* "But I stay in the dark, trapped in the body of a small child. My body doesn't feel the effects of using my powers, for it is the advantage of my power. Thank you. Thank you for the lover's kiss."

"Abigail." Vanishing before his eyes, she was gone. "I will find a way to fix it. I promise. The old Hotan may have neglected your condition, but I know rebirth can fix this for you. I can fix this for you … one day."

Hotan sat, wide awake, in the bed for hours wide. *Should I stay?* He paced the room, still dazed by his encounter with Abigail. *What a horrible fate.* The powers each came with a heavy price. He too shared the pang of the poison as it destroyed his own way of life. *We truly only have each other to depend on, under the circumstances.* Settling into the chair, he reflected on all he had learned. He still couldn't forget the kiss. *What power does she hold to be able to use it in the way she has on me? I didn't even feel it as it worked through my body. Maybe my love for Shellie blinded me to it. Or perhaps the weight of Abigail's sorrow…*

"Oh, my!" Startled by the voice, Hotan jerked up from the chair. "Well, that's a surprise not to see you in bed!"

"Saphellia." Hotan had fallen asleep at some point. "It's just you…"

"Yes." Saphellia stepped over the fallen books scattered across the floor. "I can't decide if I should ask you how you healed overnight or ask what on earth was wrong with my books being on the shelf."

"Luckily, I have one answer for both." Rubbing the sleep from his face, Hotan avoided eye contact. *I feel so ashamed about that kiss. Why can't I shake it? It's not my first kiss, but something about it… Was it her power that made us feel so connected for a moment?* "Abigail was here last night."

"Abigail?" Her teacup clattered on its saucer. "It's been ages since anyone has seen her. Are you sure?"

"No mistaking it. Shapeshifting element of Body. She was kind enough to heal me." Stretching, he avoided facing her directly. *I feel like someone can see what happened on my face today.* "Amazingly, she was able to do this much healing and not break a sweat."

"And what did she want?" Sipping her tea, her stare burned through him. "She still thinks like a child at times. She always wants to trade. It's her curse: an immortal who loses to the childish tendencies her body pushes onto her."

"It was nothing." He felt his face flush. "Just a kiss."

"Ah, that's right, I remember now. She always crushed over the old Hotan." Saphellia's laugh released his tension. "Well, that was a small payment for such a big job, for sure. Shocked you're still here then. I took you for one to run off the moment your feet were working."

"Normally, I would." Hotan flopped down on the edge of the bed, staring out the open door as he sat. "But I have no idea where here is. Plus, I decided to get some rest while I still could. Start fresh during the day."

"I'm glad you stayed." She finished her tea and placed the cup on the windowsill. "In that case, let's get going. I'm sure you need a ride home and have things to tend to after being here for so long."

"But what about Talib?" Hotan followed her out the door and down a large hallway. Her brown braid swung side-to-side against her slender back. "Won't he be mad about me leaving? About you taking me home so suddenly? Plus, I think we need to talk about what exactly happened."

"Talib knows where to find you if need be." She held a door open, leading him into a large kitchen. "Plus, he's coming with us."

"He's coming with us?" The words fumbled out of Hotan's mouth. "Are you sure about that?"

"How are you walking?" Talib's voice cut the air, catching Hotan's attention. "What is going on? You were still coming in and out of heavy sleep."

"Abigail was here." Saphellia pushed past Hotan, kissing Talib on the cheek. Grabbing a set of keys from the table in front of him, she went about her agenda. "How wonderful of her to help him heal, don't you think, dear?"

"Abigail has been lost for centuries!" Hotan jumped at the clanking of the coffee cup as it splashed steaming coffee across the table. "She was the only one I could not track. She never took on the same form. Far as I knew, she was a bird half a dozen times! Or someone's pet!"

"Let's go." Hotan admired how Saphellia disregarded the reaction and floated out the door. "Let's get this poor kid home for the time being."

"Where did you find her?" Chills ran down Hotan's neck at Talib's intense glare. "You must have found her and failed to let me know."

"Look! I have no idea where she came from! All I know is she scared the shit out of me last night." Hotan bellowed back, having no patience for Talib's condescending tone. "I thought I was losing my mind when a cat appeared and started giggling, talking to me! Imagine how I felt!"

"A cat?" There was a moment of silence as they stared each other down and finally, Talib started to laugh. "A cat, huh?"

"Yeah, a talking cat." Blinking, Hotan couldn't get over the smile across Talib's face. "I wasn't sure what was going on when she woke me up."

"I guess I cannot blame you for the mischief of a little girl." The tension broke between them as Hotan ventured to the door. "Go on. I will follow you out in a moment. I want to finish my coffee first."

"Okay." *Talib is actually smiling and laughing. That little outburst was cathartic, and now, it feels we can move forward all of a sudden.*

"I told you he liked you. He really does care." Saphellia winked at Hotan as he slid into the back seat of the compact car. "And he's scared, too. I don't think you'll ever know how relieved that man is to see you walk out of the room on your own accord. He didn't think you would fully recover from your little stunt last month."

"He was probably right to think that. From how my body felt, I was going to be down for a long time." Sighing, Hotan pumped his fist, marveling that there were no remnants of the cold, heavy sensation which had hobbled him the night before. "Is it always so cold and dead feeling when you exert too much power?"

"Yes." Saphellia's breathing changed at the thought. "It is quite the opposite of what you feel when using your power. For you, it's a new sensation all around. For us, we have never known the freezing sensation until now. Deep down, we are all afraid of going too far and not knowing until it's too late. We were never limited before, and it's terrifying."

"Has anyone died from it?" He saw her shoulders slump.

"Not to our knowledge. The worst case we've seen was me. I had gotten myself in an unpleasant situation. I found myself falling off a building, and by the grace of God, somehow awakened in time to save myself. But at a heavy price."

"From falling?" His eyes widened as she told her story. "How? How did you save yourself?"

"I'm the element of Wind. I managed to call upon it to catch my fall. The sudden large expulsion of the full extent of my power put me into a deep coma." She turned, and the heat of her glare hit his soul with terrible grief. "I woke up roughly five months ago, precisely when your power peaked for the first time. When you released the first wave in the cathedral, I came soaring out of my 80-year-old coma. Otherwise, I would still be in that very same bed you found yourself in."

What can I possibly say to that? It's clear how lucky I am to be awake, let alone walking. Her rigid expression demanded that he realize the seriousness of his capabilities. *My power affects everyone, whether directed at someone or not. Train wrecks on top of train wrecks have been going on this whole time because of my powers being in limbo. Talib had too much thrown at him in such a brief time. How selfish for me not to realize how they've been riding the coattails of disaster left behind by the old Hotan. Every day, they watched their world fall apart.*

Breaking from the silent understanding, they sat lost in their own boiling pots of emotions. *The old Hotan really turned their world upside down. This whole time I've been upset with my life being a mess when these poor people have been tormented for centuries. Especially Talib.* His mind slipped, and he revealed his thoughts. *I couldn't imagine watching Shellie in a coma for 80 years. Talib I'm sorry. I had no idea.*

Let us move on then. The car door opened, and Talib shot him a quick look. "We need to get you home. I'm sure Shellie and a few others are worried about you."

"Thanks." The car ride was agonizingly quiet as Hotan lost his need for seeking out information from Talib. *He doesn't know either.*

"You said a while, but over a month?" Worry didn't even describe the look on Shellie's face as she held back tears of relief. "Over a month! Your bike was there, no one home, no signs of you anywhere! Then when you missed our shows at 7even's, I started panicking!"

"I'm sorry, Shellie." All Hotan could think of was to hug her. "It didn't go as planned. I'm lucky to even be back this soon."

"I was so scared." Her body shook as she sobbed against him. "What exactly happened to you?"

"If I could tell you, I would." Pain and sorrow filled Hotan as he held her tight, still feeling the guilt from kissing Abigail. "It's done and over with. For now, I can take some time to heal."

"Heal? How badly were you hurt?" Her green eyes were so wonderful to see. "Hotan, you can't be serious? You're going to kill yourself going on like this."

"It's complicated." For the first time, he saw her fully with no fear of it fading away: her peachy skin, her brown hair that gave a shimmer of red in the sunlight, her rosy lips. "Let's just say, I'm feeling better. The best part, I'm no longer colorblind."

"No longer?" His lips pressed hard against hers.

The warmth of her made his heart whirl. After being in that horrible cold dead sensation, he'd grown to enjoy the warmth. She pulled back as she wiped the last of her tears on her sleeve. Regaining her composure, she managed a smile.

"I wasn't alone in my struggle this time," he reassured her. "If I had tried this alone, I wouldn't be here with you. That much I'm sure of."

"You can see color, you say." Amused, she looked intensely into his silver eyes. "Then what does my shirt look like."

"It's green with red stripes." Watching her eyes widen, he couldn't help but smile. "And your watch is blue, and the house is a pinkish color like a conch shell. What a horrible color for a house."

"How on earth were you able to—" She couldn't find the words to ask. "Will I ever know what happened to you this past month?"

"No, I don't even want to think about it. All that matters is I'm back. I want to take some time to focus on my life for a change. I learned a valuable lesson, not to rush things, and I plan to slow down. How did you guys manage without me at 7even's?"

"Well, we got lucky. Hisota showed every night, and with Metsy helping, we were able to put on a decent show. Still was lacking, didn't do many of our usual songs. We all agreed there are just some that you sing, and we couldn't possibly do even half as well." She came in for another hug. "We've all been so worried about you! Kyle insisted that he had heard from you, and you would be back soon."

"Sounds like you were the most worried about me." Sighing, he kissed her passionately again. "I'm heading home. I need to get some rest, but I'll see you tomorrow, Shellie. Love you."

"See you tomorrow." With one more squeeze, she reluctantly let him go. Hearing the exhaustion in his voice, she knew he needed the rest. "I love you, too."

It was nice being in his apartment again. Small, quiet, and dark. It was just as he had left it over a month ago. Dropping onto his couch, he stared up at the ceiling as he mulled over all the information he had obtained. There was so much to consider, and he now realized how much his power affected the others. Chills crawled across his skin. He was pulling the strings and jerking others in several directions. *Hotan must have known he was able to do this, but he lacked the will power to move past losing his family. This has to be what started this mess.*

Rubbing the cold sensation back out of his arms, he sat up, staring at the photo album on the table. *Abigail retrieved this from the trash. I was never supposed to see this album. Thanks to a twist in destiny and pure luck, I am able to have something of my mother's.* The dainty necklace and charm he wore made itself known to him constantly. Pulling it out of his shirt, he looked it over. *She had thrown this out, but I remember her wearing religiously at one point. It was also a constant reminder of who had broken her: the nameless father who smiled so smugly in all the photos and fueled my hatred for the ruined lives we lived.*

A voice interrupted his thoughts. *What have you done?* Immediately, he knew it was Callan. *What have you started?*

It's been a while since we last spoke. Lugging himself off the couch, he started the shower, hot water blazing. *I've gotten my power under control.*

Geliah is pissed. The voice sounded shaken. *He's tearing the place apart. He's been unable to track you for a few weeks now.*

And that's bad? He jerked his shirt off, freeing himself from clothes worn for God knows how long. *I needed to seal the leaks, and I guess he noticed. Good.*

Be careful. He will not keep his promise. Staring at himself in the mirror as he listened to Callan's words, he knew what that promise was. The same one that Talib refused to tell him about months ago. *He wasn't planning to wait a year anyway.* At least he could recall the night in the church. *I'll take it one step at a time.*

He knows about the girl. Do not underestimate him in terms of using those around you to his advantage. Hotan felt the desperation in Callan's voice as he tried to make him understand the trepidation involved. *I am stuck here. I want out, but I'm far too weak. I can't get past his ability to control my own fears. At least I can be your eyes when I'm able to push beyond his hold on me.*

I'm sorry. Hang in there; this can't continue much longer. He finally broke his gaze from his reflection and embraced the hot water that beat upon his head and muscles. *I will get you out of there.*

So many of them need my help, and I barely know what I can do. I don't even know what started the whole mess exactly. His body relished the hot water. *I never want to feel that close to death again. It was like being trapped in a cold husk with no way out. If it wasn't for Abigail, I would still be there. I'm lucky to be conscious. Saphellia is proof that I should have been completely unreachable, comatose to the world for eternity. She spent eighty years like that, with only Talib nurturing and watching her all that* time. Naturally, Saphellia saw better than everyone else what Talib *was feeling and thinking. He is broken, heart and soul. Dealing with all this chaos and this last leg of the race proved too much for him. Talib is shutting down and closing the doors to everyone, despite the situation in front of us. His judgment has been com-promised, just as Hotan's leadership was all those centuries ago. Mistakes proved most devastating.*

He abruptly shut the water off, stuck his arms out, pushing against the tiled wall as he watched the last of the water go down the drain. He had a lot riding on his shoulders. *Hotan was right to fear making any mistakes. It cost him everything, and if I'm not cautious, I'll suffer the same fate. Being down a month was a huge set back, but at least I'm able to defend myself and communicate with ease. I have learned so much. Tomorrow, I'll sit and talk with Talib. I'm now their leader, but I'm more blind than the old Hotan ever was all his life.*

20

THE NOOSE

"Hello there, my son." It was the first time Hotan had seen a priest in the cathedral, and he slowed his steps as the man greeted him. "How may the Lord help you? Is there anything I can do for you?"

"I'm actually looking for Talib." Hotan eyed the man carefully. *There's something about him, a faint radiance coming from his very being.* "He said I could find him here. He does know I'm coming."

"Ah, yes, he is in the back. I will get him." There was no need for the three steps he made. "Oh, he must have felt your presence."

"Thank you for tending to the visitors, Lucius." Talib exchanged a bowed head with the blonde-haired priest. "It helps make it look legitimate."

"Nice touch." As Hotan watched the priest, an awareness buzzed through him as if both foreign and familiar. "Who is that? He seems … off."

"He is Lucius, the element of Light." The door echoed as it closed behind Father Lucius. "Do you remember him somehow?"

"No. I just had this overwhelming sensation. I feel like I have a built-in radar but haven't learned how to use it." Hotan sat on the pew and slid over for Talib to sit. "Every nerve in my body wanted to shout the answer, but I have no way of knowing otherwise. I didn't inherit any memories from your brother. I suppose they were his to keep."

"I hoped some information would transfer to you. I guess that was asking for too much." Talib stood in the aisle, his eyes distant and sad. "What do you need from me? You said you had some questions that you wanted to ask me in person."

"I need to find out some history. The book talks about the timeframe and where you came from, but after that, nothing." Rubbing the back of his neck, Hotan tried to be as forthright as possible. *I've accepted that he can't answer power and element questions, but he should be able to answer questions about our origins.* "In fact, I have no idea when you went into watcher mode and no clue when the first one woke up. You might have covered some of it before, but now, you have my full attention. I no longer question if this is real."

"I imagine that does leave many unanswered questions." To Hotan's relief, Talib sat down next to him. "Jacob told me you had recovered the book, and one day you might decide to share it with me. Until then, let's see how much I can assist. Are you familiar with the Bible?"

"Sort of?" Hotan hadn't spent very much time in actual church and less reading the Bible. "I know about Adam and Eve, Moses, Noah, and stuff."

"Well, that is a good start. When Moses came to the new land, thirteen tribes were divided and laid out across the land. Israel, to give you an idea of what part of the world we are from, is close to where we lived. Our tribe was the smallest, but we were given a small lot of land which happened to produce strong animals and an abundance of food. On top of that, we were promised the firstborn child from the other tribes to ensure our prosperity and continued production of priests and diplomats. In the end, there were three fates given to our people, the Levites." A sigh of remorse escaped his lips as Talib paused. "Immortality, death, or enslavement. We are labeled in the scripture as the Levites, slaves that tended to the Tabernacle for the other tribes. It is described in every existing Bible."

"It must be sad to see yourselves written out of history." Staring into Talib's silver eyes, he knew deep down there was no deception to his story. "But the few of you that escaped made it to an island. That's where you became immortal, right?"

"Yes, we called it Nirvana or our very own Eden. My brother was in a deep depression after that point. He never regained himself, despite all my efforts to soothe his heart." There was no denying how much he cared for his brother as Talib stiffened while he continued. "When we left, we hoped to show our forgiveness toward the kin of our debtors and trespassers. We split and traveled the world, far and wide. Our goal was to teach goodness and better the lives of our fellow man. Instead, we only found heartbreak. The world was soaked in greed and corruption. Lives cursed for generations for the sins they had committed in the time we were gone."

"For every good man, there always seem to be three bad ones stepping over them." Flashes of Hotan's father's pictures and Geliah crossed his mind, the anecdote still relevant. *The world is full of shitty people.* "It just sucks that it works that way, one bad apple to spoil the bunch."

"Yes, all we accomplished was teaching them better ways to hurt one another. Many wars broke out. For every good deed, five sins followed. We decided that we were speeding up the destruction of mankind. For the first time in hundreds of years, my brother spoke up. He proposed an endless cycle of reincarnation. We all agreed, except Geliah. I distorted his judgment to support my brother's will. That was my first mistake in a long line of misjudgments. My brother's despair had infected me, and after that point, I became obsessed with uncovering his wrongdoing." Talib covered his face.

"Hotan had stopped leading that whole time until that point? Where was he last before you met up? Where did he spend most of his time? Something must have happened during that time while everyone was under the spell. I have a feeling whatever started this, started with him, not you. He was hiding something. He made it clear that he had done something sinful with his power. I haven't figured out what it was, but it led to a lot of deaths," Hotan reassured Talib. *Does he know about Hotan trying to bring his wife back? Surely, he would. Do I have the right to ask?*

"Yes, I suppose it did all start with him. He had taken a vow of silence before we left Eden. He was in Greece for some time, then traveled to Japan. He spent a long time in both places, living as a hermit. He was the only immortal who did not attempt to help anyone." Hotan could see Talib thinking long and hard. "Something had startled him back on the island, and he never revealed it to me. I assumed it was something dealing with his power, but he locked that away deep in his mind. Being his brother all this time, he never said a word. He just had that deep, lost look in his eyes, and there was only fear."

What can I even say to that? Could it be that Talib doesn't remember? Has he lived too long to recall all the details over the centuries? Hotan stood, shaking Talib's hand. "Thank you. Perhaps we can talk more later."

Hotan had spent months digging through history books, but he couldn't find anything. Many folklores and myths caught his attention, but nothing was factual. Desperately hoping for a clue, he sought to find a hint written down somewhere about them, more so about Hotan. There were too many possibilities. Considering their abilities, a lot of technological advances, early medieval improvements, alchemy, all screamed that they had a hand in it. It helped that Fae had agreed to help him search through everything.

Talib revealed to him that Fae, the element of Intelligence, had been the first to awaken in the seventeenth century. He was startled to discover that the reincarnation had lasted for approximately four thousand years when her abilities awakened. Talib described how when she awoke, it was like a pin dropping in the dead silence. She had gotten herself in quite the mess when Talib had found her. The Spanish Inquisition had hit her village, and she hadn't held her tongue. Fae was quickly labeled a witch; using her power and slipping in and out of comas in attempts to save herself had only made her appear as if she were possessed.

Hotan waited for her there in the library. Frustration got to him as he flipped through yet another book in hopes of some clue, something to pop out at him. It was musky there at the table deep in the library.

Hotan grinned to himself as he recalled the librarian's face upon seeing him again. She had immediately looked behind him to see if Kyle was there. *Amazing how he made that much of an impression on her. Then again, who could have ignored his loud, crude behavior?*

"I still cannot get over how much you look like him." Fae's voice surprised him. Hotan looked up at the woman with her copper-framed glasses perched on her nose, brown hair in a bun, and a stack of books in arms. "You need to be careful not to get yourself too absorbed into something."

"Fae, right?" Hotan watched her sit down and smooth her black pencil skirt. "You look familiar."

"I hope so. You passed me in the bookshelves a few months ago when you were last here. I've been here this whole time." Separating her books across the table, she gave him a coy smirk. "Like I said though, you should've noticed me approaching, but you had engrossed yourself into the book."

"You're right. Is that normal? If we concentrate too much on something we become blind to everything else?" She seemed meticulous about the books and counted them twice. "I sensed Lucius, but I had given him my attention."

"Unfortunately, it's one of our downfalls, next to exhausting our bodies. It's also a new issue we've inherited." Sighing with satisfaction, Fae stopped fussing with her books and gave him her attention. "I've done some research, and with what I can see, Hotan, er the old Hotan, was staying low. Nothing in the books could be old Hotan's doing."

"I had no luck either." Leaning back in his chair, Hotan felt once more that he had wasted his time. "Nothing that I saw caught my attention either."

"However, I did find instances when many of us influenced cultures. I confirmed it with those I contacted about their whereabouts during those decades. Some cultures had beliefs and stories that I traced to before we left the island as well." Leaning in closer, Fae clasped her hands together and cleared her throat. "But I found some very odd information. Events similar to the ones we made, both intentionally and by mistake. Only problem, it was none of us."

"None of you? Then it had to be Hotan." Something stirred in the depths of his mind. "But I think, I think you may have found the clue I was looking for."

"Hotan's powers remained undetectable until you came along, *mon cher*. After talking to Talib though, I was able to confirm something odd. These events end in high death and destruction. Everything from mass wars to entire colonies turning up missing or dead. It started before we arrived back in the homelands and more disturbingly, continued while we were all under the spell." Her eyes commanded him to take in her next words. "But Hotan was sighted in the area just before, always leaving moments before the destruction. It is as if he were running away from something. Whatever or whoever it was slipped under Talib's radar."

"Something was hunting him down. You think it was Geliah?" He refused to break the connection with her dark blue eyes. "Or was he not awake for the majority of this either?"

"*Oui*, he has only been awake for the last 50 years. He was a bodybuilder, which gave him an advantage to use his power; his body was trained for high endurance. I have no idea if it's a person or something demonic who was chasing Hotan. I'm sorry." The muscles in her cheeks twitched. "I don't think it's gone either. I think it's still looking for him. Perhaps it's another unknown immortal? In all our years, we have never seen anything that could reflect the myths and folklores time has painted. Demons and such do not exist, but here we are. Perhaps this immortal has a tendency for doing the world harm."

"My power and appearance make it so I'm the original Hotan, essentially just a different soul. If this thing is still looking for him, then I'm sure my latest stunt gave it a clear path to find me." Hotan's body tensed. "We'll find out what we are dealing with soon enough. I released a beacon, so it's only a matter of time before it reveals itself to me."

"I'm afraid so." The atmosphere grew grim as they toiled over the information. "Please remember you're not alone. We're here for you and will help you in any way we can, *mon petit*."

"Thanks." Standing up, Hotan nodded goodbye. "Thank you for the information. I assume I can find you here at any time?"

"*Oui*, I'm always here, night or day." Fae waved goodbye, finishing with her graceful French. "*S'il vous plaît soyez prudent*." *Please be careful.*

Hotan had one more stop to make before meeting everyone at 7even's. He had missed every show, and the Battle of the Bands was a couple of weeks away. *I owe the others one last round of being part of the band before giving up my dream. There is no use in keeping such a public dream with the current circumstances. A lot of things will have to change in my life. Being immortal has its limitations and need for concealment.* He parked behind 7even's and walked to Tina's bookstore. Hotan felt the tingling sensation as he neared the little store. It would take time to get used to his new ability, to sense and hone in on who was who. *As of right now, they all feel the same to me.* Worse, he had to be careful not to get distracted. If he let his attention stray too far one way or the other, he wouldn't be aware of his surroundings.

"Hotan…" Tina's voice echoed through the musky bookstore. "You're alone now, so lonely."

"I was always alone." Once again, he couldn't see Tina anywhere. *Then again, who could make out anything among the clutter and cobwebs that fill this place.* "Where are you?"

"You had a friend in there, in your head." Books fell from a mountainous stack in the center aisle, and she came crawling over them. Stopping at the floor, lying on her back, she grinned up at him. "Where did he go, the man in the shiny ball?"

"He went away." *I had a feeling she knew more than anyone else…* Having no patience for where her conversation would lead,

Hotan laid the book on the counter along with a large bag of chocolates. "Here. I'm done with this book now. As promised, I brought chocolate."

"Chocolate!" Hugging herself as she rocked on the floor, she looked beyond happy. "Bye-Bye, Mr. Hotan."

Hotan didn't give her any chance to talk. She'd hit a sour note by mentioning her awareness that the old Hotan previously sat huddled inside his depths of his mind. *How ignorant for me not to feel it, to know it for myself.* In fact, it took all his patience to hold back the flood of anger that wanted to spill forward. *The element of Insanity knew about the issue but never spoke of it. Why did I have to be the last one to find out and destroy him? What good did it do to leave me out of the loop on that important detail?*

Nearing the club, Hotan started to pick up the tingling sensation again. *Kyle must be here already.* He hadn't seen or talked to Kyle since he'd been back on his feet. At least everyone had given him room to recover. As he passed the locker rooms, the hairs on his arms were standing on end. He wasn't just feeling one immortal but two. He paused, trying to hold the panic at bay as thoughts of Cassandra or Geliah invaded his thoughts. *No, this wasn't a threat, but who else do I know who's an immortal? Jake? Or is someone else here?* He let his mind reach out as far as he felt the energies. He was getting better at being able to block everyone except who he wanted to talk to.

Who else is here besides you? he pressed Kyle for an answer.

It's safe. I promise. Come out and see if you can tell who it is. Kyle answered reassuringly, allowing Hotan's tension to recede as he came out onto the stage with his guitar.

"Oh! Look here!" Hisota was quick on the draw as Hotan walked up to them. "I was wondering if you were part of the band anymore!"

"I could have said the same about you months ago." Searching, Hotan went from person to person, eager to figure out who the other immortal was in the group of familiar faces. "At least my excuse was for health issues. You just didn't show."

"All right, I'll back off this time." Scoffing, Hisota pulled a curly, black-haired girl to his side. "By the way, this is Charlotte."

"Nice to meet you." Waving, he took account of everyone there; *Shellie, Kyle, Hisota, Charlotte, then there is Metsy.*

"Oh, hey there, Hotan! Sorry I was busy fixing my case." Metsy squatted behind everyone on the floor with some purple duct tape. "I somehow managed to bust open this one corner, and it's driving me crazy. Luckily, I always carry purple duct tape with me. Never know."

It's you, isn't it? I can feel it strongest in your direction when I focus on you. The smirk took its place on his face as he came over and squatted next to her to assess the damage. "Need help?"

I'm so sorry. I should have said something sooner, but, well… Her smile was warm and genuine. "I got it. Thank you." *We were hoping you'd wake up. Sorry about this mess.*

It's okay, I understand. Standing up, he turned his attention to everyone else on the stage. "Let's get this show back on track. I have a new song I want to sing tonight, if you don't mind. Perfect Circle's 'The Noose.' It's slow, but I'm in the mood for something steady, even a little dark. I'm sure Kyle wouldn't mind doing it."

"It's cool with me, man." A wink went out as Kyle's green eyes glowed. "At least I get to lead the beat on that one! It's gloomy and slow, anything you want, you're the boss."

There were no signs of Cassandra or Geliah, and it made Hotan nervous. All he heard was Callan's brief, expressing warning that

Geliah was fuming with rage. *All I can do is keep an eye and ear open for any signs of them.* Hotan was more concerned about Shellie. *Would he target her?* He stayed close to her and spent as much time with her as he could. *There's no way to tell how much longer I can keep this relationship going with everything riding on my shoulders. Every day, my gut screams about the dangers and complications of being immortal now.*

Shellie became their band manager. She came to every practice and adjusted equipment. Having a set of ears with only the task of critiquing was an immense help. If it sounded off at any point, it could cost them the chance of making it to the last round. *This is the least I can do for everyone. One last round of playing with them and a chance to see how far we can go, for old time's sake.* It was going to be the last chapter of his normal life—a life his destiny would never allow him to have in the end. The event was in full swing as they came through the back doors, flashing their badges. They had gotten the call about making it to this round while Hotan was away, and now it was time to show what they could do. Hordes of people piled into the event. The energy of the sold-out show was intoxicating. At least his final goodbye to mortal life would give him a moment of feeling like a rock star. *This will answer if I even had a chance at being the mortal me.*

"Are you sure you don't want to stay backstage with us?" Kyle pleaded with Shellie among the hustle and bustle of people carrying band equipment. "It's no fun to play up here if I can't hug you right after the performance."

"No, I want to see what the audience sees." Shellie chuckled as she gave Kyle a hug. "Plus, you're always sweaty after every song. That's the grossest hug ever."

"Shellie, just be careful." Hotan adjusted the strap on his guitar as he watched her finish her hug with Kyle. *Do you think she'll be safe?*

I don't know. Kyle and him exchanged the same worried expression with each other. *It seems a little too far but...*

"You said you'll be up front, right?" Hotan reaffirmed with Shellie.

"Yes, don't worry so much!" Shellie rushed over and kissed him. "Good luck, I'll be front and center."

"All right, Shellie." Hotan grabbed her arm, swinging her back to him and gave her a kiss once more, deepening it before pulling away to whisper, "That's better. I feel luckier after that one."

"Oh! They said we're next!" Metsy was on the other side of the backstage crowd, waving her arm high to gain attention. "Get ready!"

"See you out there!" Shellie rushed off out of view, disappearing in the crowd.

"You think she'll be okay out there?" Kyle shot him a serious look. "We aren't sure where Geliah is, but with this commotion, we're all going to have a hard time sensing him."

"It's probably safer for her to be in the middle of a crowd." Hotan sighed as he watched Hisota flirt with Charlotte in a dark corner. Unlike them, he didn't have a worry in the world. "Plus, there's too much going on around here for anyone to notice what someone else is doing. It'll be for the best. I can relax if she's out there and not alone back here."

"That's true. Thank you, by the way." Kyle watched the couple as they laughed and whispered into each other's ears. "It's nice to have this farewell to a mortal way of living. It means a lot to me, too."

"I didn't know it meant that much to you. It was my dream, but I suppose for you to have been here so religiously, you must have felt just as attached." It didn't cross his mind that this last chronicle was about more than himself. "I was doing it purely for my own selfish reasons to be honest, Kyle."

"I know that," Kyle said, once more giving an encouraging smile and pat on the back. "But that doesn't mean we feel that way, too. It doesn't mean choosing for yourself was wrong at all. We're all envious of the lives that flow with the tide of time."

Metsy made it across. Compared to the other bands, their group looked like they plucked people from a hat at random. Hotan always had a grunge look, Kyle the punk rocker, Hisota the preppy boy-band singer, and now, Metsy in her Gothic style. By the time they peeled Hisota away from Charlotte, the red light was flashing, indicating staging, and they scrambled onto the stage. For their first song, they chose "So Cold" by Breaking Benjamin. It had a good slow start that quickly sped up. Hotan had always loved the lyrics to the song, making it easier for him to get into the music.

This is my goodbye to my childish dreams. To the mortal life I was lousy at living anyhow…

As Hotan looked across the crowd, he was able to spot Shellie. *Front and center as promised. She's right there next to security. If anyone tries to take her against her will, it'll be noticeable.* Hotan focused back on the music as he bounced across the stage, walking over to Metsy as they grinned ear to ear. Their excitement on the stage tingled across them all, including the audience. Clearly, Metsy used her ability as the element of Spirit to increase the positive energy across the area, making sure it was a fun time.

Amazing to think someone can persuade people to feel this.

It was a wonderful feeling when one of the stagehands informed them that they had advanced to the second round. Backstage was becoming less crowded as bands were sent home or at least out of the area. Hotan walked over to another stage-hand who directed him to a table next to the stage entrance.

"Hey, I was wondering who else made it to the second round." The curly haired girl pushed up her glasses, and Hotan recognized her as the receptionist from the radio station. "Now that there are less people back here, I figure it's worth my time to see who's who. Get a feel for what I'm up against."

"Yeah, no problem! I was just printing out the list." She handed him a paper from the printer and went back to work on her laptop. "Good luck!"

"Thanks." Hotan walked away, heading toward the rest of the band when he froze, his eyes reading one of the lines twice. "He's here."

What's wrong? Kyle's voice asked in his head; he was watching him from afar. *Are you okay?*

Geliah is here. Searching from one end to the other, he looked for any sign of Geliah. *He's here, apparently with his very own band. They are on the second-round list, and it clearly reads: "Geliah, Cassandra, and Callan." There's no mistaking it.*

How did we miss all three of them? Kyle sounded just as alarmed as Hotan. *Good thing Shellie is out in the crowd and not back here then.*

Let's hope so. They spent the next several minutes scanning for any signs of the three, but there were none to be found.

The second round moved much faster than the first. There were still no signs of Geliah or Cassandra in all the commotion, despite there being half as many bands. He wasn't worried about Callan; he only worried about Shellie's safety. Hotan couldn't get his nerves to lay still knowing the three of them had slipped in under even Kyle and Metsy's radar. *We just have to stay on high alert while finishing the task in front of us.*

Once more, the stage light beamed red, and it was their turn again. Sweat trickled down Hotan's temple as they walked out. His heart stopped. *Shellie's gone. Her spot is empty, almost as if she is still there. Geliah has Fear in effect. They are scared to touch her spot.* The people near the opening eyed it suspiciously and fought against the pushing crowd to not step foot in the void. Frantically, he searched the crowd, but the twisting in his stomach told him what he already knew. *Geliah found what he was looking for.* Without hesitation, he threw his guitar to the ground, snapping the neck in half from the force. In his moment of panic, Kyle ran out ahead of him, long out of his sight. *Right now, I'm lucky to have lost the old Kyle; having a braver one in his place is already proving its weight in gold. I have to head for the alleyway out back where I sense Kyle went.* Metsy was right behind him until she was caught by the stage manager, demanding answers for the odd reaction.

As he burst through the door, he caught sight of a column of earth slamming Kyle against the brick building across from where he stood. Flames extinguished as Kyle fell to the ground with a sickening thud. *Is he dead or passed out?* Cassandra stood, laughing, not far from his right. Her short, choppy hair bounced around her face; she wore knee-high leather boots and a provocative miniskirt, completed with a tube top, adding to her villain persona. Hotan jumped over the railing, running for the heap on the ground, hoping Kyle was alive. Much to his relief, he was breathing, but cold and clammy feeling. *He overexerted himself.* Standing, Hotan turned his full attention to Cassandra as she smiled wildly. Her dark red lips and black eyes danced as flames from a nearby trash heap whipped high into the air. Her tattoo spotted her skin, and she glowed with a faint blue aura.

They've gone out of their way to regain their endurance in order to use their powers like this. Kyle never had a chance. Maybe Talib might, but... Hotan clenched his jaw.

"What's wrong, kid? You look like you're missing something?" Cassandra slowly walked toward him. The ground beneath him quivered and rumbled. "Maybe she'll enjoy her date with Geliah."

"Where is she?" Heat rose within him as his feelings about Shellie and Kyle boiled up from his core. "I refuse to let you get away with hurting Kyle, and you'll pay for taking Shellie."

"Big words from a little punk who can't use his powers." Her left arm lifted, and he could feel his feet go with it. "I was told not to kill you, but I'm going to have some fun first."

The ground beneath him swept out from under him like a rug. He scrambled back to his feet, only to see a large column, larger than what had hit Kyle, coming right at him. He closed his eyes in fear, preparing for what was flying toward him. He heard the rumbling pile of dirt, then something caught his attention—the rev of a motorcycle. His eyes flashed open; someone was speeding in their direction. The sound interrupted the momentum of the wall of earth before it could reach him. Hisota slid his bike across the ground. He flung himself from it, rolling off to the side and sending the motorcycle skipping across the ground right for Cassandra.

Her column of dirt retracted from its current path and blocked what it could of the surprise attack. Knowing he had no time, Hotan ran straight at her. She was panting, and he could see she was at her limit as she struggled to keep her glow. Tackling her to the ground, he hit her with the force of a bus. Her head hit the asphalt as they slammed into the ground. There was no room to be soft at this point. Jumping to his feet, he was relieved to see she had passed out, whether from exertion or the smack to the head, Hotan wasn't sure. He jogged over to where he saw Hisota roll away, but as he turned around, he was limping toward him. Hisota was grinning, despite having to hold his injured arm, and they were happy to see each other safe. *I never thought I would see Hisota risk himself for anyone, but he proved me wrong. He even sacrificed his bike.* It pained Hotan to feel that he was so wrong about Hisota.

"Are you okay?" Hotan looked at Hisota wide-eyed as he took in the scrapes and cuts. "I can't believe you did that!"

"Heh." Hisota eyed Cassandra on the ground. "Who or what the hell is she?"

"It's a long story." Hotan walked back to Kyle, propping him up against the wall. "Any chance you saw Shellie?"

"No, why?" Hisota tapped Cassandra with his foot, and she moaned in response. "Good, she's out cold."

"They took her." Satisfied at how Kyle was doing, he passed Hisota and marched toward his bike. "I'm going to get her back."

"Have you lost your mind?" Hisota hobbled behind him. "Hotan, I just saw this chick move dirt like something out of a sci-fi movie! You can't be serious!"

"You don't understand. If I don't go, he'll kill her. He wants me, nothing else." Sirens screamed in the background. "Look, stay here. Make sure Kyle gets help. Metsy must've called Jacob for back up. Tell them I went to the cathedral."

"That old church next to school? Wait, who's Jacob?" Hotan's bike roared to life on the first try, and he spun it back around as he goosed it. "This is just insane!"

Let's hope I live to explain it all to you. Sorry I ever doubted you as a friend, Hisota. Hotan lay on the accelerator, leaving Hisota in the dust.

21

SO COLD

The wind whipped his hair across his face, but he paid no heed to the stinging pain. His heart pounded in his throat with each passing second. *Geliah has Shellie, and who knows what he will do.* The tires squealed at every turn as he gunned his bike, pushing it as far as it would go without losing control. The cathedral's silhouette grew taller against the night sky as he came down the last stretch. *My worst nightmare has come true. I put Shellie in trouble. No, worse, I put her very life at risk!* He skidded to a stop on the street out front, dropping his bike hard on the asphalt as he raced toward the doors. Hotan felt queasy as he held his breath, unsure of the scene that would appear before him when opened the doors.

"Finally! You've joined the party!" Geliah laughed as he jerked Shellie closer to him, causing her to squeal and sob. "I was wondering if you'd have the balls to even show up!"

"Let her go, Geliah." Hotan took a cautionary step forward, but it didn't intimidate Geliah at all. "This fight is between us. She's nothing to you."

"Oh! But she's something to you, is she not?" His amber eyes grew eager as he grinned wider, excitement trembling through him. "She does look a lot like the last one you lost."

"You might as well give up on using the past to stir my nerves. I'm not the Hotan you think I am, but I am what you're looking for." Hotan took an uneasy swallow, unable to read Geliah's thoughts or actions. *Dammit, I can't feel his power very well.* His new skills weren't doing him any good. "I don't care that you made a deal with Talib to wait a few more months. We can settle this now."

"Oh, but that would be too convenient for the both of us." He jerked Shellie's face up against his own, cheek to cheek. "Wouldn't it, my dear?"

"Please, please let me go," Shellie sobbed heavily, her green eyes terrified and wild.

"What do you want? Tell me now!" Hotan didn't break his stare on Shellie as Geliah handled her roughly. "Name it! Anything Geliah!"

"I don't think you want to pay the price," Geliah growled, his grin never faltering as he glowered at Hotan. "You see, what she's seeing now is much more frightening than me."

"How dare you." Hotan worked his way closer to Geliah, who stood below the crucifix bearing witness to the events unfolding. "What did you do to her?"

"Oh, just a simple trick." He jerked her once more, placing his blade tight against her throat and sending her into a tearful panic. "Nothing out of the ordinary, really."

"Please," Shellie begged, her voice hoarse from her long excursion through Hell. "Please Hotan, don't kill me. Please, I love you. Don't kill me, Hotan. I don't know why you're so angry with me. Whatever is going on, I can help. Just please, not this."

"You bastard!" Hotan's blood boiled at the thought of Shellie seeing him as the one threatening to take her life away. "Stop this! This is insane, it's uncalled for! You've had your fun with her! Now stop it!"

"Is it now? Uncalled for?" Geliah laughed, enjoying the game he had laid out. "Or else what? You'll use those non-existent powers of yours to stop me?"

They stood in silence. Hotan had no idea what to do, especially with the way his chest ached at the idea that he was the person causing Shellie's fear. *If I could just tell her that I'm here to rescue her. That it isn't me, that it's Geliah, but—* He knew no way of clearing the spell that held her mind and eyes. *I can't focus enough to sense how he's using his ability. What should I do? I haven't figured out my own powers. To battle Geliah now would be suicide.* Her bottom lip trembled as tears continued falling. *Suicide will have to do if it means saving Shellie. She made life worth living, no matter how horrible it seemed. Where is Talib? Even Jacob? I hate that I can't do anything. I need help, but they're all probably on the other side of town still. He made a commotion there with the crowd to pull everyone away, so he'd have me to himself.*

"Oh, that's right! It almost slipped my mind!" Geliah released Shellie, and she dropped to her knees, revealing the shackles chained to the statue behind her. "Cassandra, my dear, bring in the rest of our tea party guests!"

Who else? Who else does he have? Cassandra was passed out! I made sure of it before I left! Hotan's eyes grew wide as he watched Cassandra and Callan drag in Talib and Jacob. They were shoved to the ground, pale and barely conscious. *Jacob might have overextended his power, but Talib, too? Did they catch him off guard?* Hotan's chest tightened, realizing he was on his own. *I pray that Kyle is on his way to the hospital thanks to Cassandra's ambush earlier. I hope that means the same for Hisota.* Now, the people he depended on the most for power had failed to stop the nightmarish movie playing in front of him.

Alone, again.

"Here you go, baby." Cassandra blew Geliah a kiss as she propped her heeled boot on Talib's back, making him flinch and moan. "I believe that finishes roll call for this evening. Maybe you should have enrolled in sports, sweetheart. That tackle was weak."

"What now, oh, great wise Hotan?" Geliah's delusion continued as Hotan's blood went from boiling to ice. "You have no one left, and you were so careless; all your friends got hurt playing with us. What a shame."

"This is insane." Hotan breathed as he painfully stared from one hurt face to the other, stopping on Shellie's terrified face full of tears. "I'm so sorry. If I knew, if I could..."

"Aww, he's getting weepy on us, honey," Cassandra mocked, watching with the same lack of compassion as her lover. "Are you going to cry, little Hotan?"

"Well, I think everything is in order." Geliah walked up the steps, stood in front of the statue, and stretched out his arms. He let out an excited scream much like a singer on stage, yet primal. "Oh, am I going to love watching you be so helpless! I hate you for making me live all those futile lives, so weak and disgusting! An insult considering what we went through!"

"I'm so sorry. This is my fault. Everyone's hurt because I couldn't figure it out." Hotan started to shut down as his emotions swallowed him into the deepest and darkest place it could. "Just kill me. End it now."

"Oh? That would be too easy." Geliah took in a deep, refreshing breath as he stared him down. "I prefer to let you suffer. Let's see, I have the choice between the brother and the lover, which to start with?"

"Leave them out of it. I'm what you're after." Every muscle in his body burned as he fought not to shake in fear and anger. "Your curse was my doing, and only my death can undo it. Just kill me. Take me instead. I can't fight back; what more could you ask for?"

"Feh, you're no fun." Geliah's smile faded as he looked across the room, admiring his masterpiece of devastation. "Alright, I'll allow you to say your goodbyes before I finish you off."

"You mean it. You'll let them go?" Mouth dry, throat hurting, Hotan looked at Shellie, his heart racing in terror and hope. "After they go, we'll finish this?"

"Sure, I'll let them go. Here." Hotan flinched as keys landed at his feet. "I'll even let you unlock your girl's shackles personally. Hell, even exchange kissy faces a little for kicks! Make a good show of it!"

"It's a deal then." Hotan crouched down and picked up the keys, still watching Geliah, cautious of what he may do next. "I'll say my goodbyes, and we'll get down to business, just you and I, no one else."

"Deal." The grin on Geliah's face sent chills through him as he cautiously walked over to the heap that was Shellie. "Shellie? Are you, are you okay? It's me, the real me. I won't hurt you. I would never hurt you. God, I am so sorry. Please forgive me. Please, I'm sorry."

"Please, please don't hurt me," she mumbled as she stared at the ground, drained of willpower. "Please let me go, Hotan. Please."

"It's okay. Everything's going to be okay. Be strong." He helped her to her feet and began to undo the shackles around her ankles, his chest feeling as if it was going to explode from distress. "This nightmare will be over soon enough. I'm so sorry. I should've been there for you more. Please forgive me, Shellie."

"Hotan?" She stared at him, backing up as she stood. He placed his hands on her shoulders. "But you, you're, please Hotan."

"Please, for the love of God, forgive me." A tear slid down his cheek as he stared into her lush green eyes which had been hurt so horribly. "I never would've put you in danger like this if I had known."

"Hotan, it's really you—ugh!" A ripping agony burned through his abdomen as he watched her face contort and eyes go out of focus. "Hotan…" she stuttered.

"Shellie!" He held onto her as the horrendous metal blade removed itself, and they fell backward onto the cold marble floor. "Augh!"

Geliah stood over them. Hotan had failed to keep an eye on him and paid the ultimate price. Geliah had swooped down like a hawk, running his wicked blade through Shellie and into Hotan's own gut. The pain burned through him, and he felt the warm rush of blood as it waved over his body. He had failed to protect Shellie. She lay limp and heavy on top of him, pulse fading, as the warmth from her body drifted away to a lifeless chill. He rolled her to the side, frantically brushing hair from her face, sobbing as he shook her, ignoring his own bleeding injuries. Blood spread out around them as it crawled away from her body.

"No! Shellie! Please, please wake up." He was heartbroken. She wouldn't open her eyes, and he could feel her fading away. "Don't leave me. I need you. Don't leave me alone here. Please, why, why you?"

Hotan shook her repeatedly, desperate for some signs of life. At last, he realized she was gone. *I failed her, I lost her. Alone, I'm all alone.* She was cold, her eyes faded, no longer alive with the deep green that he had grown to admire. Shellie would never be there by his side. He was alone in the world. He hugged her bitterly limp body close to him as he cried and screamed, rage consuming him as he did so.

Geliah watched the aftermath of his deceitful act with satisfaction. The floor around Hotan slowly stained red as he rocked her in his arms, falling into a remorseful silence. *I'm so sorry, Shellie. I should have protected you. I was careless. Please forgive me. I only hope you realize it wasn't me who brought you such fear in the end. I will make Geliah pay for what he's done to you. What he has done to Kyle and everyone else. It stops now, even if it costs me my life. I will make it up to you.*

"I kept my deal. I let her go." Geliah's growing chuckle added to the wintry atmosphere. "I never said I would let her go alive! Tsk-tsk, will you hold up your end of the bargain? We made a deal! Bahahaha!"

"You!" Hotan growled as he embraced Shellie, his love. "I will do more than hold up my end of this bargain."

Hotan burned inside, both from his gushing wound and fury. Geliah pushed him too far. *He will pay for his crimes. Geliah spent years terrorizing the others and who knows how many innocents like Shellie. I'm the only one person strong enough to take him out; if only I had my powers, or at least knew what they were. I can put an end to this if I just… I want to put an end to this. He's hurt everyone I care about. I will make sure I end this.* Hotan's emotions washed over him as played out those last seconds over and over. The blood he sat in began to steam. The smell of copper and iron filled the large cathedral. Geliah watched, aroused as the blood began to boil and glow blue. He had done it; he had awakened his powers, and a fight worth fighting was upon them.

Laughter from Geliah grew more excited, seeing he had struck a nerve. "Now it's a party!"

Hotan kissed her icy lips and laid her softly on the floor as he raised himself, and steam swirled around him. Blood dripped from the gaping gash in his stomach as he clenched his fists at his sides. The glowing blue grew larger until it seemed as if he were on fire with large flames whipping toward the ceiling. Black marks crawled and veined across his skin as he looked up at Geliah with insufferable hatred. He had paid a horrible price to gain access to these powers, and he was going to make sure Geliah felt the full extent of his abilities. *I will avenge her.*

"Well, that's a pretty light show, don't you think?" Cassandra whistled as she shot a glance at Callan who remained silent. "You never say much, do you?"

"You've all made a grave mistake." Callan's dark eyes glared at her, his pale gaunt face baring a mournful look. "You two will pay for what you've done here tonight. I will not pity you for the punishment the boy will give you. There will be no mourning the loss of you or Geliah. You have tortured us all long enough."

"Now those are the kind of powers I'm talking about!" Geliah spun around. "I'm going to have a *real* fight. I love it when a plan works like clockwork!"

"I'll make short work of you, Geliah." Hotan felt power surging through him, telling him all the secrets he had been trying to find. They flooded the empty spaces within him, and for the first time in his life, he was whole. "I promise you that."

"I doubt it." Geliah raised his crimson-colored sword, still wearing Shellie's blood, and pointed it at Hotan. "I'm afraid you don't have a chance."

Despite the swiftness of Geliah's strike, it all appeared slow to Hotan. He was no longer on the same playing field; he was beyond it. The sword came quick and hard as Geliah sent a slicing cut toward his head. Hotan's body reacted on its own accord. He reached up and caught the blade with his bare hand,

and the sword rusted, crumbling from the touch. In a blink of an eye, he had aged the material in fast forward. Geliah's eyes went wide as he paled. Behind him, Cassandra cried out, and her heels cracked like lightning across the marble as she ran toward them. Hotan grabbed Geliah's throat as he stared him down, drinking up the fear he saw. He had come into his powers much further than anyone could have predicted.

"But, but how," Geliah choked.

"This will be your punishment." Hotan grinned wildly at Geliah, returning all those tortured moments. "You thought you had it bad before? This is the appropriate retribution for the crimes you committed against your own kind, and more importantly, taking her life. Enjoy your trip to Purgatory, asshole."

A scream of pain echoed through the church as Cassandra pinged off the wall of blue flames. Hotan had surrounded them in a barrier. She was next on his list after he finished with her lover. He gripped Geliah's throat tighter, cutting the air from him. There was an explosion of blue fire, accompanied by a deafening sound of something imploding. Hotan let go, allowing Geliah to fall limp on the ground. Towering over him, the only sound heard was Cassandra's hysterical crying. *It is done.*

"I refuse to lower myself to your level. I'm no monster." Hotan let out a disheartened sigh, almost regretting that his conscience wouldn't allow him to take a life in return. "But this should be a fair enough for you."

"You killed him!" Cassandra crawled over to Geliah as the flames absorbed back into Hotan. "Geliah! Geliah!"

I'm so sorry. Callan's shaken words did nothing to ease what had happened. *I couldn't do anything; I was too weak, and I—*

Geliah suddenly took in a gasp of air, desperate to refill his lungs. He began to cough and hack as he struggled to sit up. He pushed Cassandra away as he tried to recall what just happened.

Enraged by being defeated so flawlessly by a boy, he croaked, trying to regain his voice. For several minutes, Geliah gasped for air, continuing to push Cassandra to the side as she frantically tried to aid him. Hotan looked over at Callan as he released the bindings on Jake and Talib. At least his assumptions about Callan were right. *He had no intentions of aggression. Just another victim to Geliah's and Cassandra's games with no way of getting himself out.* Callan had simply done as his element would have done: flowed like water, hoping to ride the current out to peaceful waters. They exchanged reassuring nods before he returned his glance to Geliah.

Geliah wobbled weakly onto his feet. "What have you done to me?" He glowered at Hotan as he struggled to stand. "What the hell have you done!"

"I did what should have been done a long time ago. You no longer possess any power." Hotan's mournful stare gave no pity to Geliah. "And you're now truly a mortal. You are no different from all those you've ever tortured or killed over your long years. I recommend you use your time wisely. It's going to be your last before the Devil himself drags you to Hell."

"Damn you!" Geliah's balance faltered, and he fell to his knees, banging his fist onto the floor. "I'd rather be dead! Just be a man and kill me!"

"I'm glad to see you won't enjoy your time—" Hotan was interrupted as Cassandra rushed him, but he didn't flinch.

"Undo it! You have no right to take his power from him!" Cassandra pounded fists against Hotan's chest, mascara streaming down her face.

"Oh, yes. I almost forgot." Grabbing her by the wrists, Hotan looked her in the eyes.

She froze, shivering in his grip as tears fell. Just as before, a loud sucking sound consumed the cathedral. Her eyes rolled back in her head, and he released her. She fell with a thud next to Geliah, who was still submerged in his own self-pity. Geliah neglected to spare even a moment's glance in her direction as he spat curse after curse at Hotan, howling like a mad man. Geliah was still too weak, and he failed at his attempts to remain standing.

"What a shame that you throw her love for you to the side." Hotan empathized with Cassandra as he walked away, hearing her gasping and coughing on the floor behind him. "How horrible for her."

Hotan fell to his knees next to Shellie. All he could do was stare at her lifeless body as it lay cold and empty. *She's gone.* His hand reached out to close her eyelids. It hurt to see her dead and barren. He wasn't sure how much time had passed when Talib and Jacob woke up and approached the blood bath that lay around him. They gasped as they came closer to him. He couldn't rip his eyes from her lifeless body; his entire world lay there on the cold, hard floor in front of him.

Alone.

"Hotan." Jacob's voice was low and stunned as he knelt on the other side of her body. "She's gone. We need to get you out of here. I wish I could have prevented this. I tried, and I let you down. I'm so sorry."

"I let you all down." Wobbling, Talib leaned on a nearby pew. "I let my guard down. I did not want it to end this way. It should have never gone this way. Hotan, Hotan you need to leave."

Tears poured down Hotan's cheeks as he listened in silence. *They all tried so hard to stop this from happening, but it was out of everyone's control. No one was able to prevent, let alone predict, the outcome.* His anger receded, content that he gave Geliah a fitting punishment. *He hated being a mortal more than death itself.* It was all he could think of. His heart and soul wouldn't allow him to take another person's life. *Killing Geliah would have been an easy out for him, and I want him to suffer. It is only fair.*

"What should we do?" Jacob's purple eyes were watery with despair as he looked over at Talib. "He's in shock. I hate to move him, but the police are bound to be on their way. I can only do so much explaining."

"Saphellia is on her way." Sitting on the pew, Talib placed his face in his hands. "She will take him to my place. I will stick around and use my power to help smooth this over."

"I can bring her back." Hotan managed the words, choking on the tightness in his throat. Whispers murmured all the dark secrets that the element of Rebirth had to offer. "I could bring her back. I know how."

"What?" Talib looked up at Hotan as he knelt beside her. Years of fear danced in his eyes. "Bring her back?"

"I have the power to bring her back." Breaking his stare from her body, he looked Talib in the eyes. "But it wouldn't be her any-more. It wouldn't be her at all."

"What do you mean?" Jacob shuddered as he caught a glance of the wound, still dripping blood, from Hotan's abdomen. "We need to get you to the hospital, Hotan."

"It wouldn't be her anymore," Hotan muttered over and over. He was cold, tired, and broken.

"You can resurrect the dead?" Stumbling to his feet, Talib worked his way over to him and placed a heavy hand on his shoulder. "You can bring her back?"

"No, not her," Hotan murmured. "It would be another person, a look alike, a fake. Shellie would still be gone. She left. It only works if they are still here, and she left so fast… I don't under-stand why."

"Hotan." Tears slid down Jake's cheeks as he came over to help Talib pull him to his feet. They urgently increased the distance between him and Shellie's body and tugged him toward the door. "I'm so sorry, kiddo. I hate that you are… I'm sorry I was too dumb to figure this out in time. I should have tried harder to put a warrant out for his arrest, but…"

"It would be Shellie without her soul, her body holding another soul." Mumbling was the only thing Hotan could manage as they ushered him out the door and toward the car waiting outside. "Shellie is gone. I've lost her. I failed her. Alone, I am all alone."

"Jesus." Saphellia's face drained of color as she watched them drag him, soaked in blood, wound dripping. "Is he going to make it?"

"I, I don't know." Jake gave her a solemn expression. "He may be too gravely injured to even make it to the hospital. He was wounded before I even came to, and that was quite a while ago."

"Let's get him in the car quick." Saphellia jerked the backseat door open and rushed to pick up his feet to speed the process along. "Please don't die on me, kid. We've only just met!"

They dragged Hotan into the backseat. It was getting harder for him breathe, and his body felt numb and cold. *I should follow her…* He felt the pain but didn't care to give it any attention. It was the only feeling he had left that made him feel alive. *Can I die? I might be immortal, but…* Watching as they exchanged words, he stopped listening to them. He wanted to close his eyes and fade away. *Just let go.*

"Hotan!" Talib yelled, holding him by the jaw.

It hurt, so he cracked his eyes open to see why he was being disturbed. *Just let me die.*

"Heal yourself! I know you can do it. Damnit, heal yourself!" Talib's voice broke in desperation.

"Why?" Closing his eyes, Hotan was annoyed at the interruption. "I don't want to live. I'm dead."

"I said to heal yourself." Heat came crawling into him, and he didn't have the will left to fight it. "I'll make you, if I must. You hear me, Hotan? I will make you live!"

22

BROKEN

It smelled dark and musky in the apartment. Hotan allowed it to go unattended, spending most of his day on the couch or on the mattress. Bothered by the light from the window in the living room, he took another band poster and covered it. *Nothing seems bright or warm anymore.* There was just the hurt from the gaping hole where Shellie used to be. His worst fear had happened. No one even had a chance to stop it. He thought a public space was sufficient enough to discourage Geliah, but that had been a foolish comfort. *I should have been by her side.*

Geliah and Cassandra were rotting in a mental institute for an extensive list of crimes, including the murder of Shellie. He regretted not taking their lives, but he knew deep down it wouldn't have satisfied the pain of her loss. In the end, there would have been a severe recoil for using such an action. Many of his friends had come and gone, trying to take care of him or at least cheer him up. So many questions and feelings overtook him, and all he could do was sit there, letting them wash over and drown him repeatedly.

There was no denying that he had come into his immortality. He was aware of his abilities and the curse of the element of

Rebirth. *I no longer need to eat or require anything which qualifies as a normal human function.* All that remained was the body that imprisoned him there in that tiny apartment. Hotan had every right to fear his own abilities. *I'm practically a god, but it did me no good. It wasn't enough to save Shellie or even bring her back. I'm all alone in the world.*

Why did I let Talib force me to heal myself? I could have left with her that night. Instead, I allowed him to access my abilities, healing myself in a flash of blue. I was afraid of dying, deep down. What would that resolve? Laying there on the mattress, staring endlessly at the ceiling, he rubbed his abdomen. A tiny, thin scar remained where he was torn open by Geliah's blade. There may have been barely any signs of his wound, but he wouldn't forget the pain it had induced. Time had passed, but he had no idea how many months had come and gone in his sulking.

He felt broken.

Hotan managed to attend her funeral. He took his acoustic guitar and sung Seether's "Broken" in tribute. It was the only song that expressed how he felt losing her. *Never again will I see those green eyes.* It was hard seeing her parent's faces that day. *Do they blame me for not protecting her? No, they had no idea I was even there…* Sighing, he rolled to his side. A black cat with yellow eyes sat there, watching him. She had shown up immediately after Shellie's death, but he didn't have the willpower to figure out if it was really Abigail in disguise. He assumed it was, but she hadn't spoken a word to him. In fact, he hadn't even heard even a giggle. He slowly sat up, careful not to break his stare with her. Something stirred deep inside him, and he couldn't ignore it. *I made a promise, and I intend to keep it.*

"Abigail, I did promise you, didn't I?" The cat simply tilted its head at him, flicking its tail back and forth. "I'm sorry for neglecting to do as promised and not getting to it sooner."

"You've lost your love." The whiskers flicked, and the cat furrowed its brow. "It hurts so much to see you so sad." Abigail came closer, nudging her feline head on his leg. "I'm so sorry."

"There was nothing any of us could do." Shuddering, Hotan attempted to shake the wave of sorrow that engulfed him. *Their apologies bring me no comfort.* "Shellie would want me to move on, to move forward, to honor her leaving this world. How long have I allowed myself to rot here in my own torment and regret?"

"I don't think you want to know that." Changing into her true form as the dark-haired little girl, she sat next to him and leaned her head on his shoulder. "You have been here like this for a very long time."

"Several months, I suppose." Rubbing his face, he couldn't help but feel dirty and grimy. "A good six months? Tops?"

"Longer." He could barely hear her. "Over a year."

"A year." Nausea waved over him to think that he'd allowed himself to grieve in filth for that long. *I've grieved for over a year. Not eating, not living, just tormenting myself in my own private purgatory. I've punished myself enough for what happened...* "I can't sit here like this. It does no one any good. It does nothing for me, nothing for her." The weight of his shame made his chest ache.

"Hotan." Abigail sniffled, rubbing tears away from her cheeks with her fist. "I was too scared to help..."

"I'm at fault, but I've been sorry for far too long." Jerking to his feet, he headed for the shower. "I need to clean up my act. The old Hotan made this mistake, I will not follow his path of destruction. I refuse to repeat history."

Hotan could feel the grime of his lament wash off his skin, allowing it to be swallowed down the drain. *This is horrible. I should have never let myself waste away for this long. Shellie would have disapproved of a few months, but over a year is beyond mourning her loss. It's refusing to live. I didn't allow myself to grieve this long for my mother, and there is no reason for it now. It was only right to honor losing a life by living your life to the fullest. Anything other than that was disrespectful.* His skin fresh, he could feel part of the world for a fleeting moment. Shutting the shower off, he leaned his head against the shower wall, taking in deep breaths. He needed to start making plans to set himself up. *I'm immortal, but now is the time to take care of unfinished business.* If he had goals to make, this was his only moment in the never-ending life to do them as himself and not the mysterious, undying entity.

Finally, he was thinking outside of the black pool of heartache. With a towel around his waist, he walked out of the bathroom, drying his hair with a second one. Abigail's cheeks were red, and she looked away as he sat on the couch. *The poor girl is stuck in a child-like state, yearning to be an adult, fighting to be herself all this time.* There was nothing intimate or personal about having to change yourself to meet your desires. This obviously weighed on her heart heavily. His sorrow shifted for her at that moment. Despite looking away, she didn't dare move from the couch where Hotan sat enjoying being clean and awake.

The first thing I want to do is help Abigail. He leaned over and kissed the top of her head, and a pulse of power drummed from the soft touch. She turned to him in disbelief as blue steam lifted off her body. As if time itself had sped up, she started to age before him. She glared at her little hands as they slowly became the hands of an adult. *Twenty-three should be a good age for her.* Hotan walked into his bedroom with a content grin on his face.

"What, what did you do?" The steam slowly faded as she marveled over her long legs and her new arms and hands. "Is it real? Will it stay?"

"I hope this age suits you." He tossed some clothes next to her on the couch. "I'm sorry, I didn't think about your dress becoming too small after the change. Here are some clothes. Keep them. Sorry if I embarrassed you any."

"Oh?" Abigail blushed, realizing her tiny dress had survived as an awkward shirt with popped stitches and holes in a few places. "Oh, no."

"Take your time." He quickly returned to his room to give her privacy. "Feel free to use the bathroom and anything else."

There was a long moment of silence between them as he dressed and removed the poster that covered his bedroom window. As he opened his window, a cool breeze swept in, flushing out the stale air. *This is long overdue.* Hotan leaned out on the windowsill, squinting as the sun beamed brightly. *It's weird how I can feel my power snaking through me now. Whispering things to me as if revealing all its riddles, so I may do what I please with it.* The next agenda it murmured to him was to find replacements. He was holding the elements of Fear and Earth within himself, and he couldn't keep it that way if he wanted to balance his own power. *Who will I choose to become immortal and live with this curse?*

"Thank you." Abigail was beautiful with her athletic build. With dark pools for eyes and long, wavy black hair past her hips, she could have been a model in another life. "I never knew it was even possible. I don't know how I'll ever repay you. But for now, thank you."

"It's the least I can do for you. You helped me when you didn't have to." He smiled warmly at her, enjoying the red in her cheeks. "You can just continue to keep me company. I'm in no mood to be alone. Despite my state, you've been with me every second for over a year, Abigail. Thank you for making sure I was never alone. I hate being alone…"

"Thank you." She tugged at the baggy shirt and pulled up the cargo shorts, trying to adjust to her new body. "I would like to stay longer, as long as you're okay with that. I have been on my own for far too long as well. I need to … grow up some more."

"I hope it's easier now that your mind and body aren't competing with one another, causing you to regress. I hate that he didn't solve this for you sooner." She rushed him, hugging him tightly, and he found himself smiling once more. *My life is changing ever faster now. Normal life is gone, and I suppose it's time to start thinking like an immortal.* "Let's get you some better fitting clothes. You look close to Annie's size, so let's go pay her a visit. She must be worried sick over how badly I've been doing."

Abigail followed close behind him like a lost puppy. Musing over her legs and enjoying every step, he heard her giggling behind him. *At least I'm able to do something good with the powers I hold.* He felt an immortal close by as they worked their way down the stairs. Hotan had to catch Abigail a few times as she fumbled over her legs. Laughing, she grew more excited about what it was like to be in a true adult body. As he made the corner toward Annie's door, Jacob was leaning on the wall, smoking a cigarette.

"Hotan!" Jake's eyes sparkled as he saw him. "Oh, I'm so relieved to see you up and about! Out of the apartment finally!"

"Thanks, I just wish someone had pulled me out of that sooner." Hotan laughed as he watched Abigail run down the hallway, holding the shorts up as she went. "But I'm trying to make up for the lost time now."

"Who's the girl?" Jake grinned goofily as he watched her run back to Hotan, panting from the sprint. "I don't recognize you, but I do feel you're one of us. Did I miss something?"

"It's me!" Huffing, she swallowed as she slowed her breathing. "Abigail!"

"Abigail! Since when do you pose as an adult, young lady?" Jake shot a look at Hotan, then returned his stare to her. "Or did something happen?"

"Nothing like that." Heat poured over Hotan's face as he realized what Jake was insinuating. "Nothing like that at all! I used my power to age her forward a few years, so she isn't stuck as a little girl anymore. It didn't seem right, especially since I know he could have fixed it so long ago."

"Sure, but you did nothing else?" Jake winked at Hotan as he finished his cigarette, putting it out in the nearby ashtray. "Let's get Annie. She's been worried sick about you. I was running out of excuses, ya know."

"I figured as much. Plus, Abigail needs some clothes that won't fall off." They followed Jacob into the apartment where the smell of Annie's famous spaghetti filled the air. "Now, I feel hungry." *What a relief that I'm not completely void of this sensation!*

"We've got company, babe." They heard the oven closing in the kitchen.

"Who? Did you invite someone over without telling me again?" Annie laughed as she finished her task before turning to see who Jake had dragged in. "Hotan! Oh my God!"

Annie was across the apartment in a flash, hugging the air from Hotan's lungs. She had always been like a maternal big sister to him. He squeezed her back, happy to be out of his self-made prison. Allowing the warmhearted greetings to smooth over the last of the sharp edges of his sorrow, he was finally back on stable ground. It was nice to know that everyone had missed his presence and was thrilled to see him on his feet. *I was dumb to think I was alone, and they wouldn't miss me...*

"Oh, my! Who's this?" Making eye contact with Abigail, Annie pulled away from the hug to exchange a tender smile with her. "A new friend? Hi, I'm Annie."

"Not exactly, I, uh, well it's hard to explain, but if you have any spare clothes, she could really use them. Mine don't fit her very well." Scratching his head, Hotan contemplated how he was going to explain Abigail to Annie. "Her dress got ruined earlier today?"

"Her name's Abigail. She's the one I was telling you about a few days ago." Jake's voice was smooth and calm. "She's one of us."

"Oh! The little girl who turns into things." Annie nodded as she took Abigail by the hand and led her to her bedroom. "Come on, sweetie, let's take care of this."

"Wait, you told her?" Astonished, Hotan gaped at Jake, amazed once more by the man's actions. "Did you tell her about me?"

"Yup, I told her everything." Jake stared coolly at Annie's bedroom door. "There are some things in this life that are worth the risk. I genuinely love that woman, and spending a portion of this immortal life with her is worth everything to me. It's best to share everything I know with her to keep her even closer. This one is going to hurt the most though. As you may have assumed, I've loved and lost many lovers over the centuries. There are only a small few who are like Annie. They aren't kidding when they say you only find a girl like that every other century."

"Hurt the most?" Hotan asked.

The sparkle had faded from Jake's purple eyes, and they looked distant as he stared heavily at Hotan. "I always hate outliving them. Watching them slowly lose themselves or passing. I have loved many, but there's something about Annie that pulls at me. Truly one of a kind, you don't find her type very often. I know it'll hurt, but I don't want to miss out on being with her.

Sometimes the hurt is worth every minute. Remember that. I can vouch that it is better to have loved and lost than to have never loved at all. I have tried both ways…"

"I can fix that." Hotan spoke before he could stop himself. "I can make her one of us. She is a perfect fit for what I need her to be."

"You can't be serious?" The color bled from Jacob's face. "Hotan, as much as I appreciate the offer, I couldn't bear making someone live this long. It's tearing all of us apart as it is."

"I know," Hotan mumbled low as he fought the facts in his head, desperately arguing with himself on the matters that still needed to be addressed. He quarreled with the boiling power that barked its commands and needs at him like the caged animal it truly was. "But I have a problem: I need to find replacements for Cassandra and Geliah. I'm out of balance, and it wreaks havoc on me if I allow it to continue for too long. It'll start causing imbalance in everyone else as well if it goes unresolved. We need people to take over Earth and Fear."

"Replacements?" Jake ran his hand through his short blonde hair, staring hard at Annie's bedroom door. "I, I just don't know. I guess it makes sense that you merely absorbed their elements. Now, we just need to give them to better users. Better people. Damnit, to have to drag people into this curse just makes me sick to my stomach."

"She would make a great host for Earth. She is nurturing and strong." Hotan felt exhausted; thoughts bubbled over in his head repeatedly. "It has to be done. I care about Annie like a sister, almost a second mom. I don't think I could bear watching her go through this curse either, but I don't like knowing that I will eventually lose her in the end, no matter what happens."

They stood in silence, pondering over the idea. The girls came giggling out of the bedroom. Annie had dressed Abigail in a black tank top, white over shirt, and a black, frilled mini skirt. Hotan noticed once more how beautiful she was. A complete opposite of Shellie but just as attractive. The sting of her kiss that night came back to the surface, and his face heated. *Maybe I can learn to love again. Shellie would be more than happy to share me now that she is gone. She was always giving in that way. Let her be safe in the afterlife and give me courage for what I must face. Life is never-ending for me. I'm sorry, Shellie, that I won't even get to see you in the afterlife either. But I promise to pick myself up and be happy... you were always worried about me being alone, and we won't have to ever fear that fate for me.*

"I'll have to talk to her about it." Jake's voice cut through Hotan's thoughts. "It's her decision, not ours."

"I wouldn't be so cruel to force anyone into this mess. I had no choice, and I still struggle with it."

Both sighing, they turned back to the girls.

Hotan fell further back down to Earth with each passing moment. Unfortunately, he was still distracted by the whispers from his fluctuating power, telling him, screaming at him about the importance of balance. *No wonder the old Hotan struggled and fell about. Grief teamed with the malicious needs of Rebirth could break a person instantly.* He had someone for Earth in mind, but another name and face told him whom the element of Fear belonged to: Hisota. Everyone had been brought together due to the underlying currents of their immortality and power, but Hisota was not one of them. *Why was Hisota drawn to the group? Is he a predetermined replacement for Geliah? If so, this is even beyond me. Above what any of us realize, we have no control of our fates. Even with my own incredible power, I have no say in what may happen from this point. We are at the mercy of life and nature itself.*

"I'm ready." Annie's voice was solid, and the look in her eyes told him all that he needed to know.

She accepted the impossible task before her. Hotan looked from her to Hisota. With a confident nod to one another, he too confirmed that he was ready. Hisota didn't hesitate to take him up on the offer of becoming the immortal element of Fear. He was infamous for striking fear in others with his relentless bullying, yet he had set aside his own fears and stood against the unknown without pause. In Hotan's eyes, Histota had risked his own life without a shred of fear that day with Cassandra. Furthermore, out of the three friends, he was the only mortal. It seemed as if he was meant to join their ranks according to some divine plan. *I can't ignore that all the puzzle pieces fit far too well.* He had found the replacements for the elements of Earth and Fear. They were far better people than the ones who had possessed the power for all this time. Feeling confident they fit the bill, Hotan took a steadying inhale.

"Okay, here we go," Hotan said softly as he reached his hands out, one toward each of them.

Delicately, he tapped their foreheads with the palms of his hands. He couldn't keep them from shaking with the weight of their duty. Blue light filled their eyes as they gasped, and the blue flames sucked into them as if it were a breath of air. Luckily, Jacob and Kyle were behind them as they collapsed. Sweat beaded across their skin as the blue faded. *It's done, they're immortal.*

After an hour or so, they started to moan and move; relieved, everyone in the room breathed easier. Their muscles released the worried tension held during the event. Jacob snuggled closer to Annie, kissing her head as a tear slid down one cheek. *I never realized how passionate he is, and I'm glad someone with a large heart is the element of Lust, no, the element of Love. Jake moved those around him by his love, and in return, he was moved by their kinship even more so.*

"Wow." Annie rubbed her eyes as she struggled to sit up straight. "That was amazing. The warmth was… It was simply miraculous."

"You okay?" Jacob nuzzled her as he pulled her head to his chest. "You should probably take it easy and remember what we told you two."

"Yeah, yeah, be careful using our powers, we can really get ourselves in a bind." Hisota leaned onto his knees, rubbing his face. "It really feels different being like this. Exciting and frightening. I can feel… I feel the fear you all have about this. It's so strong, yet intoxicating. No wonder Geliah encouraged chaos."

"Yes, it feels like you are cursed in a way." Hotan reminded them of the powers and his own tribulations. "Just remember, there are several of us in the city. We are still missing some, but as far as we know, they are still in a state of reincarnation. I prefer we leave them alone. It's best that they enjoy it while it lasts. As more of us awaken, it will draw the remaining sleepers to us."

Electricity seemed to shoot through everyone in the room. They all stood in one swift jolt, all staring at the ceiling. The power that wafted down from above was chilling, and it didn't feel right. In fact, it didn't even feel alive. Hotan's spirit rattled as he recognized the essence of what stood on the building above them. *It's the shadow figure from my dream. Death incarnate.* He had been too drained to pay attention to the repeating dream. It had only increased since Geliah, but he ignored it, thinking it was all related to holding the element of Fear. *What or who is this bringer of death and destruction? Is it the same entity who has been hunting me for centuries? Has Death finally come to claim me?*

23

ALREADY GONE

"Talib!" Hotan made it out of the door first, scrambling onto the rooftop in time to see a pale Talib hit and slide across the gravel toward him. "No! Talib!"

Hotan rushed to him, flipping him over to see ashen skin and hazed eyes of death. *Talib's dead.* Hotan screamed, crazed with sorrow as he pounded Talib's chest. Shaking in choking sobs as he knelt there, he felt the cold and decayed aura as it approached him. Laughter rolled from the shadow figure. *I have heard that laugh time and time again in my nightmares, and I hate it. I'm tired of it. It needs to go away, forever.*

"Hotan! I shall take my revenge." The animosity in the voice gripped Hotan's soul. "I wish to thank you for my tortured life for all these centuries! I'll send you to a lonely darkness equal to the one you gave me!"

"I hate you!" *It can't be. The dark hair, the dark eyes. This has to be a nightmare. Why him? Of all the people in the world, why did the shadow figure have to be HIM!* "You, why you? Why now?"

"I have searched the world over for you!" The man in black lifted Hotan by his throat, choking off the air from his lungs.

I know who you are! You asshole! Hotan's mother's necklace broke loose as he glared into the face he had spent his entire life loathing.

"I must say, this is the first time you've stayed long enough to see me in quite some time." Gritting his teeth, the man seemed furious and filled with hatred. *This will be the last time you escape me!*

"It can't be. Not you." Hotan struggled for air; he could feel his soul being sucked out of him from the touch of the man's hand to his skin. *Why does it have to be you? If Mom knew…*

"Huh?" The sunlight was being drawn away by the black flames that whipped off the man as he picked up the small object that had broken loose under his grip. A flash of recognition made his anger falter, and he let go of Hotan. "Where did you get this?"

Landing hard, coughing and gasping, Hotan looked up bewildered at the man in the black trench coat. "You should know that already. You remember where—"

"Answer me!" The kick to the ribs sent him rolling over Talib's cold body. "How dare you come near her!"

"She was my mother! You left us behind!" Hotan's cracked rib throbbed as he desperately tried to maintain eye contact with his father, identical to the photos taken so long ago. "You left her, pregnant and helpless!"

"Your, your mother?" Fear overtook his eyes as the flames faded and he stood, shocked as feelings long forgotten made themselves known to him once more. "But, but you're my father. Hotan, you brought me back into the world only to cast me out. Ashamed of me! Cold and lonely, only death kept me company in my first days on this Earth! You are the one I have been tracking over these tormented years."

"I am not Hotan." Rolling onto his feet, he spit blood onto the rooftop; he wheezed and whined as pain shot through with each breath. "I'm your son. I was that child you thought was impossible. The son you damned to misery, cursed to be alone."

"Why would he do something so cruel to me? He left me behind … again." Hotan's father stabbed his katana deep into the rooftop, roaring like an animal.

"Tell me your name," Hotan demanded as he healed himself, building up the courage and focus he would need. "I WANT YOUR NAME, YOU BASTARD!"

"Iapetos." The dark eyes stared into him as if the Devil himself had caught sight of his soul. "Rightfully, one of the Titan Gods. Is that not what we are?"

"We are not gods. We are the cursed ones." Hotan allowed his power to let loose. It boiled out as it overfilled him. "You have brought enough destruction and agony on this Earth. I have waited a long time to meet you, and now that I know who you are, I'm not afraid."

"Not afraid?" Laughing, Iapetos stretched his arms out, revealing large, decaying wings with sparse clumps of black feathers clinging to what remained. "Oh! You should be afraid! You may be flesh and blood, but I will take that soul. It still smells like him. I can taste it. His soul will be mine!"

"My God…" Saphellia had appeared from thin air. She stood, shaking, before sliding to her knees. Fear overcame her as her eyes reflected the image of the Dark Angel. "May God have mercy on us."

"I could not care less what affairs you had with Hotan. You are dealing with me, your son, not your father."

This is the crime, the sin, and the fear that the old Hotan had hidden from us all. His older brother lay dead. People had been hurt and killed over the centuries because he hid—no, ran—from his own son whom he had brought back to life. It wasn't what he wanted. He wanted to bring Liora back, and all he got was something cold and dead, something that wanted to be with him but was cast to the side.

Iapetos had cast me to the side with the same fear and resentment. He will pay for the innocent lives he has carelessly destroyed while chasing a coward, a broken man. I will show him the man I have become… that he failed to be.

They ran at each other. Each crying out, glowering at one another, ignoring the others who had made their way to the rooftop. As they came ever closer, black and blue flames collided and blinding light sparked, blocking what happened. Light is all that they saw.

To be continued in Judgment…

BOOK CLUB DISCUSSION QUESTIONS

1. What is the significance between the element of Rebirth and how it's portrayed in the book through Hotan?
2. Did Hotan have the right to use force to take the power for himself?
3. Though Hotan expresses how alone he is in the story, do you agree with him?
4. When the Shadow Figure is revealed, was this the person you thought it would be?
5. Discuss how the story encompasses the phrases: "Facing death itself" and "Learning to live."
6. Do you think Hotan will be able to find his own sense of family without clinging to his past?
7. What do you believe the old Hotan actually did?
8. Do you think it was right for Geliah to force others out of the reincarnation spell?
9. Do you believe the old Hotan cast the spell to hide something? Or someone?
10. Talib has been silent and conflictive throughout this endeavor. Do you think he was wrong, right, or traumatized from his past?

AUTHOR BIO

Valerie Willis is the COO at 4 Horsemen Publications, Inc., an expert digital typesetter, co-host to Drinking with Authors Podcast, and an award-winning Fantasy Paranormal Romance author. Her works include a workbook series, *Writer's Bane*, starting with *Research* and *Formatting 101*, and novels inspired by mythology, superstitions, legends, folklore, fairy tales, and history such as in *The Cedric Series*. Many have experienced her hosting workshops or being a guest speaker at events where she shares her expertise in publishing, novel writing, research for fiction, worldbuilding, character development, book design, reader immersion, foreshadowing, and more.

www.WillisAuthor.com
https://linktr.ee/WillisAuthor
OR
Instagram: @WillisAuthor
Facebook: facebook.com/ValerieWillisAuthor
Twitter: @Valerie_Willis
TikTok: @willisauthor
Email: Willis.author@gmail.com

JUDGMENT

I

DIE TRYING

Present Day

I fear I have failed my brother.

The start of my inability to protect him was a slow fall from grace before I plummeted into the endless pit of despair.

The day they fell under his reincarnation spell, I should have known something was not right with Hotan. He carried a distant look in his deep, green eyes; he kept secrets from me. Ignoring it was a dire mistake that would endanger all of us, even the innocent people of the world. I was their watcher, protector. I don't know exactly what created this chaos which surrounds us now. So much has been destroyed for our sins; it makes me sick with guilt.

Decades ago, I decided I could no longer allow myself to watch without intervening. My dreams are forever haunted by the faces of my fellow Levites, seeing them reborn only to die again. My memories are filled with centuries of disasters and horrific wars. Many of these I have seen and experienced firsthand in my efforts to track the others as promised. It took centuries for me to realize that idly watching their lives was not enough. This was my mistake.

I am troubled by my brother's hidden sins. It is time I set things right. I must atone for my own failures by doing what my brother could not. Life was complicated in the beginning. I trusted Hotan, but at some point along the way, he lost trust in himself. Am I not remembering some important clues from so long ago? There are so many gaps in my mind where memories should be… Have I lived too long? Is this the cost of remaining awake, unlike the others, as time went by?

With a gasp, Talib snapped out of his darkening thoughts. A wave of power echoed through his soul with an icy sensation, stinging and pulling at him. He had associated this power with his brother in the past, but with the old Hotan dead, it meant this was another entity—one which sought out his brother and now, the new Hotan. The power tugged at him to look north toward the unseen beacon. Silence fell over him from where he stood sheltered within the cathedral. A cold sweat slithered across his temple and his jaw tightened; this power easily matched his own. *No, it is stronger.*

Swallowing back the choking sensation of fear, he whispered, "The power that haunted my brother has returned."

"What has returned? What are you talking about?" Lucius turned away from the candles by the holy water fountain to the paling gentlemen behind him. "Talib, what on earth is going on?"

"There is no time to explain." He ran down the aisle between the rows of pews, pulling off his white suit jacket in hopes of freeing himself of any physical restrictions. "It is coming for Hotan!"

With amazing agility, he slid across the black hood of an Audi A8, his silver hair flashing in the sunlight. He rolled himself upright and jerked the driver door open. There was no time to worry about the consequences for what he was about to do. The tires screamed as he floored the gas pedal. He needed to reach the source of the terrible power before it found its target. Gripping the steering wheel tighter, his palms were clammy, and his jaw ached from clenching his teeth. Every muscle in his body grew taught under the pressure of the approaching, unavoidable battle.

The power being released shared a presence similar to Rebirth but took on a more negative tone. Instead of an exertion of power and life, this one consumed it—a black hole void of compassion. He could safely concur this was the element of Death. A coldness struck deep into his core, the grip of it making breathing painful and rattling his nerves. There was no other explanation; this was an immortal who became the embodiment of a terrible element, the one element none of them truly possessed. Whether Death realized Hotan was not the same entity it had chased in the past was unknown.

The Audi raced down busy roadways, disregarding street signs, traffic lights, and even the pedestrians crossing his path. Talib let his power free, allowing it to stretch ahead like a tidal wave. This was something he had not done in hundreds of years, and unlike the others, it did not exhaust him to unleash his element to this magnitude. People were baffled as they stopped their cars at green lights, pulled their vehicles off to the side, or found themselves sitting down on the sidewalk for no apparent reason. Being able to control the element of Judgment had its advantages as his power cleared the route.

Hotan's apartment building drew closer, and he felt the presence of other Levites. Hotan, Jacob, and several others were under the cold presence which loomed above them. The demon sat on the rooftop like a vulture, waiting patiently for the perfect moment to swoop down to its meal. The weight of the immortal's presence sent chills across his skin as he caught a glimpse of the shadowy figure.

Fae, the element of Intelligence, had concluded that something had been chasing his brother all these centuries. The clues left behind in books and records left a pathway of mass destruction which devoured an unfathomable number of lives. Entire cities, nations, and cultures had been wiped out in its wake. He hadn't revealed his knowledge of the destruction, but for her to recognize it within the history books was horrifying. She pinpointed events, huge and small, with similar characteristics, but the entity responsible for all of it was still a mystery. Disappearing colonies, unexplained wars, and natural disasters all happening within isolated areas were linked to this phenomenon. It started shortly after they left the island of paradise that they had called home, and sadly, escalated at an alarming rate.

What did my brother do to create something so evil? Why did I fail to notice this was a separate entity? I was there to help him; all he needed to do was ask. Was he too ashamed of what he had done to even tell me? And now, this child who bears Hotan's legacy must face the sins of my brother before he can master his powers. Lord, this cannot be the way you want this to end. A child against a monster is never a fair fight.

He slammed on the brakes. The tires squealed in response but failed to stop fast enough. He yanked the emergency brake lever up and sent the car sliding. It turned ninety degrees before skidding to a complete stop. The air filled with the pungent smell of burnt rubber as he flew out of the car; the streets were too congested here to move all of them out of the way. Even with the aid of his powers, the bumper-to-bumper traffic left no room to move all the cars without causing injury.

Bursting into a full run, he left the car far behind. Stepping up and over car after car was proving too slow. Sprinting off to the right, he took an inhuman leap to the top of the nearest building; centuries of physical conditioning and the advantage of immortality allowed him to do the impossible. He ran with urgency toward the power source, leaping effortlessly from roof to roof, drawing closer with amazing speed. Reaching his destination, he skidded to a stop, spraying pea gravel across the rooftop. Panting, he quickly caught his breath, quelling the stinging in his lungs.

He looked wearily toward the back of a black trench coat flapping in the wind. The man's black hair gave way to the wind as he remained as motionless as a statue, unbothered that he was no longer alone. They stood there with nothing more than the slapping of the coat filling their ears. His chest ached from the frightening sensation urging him to flee. His mind flashed a lifetime's worth of glimpses reflecting those same broad shoulders.

Why do I feel like I know him? I have seen this man many times at different times and centuries, but...

The full scale of those memories and where they came from were beyond him, far out of reach. The nostalgic chaos of emotions inside his soul told him he had found the source of his brother's sins, but it was a threat he had lost memory of somewhere during his lifetime. This was the man in black which plagued the deepest reaches of his own mind and the nightmares Hotan suffered.

"Stop!" The determination in his voice was startling even to him; standing tall, he was prepared to do anything necessary to stop the element of Death. "He is not who you think he is!"

"Who are you?" Standing motionless, the deep, calm voice mused, "I've never had anyone find me. Let alone be brave enough to speak to me in that tone."

"I am Talib. I was the brother of Hotan." As his lips hit the last word, there was a change in the man's power.

He is targeting him.

"Brother of Hotan?" The man shifted to peer over his shoulder, revealing the dark pools of black which glowered back at Talib. "My, my, you definitely must be. No one carries the genetic coding for silver hair in today's time. I guess I can call you uncle."

"Uncle?" It all made perfect sense. *I have been so blind.*

My brother attempted to bring her back, but that is not what came to him. There is no time to be shocked or question what was revealed in this instant. I can only take the information and run with it…

"I am so sorry. My brother, your father, is gone. I cannot undo what crimes have been committed against you, but please understand, this boy is not who you think he is. The person within this building is someone who looks like him and holds his powers, but Hotan's soul is gone. The boy knows nothing of my brother's wrongdoings. If you wish, we could finish that business here between the two of us."

"Then a look-alike will suffice." Sneering, he turned around to face him, his wild smile sending chills through Talib's entire being. "And will you attempt to stop me?"

"Yes." His body tensed. He planned to use the small revolver tucked in his back holster, and the handle of the gun urged him to shoot. "You have no right to take innocent lives. So many have been killed by your hand and had nothing to do with your endeavors to kill my brother. It must end; I will not allow this slaughter to continue further."

"Sorry, I guess I have a nasty habit of losing my temper." The nonchalant shrug was followed by a step forward. "Do you even realize who or what you are facing, Uncle?"

He is trying to play mind games with me; it won't work.

"I do not care what or who you are." He pulled the gun, and the man responded, black flames leaping off his skin, crawling outward like snakes. "You will be stopped here. I am his protector, and I owe that child my life for what my own brother has done to him."

"So be it, Uncle. Know that Iapetos, harbinger of Death itself, was the one who ended your life. Reborn from the cold womb of the dead and rejected by its own father." The black irises became glassy as he continued his growling speech. Another step closer sent Talib's heart racing. "I will not be satisfied until I have sucked the life from the soul that once was my father's. I will devour it; it will be mine."

"It pains me to know such evil was created by my own flesh and blood." As his fear mounted, he took an involuntary step backward. The man's power resonated through him like bony fingers of ice scratching at his soul.

You cannot take Hotan away from me!

An eerie calm washed over him.

BANG!

He squeezed the trigger.

The kickback from the revolver shook his arm and left his ears ringing, but his aim was impeccable. Gunpowder stung his nostrils as he sighed. He had landed the shot front and center—a single hole in Iapetos' forehead. His head fell back, still wearing the maddening grin. The relief was short lived, however, and Talib's blood ran cold as Iapetos started laughing. Tilting his head forward again, Iapetos stared him in the eyes again. Talib emptied the revolver into the demon before him. There were no more chances for negotiations or patience to entertain mind games. He hit the heart and neck, anywhere deemed vital to assure a kill shot, praying it would do damage or at least slow him. To his horror, Iapetos' laughter grew hysterical, and the small black holes lacked any sign of blood.

How does one kill Death itself?

He threw the empty gun to the ground in frustration, but his resolution to stop Iapetos stood firm. Swallowing down his fear, he ran toward his opponent. Pulling a hidden dagger from his shirt sleeve, he plunged the silver blade deep into the neck of the soul-eating beast. It was then that he felt something demonic in nature. He had only succeeded in entertaining the harbinger of Death. Before he could withdraw from his dire mistake, a firm hand had grasped his neck. Coldness like nothing he had ever felt snaked its way into his body and soul. His power had no sway here, and he felt his life seeping into Iapetos' fingers.

I have failed again.

Is this the coldness everyone feels when they begin to die? What a terrible, comfortless sensation. I have felt sorrow so many times but never the heartlessness of cold such as this.

How horrible to die with no chance of aiding others, unable to send even a simple warning, as his power pulls my soul so far from me. Even my powers have been yanked from me. Dear God, the others do not stand a chance against this immortal named Iapetos.

He could do nothing. He was flung away from his killer like a wet rag. As he hit the ground, the last thing he saw was the rooftop door opening, revealing Hotan's shocked face. His eyes rolled back as the darkness of death pulled him from the present, muffling the shouts and numbing the grip of those rushing to his body.

Why must he be so much like my brother in appearance? Run away, child. A demon is here to devour your soul. Can you not see he has killed me?

Ah, I hear music now.

Yes, the song Hotan sang at the club before Shellie's own death. Jacob said it was "Die Trying" by Art of Dying. What an appropriate song for me to hear as I fade away into the next life.

Oh, my dear Saphellia! I finally got you back, and here I go, leaving you behind. I am so sorry, my dove. Please understand my intentions. You always understood me so much better than I understood myself.

I wonder if it is true that one's life flashes before them as they arrive at Heaven's Gate…

Uncover the secrets of Talib's past in book 2! Will the secret to taking down Death be revealed? Can he fight against the power and save the new Hotan?

MORE BOOKS FROM
4 HORSEMEN PUBLICATIONS

PARANORMAL & URBAN FANTASY

AMANDA FASCIANO
Waking Up Dead
Dead Vessel

BEAU LAKE
The Beast Beside Me
The Beast Within Me
Taming the Beast: Novella
The Beast After Me
Charming the Beast: Novella
The Beast Like Me
An Eye for Emeralds
Swimming in Sapphires
Pining for Pearls

**CHELSEA
BURTON DUNN**
By Moonlight

J.M. PAQUETTE
Call Me Forth
Invite Me In
Keep Me Close

JESSICA SALINA
Not My Time

KAIT DISNEY-LEUGERS
Antique Magic

LYRA R. SAENZ
Prelude
Falsetto in the Woods: Novella
Ragtime Swing
Sonata
Song of the Sea
The Devil's Trill
Bercuese
To Heal a Songbird
Ghost March
Nocturne

MEGAN MACKIE
The Saint Liars
The Devil's Day
The Finder of the Lucky Devil

PAIGE LAVOIE
I'm in Love with Mothman

ROBERT J. LEWIS
Shadow Guardian and the
Three Bears

VALERIE WILLIS
Cedric: The Demonic Knight
Romasanta: Father of Werewolves

The Oracle: Keeper of the
Gaea's Gate
Artemis: Eye of Gaea
King Incubus: A New Reign

YOUNG ADULT FANTASY

BLAISE RAMSAY
Through The Black Mirror
The City of Nightmares
The Astral Tower
The Lost Book of the Old Blood
Shadow of the Dark Witch
Chamber of the Dead God

Honorable Darkness: Story of
Hex and Snip
A Love Lost: Story of Radnar

**LESLIE &
JANICE SOMMERS**
Brighde Reborn

C.R. RICE
Denial
Anger
Bargaining
Depression
Acceptance
Broken Beginnings:
Story of Thane
Shattered Start: Story of Sera
Sins of The Father: Story of Silas

M.E. BATT
The Syphon's Daughter

VALERIE WILLIS
Rebirth
Judgment
Death

**DISCOVER MORE AT
4HORSEMENPUBLICATIONS.COM**